TWILIGHT OF THE GODLINGS

Throughout the recorded history of Britain, belief in earthbound spirits presiding over nature, the home and human destiny has been a feature of successive cultures. From the localised deities of Britannia to the Anglo-Saxons' elves and the fairies of late medieval England, Britain's godlings have populated a shadowy, secretive realm of ritual and belief running parallel to authorised religion. *Twilight of the Godlings* delves deep into the elusive history of these supernatural beings, tracing their evolution from the pre-Roman Iron Age to the end of the Middle Ages. Arguing that accreted cultural assumptions must be cast aside in order to understand the godlings – including the cherished idea that these folkloric creatures are the decayed remnants of pagan gods and goddesses – this bold, revisionist book traces Britain's 'small gods' to a popular religiosity influenced by classical learning. It offers an exciting new way of grasping the island's most mysterious mythical inhabitants.

FRANCIS YOUNG has written eighteen previous books in the fields of folklore and the history of religion and supernatural belief, including – most recently – *Magic in Merlin's Realm* (Cambridge University Press, 2022). A Fellow of the Royal Historical Society, he teaches courses on history, myth and religion for the Department for Continuing Education in the University of Oxford. In addition, he broadcasts regularly on folkloric and religious subjects for the BBC, and has been shortlisted three times for the prestigious Katharine Briggs Folklore Award awarded annually by the Folklore Society.

'As Francis Young acknowledges, folklore studies have moved away from the question of origins because of problematic past approaches. His new book boldly returns us to this question by reminding us of an important fact: that folklore is history and can (and should) be studied from a historical perspective, drawing on literary and material evidence to trace the development of folkloric figures. Because of its novel approach, the book will certainly appeal to historians and folklorists alike, bridging the divide between the two – and, with any luck, convincing each of the benefit of the other's viewpoint. Because of its accessibility, the book will also attract the general reader interested in folklore and history. *Twilight of the Godlings* is a brilliant achievement.'

– **Ceri Houlbrook, Lecturer in Folklore and History, University of Hertfordshire**

'This is a bold, erudite, exciting and genuinely original attempt to solve one of the most intractable of questions concerning medieval British culture. It is very readable and enjoyable, and undoubtedly makes a notable contribution to debate.'

– **Ronald Hutton, Professor of History, University of Bristol, author of Pagan Britain (2013)**

'*Twilight of the Godlings* is nicely combative, making considerable and justifiable claims for its own originality: tracing the history of various folkloric beings through from Roman Britain to the late medieval period. The author firmly eschews outmoded ideas of a 'Celtic hypothesis' – the belief that later

Celtic-language tales, in particular in Irish, can explain the origins and development of such creatures. Dr Young has a background in classical literature and an unusual competence in comparative religion, which is very useful in broadening his comparative frame of reference. He writes clearly and authoritatively and his book is both timely and persuasive.'

— *Carolyne Larrington, Professor of Medieval European Literature, University of Oxford, author of* **The Land of the Green Man: A Journey through the Supernatural Landscapes of the British Isles (2015)**

'This is a magnificent book and I am very proud to have my name associated with it. The real proof of its magnificence is that I disagreed with large parts, but still loved reading it. *Twilight of the Godlings* will stir up debate and act as a fantastic stimulus for supernatural folklore studies. The critical accompaniment is always fascinating and provocative – and at times intoxicating. Packed with fruitful ideas, it is the only post-war volume to look at the development of British fairylore from earliest times to the Middle Ages.'

— *Simon Young, Lecturer in History, University of Virginia (CET), Siena*

Niamh of the Golden Hair by Alan Lee

TWILIGHT OF THE GODLINGS

The Shadowy Beginnings of Britain's Supernatural Beings

FRANCIS YOUNG

Shaftesbury Road, Cambridge CB2 8EA, United Kingdom

One Liberty Plaza, 20th Floor, New York, NY 10006, USA

477 Williamstown Road, Port Melbourne, VIC 3207, Australia

314–321, 3rd Floor, Plot 3, Splendor Forum, Jasola District Centre, New Delhi – 110025, India

103 Penang Road, #05–06/07, Visioncrest Commercial, Singapore 238467

Cambridge University Press is part of Cambridge University Press & Assessment, a department of the University of Cambridge.

We share the University's mission to contribute to society through the pursuit of education, learning and research at the highest international levels of excellence.

www.cambridge.org
Information on this title: www.cambridge.org/9781009330367

DOI: 10.1017/9781009330343

© Francis Young 2023

This publication is in copyright. Subject to statutory exception and to the provisions of relevant collective licensing agreements, no reproduction of any part may take place without the written permission of Cambridge University Press & Assessment.

First published 2023 (version 2, June 2023)

Printed in the United Kingdom by TJ Books Limited, Padstow Cornwall, June 2023

A catalogue record for this publication is available from the British Library.

ISBN 978-1-009-33036-7 Hardback

Cambridge University Press & Assessment has no responsibility for the persistence or accuracy of URLs for external or third-party internet websites referred to in this publication and does not guarantee that any content on such websites is, or will remain, accurate or appropriate.

For Jimmy Altham
εἶναι γὰρ καὶ ἐνταῦθα θεούς.
— *Heraclitus*

CONTENTS

List of Plates	*page* xii
Preface	xv
List of Abbreviations	xviii

	Introduction	1
	Supernatural Beings: The Search for Origins	6
	Approach of the Book	25
	Sources	30
	Structure of the Book	33
1	A World Full of Small Gods: Understanding Godlings	37
	Di nemorum: Ancient Understandings of Godlings	40
	Godlings in the *longue durée*	47
	Animism, 'Shamanism' and Therianthropy in the British Iron Age	60
	One or Many, Male or Female?	70
	Godlings, Hags and Witches	74
	Spirits of the Waters	78
	Conclusion	87
2	Menagerie of the Divine: Godlings in Roman Britain	89
	Interpretatio Romana	94
	The Nymphs	99
	Goddesses of Destiny	103
	The Lares and Penates	110

	Faunus, Silvanus and Bacchic Cults	112
	Genii Loci	129
	Conclusion	133
3	The Nymph and the Cross: Godlings and Christianisation	136
	An Interpretative Model: Demonisation, Undemonisation and Re-Personification	142
	Understanding Christianisation and Syncretism	156
	Christianisation and Godlings in Late Roman Britain	167
	The Evidence of Penitentials	181
	Anglo-Saxon Pagans in a Roman Landscape	187
	Conclusion	193
4	Furies, Elves and Giants: Godlings in Early Medieval Britain	194
	The Influence of Learned Traditions	196
	The Brittonic Linguistic and Onomastic Evidence	200
	Fauns, Woodwoses and the Origins of Male Fairies	212
	Elves	222
	Female Godlings in Early Medieval Britain	225
	Pygmy Otherworlders	238
	Work of Giants	243
	Conclusion	248
5	The Fairy Synthesis: Godlings in Later Medieval Britain	250
	Medieval Fairies	252
	The Norman Cultural Revolution	256
	From Elves to Fairies	260
	From Fauns to Fairies	263
	Parcae, Fates and Nymphs	273

Contents

Fairy Kings and Fairy Otherworlds	278
Medieval Folklore	283
Fairies and Romance	292
Fairies in Ritual Magic	298
Conclusion	302
Epilogue: The Fairy Legacy	305
The Classicising Legacy	310
Almost Human, Not Quite Divine	317
Bibliography	322
Index	349

The plate section is to be found between pages 192 and 193

PLATES

1. A Roman relief of dancing godlings, Peterborough Cathedral
2. The nymph-goddess Coventina and companions, Carrawburgh
3. St Anne's Well, Buxton
4. Three nymphs in the 'nymph room', Lullingstone
5. A Roman relief of the Parcae, Calne
6. Spoons from the Thetford treasure bearing a mixture of pagan and Christian symbolism
7. A satyr on a gold belt buckle from the Thetford treasure
8. The Bacchic *thiasos* on the Great Dish of the Mildenhall Treasure
9. A Mother Goddess with the Genii Cucullati, Cirencester
10. A figure of Minerva carved into the side of a quarry, Chester
11. Stone chapel, near Faversham
12. Medieval satyrs
13. A woodwose on the font, Waldringfield
14. The stoke-hole of a Roman hypocaust, Richborough
15. Anglo-Saxon-era lead amulet bearing the runic legend 'the dwarf is dead', found near Fakenham
16. The conception of Merlin by an incubus
17. A reconstructed nymphaeum, Vindolanda Roman fort

List of Plates

18 Robin Goodfellow as Pan or Faunus (1639)
19 A faun surrounded by fairies (1840)
20 An early modern handbill advertising 'the Ethiopian Satyr, or Real wild-Man of the Woods'

PREFACE

'It is the supreme difficulty experienced in accounting for the origins of the fairy superstition, in finding a formula which shall express its original nature, which has inspired so many brilliant men and women to ransack the records of elfin tradition'.[1] So wrote Lewis Spence in 1946 – at a time, as he himself acknowledged, when folklorists had already 'agreed to differ' on the question of the origins of the supernatural beings of British folklore. The discussion was already, in other words, an unfashionable one because it risked leading the scholar down an unprofitable cul-de-sac where there was only endless argument and no satisfactory answers. As a consequence, the question of the ultimate origins of Britain's supernatural beings – for to classify them only as 'fairies', as we shall see, is far too restrictive – has been largely neglected since, and was touched upon only lightly and speculatively even by great folklorists such as Katharine Briggs.

It is the premise of this book that the time for such silence and reticence is over. The methodological advances made by historians, folklorists, archaeologists, linguists and others over the past eighty years have transformed the intellectual landscape, more than justifying a return to the question of the ultimate origins of Britain's attachment to those beings named as 'godlings' in the title

---

[1] Spence, *British Fairy Origins*, pp. v–vi.

of this book. Whether *Twilight of the Godlings* successfully peers through the half-light and adequately answers the questions it poses is for the reader to judge; however, this book is not intended as a reductive polemic that offers a single simplistic explanation for the origins of those elusive supernatural beings we now generally call fairies. The book is, rather, intended to illustrate the complexity of a difficult historical and folkloristic problem, and to mark a possible path through the maze. There are no simple answers to the questions addressed by this book, but there are certain concepts and processes we may wish to adopt that could lead us closer to the truth, as well as outdated assumptions and approaches we can profitably lay aside that have hitherto hindered understanding or led researchers down blind alleys.

While fairy lore and fairy stories have fascinated me since childhood, the idea for this book emerged from the process of writing my earlier book, *Suffolk Fairylore* (2018), which first led me to ponder questions about the ultimate origins of fairy belief in Britain. Clearly, those questions could not be adequately addressed in a book focussed on the folklore of a single English county, but I found them insufficiently explored (or dealt with summarily) in much of the literature. Then, in writing my book *Pagans in the Early Modern Baltic* (2022), I again found myself considering the nature of those beliefs that hover on the unstable boundary between religion and folklore, in the context of the definition of paganism and traditional religions. The need for an up-to-date study addressing the origins of supernatural beings in Britain – a country that has produced much of the literature on the subject over the past two centuries – seemed to me acute.

Preface

I am very grateful to Alex Wright for his faith in this project, and to the rest of the team at Cambridge University Press for bringing it to fruition, as well as the anonymous reviewers commissioned by the press for their helpful and constructive criticism of the manuscript. The late Susan Curran, who supported me in the writing of *Suffolk Fairylore* (which led to this book) is also deserving of thanks. I thank Dr Simon Young – who, incidentally, is no relation – the foremost chronicler of Britain's fairies, for pointing me in the direction of crucial sources for this book. I am grateful to Danny Bate for providing expert advice on linguistics, and to Dr Nicholas Wilkinson for many inspiring conversations on folklore over the years, as well as for reading over the book's Epilogue from the perspective of a biologist. I thank Simon Knott for sharing his knowledge of woodwoses in church art, and Dr Margaret Hilditch for her generosity in sharing her personal library.

I am grateful to Simon Knott, the Trustees of the British Library Board, the Trustees of the British Museum, the Wellcome Collection, the Corinium Museum at Cirencester, the Portable Antiquities Scheme and the Wiltshire Museum, Devizes, for permission to reproduce images from their collections, and I acknowledge with thanks the helpful staff of Cambridge University Library, the British Library and other libraries whose digitisation of their manuscripts has greatly aided my research. As always, my greatest debt of gratitude is to my wife Rachel and daughters Abigail and Talitha for sustaining me and supporting my scholarship.

Translations from other languages are my own unless otherwise stated.

ABBREVIATIONS

BL	British Library, London
GPC	*Geiriadur Prifysgol Cymru*, geiriadur.ac.uk/gpc/gpc.html
ODNB	*The Oxford Dictionary of National Biography* (online edition), oxforddnb.com
OED	*Oxford English Dictionary*, oed.com
PL	Migne, J.-P. (ed.), *Patrologia Latina* (Paris, 1844–64), 221 vols
RIB	Roman Inscriptions of Britain, romaninscriptionsofbritain.org
RMLWL	Latham, R. E. (ed.), *Revised Medieval Latin Word List from British and Irish Sources* (Oxford: Oxford University Press, 1965)

Introduction

On the west wall of the south transept of Peterborough Cathedral, the last great Norman building of medieval England, is a curious and much-worn limestone Roman relief depicting two dancing figures in flowing robes, wearing pointed hats (Plate 1). The sculpture was reworked in the Middle Ages and long misidentified as a portrayal of two medieval abbots. In reality, the figures represent a man and a woman; they do not hold croziers but spears, and wear not mitres but the Roman *pileus* (the emblem of freedom), while they carry a bivalve shell between them to evoke their watery identity. Peterborough's dancing figures are, in all likelihood, 'a water god and his nymph consort' once worshipped at the Romano-British shrine that almost certainly once stood on the bank of the River Nene where the medieval cathedral would one day come to be built.[1]

As in so many cases where we encounter unique religious iconography from Roman Britain, we know nothing of the dancing godlings of Peterborough; except that by some strange chance their images survived in a Christian church, mistaken for something else, while the cult images of so many other shrines were buried, lost or defaced. Yet these dancing figures are at once strange denizens of an entirely alien religious world and

---

[1] Coombe et al., 'A Relief Depicting Two Dancing Deities', pp. 26–42.

unexpectedly familiar figures. For we know these divine dancers of unearthly beauty, unconstrained by human rules, albeit under another name and accompanied by a different set of cultural associations. All that remains of the divine dance of the nymphs is the ring of mushrooms or lush grass that children call a fairy ring, while the *pileus* now seems reduced to the red hat of the garden gnome.

This book is about those lesser divinities of Britain who, like the Peterborough pair, dance their way in one way or another through the history of the island: 'small gods', to borrow a phrase coined by the fantasy author Terry Pratchett. The 'small gods' or godlings are the nymphs, the gods of nature, the fauns and satyrs and the deities of fate and chance. They are a class of beings that while difficult to define, were still known to the inhabitants of this island in 1300 as they had been a thousand years earlier: before Christianity, before England and before the English language. Yet these small gods were by no means a fixed class of beings, and the godlings of 1300 and the godlings of 300 looked very different indeed. Whether any direct lines of descent can be traced between the godlings of medieval England, Wales and Scotland and the small gods of Roman Britain is a difficult question that this book seeks to address. But the story of Britain's godlings is more interesting than a mere narrative of survival: it is a story of loss, invention, re-invention, imagination, subversion and the re-animation of belief.

Folklorists do not always spend very much time examining the origins of popular beliefs. An earlier generation of scholars was excessively confident in simplistic explanations for the origins of folkloric beings; partly in reaction to that, folklore studies has drifted towards

Introduction

comparative studies less focussed on the question of origins, while few historians have shown an interest in the roots of folklore. The idea that the building blocks of British folklore emerged in the post-Roman twilight of early medieval Britain is, in and of itself, uncontroversial; but it is an assertion often presented as an epistemological 'black box'. Romano-Celtic and Germanic beliefs went in and, somehow, fairly familiar supernatural and folkloric beings came out. What happened in between is often presented as an irrecoverable mystery. It is the contention of this book that the black box is worth examining, especially in light of new methodologies and perspectives. Questions that seemed not only unanswerable but even *unaskable* a few decades ago are worth revisiting in light of the most recent scholarship, and among those questions is 'Where did the supernatural beings of British folklore come from?'

The purpose of this book is to draw on the latest perspectives and methodologies to examine the origins of Britain's folkloric fauna. It explores Britain's godlings in the *longue durée* of the millennium between the Claudian and Norman invasions, and on into the High Middle Ages to the threshold of the early modern era. In doing so, *Twilight of the Godlings* deliberately transgresses the usual scholarly divide placed between Classical and medieval studies, which has traditionally been a particularly stark one in British history. But it is precisely the fact that folkloric beings seem to bridge the unbridgeable chasm in time between Roman and early medieval Britain that makes them a particular object of interest, and of importance not only for the history of belief but also for understanding the origins of medieval Britain.

Introduction

Ever since Stuart Clark argued that 'thinking with demons' was a key to unlocking some little-understood aspects of the early modern world,[2] historians have been increasingly willing to accept that studying culturally constructed beings – whether demons, angels, saints, or 'small gods' – has the capacity to illuminate the past in a unique way. The question of whether supernatural beings 'exist' is, of course, beyond the capacity of the historian or the folklorist to answer – but that they exist as cultural artefacts there can be no doubt, and they are more than simply ideas. In societies where they are accepted as real, supernatural beings function as a category of person, and have all the capacity of real people to be embodiments of a society's preoccupations. The supernatural beings whose existence is accepted (or indeed contested) within a community reveal its self-understanding, its inner tensions, its taboos and its understanding of the familiar and the unfamiliar, the normal and the strange.

To Clark's 'thinking with demons' Simon Ditchfield later added the idea of 'thinking with saints',[3] while others have made a similar case for the historiographical potential of belief in angels.[4] Michael Ostling, meanwhile, has advocated 'thinking with small gods' (the enduring godlings of folklore) as a means of engaging with wider questions of 'continuity and change, tradition and modernity, [and] indigenous religion and its redefinition'.[5] This book takes Ostling's observation as its inspiration, arguing that understanding the 'small gods' of Britain in the

---

[2] Clark, *Thinking with Demons*.
[3] Ditchfield, 'Thinking with Saints', pp. 157–89.
[4] Raymond, 'Introduction', pp. 1–21.
[5] Ostling, 'Introduction: Where've All the Good People Gone?', p. 2.

longue durée opens hitherto unexplored perspectives on questions of cultural and religious survival, creativity and adaptation in the millennium-long transition from the Romanised Iron Age society of Roman Britain to the medieval Christian world.

'Folkloric beings' are non-human supernatural entities of folklore, usually endowed with a human-like personality or living in human-like societies, and called by a great variety of names across cultures (and even within the cultures of the island of Great Britain). As I shall argue in Chapter 1, the names by which these beings are called are usually less important than the cultural 'niches' they occupy. Indeed, focusing on names can be a hindrance to historical understanding, cementing stereotypical and limiting notions of what we expect these beings to be. Because they are cultural creations, folkloric beings can change almost unrecognisably over time, and names thus serve as a poor guide to their nature. The 'demon' of today's Christian mythology is quite different from the *daimōn* of ancient Greece; and if we did not know the process by which a name given to godlings and spirits in Greek religion came to be adopted for evil spiritual beings in modern Christianity, the etymological connection between the two words, in and of itself, would be almost entirely useless.

While the existence of folkloric beings undoubtedly helped people in the past to account for events and aspects of the surrounding world that were not otherwise explicable or subject to their control,[6] reductive

---

[6] On the possible 'functions' of fairy belief see Thomas, *Religion and the Decline of Magic*, pp. 730–34.

or functional explanations of such beliefs are ultimately inadequate because the things people believed about godlings and fairies clearly far exceeded any functional social, psychological or 'pre-scientific' purpose we might propose. Godlings cannot simply be 'explained away' as psychosocial phenomena, because these beings caught people's imaginations. While speculations as to the functions of popular belief can have value – and this book does not entirely hold back from such speculations – if we are forever seeking 'rational explanations' for folkloric narratives, there is a danger that we will be blinded to the significance of those narratives to most people at the time when they were originally told. This book therefore approaches godlings as experiential and cultural realities in the period under discussion, because that was how they were encountered by people at the time.

Supernatural Beings: The Search for Origins

The story of the search for the origins of Britain's supernatural beings is part of the history of the study of folklore, whose beginnings can perhaps be traced to the development of ethnography in the fifteenth and sixteenth centuries – which was in turn a response to the need to understand unfamiliar cultures left unexamined by ancient ethnographers like Herodotus. Margaret Meserve has linked the rapid appearance of the Ottoman Turks in Asia Minor and the cultural trauma of the Ottoman capture of Constantinople in 1453 with an explosion of learned interest in the Turks, as well as other Asian peoples such as the Mongols and Tatars.[7] I have shown elsewhere that European authors began to take a detailed interest in the pagan peoples of the Baltic at the same time.[8] However, it was the European encounter with the indigenous peoples of the New World that brought true urgency to the ethnographic project, for here were culturally alien peoples without writing, and without a presence in the Classical record, who could be understood only via ethnography and the recording of their stories and customs.[9] Dan Ben-Amos has argued that the encounter with the New World and the ethnographical literature it produced influenced early antiquarians in Britain (such as William Camden) to pay attention to stories and popular customs as an integral part of the antiquarian project.[10]

If the recording of folklore was part of the early modern antiquarian project from the very beginning, the first British antiquarian to devote a book solely to 'popular antiquities' (what would later come to be known as folklore) was John Aubrey. In his *Remaines of Gentilisme and Judaisme*, compiled in 1687–1688 but not published until the late nineteenth century, Aubrey presented a miscellany of folklore set alongside allusions to Classical literature that seemed to Aubrey to resemble English folk beliefs and customs. Aubrey's work imitated the structure of Ovid's *Fasti* (a series of poetic aetiologies of Roman customs and rituals), and there was nothing new about using the Classical record as a comparative interpretative framework to understand other cultures.

[7] Meserve, *Empires of Islam*, pp. 152–53.
[8] Young (ed.), *Pagans in the Early Modern Baltic*, pp. 19–24.
[9] Davies, *Renaissance Ethnography*, pp. 23–24.
[10] Ben-Amos, *Folklore Concepts*, pp. 8–22.

However, Aubrey's decision to engage in 'othering his own culture' was unusual;[11] his approach to fairy lore differs markedly from that of his Scottish contemporary Robert Kirk, for example, whose chief aim was to provide a theologically coherent account of what fairies might be rather than tracing the origins of belief in fairies.[12]

In common with his contemporaries, Aubrey's view of pre-Christian religion ('gentilisme') was informed by *interpretatio Romana*, the tendency to interpret all forms of paganism through the lens of Roman religion (a religious hermeneutic for which the Romans themselves were responsible).[13] Aubrey displayed a specific interest in popular belief in folkloric beings, following his methodology of *interpretatio Romana* to conclude that the archetypal English fairy Robin Goodfellow could be identified with the Roman god Faunus.[14] Aubrey identified the fairies with 'the nymphes, the ladies of the plaines,/The watchfull nymphs that dance, & fright the swaine', quoting Theocritus.[15] He also identified Pliny the Elder's report that 'In the solitudes of Africa a kind of men appear on the road, and vanish in a moment' as encounters with the fairies.[16] Although never articulated, the implied hypothesis behind Aubrey's speculations was that, at some time in the past – and presumably at the time of the Roman occupation – the religion of Britain was essentially Roman. The 'Country Gods' of the Romans degenerated into Robin Goodfellow and the fairies.

[11] Williams, *The Antiquary*, p. 119.
[12] Kirk, *Secret Commonwealth*, pp. 5–7.
[13] Ando, 'Interpretatio Romana', pp. 51–65.
[14] Aubrey, *Remaines*, p. 84.
[15] Aubrey, *Remaines*, p. 28.   [16] Aubrey, *Remaines*, p. 177.

Aubrey's basic thesis that Britain's folkloric beings were the degenerate remnants of pagan gods remained at the heart of most attempts to understand the origins of folkloric beings into the twentieth century, even if Aubrey's emphasis on Classical and Roman origins was abandoned in favour of a 'British' or 'Celtic' mythology, supposedly more ancient than the imported mythology of Greece and Rome.[17] Even today, the idea that the supernatural otherworlders of European folklore are gods who have somehow been diminished or demoted and become fairies is a dominant strand of thought about the origins of folklore. But while such demotion can sometimes be argued convincingly in individual cases, the idea that all folkloric beings are diminished gods ignores the fact that ancient pagans, too, had minor spirits as part of their belief systems. The application of Occam's razor to the problem should guide us to examine the 'small gods' of antiquity first, before the formulation of any thesis of 'demotion' or diminution becomes necessary.

The idea of 'Celtic' mythology largely derived from the twelfth-century imagination of Geoffrey of Monmouth, giving rise to tales of ancient British kings such as Lear, Cymbeline and (most notably) Arthur. The eighteenth- and nineteenth-century rediscovery of the medieval Welsh imaginative literature contained in the *White Book of Rhydderch* and *Red Book of Hergest* (known today as the *Mabinogion*) further transformed understandings of 'Celtic' culture, although perceptions of 'British mythology' were also distorted by the forgeries perpetrated by

[17] Sims-Williams, 'The Visionary Celt', 71–96.

Iolo Morganwg (1747–1826).[18] Directed interest in folkloric beings first stirred at the turn of the nineteenth century, motivated by a mixture of Romanticism, patriotism and literary-critical interest in earlier writers who made use of the fairies, such as Chaucer and Shakespeare.[19]

Sir Walter Scott's 1802 essay 'On the Fairies of Popular Superstition' in his *Minstrelsy of the Scottish Borders* represented an early detailed exploration of the origins of fairy lore. Scott argued that the origins of Britain's folkloric beings 'are to be sought in the traditions of the east, in the wreck and confusion of the Gothic mythology, in the tales of chivalry, in the fables of classical antiquity, in the influence of the Christian religion, and finally, in the creative imagination of the 16th century'.[20] Whatever we may now think of Scott's interpretation, his basic insight that the origins of folkloric beings are composite and complex remains valid, and represented a significant advance from Aubrey's simplistic attempt to equate beings across disparate cultures, like Faunus and Robin Goodfellow. In his *Letters on Demonology and Witchcraft* (1830), however, Scott supplemented his earlier theories with an additional hypothesis that would prove very influential throughout the nineteenth century and beyond:

There seems reason to conclude that these *duergar* [dwarves] were originally nothing else than the diminutive natives of the Lappish, Lettish, and Finnish nations, who, flying before the conquering weapons of the Asae, sought the most retired regions of the north, and there endeavoured to hide themselves from

---

[18] Constantine, 'Welsh Literary History', pp. 109–28.
[19] Silver, 'On the Origin of Fairies', pp. 141–42.
[20] Scott, *Minstrelsy*, vol. 2, p. 173.

their eastern invaders. They were a little diminutive race, but possessed of some skill probably in mining or smelting minerals, with which the country abounds; perhaps also they might, from their acquaintance with the changes of the clouds, or meteorological phenomena, be judges of weather, and so enjoy another title to supernatural skill. At any rate, it has been plausibly supposed, that these poor people, who sought caverns and hiding-places from the persecution of the Asae, were in some respects compensated for inferiority in strength and stature, by the art and power with which the superstition of the enemy invested them. These oppressed, yet dreaded fugitives, obtained, naturally enough, the character of the German spirits called Kobold, from which the English Goblin and the Scottish Bogle, by some inversion and alteration of pronunciation, are evidently derived.[21]

Scott's attempt to 'euhemerise' folkloric beings (identifying them with historic human populations), freighted as it was with racial and colonial prejudices, was enthusiastically taken up by subsequent authors and became a regrettable cul-de-sac of Victorian speculations about the origins of folkloric beings. The instinct to euhemerise, and to find a 'scientific' or historical-realist explanation of fairies in a half-remembered history, was rooted in the Enlightenment. The earliest British writer to suggest that the fairies might be a hidden race of diminutive humans was John Webster, writing in 1677:

In a few ages past when Popish ignorance did abound, there was no discourse more common (which yet continueth among the vulgar people) than of the apparition of certain Creatures which they called Fayries, that were of very little stature, and being seen would soon vanish and disappear.

[21] Scott, *Letters on Demonology*, pp. 120–21.

Introduction

After a discussion of the reality or otherwise of pygmy races, Webster concluded that pygmies probably did exist, and that fairies

> have been really existent in the World, and are and may be so still in Islands and Mountains that are uninhabited ... they are no real Demons, or non-Adamick Creatures, that can appear and become invisible when they please, as Paracelsus thinketh. But ... they were truly of human race endowed with the use of reason or speech (which is most probable) or at least ... they were some little kind of Apes or Satyres, that having their secret recesses and holes in the Mountains, could by their agility and nimbleness soon be in or out like Conies, Weazels, Squirrels, and the like.[22]

Although Webster does not say it outright, he implies here that pygmies may once have lived in Britain (in order to account for belief in fairies). This approach reached its apogee in David MacRitchie's 'pygmy theory' of fairy origins, which theorised that fairy lore represented folk memory of diminutive peoples driven to hills and caves by invaders.[23] The 'pygmy theory' would even inspire an entire subgenre of Victorian literary fiction by authors such as Arthur Machen and John Buchan, in which modern-day Britons unwittingly stumble upon savage races of troglodytes.[24] Remarkably, even one popular book on folklore published in 2022 could still be found advocating the theory.[25]

However, MacRitchie's racialised euhemerism was never entirely triumphant in the study of fairy origins. The influential folklorist Thomas Keightley, whose *Fairy*

---

[22] Webster, *Displaying of Supposed Witchcraft*, pp. 283–84.
[23] Silver, 'On the Origin of Fairies', pp. 149–53.
[24] Fergus, 'Goblinlike, Fantastic'.
[25] Webb, *On the Origins of Wizards*, pp. 118–20.

Mythology (1828) was an early work of serious folklore studies in English, was influenced by the comparative approach of the Brothers Grimm. Keightley's understanding of fairy lore was rooted in a kind of functionalism that posited universal 'laws' by which primitive peoples arrived at belief in both gods and godlings:

> In accordance with these laws, we find in every country a popular belief in different classes of beings distinct from men, and from the higher orders of divinities. These beings are believed to inhabit, in the caverns of earth, or the depths of the waters, a region of their own. They generally excel mankind in power and in knowledge, and like them are subject to the immutable laws of death, though after a more prolonged period of existence.[26]

Keightley considered it most probable that the word 'fairy' derived from the Persian word *peri*,[27] and mentioned only in a footnote the Breton antiquary Jacques Cambry's (broadly correct) view that French *fée* could be linked to Latin *fatua*, as articulated in Cambry's *Monumens Celtiques* (1805):

> *Fatua*, the good goddess, is the same word as *fée* [in French]; *fata* in Provencal; *fada* in Italian; *hada* in Spanish; the Celto-Breton *mat* or *mad*; in construction *fat*, 'the good woman', from which [derives] *madez*, a child's nurse and English *maid*, 'a virgin, a girl'. The Romans called the good goddess indiscriminately *fatua*, *fauna* or *bona dea*; in effect, *fauna* comes from *bona*, and *bona* is nothing but the translation of the Celtic *mat*, *fat*, from which [we derive] *fatua*. It is a proof that the Romans knew the fairies, and that they knew them under the same name as the Celts.[28]

---

[26] Keightley, *Fairy Mythology*, vol. 1, pp. 6–7.
[27] Keightley, *Fairy Mythology*, vol. 1, p. 9.
[28] Cambry, *Monumens Celtques*, p. 337.

Cambry was by no means right about all of this ('maid', for example, is a thoroughly Germanic word), and his suggestion that 'the Romans knew the fairies' will be discussed at length in this book. However, Cambry's basic insight that 'fairy' can be linked to a cluster of etymologies around the Latin verb *fari* (from which *fatua* derives) has stood the test of time.

Keightley's decision to ignore the possibility of a Classical origin for the fairies may speak to his insistence on seeing fairy lore as a belief of primitive peoples and therefore unconnected with the prestigious civilisations of Greece and Rome. Furthermore, his decision to promote a Persian origin for the word 'fairy' contributed to an exoticising tendency that strained to see Eastern origins in European folklore. In the second half of the nineteenth century, the popularity of Spiritualism led some to speculate that Britain's folkloric beings were best understood as the psychically evolved humans of remote antiquity. However, Spiritualists were also drawn to the idea of fairies as 'psychic insect life', and the affair of the 'Cottingley Fairies' (in which Sir Arthur Conan Doyle was duped into advocating the reality of a set of fabricated fairy photographs) merely encouraged the idea of insect-like 'flower fairies'.[29] Needless to say, insectoid fairies are without any basis in folklore; they are instead a literary creation of seventeenth-century poets like Robert Herrick.[30]

---

[29] Silver, 'On the Origin of Fairies', pp. 153–54.
[30] Hutton, *Queens of the Wild*, pp. 107–8 (see, for example, Herrick, *Hesperides*, pp. 101–5). Hutton, *Queens of the Wild*, p. 90, notes that the Scottish poet Robert Henryson imagined insect-sized fairies in his poem 'King Berdok', although there is no evidence that Henryson initiated a literary tradition.

The scholarly impetus to understand fairy lore in the twentieth century emerged from literary criticism, particularly the attempt to understand the origins of the fairies portrayed in medieval romances.[31] Shakespeare studies – particularly interest in the fairies of *A Midsummer Night's Dream* – also played a key role, and no-one is more closely associated with the study of Shakespeare's fairies than the folklorist Katharine Briggs, whose 1952 doctoral thesis dealt with 'Some Aspects of Folk-Lore in Early Seventeenth-Century Literature'.[32] Briggs' 1957 article in the journal *Folklore*, 'The English Fairies', launched a lifetime of scholarship devoted to fairy folklore. In that article Briggs' opening observation about the study of British fairy beliefs remains as true now as it was then:

> No single explanation seems to fit the whole subject. It is as if we were reading a detective story in which the crime turns out to have been committed not by one main criminal but by a number of fortuitous minor criminals, who has each unwittingly contributed to the main crime, and who have scattered clues about with bewildering profusion ...[33]

Here, as in her subsequent work, Briggs adopted a taxonomic approach to the fairy realm (the very title of her 1959 book *The Anatomy of Puck* seems to jest with the idea of bringing a scientific level of precision to what might appear the most unscientific of subjects) and her classifications of trooping, solitary, tutelary and nature fairies remain influential. Briggs differed from earlier authors

---

[31] Hutton, 'Making of the Early Modern British Fairy Tradition', pp. 1135–36.
[32] Davidson, *Katharine Briggs*, p. 107.
[33] Briggs, 'English Fairies', p. 270.

by insisting on the need to engage with folklore on its own terms without the intrusion of functionalist and historical-realist speculations. She advanced the theory that fairy belief was in some way connected with the dead,[34] which in turn suggested the idea that the fairies were in some way the decayed remnants of a cult of the ancestors associated with prehistoric landscape features like barrows.

In *The Fairies in Tradition and Literature* (1967) Briggs continued to grapple with the difficult question of fairy origins, concluding that

> the flourishing time of fairy belief must be pushed back to the earliest historic times on these Islands, almost to the verge of prehistory ... [T]here is little doubt that [pagan gods] can claim their part in the building of the fairy tradition as well as the half-deified spirits of the dead and the spirits of woods and wells and vegetation.[35]

Briggs' work continues to form the basic foundation for the study of British fairy lore today, although there are aspects of her approach that might now give us pause. Her preferred theory that fairies are remnants of a cult of 'half-deified spirits of the dead' is unaccompanied by much evidence that such a cult existed beyond prehistory. The Romans venerated the *di manes* but there is no compelling reason to believe that veneration of the dead in Roman Britain was much different from anywhere else in the empire, and the pagan Anglo-Saxons' preference for establishing cemeteries close to prehistoric features like barrows constitutes insufficient grounds to propose an

---

[34] Briggs, 'English Fairies', pp. 277–78. [35] Briggs, *Fairies*, p. 4.

ongoing cult of the ancient dead. If fairies are associated with barrows and other human-made earthworks, they are equally associated with natural mounds and hills. It is difficult to avoid the conclusion that Briggs, like many folklorists of her generation, was drawn into advocating continuities of belief from remote prehistory that seem rather unlikely.

A further problematic aspect of Briggs' approach is her liking for taxonomizing supernatural beings, which culminated in her multi-volume *Dictionary of Fairies* (1976). As Simon Young has observed, in 'the drive to order British supernatural creatures ... dialectal differences have been unknowingly turned into folklore differences',[36] which is just one of the problems that can arise when trying to separate folkloric beings like species of real-world fauna. Briggs speculated that 'the lesser deities' of the Roman world 'had descended into being fairies', but did not offer any explanation of how this process occurred.[37] It is unclear whether Briggs presumed that such an enquiry was impossible or considered that it lay beyond her expertise – or whether, as a folklorist interested primarily in folklore since the early modern period, questions about the more remote origins of fairies did not particularly interest her. More recent authors have followed in Briggs' footsteps by setting aside the question of the fairies' historical origins; Richard Sugg, for example, while thoroughly discussing folkloric explanations for where the fairies came from, makes little attempt to explain where he thinks they *really* came from.[38]

[36] Young, *The Boggart*, p. 211.
[37] Briggs, *The Fairies in Tradition and Literature*, p. 11.
[38] Sugg, *Fairies*, pp. 17–45.

Introduction

Keith Thomas reflected the attitude of many scholars of early modern fairy belief in showing more interest in its social and cultural function than in where it came from, observing only that 'Ancestral spirits, ghosts, sleeping heroes, fertility spirits and pagan gods can all be discerned in the heterogeneous fairy lore of medieval England, and modern enquiries into fairy origins can never be more than speculative'.[39] Similarly, referring to godlings, Euan Cameron declared that 'It is ... an open question as to whether the raw material of supernatural beliefs actually has a history'.[40] Thomas' and Cameron's scepticism has also been echoed by Ronald Hutton, who considers that the 'ultimate root' of fairy beliefs is irrecoverable.[41] Indeed, Hutton has argued that, in contrast to Olympian gods who survived under the form of cultural allegories, the 'small gods' of the ancient world disappeared.[42] However, he is somewhat less pessimistic than Thomas, arguing that late medieval and early modern fairy belief is essentially a literary construct built around a variety of folkloric beings who existed in popular belief within no particular conceptual framework: 'a late medieval development, achieved originally in a literary context, which found a wide and rapid acceptance'.[43] This is displayed in works such as *Sir Orfeo*, a romance composed around 1300 that retold the myth of Orpheus and Eurydice while replacing Hades with the 'King of Fairy' and the Greek underworld with a fairy kingdom. In Hutton's view, the

---

[39] Thomas, *Religion and the Decline of Magic*, p. 724.
[40] Cameron, *Enchanted Europe*, p. 74.
[41] Hutton, 'Making of the Early Modern British Fairy Tradition', p. 1136.
[42] Hutton, 'Afterword', p. 351.
[43] Hutton, 'Making of the Early Modern British Fairy Tradition', p. 1155.

idea of the fairy kingdom then migrated from literature into folklore, becoming an established popular belief by the fifteenth century.[44] Hutton considers the fairies to be the descendants of 'land spirits' and 'rural spirits which had no obvious place in Christianity'. While water spirits and household spirits can be found throughout Europe, the 'fairies proper' who constitute a parallel society with its own hierarchy are 'strictly a northern tradition', and these fairies can be considered 'neither personifications of nature nor deities'. Hutton concludes that the fairies

were a survival from pagan belief which the new religion had found more or less indigestible, but which gave it little trouble in practice because few if any people attempted to worship fairies so they did not tangle with issues of allegiance or salvation.[45]

While it is certainly possible for literary tropes to cross over into the realm of folklore, Hutton's thesis that popular English fairy belief is an essentially literary construct of the late Middle Ages lacks plausibility. Many individual instances of folklore originated in literature, but there is no obvious precedent or parallel for a set of beliefs so widespread and deeply held as belief in the fairy realm crossing over into folklore within a fairly short period. Furthermore, parallels to English, Welsh and Scottish belief in a fairy realm can be found in Ireland and Brittany, suggesting a more ancient and fundamental origin. On the other hand, Hutton's argument is a helpful corrective

---

[44] Hutton, 'Making of the Early Modern British Fairy Tradition', pp. 1142–56.
[45] Hutton, *Pagan Britain*, pp. 379–80.

to the long-established tendency to assume, uncritically, that folklore *always* has ancient and immemorial origins. As he has argued recently, 'Christian Europe, both in the Middle Ages and after, was capable of developing new superhuman figures which operated outside of Christian cosmology'.[46] It is the argument of this book that fairy belief, rather than being constructed from literary sources at a particular moment in time, is the result of sustained interaction between learned and popular culture over an extended period – and the fairies were just as likely to be novel creations as survivals from the immemorial past.

Alaric Hall's definitive work on elves in Anglo-Saxon England has shown the potential of attentive study of linguistic sources like glosses to clarify the nature of different supernatural beings mentioned in Old English texts. Hall introduced a new standard of rigour to the field that should serve as a model for future study of the origins of folkloric beings, and makes it impossible to return to the vague generalisations of some past scholarship.[47] Hall's analysis also reveals how little can be stated with certainty about Anglo-Saxon belief in elves, in spite of the fact that the name of the elves migrated into Middle English as a term for the beings later called fairies. On the way, however, Hall highlights the richness and complexity of Anglo-Saxon England's supernatural fauna, a theme subsequently taken up by scholars such as Sarah Semple and Tim Flight.[48] Hall's work throws into doubt another traditional view of the origins of England's fairies

[46] Hutton, *Queens of the Wild*, p. 196.   [47] Hall, *Elves*.
[48] Semple, *Perceptions of the Prehistoric*, pp. 143–92; Flight, *Basilisks and Beowulf*.

as the unproblematic descendants of the elves of Anglo-Saxon England, which seems unsustainable insofar as Hall shows the elves were very different beings from the fairies who later assumed their name.

In addition to Hall, three scholars who have made important contributions to the enquiry into the origins of Britain's folkloric beings are Emma Wilby, Diane Purkiss and Michael Ostling. Through an analysis of the evidence of Scottish witch trials, Wilby argued that there was evidence of ongoing animistic and shamanistic belief underlying Scottish popular religion, suggesting that fairy belief is perhaps best understood as the persistence of an animistic understanding of a deified nature as an undercurrent to other religious beliefs.[49] While this book is not uncritical of Wilby's approach, nor of the application of the concept of animism itself, her basic insight that fairy belief may be linked with animism is not one that ought to be set aside entirely – and, once again, it serves as a helpful corrective to the idea of fairies as diminished deities.

Diane Purkiss' *Troublesome Things* (2000) is undoubtedly one of the most important books of recent decades on folkloric beings, and while its psychosocial approach is not primarily directed at the question of historical origins (as Purkiss acknowledges), Purkiss was prepared to challenge many of the long-held assumptions (largely derived from Briggs) about fairy origins. Purkiss stressed the parallels between 'Celtic' and Near Eastern beliefs and even went so far as to suggest that Celtic ideas about the fairies could have come from the Classical world.[50]

[49] Wilby, *Cunning-Folk*.   [50] Purkiss, *Troublesome Things*, pp. 11–51.

While Purkiss' specific proposal of Greek influence on the pre-Roman Celts seems rather unlikely (and considerably less likely than Roman influence on Britain during the period of occupation), she can be credited with reviving the idea of Classical influence in general as an explanation for fairy belief. Purkiss' insight has been taken forward by at least one scholar, Angana Moitra, who has sought to trace in detail the origins of one figure, the Fairy King, over the cultural *longue durée*.[51]

Beyond the English-speaking world, the French historiography of fairy origins has generally been focussed on explaining the origins of the folkloric themes of the medieval romances. This is a historiography that cannot be neglected in a history of British folkloric beings, because the stories of British and French folklore intersect in the territory of Brittany: an area that is geographically France but historically, culturally and linguistically Brittonic. For Francisca Aramburu, Catherine Despres, Begoña Aguiriano and Javier Benito, medieval fairy belief was a complex amalgam of cultures, yet fairies could nevertheless be said to conflate the Parcae, the Gaulish Deae Matres and the godlings of nature and birth.[52] Claude Lecouteux's emphasis, by contrast, was on the fairies as embodiments of dream, destiny and fantasy, as well as on the fairy's role as a psychic double,[53] while Pierre Gallais eschewed a historical approach altogether, emphasising the universality of the figure of the fairy across all

---

[51] Moitra, 'From Pagan God to Magical Being', pp. 23–40; Moitra, 'From Graeco-Roman Underworld to the Celtic Otherworld', pp. 85–106.
[52] Aramburu et al., 'Deux faces de la femme merveilleuse', p. 8.
[53] Lecouteux, *Fées, sorcières et loups-garous*, p. 83.

human cultures.[54] Laurence Harf-Lancner echoed Keith Thomas' scepticism, arguing that since medieval folklore of fairies is now subsumed entirely in literary sources, it is impossible to recover.[55] On the whole, the focus of French historiography is not so much on the historical origins of fairies as on their functions, universality, archetypal character and roles in literature.

Notable recent advances in the understanding of the origins of fairy lore have been made by Michael Ostling, Richard Firth Green and Ronald Hutton. In an important volume that brings together scholarship on belief in godlings across the world, from Estonia to Zambia,[56] Ostling has made the case for reclaiming 'small gods' from a realm of cultural studies that tends to take them out of space and time, and returning them firmly to history.[57] By adopting a broad understanding of 'small gods' as 'animistic "survivals" problematically present within a Christianity that attempts to exclude them',[58] Ostling and his fellow contributors are able to advance the comparative study of folkloric beings in both a European and an international context. Ostling's firm insistence that 'small gods' are a category in their own right, found in both pagan and Christian contexts, is an important corrective to the old idea of folkloric beings as diminished gods. A further significant contribution to the historiography of fairy belief has been made by Richard Firth Green, who has challenged the 'Celtic fallacy' that has hampered the study of what is, in reality, a set

[54] Gallais, *La fée à la fontaine*, p. 12.
[55] Harf-Lancner, *Les fées au moyen âge*, p. 8.
[56] Ostling (ed.), *Fairies, Demons, and Nature Spirits*.
[57] Ostling, 'Introduction', p. 2.   [58] Ostling, 'Introduction', pp. 4–11.

of beliefs found throughout Europe.[59] While sceptical of attempts to trace the origins of fairy lore or taxonomise the fairies, Green expanded the evidential base for the study of medieval fairy belief by noting that many stories of demons in sources such as pastoral literature and saints' lives were, in fact, narratives about fairies. Similarly, Ronald Hutton's insightful recent study of the figure of the Fairy Queen in his book *Queens of the Wild* builds on his earlier scholarship on the origins and antecedents of fairy belief.[60]

Between them, these innovative scholars have brought the study of the origins of folkloric beings out of the 'Celtic twilight' in which it had long languished, contributing important insights that, collectively, transform the conversation about folkloric beings. Firstly, the study of folkloric beings should be conducted as rigorously as any other historical investigation, and should make use of all available evidence, including the linguistic and the archaeological. Secondly, folkloric beings should be seen as the product of continuous interactions between oral and learned culture, including literature. Thirdly, folkloric beings may be viewed in the context of underlying animistic worldviews across the *longue durée* of cultural history, even if the persistence of 'animism' should sometimes be treated with a degree of scepticism. Fourthly, there is a strong element of influence from the Classical world in Britain's folkloric beings. And fifthly, Britain's 'small gods' are best understood not in isolation, but in their European and international context.

---

[59] Green, *Elf Queens*, pp. 5–7.
[60] Hutton, *Queens of the Wild*, pp. 75–109.

Approach of the Book

In 2014 Ronald Hutton observed that there existed no modern history of British fairies, in the sense of a book that approached fairies historically with a focus on 'change over time'.[61] By contrast, ambitious studies of the history and origins of other classes of folkloric being have been undertaken, such as Daniel Ogden's study of dragons and Simon Young's work on boggarts.[62] It is this deficit that the present book seeks to address, while avoiding (as far as possible) a teleological approach that merely explains how the fairies of Shakespeare (for example) or the fairies of nineteenth-century folklore came about. Most studies of British fairy belief have hitherto been hampered either by insufficient curiosity about (or willingness to investigate) the question of origins, or by a methodological aversion to a historical approach to folkloric beings. As the Classicist T. P. Wiseman has observed, however, anthropological and comparativist approaches to beliefs and customs have a tendency to argue synchronically, taking inadequate account of change over time. In reality, 'any community's dealings with its gods must reflect, at some level, its own needs and preoccupations, and adjust, with whatever time-lag, as those needs and preoccupations change'.[63] Similarly, belief in 'an essentially constant rural popular cosmology that persisted through all the dramatic developments in elite and official belief' is ahistorical.[64] The discipline of folklore on its own lacks

---

[61] Hutton, 'Making of the Early Modern British Fairy Tradition', p. 1135.
[62] Ogden, *The Dragon in the West*; Young, *The Boggart*.
[63] Wiseman, *Unwritten Rome*, p. 54.
[64] Hutton, 'Making of the Early Modern British Fairy Tradition', p. 1136.

Introduction

the methodological resources to investigate a question – the origins of Britain's folkloric beings – that requires the analysis of such a variety of sources, over such a long period, that an interdisciplinary approach is required, drawing on the perspectives offered by history, Classics, linguistics and archaeology. At the same time, the present study does not claim to be a complete study of the totality of British lore of supernatural beings, and is fairly narrowly focussed on questions of origins and development.

A history of folkloric beings can be written either from the present to the past or from the past to the present. If it is written from the present to the past, its focus will be on discerning the building blocks of modern belief in the past; but a shortcoming of this approach is that it presumes the character of modern folklore is the final goal towards which history has been moving. Yet the history of popular belief is full of extinct strands of belief that have had very little influence on the present, but are no less historically important for that. However, the alternative approach – telling the story of Britain's folkloric beings from the past to the present – also presents a difficulty, because it requires us to start off with some idea of the kind of beings we are pursuing through time. Since folkloric beings are cultural constructions rather than empirical realities, this requires us to understand the factors that may have led to particular cultural constructions at particular times – a very challenging demand for remote and poorly evidenced eras of the past.

Tracing the history of belief in 'small gods' is difficult, certainly, and it will always be an enterprise that produces only partial results. It is a cliché of historiography that most historical sources are produced by elites, and belief in 'small gods', for much of the period under discussion, was characteristic of the secular culture of the unlearned elite and the non-elite lower echelons of society. Yet historians are now well accustomed to the challenge of extracting the traces of non-elite culture from elite sources, and there is no reason to think that a history of fairy belief should be harder to write than, say, a history of Romano-British religion, where the evidence is similarly scattered and problematic. Furthermore, as Richard Firth Green has observed, there is no reason to believe that fairy beliefs were not generated (as well as consumed) by elites, and the assumption that such beliefs always came 'from below' is itself a projection of modernity onto the past.[65] It is my contention, therefore, that historians have hitherto been excessively pessimistic about the potential of tracing the origins of Britain's folkloric beings. While this book keeps in view the question of how late medieval and early modern fairy belief came about, its focus is primarily on examining the development of belief in broadly defined 'small gods' in Britain from beginning to end, on the basis that (as I shall argue in Chapter 1) it is possible to trace the outlines of the kind of being we might consider a 'small god'.

Ferdinand Braudel observed in the 1960s that basic human relationships with nature lie beneath the ever-changing drama of history, as well as the shape of the human mind itself. These are factors that undergo slow processes of change – if, indeed, they change at all within historical time.[66] Since belief in godlings is entwined

---

[65] Green, *Elf Queens*, p. 43.
[66] Salisbury, 'Before the Standing Stones', pp. 20–21.

intimately with humanity's relationship with nature – to a greater extent, perhaps, than other aspects of religion and belief – its history is an ideal subject for a survey in the *longue durée*. As Joyce Salisbury has argued, 'if people believed the same things in two separate periods of time, we might assume a similar belief in the central, though undocumented period', and the potential of a *longue durée* examination of belief in godlings from the Roman period to the later Middle Ages has not yet been explored.

Archaeologists of prehistory and anthropologists are accustomed to making use of 'cable-like' arguments that contain distinct, separate strands of evidence, and allow for the other strands to cover the gap if there is an evidential lacuna – as often occurs when dealing with the prehistoric world.[67] Some of the 'cables' that can be constructed for the study of folkloric beings in Roman, post-Roman and early medieval Britain are significantly stronger than those deployed by archaeologists to account for religious behaviour in prehistory, although the presence of evidential lacunae is no less of a problem. However, the historical and conceptual advances made in the understanding of godlings by the scholars already mentioned in this introduction should dispel the notion that Britain's folkloric beings cannot be studied historically, as cultural artefacts within time. This study takes those scholars' determination to study godlings historically as its inspiration.

A study of Britain's godlings in the *longue durée* has the capacity to challenge many cherished assumptions about the origins of British folklore, such as the 'Celtic myth' that folkloric beings such as fairies can be traced

---

[67] Lewis-Williams, *A Cosmos in Stone*, p. 137.

to an imagined 'Celtic twilight', either before or after the Roman occupation of Britain – or to the pagan religion of the Anglo-Saxons, of which we know virtually nothing. Related to the 'Celtic twilight' myth is the more or less uncritical use of sources from medieval Ireland to support arguments about Britain. While it is true that theonyms (names of deities) in Irish and Welsh are sometimes linguistic cognates, and therefore it would be absurd to deny any sort of religious or cultural connections between the two islands in ancient times, the belief that Irish mythology can illuminate ancient British beliefs rests on assumptions about a pan-Celtic cultural identity that is more of a nineteenth-century construct than a historical or archaeological reality. Even if, for the sake of argument, we imagine that Irish and British beliefs were more or less identical in the pre-Roman Iron Age (which is unlikely), the historical paths taken by Ireland and Britain in the Roman and early medieval periods were so dramatically different that we should not expect much similarity in folk beliefs about the supernatural by the time of the Anglo-Norman invasion in the late twelfth century. That invasion resulted in the eventual imposition of English words like 'fairy' on Ireland's supernatural beings, but Iron Age Ireland did not experience directly the religious influence of Rome, encountering it only secondhand through a Christianity transplanted from late Roman Britain. Ireland's supernatural world is a unique one, which cannot and should not be imposed as a framework on other cultures.

As well as setting aside the myth of a common 'Celtic' identity, this book challenges the idea that buried ancient mythologies can be constructed from medieval literary sources – whether from Britain or Ireland – that are, in fact, works of imaginative fiction. It is the argument of this book that the 'small gods' of early medieval England were largely fresh cultural constructions of the period, confected at need in the aftermath of Christianisation and under the influence of Christian learning, against a background of the detritus of Roman, Brittonic and Anglo-Saxon paganisms. The idea that Britain's godlings were 'pagan survivals' should be largely (albeit not entirely) set aside. The 'small gods' that later became Britain's elves, fairies and giants are not Christian, but they are the non-Christian artefacts of a Christian culture. Owing to the influence of learned commentary on popular culture, and the significance of Latin and Classical learning within that commentary, it is the contention of this book that Roman pagan religion was by far the most important cultural background for Britain's early medieval godlings – albeit rarely directly, through a process of direct survival from Roman Britain. Instead, Roman religion came to influence British folk belief through the writings of the Church Fathers. If the 'small gods' are not the children of Rome, they are at least Rome's grandchildren.

Sources

The sources for the study of a question as large as the origins of Britain's folkloric beings are very diverse indeed, ranging from the insights of lexicographers to the discoveries of archaeologists. Popular belief in godlings is, by its very nature, very difficult to trace owing to the truism that most written evidence was produced by elite sources who were less likely to mention or discuss such beliefs. In the case of Roman Britain, our direct evidence for godlings is almost entirely archaeological and epigraphic, depending on figurative representations and inscriptions. However, our understanding of that artistic and epigraphic information depends in turn on the written evidence for Roman religion in Rome itself, especially those writers (like Ovid and Varro) who provide the most information about popular religion. The likely distance that existed between Roman belief and practice in Roman Britain and more richly textually evidenced provinces of the Roman world makes the use of such sources problematic but, nevertheless, unavoidable.

The evidence for early medieval belief in godlings is to be found in a diverse range of sources, including saints' lives, chronicles, glosses, penitentials, imaginative literature and learned commentaries on the Bible and Classical texts. One source of evidence for fairy lore that (as Simon Young has observed) has been overlooked until recently is place names.[68] This is a source extensively explored by Sarah Semple in her analysis of folkloric beings in the English landscape.[69] Literary sources for belief in folkloric beings are difficult to use for a number of reasons, including differences in language between the text and the language used by those who held the beliefs discussed. Since folkloric beings are cultural creations whose conceptual character is closely tied to the words used to name them in specific languages, such linguistic gaps can be very significant indeed. Thus we are often faced with sources in Latin discussing belief in beings by Old English speakers, when those beings' Old English names

[68] Young, 'Fairy Holes and Fairy Butter', p. 83.
[69] Semple, *Perceptions of the Prehistoric*, pp. 143–92.

are not given. If a Latin source by an Anglo-Saxon author names *nymphae*, for example, we have no way of being sure what Old English speakers called these beings.

Furthermore, literary sources were produced by people with a much higher level of education than most ordinary people, so it is imperative to be sensitive to the importation of learned assumptions when folkloric beings surface in medieval sources. A learned commentator with a theological education might be more inclined to demonise folkloric beings, for example, than the majority of people for whom those beings were a cultural reality. Literary texts, especially in the early Middle Ages, often date from decades or centuries after the events they describe, and we must always be attentive to the importance of the genre and character of texts. A sceptical stance regarding what can be recovered of popular belief from elite sources is always possible, and often justifiable, but the notion that all early medieval writing was a conversation between the learned that bore little or no relationship to ordinary people's beliefs is one that stretches credulity. People in early medieval societies who worked for the church and acquired Latin learning were not thereby cut off from their communities or from the societies they grew up in, and if we set up an excessively rigid dichotomy between elite and non-elite culture we are in danger of reviving the old myth of a pagan peasantry co-existing with a Christian elite.[70]

The tendency to give undue weight to medieval works of imaginative literature as reliable accounts of folklore

---

[70] On this myth see Hutton, 'How Pagan Were Medieval English Peasants?', pp. 235–49.

has been a persistent hindrance to the study of the origins of fairy lore, although it is also important not to neglect texts of a literary character. However, scholars of the fairy theme in medieval literature such as James Wade now often focus on the 'internal folklore' of the text rather than on attempting to draw connections with the putative world of belief that lay beyond it.[71] The approach adopted in this book is to treat the fairy theme in the medieval romances as an indication of the importance of fairies in medieval culture, but not as a source from which it is possible to mine or recover folklore or popular belief. In the same way, the idea that the beliefs of distant ages can be reconstructed from folklore collected in the nineteenth and twentieth centuries is not a proposal that the historian should seriously contemplate.

Structure of the Book

The structure of the book is partly chronological and partly thematic, with Chapters 2, 4 and 5 tracing the evolution of belief in godlings between the Roman period and the later Middle Ages while the focus of Chapters 1 and 3 is on questions of definition and the impact of Christianisation, respectively. Establishing what we mean by 'godlings' and 'small gods' is crucial to studying their origins, and therefore Chapter 1 deals with the issue of identifying godlings. The chapter approaches ancient understandings of minor spirits in the Roman world and considers how godlings can be studied over the *longue durée*, in this case the millennium or more

---

[71] Wade, *Fairies in Medieval Romance*, pp. 1–3.

from the Roman Iron Age to the later Middle Ages. The chapter evaluates the significance and appropriateness of the concepts of animism, 'shamanism' and therianthropy to understanding the phenomenon of godlings in ancient Britain, before suggesting certain key characteristics of 'small gods': for example, ambiguity as to number and gender. The nature of Britain's godlings is illustrated through a study of the parallels between the godling, the hag and the witch, while the question of long-term survival is considered through the most promising example of possible genuine survival of veneration of godling-like beings: the spirits associated with water sources throughout Britain.

Chapter 2 turns to a more chronological approach, examining the 'menagerie of the divine' that was Roman Britain. Here there is a great deal of archaeological and epigraphic evidence for the veneration of a multiplicity of divine beings – albeit often accompanied with little context that helps us to understand exactly what the significance of such cults was. The chapter introduces the main categories of godlings in Roman Britain, including genii loci, nymphs, mother goddesses and deities of nature, arguing that such cults became much more significant during the fourth-century 'pagan revival' that followed the accession of the pagan emperor Julian in 361. In particular, the extraordinary cult of Faunus revealed by the Thetford Treasure – along with other ecstatic nature cults apparently testified by the archaeological record – suggests that the fourth century was an important time for the development of distinctive and inventive Romano-British interpretations of Roman pagan religion. However, the relationship between Romano-British cults and subsequent strains of belief

Structure of the Book

remains unclear, and no definitive link can be established with the early Middle Ages.

Christianity was a growing religion in Britain from the 330s onwards, and Chapter 3 tackles the difficult question of the relationship between Christianity, Christianisation and godlings. The chapter examines the phenomenon of the Christian demonisation of pagan cults, arguing that it was a more complex process than mere condemnation and suppression. Demonisation inadvertently produced the potential for the survival (and even re-invention) of some of the beings it targeted. Through comparisons with the better evidenced Christianisation of other cultures in Europe and further afield, the chapter develops an interpretative framework for the likely changes undergone by popular religion in the lengthy conversion period. The framework includes the likely 'undemonisation' of formerly demonised entities and the creative 're-personification' of supernatural forces to account for the survival and reinvention of godlings in a Christianised society – where godlings should not so much be seen as 'pagan survivals' but rather as non-Christian artefacts of the Christianisation process.

Chapter 4 examines in detail the early medieval evidence for godlings in Britain, from both Brittonic and Anglo-Saxon sources, dealing in turn with the main categories of folkloric beings such as fauns, elves, the various categories of supernatural women, pygmies and giants. The chapter stresses the interaction between folk belief and learned commentary, identifying biblical commentary and the work of Church Fathers such as Isidore of Seville as the main source of discussions about godlings and, perhaps, as the source of much of the folklore itself.

It is the argument of the chapter that by the time of the Norman Conquest, the various elements of fairy lore were present in British popular belief but had yet to be brought together into a single synthesis. These elements included a belief in wild 'men of the woods' gifted with prophetic powers; belief in elves; belief in supernatural women, often in a triad, governing the fates of human beings; belief in diminutive otherworlders, sometimes living beneath the earth and belief in heroes who had somehow become supernatural beings.

The book's final chapter argues that the various elements of fairy belief as we might recognise it, including belief in an underground otherworld inhabited by sometimes pygmy-sized otherworlders, the connection between fairies and fate and fairy sexuality, were brought together as a direct result of the Norman Conquest. The key role played in the Conquest by Breton nobles who felt a cultural affinity with the Cornish and Welsh, combined with the Normans' desire to escape the English past, resulted in the crafting of a new 'British' identity for the whole island of Great Britain by authors with a Brittonic cultural background such as Geoffrey of Monmouth, Gerald of Wales and Walter Map. These authors united elements of English and Brittonic folklore to fashion a new fairy world that was subsequently adopted as the setting for literary romances. The fairies of romance soon took on a life of their own and fed back into popular culture as a source of fairy lore, creating a complex amalgam of belief that was not fully described until the early modern period.

I

A World Full of Small Gods

Understanding Godlings

~

In the seventh century an Irish monastic writer, Tírechán, described an incident that supposedly occurred during St Patrick's mission in Ireland in the fifth century. Two pagan princesses arrived early one morning at a spring, where they encountered Patrick and his companions. Not understanding who the missionaries were, the princesses suspected they were 'men of the *sídhe*' (*viros side*), 'of the terrestrial gods' (*deorum terrenorum*, perhaps a later gloss) and even 'an illusion' (*fantassiam*).[1] Realising that the missionaries were really just human beings, however, the princesses agreed to hear the message of the Gospel. An interesting feature of Tírechán's account is his direct interpolation of the Irish word *side* into a Latin text. It suggests that Tírechán may have found the Irish concept of the *aos sí*, known in later tradition as the fairies, untranslatable. He made no attempt to identify the *sídhe* with beings of Classical mythology, such as fauns, Parcae, nymphs or genii, in spite of the richness of Classical learning in Ireland at the time.[2] Perhaps even more surprisingly, Tírechán also made no attempt to identify the

---

[1] Gwynn (ed.), *Book of Armagh*, p. 23.
[2] The name of the god Faunus was variously rendered *Phuinn*, *Puin*, *Fuin* and *Thuin* in the medieval Irish translation of *Aeneid* VII (Calder (ed.), *Imtheachta Æniasa*, p. 94).

sídhe with the demons of Christian belief. The godlings stood apart from classification.

Tírechán's approach was, in one way, distinctively Irish; Irish writers generally portrayed Christian missionaries in conflict with idols, druids or demons but not with the *aos sí*, who stood apart as an unclassifiable other.[3] But the infuriating indefinability and ambiguity of the 'small gods' of Britain and Ireland is a consistent feature of these beings found across the different cultures of the islands. Even deciding on a suitable label for them through time is difficult, let alone classifying their characteristic features and tracing their presence in British religion and folklore across the *longue durée* of more than two thousand years. Nevertheless, this chapter attempts to establish a conceptual framework in which the 'small gods' can be understood, at least partially. It does so by examining, first of all, ancient understandings of lesser gods and spirits, before exploring the idea that such beings can endure while undergoing profound transformations over a long period of time. The chapter considers the theory that the roots of Britain's small gods lie in Iron Age animism and shamanism, as well as focussing on some key characteristics of godlings such as their plurality, their fluid nature and the association between godlings and witches. Finally, the chapter addresses the strongest British evidence for the continuity in belief in godlings from the remote past: the association between godlings and bodies of water.

The word 'godling' used in the title of this book is deliberately vague. As I noted in the Introduction, the use of more specific titles is unhelpful when dealing with the

---

[3] Bitel, 'Secrets of the *Síd*', p. 82.

deep history of folkloric beings, since it implants certain expectations in the minds of both researcher and reader. A focus on the 'final' (or most recent) cultural form that such entities assume might render a search for their origins excessively teleological – in which all that counts is evidence of the development of characteristics that are manifested in contemporary and near-contemporary belief. This is why attempting to trace the 'history of fairy belief', for example, would be a misguided exercise: it assumes that the beings that became the fairies were always fairies in some meaningful sense. Once again, the semantic evolution of the Greek word *daimōn* is the *locus classicus* of dealing with the history of supernatural beings. It would be a grave injustice to the *daimōn* of ancient Greece to study only those characteristics of the *daimōn* that resemble the demon of contemporary Christian belief. Such an approach would ignore not only the cultural context of ancient Greek belief but also the complexity of the worlds of belief that have accumulated on top of that original belief – worlds of belief that, in some cases, have long since been and gone.

If it is problematic to seek to trace the origins and development of supernatural beings over time, the comparison and identification of supernatural beings across disparate cultures presents even greater challenges and pitfalls. Rather than aiming at such identifications, a number of scholars are now more inclined to use open-ended terminology for folkloric beings that can be applied in a general way in multiple contexts: 'land spirits' and 'small gods' are popular alternatives to 'godlings', while C. S. Lewis preferred the esoteric 'longaevi' on the grounds that the word 'fairy' was 'tarnished by pantomime and bad children's books with worse illustrations'.[4] My choice of the single word 'godling' over these other terms in the title of this book is primarily a matter of economy, although it is also designed to convey the fact that these beings were, at one time, often venerated in religious or quasi-religious rites. It is the argument of this book that tracing the persistence of godlings – or at least the *idea* of godlings – over the *longue durée* is worthwhile. However, the nature of that persistence has often been misunderstood as something much more definite than it really is, with the result that many straightforwardly 'survivalist' representations of supernatural beings ought to be set aside.

Di nemorum: Ancient Understandings of Godlings

While the Greek words *daimōn* and *theos* may once have had similar meanings, by the fourth century BCE Greeks had begun to distinguish higher and lower divine beings by these terms. The *daimōn* as a subordinate divine being was essentially a creation of the Hellenistic period, elaborated from hints found in the philosophy of Plato. Georg Luck associates the development of a kind of demonological *koine*, or cultural vernacular – which passed into the Roman world – with Plutarch and Apuleius, according to which 'daemons are spiritual beings who think so intensely that they produce vibrations in the air that enable other spiritual beings ... as well as highly sensitive men and women, to "receive" their thoughts'. In this way,

---

[4] Lewis, *Discarded Image*, p. 123.

daemons were the source of phenomena such as clairvoyance and prophecy. According to the Christian writer Eusebius, the 'pagan philosophers' of his day divided spiritual beings into gods, daemons, heroes and souls, and it was a point of continuity between pagan and Christian belief that Christians continued to accept the reality of daemons.[5] The only difference was that Christians tended to roll all supernatural beings other than God and his angels into the daemonic category, and usually portrayed all daemons as evil.

While this Greek sophistication permeated the whole Roman world through the influence of Hellenistic culture, Britain lay beyond the limits of the Greek-speaking Hellenised Roman world and it was the Latin language, therefore, that mattered most. Latin generally made no overt linguistic distinction between gods and godlings (calling both *di* or *dii*). However, a conceptual distinction between different ranks of deities was rooted in Roman religion, even if it was sometimes rather vague and fluid. The vocabulary the Romans developed for divine beings later passed into Christian cultures or inspired new coinages. The words *deus* and *divus* were frequently used in Latin for beings that do not obviously fit modern categories of what might be considered a god – such as the *di manes*, the divine shades of the dead. However, this may say more about our culture's monotheistic (or post-monotheistic) preoccupation with the idea of divine sovereignty, which leaves us consciously or unconsciously wondering how the deities of Greece and Rome fulfilled the divine functions that

---

[5] Luck (ed.), *Arcana Mundi*, pp. 217–18.

monotheistic faiths ascribe to a single deity, rather than actually examining what Roman *di* did.

As Harriet Flower has noted, if we want to understand 'the world BC' ('before Christianity') on its own terms, we need to approach pre-Christian religion 'independent of pervasive comparisons and contrasts with various monotheisms'.[6] It is unclear whether distinctions between different classes of divine beings would have meant much to ordinary Romans and Britons, even if learned Romans like Ovid were aware of the difference (and, indeed, the epigraphic evidence from Roman Britain suggests there was some confusion at times). Famously, the subtle distinction observed in Rome between the illicit direct worship of the living emperor and the licit worship of the emperor's genius was often elided and lost in the provinces.[7]

It was only with the advent of Christianity that the distinction between those impressive, celestial deities who directly competed with the Christian deity and those who occupied a less threatening subordinate position became truly apparent, and it is important to be attentive to the extent to which our image of Roman religion is formed by Christian polemic. In contrast to Islam, which incorporated morally ambiguous godlings into its cosmology as the jinn, Christianity generally tended to a dualistic view of spiritual beings other than God, who were either God's servants or his evil opponents (although, as we shall see in Chapter 3 below, there were exceptions to this dualism). The distinctions that existed between

---

[6] Flower, *Dancing Lares*, p. ix.
[7] Aldhouse-Green, *Sacred Britannia*, p. 43.

different kinds of daemons (good, bad, and morally indifferent) in Hellenistic culture were elided by Christian theologians, who also often maintained that the pagan gods themselves were evil demons who deceived people into worshipping them. However, the concept of fractally multiplying *augenblickgötter* ('gods of the blink of an eye') with responsibility for ever narrower spheres of human life may owe more to Augustine's polemic in *The City of God* than to reality.[8] Eager to satirise what he saw as the absurdity of pagan belief, Augustine explains the gods responsible for every aspect of agriculture and every aspect of the doors of houses, such as Forculus the god of doors, Cardea the goddess of hinges and Limentinus the god of thresholds.[9] While we are supposed to laugh at this multiplication of gods, Augustine leaves unanswered the question of how the Romans themselves understood these deities – whether as really existing personalities, for example, or as personifications, or as beings confected in order to accompany inherited rites whose original purpose was lost in time, but for which the invocation of some imagined god was thought fitting. The classic case of the latter scenario was the Roman rite of the Lupercalia, where the identity of the original patron god of the rites had been forgotten so Faunus or Pan was inserted.

A distinction between celestial deities and deities of nature seems to have been well understood by educated Romans, judging from Ovid's treatment of the subject in his *Fasti*. When King Numa manages to capture Faunus and Picus, in the hope of compelling them to reveal the

---

[8] Aldhouse-Green, *Sacred Britannia*, p. 42.
[9] Augustine, *De civitate Dei* 6.7.1 (*PL* 41.184).

secret of placating Jupiter in order to prevent thunder, the *silvestria numina* ('woodland spirits'), whom Numa addresses as *di nemorum* ('gods of the groves'),[10] protest that 'spirits like us have our limits; we are rustic gods who have dominion in the high mountains'.[11] Faunus was an archaic god of the Latin countryside who failed to conform to later Roman perceptions of how a god should behave. As well as his portrayal as theriomorphic and quasi-bestial, Faunus was usually worshipped in the open air rather than in a temple and provided spontaneous oracles in wild places, in contrast to the majority of Roman gods who did not communicate directly with human beings.[12] While poets like Ovid seem to have equated Faunus with Pan, others were far less sure: 'I don't know what Faunus is at all' (*Faunus omnino quid sit, nescio*), Cicero declared in his *On the Nature of the Gods*.[13]

The word *numen*, sometimes taken to mean a being a little less than a god, really had the sense of a god's divine nature;[14] the older idea that *numen* referred to a kind of *mana* or impersonal animistic spirit, which was enthusiastically advanced by comparativist scholars keen to view the ancient world through the lens of anthropology, is no longer tenable.[15] All deities, large and small, were in possession of *numen*, meaning that the word could be used as a synonym for *deus* or *divus* by way of synecdoche. Another word, *semideus* (literally 'half-god') was used by

---

[10] Ovid, *Fasti* 3.303, 309.
[11] Ovid, *Fasti* 3.314–16: *habent fines numina nostra suos. / di sumus agrestes et qui dominemur in altis / montibus.*
[12] Dorcey, *Cult of Silvanus*, pp. 33–35.
[13] Cicero, *De natura deorum* 3.15.   [14] Flower, *Dancing Lares*, p. 307.
[15] Hunt, 'Pagan Animism', p. 139.

the fifth-century medical writer Caelius Aurelianus to describe the godling Incubo, who was apparently an aspect of Faunus and would eventually lend his name as the most common Latin word used for a fairy in the Middle Ages, *incubus*.[16] However, *semideus* is an ambiguous term, since it could also be used to describe a demigod or hero like Hercules, and a demigod is distinct from a godling insofar as a godling is always a non-human entity. In Classical Latin, therefore, there was no single unambiguous term that described a 'small god' as distinct from other deities.

Later Latin partially supplied this deficit. The rare late Latin word *deunculus* (literally 'godling') occurs in a gloss of around 800 but was clearly not in common use.[17] However, in the fifth-century narrative of the martyrdom of St Susanna the word has the sense of a small idol, as well as being a pejorative way of referring to pagan gods.[18] It is possible that *deunculus* never took off as a word in medieval Latin because it was an insufficiently pejorative term for the false demon-gods of the pagans. Then, in the sixteenth century, Sebastian Castellio coined the word *deaster*,[19] initially to refer to the wooden idols of the Balts and Slavs.[20] However, by the thirteenth century the word *numen* had acquired the sense of a being of lower status than a god within a pagan culture, implying something like 'animistic' belief rather than the 'noble' paganism of Greece and Rome. Thus *numen* was used more frequently

---

[16] Wiseman, 'God of the Lupercal', p. 20.   [17] *RMLWL*, p. 143.
[18] Lapidge (ed.), *Roman Martyrs*, p. 285 n.48.
[19] Frick, *Polish Sacred Philology*, p. 104. The *OED* gives the first use of 'godling' in Lambarde, *Perambulation of Kent*, p. 437.
[20] Young (ed.), *Pagans in the Early Modern Baltic*, p. 137 n.8.

than *deus* by medieval Christian commentators writing about the spirits worshipped by the pagan Balts.[21]

In the same way that the Romans understood the gods as both a general category and one that could be divided into higher and lower echelons, so Norse religion seems to have made similar distinctions (although it should be borne in mind that much of the evidence for Norse paganism is late and was written down only in the Christian era). For the Norse, the world of the divine consisted of the Æsir, the Vanir (later incorporated into the Æsir) and the *álfar* (elves); but the term *æsir* was also a general term for gods and included the *álfar*. However, the *álfar* sometimes stood poetically for the *æsir* and the god Thor seems to have been the *áss* (singular of *æsir*) par excellence, since the term was sometimes used for him in isolation.[22] Old Norse *áss* was cognate with Old English *ós*, which survives as an element in names such as Oswald and Oswin.[23] Another cognate was Gothic *anses*, noted in the sixth century by Jordanes, and apparently having a meaning equivalent to the Latin *semideus*: 'The Goths call their leading men, as if they have won by fortune, not only men but demigods (*semideos*), that is, *anses*'.[24] The word *áss* also meant a beam of wood, leading some philologists to suggest a link with idols carved from poles (rather like the Latin *deunculus* and Neo-Latin *deaster*).[25] All of this suggests

[21] Young (ed.), *Pagans in the Early Modern Baltic*, p. 15.
[22] Lindow, *Norse Mythology*, pp. 49–50.
[23] *Bosworth Toller's Anglo-Saxon Dictionary Online*, s.v. 'ós', bosworthtoller.com/25014, accessed 19 April 2022.
[24] Jordanes, *De origine actibusque Getarum* 13.76: *Gothi proceres suos quasi qui fortuna vincebant non pares homines sed semideos, id est, Anses vocavere*.
[25] Lindow, *Norse Mythology*, p. 50.

that a sophisticated understanding of divine hierarchies prevailed in the ancient Norse and Germanic worlds as well as the Classical world, in which godlings had clearly defined roles even if the exact nature of those roles is sometimes obscure today.

Godlings in the *longue durée*

Euan Cameron argued that 'over the extremely longue durée ... The Christianization of late antique and post-Roman Europe will have generated countless instances of the transmutation, evolution, and re-expression of old beliefs in new cultural garb: classical minor deities will have become the fauns and nymphs of legend'.[26] Picking up on this observation, it is a key argument of this book that the concept of the *longue durée* – the near-permanence of certain structures of human behaviour and belief across long eras of time, as proposed by Braudel and others – is generally a more helpful one for understanding the phenomenon of godlings than is the 'survivalist hypothesis'. The survivalist hypothesis that dominated folklore studies until the 1970s was the idea, associated with scholars influenced by the anthropologist Sir James Frazer, that popular religion often represented an ancient (or even immemorial) substratum of belief that survived beneath Christianity and other organised religions, especially among rural populations. For the survivalist, popular religion is an ark of memory that transmits beliefs and rituals from remote periods to the historical era. The historian of the *longue durée*, by contrast, is not

---

[26] Cameron, *Enchanted Europe*, p. 74.

committed to the survival of specific beliefs, emphasising instead long-term trends of belief. The study of godlings in the *longue durée* does not presuppose a genealogical connection between iterations of belief in such beings in different eras. Continuity is to be found in the niches occupied by godlings within the popular religion of different cultures at different times.

Human cultural memory, in the *longue durée*, is not so much an ark as a Ship of Theseus – subject to constant repair, reinvention and renewal, yet retaining throughout a recognisable form. While it is impossible to speak of the survival of the whole ship, or even the survival of any individual part of the ship, the general form the ship retains throughout its many phases of repair give us a strong indication of its purpose; it is unlikely, even over the course of centuries, to go from being a wooden trireme to a metal-hulled oil tanker, for example. Furthermore, if individual timbers *do* survive within the ship there is no guarantee that those oldest timbers will play a crucial role in its structure – they may be of only incidental importance. If the reader prefers a different metaphor for the true nature of folkloric survival, Ronald Hutton supplies one in his book *Queens of Wild*, playing on the metaphor of 'throwing the baby out with the bathwater'. If the 'babies' are the popular rural customs once thought to be pagan survivals by twentieth-century folklorists but now known to be of recent vintage, the babies should indeed be taken out of the water. But once the 'babies' are tucked up in bed as largely nineteenth-century creations, it is the bathwater itself that remains interesting. In other words, individual rural festivities are usually of recent date, but the idea that there might have been *some sort* of antecedent festivity held at that time of year since immemorial antiquity still retains merit.[27] The 'bathwater' is the *longue durée* of human history, and the largely unchanging and harsh realities of a rural subsistence economy dependent on the seasons.

This does not mean that no effort should be made to pursue the historical genealogies of supernatural beings (and much of this book consists of just such an effort). It is not always inappropriate to speak of 'survival', as this and subsequent chapters will make clear. However, a high standard of evidence is required to demonstrate real survival, as opposed to a more generalised continuity of form in the *longue durée*. Survivalist assumptions can lead to rather unguarded claims, such as Neil Faulkner's reflection on the nature of Romano-British religion:

> [B]eneath the Romanised veneer – urban, cosmopolitan, sophisticated – there survived an ancient culture rooted in the landscape, in the native soil, and in the ancestral farmlands, much of it older than the Celts, older even than the Beaker folk, some indeed going back to the myth-time when the whole world was a wooded wilderness.[28]

The idea of immemorial traditions in rural communities is an attractive one, both to historians and folklorists. Yet the idea that rural communities preserved immemorial traditions from the Bronze Age in Roman Britain is really no more plausible than the idea that there were pagan peasants in nineteenth-century England. We do not know that Romanisation was a 'veneer' in late Roman

---

[27] Hutton, *Queens of the Wild*, p. 34.
[28] Faulkner, *Decline and Fall of Roman Britain*, p. 120.

Britain – and while there is archaeological evidence that communities remembered Iron Age sites or considered them significant, we cannot be certain they ascribed anything like the same significance to those sites as their Iron Age ancestors. The 'survivalist' mindset irrationally privileges the possibility that beliefs and practices in popular religion may derive from remote periods of antiquity, often without proper investigation of the alternative possibility: that popular religion and folklore are confected and constructed at need, and are often not as ancient as they might seem.

The notion of deliberate confection of supernatural beliefs has its limitations; clearly, within oral, preliterate and largely illiterate societies the processes by which supernatural belief arises are as much organic and spontaneous as they are premeditated by an individual or individuals. But there is no need for us to abandon historical thinking when faced with folkloric beliefs, and plunge into an imagined dark forest of immemorial, primordial and irrecoverable myth, and it is this book's contention that it is not altogether misguided to discern a degree of intentionality in the interpretations of supernatural beings adopted within a culture. It is always possible that folk beliefs really are very ancient, and it is not a possibility that should be dismissed *tout court*; but alternative explanations setting beliefs in their contemporary cultural context should first be explored and exhausted. Supernatural beings rarely survive across the *longue durée* as individual characters, because they are cultural creations; they will, then, change unrecognisably as cultures undergo transformation. While folkloric beings like the fairies are indeed, in one sense, a legacy of a world older than Christianity,[29] it would be a mistake to look for detailed information about the content of pre-Christian belief within fairy traditions.

Diane Purkiss observed, 'To say that fairies were once gods is helpful in the sense that it is helpful to say that cars were once ox-carts'.[30] In other words, while it may be true in some sense that folkloric beings descend from deities, it is scarcely a meaningful observation – because they no longer play the role of gods by the time we encounter them in folklore. Fairy lore is the diffuse and repurposed wreckage of pre-Christian religious beliefs, not their lineal successor. If we imagine that an aeroplane crashes in the jungle and its wreckage becomes a resource for those who live in the jungle over generations, it would be absurd for a visiting anthropologist to conclude that whoever wears the threadbare pilot's hat is 'the pilot'. Continuity in folkloric beings is to be found not in characters or even in classes of being, and we must always be prepared to contemplate the possibility that a belief died out entirely and a familiar name that had lost almost all significance was later picked up and applied to a new cultural creation. This latter process, which we might call 're-personification', involves the re-use of names of half-remembered supernatural beings to newly name and personify supernatural forces that have a particular cultural relevance in a time and place.

The phenomenon of personification in the medieval world and in medieval literature has been the subject of important studies by Barbara Newman and James Paxson,[31] who have shown that culturally constructed

[29] Hutton, *Pagan Britain*, p. 382.   [30] Purkiss, *Troublesome Things*, p. 7.
[31] Newman, *God and the Goddesses*; Paxson, *Poetics of Personification*.

personified figures were not mere literary devices but had real power to be used and adapted for new purposes. Martianus Capella's personification of the Seven Liberal Arts as maidens (by analogy with the Graces, the Muses and, indeed, the Fates) is one well-known example.[32] However, the lines between new characters created by personification, ancient personified beings and folkloric beings such as gods, ghosts and genii were never clearly drawn,[33] and thus understanding processes of personification and re-personification may be crucial to revealing how medieval folkloric beings came about. In an earlier book dealing with early modern supernatural beliefs I showed how a process rather like re-personification created the monastic ghosts familiar in modern English folklore (the 'black monk' and 'grey nun' who characteristically haunt houses built on the sites of England's dissolved monasteries). Apparitions of this kind were first recorded in the nineteenth century, but they were often preceded by anxieties about bad luck. This belief in ill luck proceeded in turn from a belief that sacrilege would be punished by divine providence. The ghosts that haunted former monastic sites from the nineteenth century onwards were, in one sense, a particular product of the nineteenth century; but they can also be interpreted as new cultural projections, in personified form, of much older anxieties hitherto expressed in other ways.[34] A sixteenth-century owner of a former monastic property might fear an untimely death as punishment

[32] Ross, *Medieval Art*, p. 277.
[33] Newman, *God and the Goddesses*, pp. 33–34.
[34] Young, *English Catholics and the Supernatural*, pp. 79–109.

for hereditary sacrilege, while their nineteenth-century successor might fear the appearance of spectral monks or nuns. Literary Romanticism encouraged people to personify monastic curses as apparitions, where previously the curse had simply taken the form of fears of misfortune. While we cannot expect characters to survive across time, names and (to some extent) characteristics tied to those names may survive. Language is the essential bearer of folkloric beings through time, but those beings may also persist when they are tied to enduring features of the landscape or of the agricultural year – or simply because the cultural niche they occupy remains relevant across the *longue durée* in a pre-industrial society. In a *longue durée* study of popular religion focussed on Iberia, Joyce Salisbury argued for 'deep religious needs integral to rural culture' that did not essentially change, whether Celtiberians, Romans or Visigoths were in charge. Similarly, Averil Cameron has argued for understanding the Mediterranean world of late antiquity in the *longue durée* 'in terms of continuities, [and] abiding structures'.[35] We cannot assume that ordinary rural people had the same religious needs or views as those who ruled over them, and it is a mistake to characterise popular religion as 'persisting superstitions' or as 'peripheral, archaic or deviant religiosity'.[36] Salisbury drew attention to scholars' tendency to dismiss unexpected expressions of popular religion with the pejorative and uninformative label of 'superstition'. At the same time, however, Salisbury did

---

[35] Cameron, *Mediterranean World in Late Antiquity*, p. 208.
[36] Salisbury, *Iberian Popular Religion*, p. 2.

not go as far as Emma Wilby and claim that rural people remained essentially animists.[37]

It is largely unhelpful to apply labels such as 'pagan' or 'animist' to popular religion, which is much harder to pin down than such convenient labels might suggest. Salisbury largely set aside the possibility of continuity in *belief* in the period from the Iberian Iron Age to the Visigothic early Middle Ages; instead, she argued for continuity in the *ecosystem* of belief within a rural society whose essential structure did not change as much as those who governed it. In the subsistence economy of rural Galicia, the propitiation of spirits believed to control natural processes 'represented the difference between sufficiency and starvation', and such practices persisted for as long as the church failed to provide an equivalent service. Rural people's attachment to 'superstition' was not a sign of backwardness so much as a matter of survival.[38] In late antique and early medieval Galicia, for example, Christianity had no chance of making progress in the countryside until it was able to accommodate a particular Galician reverence for mountains, which it did by associating the mountains with hermit saints who defeated the demons inhabiting the peaks.[39] In Hutton's words, 'the sheer otherworldliness of Christianity ... forced medieval people to retain memories of ancient pagan beliefs in order to cope with the present world'.[40]

Nevertheless, Christianisation was not a straightforward matter of replacing one set of supernatural beings

[37] Wilby, *Cunning Folk*, p. 15.
[38] Salisbury, *Iberian Popular Religion*, p. 25.
[39] Salisbury, *Iberian Popular Religion*, pp. 228–34.
[40] Hutton, *Queens of the Wild*, p. 37.

with another. Like the fragments of figurative sculpture that often survive high up in English cathedrals and churches, beyond the reach of even the most thorough sixteenth-century iconoclasts, godlings endured because it was too hard for new religions to reach the niches they occupied. Yet we should not be surprised if the character of these beings changed over time, sometimes unrecognisably, even when the names these characters bore are traceable to an earlier age. Etymology can be both a help and a hindrance to the historian of supernatural beings. On the one hand, tracing the sources of a being's name can illuminate its origins, but on the other hand it can easily give rise to misguided notions about the significance of that being in later ages. The folklorist Simon Young has noted that the linguistic history of 'England's supernatural fauna' has historically been neglected or 'left in the hands of dilettantes to general disadvantage'.[41] Linguistic analysis has thus simultaneously failed to achieve its potential and been allowed to perpetuate unhelpful academic myths.

Etymology can also be deceptive, even when traced with accuracy. To take one example from Irish folklore, Jacopo Bisagni has argued that the Irish word *luchorpán* (one of the origins of 'leprechaun') was created from folk etymology in an effort to gloss the older and more obscure word *lupracán*, with *luchorpán* meaning something like 'small body'. But while it is true that 'leprechaun' derives in part from *luchorpán*, the meaning of *luchorpán* reflects the cultural understanding of what a *lupracán* was at the moment in time when it was glossed as *luchorpán*, and not the original meaning of *lupracán*.[42] A similar process

[41] Young, *The Boggart*, p. 29.   [42] Bisagni, 'Leprechaun', pp. 61–62.

can perhaps be detected in the glossing of the obscure English word *colepixy* (a bogey-beast) in some dialects as *coltpixy*, with the result that the *colepixy* was imagined as taking an equine form.[43] Yet it seems highly unlikely that the *colepixy* originally had anything to do with colts. Folk etymologies can lead to the phenomenon of *lectio facilior*: the formation of new, easier-to-understand words when the original words are deemed too obscure or incomprehensible (a particular problem when it comes to words for supernatural beings). Clearly, the etymologist can easily be led astray by examining re-formations like *luchorpán* instead of the word's ultimate ancestor.

There is an established tradition of using evidence from other cultures and evidence from much later eras in the study of ancient British religion, often because there is little choice if a scholar wishes to widen their body of evidence. Study of the druids, for example, has routinely relied on comparative data drawn from early medieval Irish literature.[44] However, a shortcoming of such an approach is that it is possible medieval Irish writers introduced druids to an imagined ancient Ireland because they knew of them from Classical literature.[45] Indeed, it is even possible that druidism was in some way reinvented in later antiquity, long after any real knowledge of the druids extirpated by Roman authority had vanished.[46] The case of the druids is a reminder that the survival of a name alone is no guarantee that the original meaning of that name has been

---

[43] Harte, 'Fairy Barrows', p. 71.   [44] Hutton, *Pagan Britain*, p. 175.
[45] Aldhouse-Green, *Sacred Britannia*, p. 36.
[46] Aldhouse-Green, *Sacred Britannia*, p. 31.

preserved; the druids were and are an evocative symbol of pre-Roman Gaulish, British and Irish religion, but that does not mean we know much about who they were or what they believed. Salisbury has argued that, rather than attempting to trace the changing meaning of monuments or objects through time, historians of the ancient world should study 'the addition of changing ideas onto a fixed object', using the example of ancient Egyptian obelisks transported to Rome.[47] The same principle can also be applied to names and words as well as objects, where the name is the fixed object but the ideas added to it change and evolve over time.

Similarly, while it is probable that medieval British and Irish literature bears *some* faint relationship to the religious beliefs and practices of the pre-Christian (and pre-Roman) Iron Age, the idea that the personalities of individual Iron Age or Roman deities can be reconstructed from medieval literature is decidedly fanciful. The dearth of reliable evidence, the charisma of the literature itself, and an excessively hopeful belief in the possibility of ancient survivals in oral tradition have often conspired to produce less than critical reconstructions of 'Celtic' religion. Barry Cunliffe, for example, speculated that Iron Age religion was based on a balancing of male and female opposites, with the result that the multiplicity of gods are simply tribal names for a single male deity, while 'the many female deities are manifestations of the one earth mother seen in various local guises'.[48] One could be forgiven for thinking that Cunliffe was influenced by

[47] Salisbury, 'Before the Standing Stones', pp. 21–22.
[48] Cunliffe, *Iron Age Britain*, p. 103.

Margaret Murray's belief in an essentially duotheistic cult of the Goddess and the Horned God, the basis of the modern religion of Wicca. Needless to say, there is no evidence for the existence of this twentieth-century belief in Iron Age Britain.

It is the aim of this book to set aside both the wishful thinking of those who maintain godlings can be traced as specific characters over time, and the reductivism of those who see minor spirits as no more than functional entities whose specific identity is unimportant at any point in time. Godlings do have a history, and some attempt can be made to tell it; yet their identities are also highly fluid over time, and therefore it is not possible to formulate a straightforward definition of godlings or 'small gods' that will ever be completely satisfactory and take account of every aspect of their nature. However, it is possible to identify certain typical characteristics of godlings in the *longue durée* of British history, which can be discerned in the minor deities of Roman Britain as much as in the fairies of late medieval England.

Firstly, as Katharine Briggs insisted, godlings are non-human beings.[49] They are not to be confused with heroes, demigods or saints, because they are entities of a decidedly supernatural character even if they take a physical form and appear 'human-like'. Secondly, godlings are 'chthonic' entities, 'land spirits' connected with nature, the land or the household rather than with celestial realms. They are not to be confused with angels or transcendent gods. Thirdly, godlings are often ambiguous in various ways; they may have animal or therianthropic

[49] Briggs, *Vanishing People*, p. 26.

characteristics, rendering their classification as human-like or animal-like ambiguous, and their gender may be uncertain or fluid. Furthermore, while they may be understood and venerated as individual entities, they will often also be understood and venerated as a class of beings, such as 'the nymphs', 'the fauns', 'the Parcae' or 'the fairies'. As Jacqueline Simpson noted, the 'contradictoriness' of fairies is one of their stable attributes.[50] Fourthly, godlings are often associated with abstract concepts of fate and destiny. In this respect they are adjacent to (albeit not the same as) divine personifications, and they are entities conjured at need in order to provide a focus for anxieties about unpredictable forces.

In addition to these four key characteristics, the cults of godlings (where they have existed at all) have generally been 'complementary cults' (in Harriet Flower's phrase) that supplemented official religion.[51] We should not expect godlings to be worshipped at major city temples by an elite group of priests; their worship was not deemed a necessity by the public authorities, and was a matter of individual choice. Yet belief in godlings may also be unconnected with a cult at all, or the cult will take the form of basic propitiation rather than formal offerings and sacrifices. Godlings are, by definition, subordinate deities who will inhabit an ecosystem of the divine alongside greater gods of celestial sovereignty or colonial domination, whether the gods of the official Roman pantheon, the deified emperors of Rome or the Christian God and his saints.

[50] Simpson, 'Ambiguity of Elves [1]', pp. 81–82.
[51] Flower, *Dancing Lares*, p. ix.

Animism, 'Shamanism' and Therianthropy in the British Iron Age

The idea that early modern fairy belief should be seen as animistic, and even as an animistic survival from a remote period, has been advanced by Emma Wilby, who saw it as 'an amalgamation of many of the animistic beliefs and rituals surrounding nature spirits, deities, ghosts and so on which had not been completely homogenized into Catholic hagiolatry and the cult of the dead'.[52] A striking feature of early modern fairy belief is that the fairies were capable of fulfilling the role of almost any other spiritual being, with fairies sometimes appearing as the host of the dead (that is, ghosts), sometimes as angels, sometimes as demons, sometimes as the devil, and sometimes even as witches. The idea that fairies represented a basic experience of the spiritual world from before that world became subject to the classifications of demonologists is therefore an attractive one.[53] Fairies, on this interpretation, belong to an earlier stratum of belief that, on account of its deep-rooted antiquity, did not easily yield to classifications arising from Christian theology.

If Wilby is correct that fairy belief is ancient and animistic, we should expect to see some evidence of that animism in Britain throughout history, but there is no clear indication that this is the case. While there are sporadic instances of 'idolatry' recorded in medieval Britain, there is no plausible case that 'paganism' survived in medieval Britain in any form beyond the tenth century, at the very latest.[54] The idea that animism remained submerged and

[52] Wilby, *Cunning Folk*, p. 17. [53] Young, *Suffolk Fairylore*, p. 8.
[54] Hutton, *Pagan Britain*, pp. 340–96.

only re-emerged in the testimony of early modern witchcraft trials therefore lacks plausibility. Nevertheless, the idea that godlings per se belong more comfortably to animism than to polytheism is not a new one,[55] given that godlings are often intimately and inseparably linked with features of the landscape and the natural world. In a critique of the application of the idea of animism to Greek and Roman religion, Ailsa Hunt has argued that there is insufficient evidence from ancient sources for belief in impersonal spirits animating features of the natural world (such as trees) in the Roman world.[56] The association of words such as *numen* with sacred groves can be interpreted as a reference to anthropomorphic divine beings rather than impersonal animistic spirits, and as such the concept of animism is not a very helpful one to apply to Roman religion – and, by extension, to post-Roman cultures heavily influenced by it. Scholars have tended to find animism in Classical texts because they have been looking for it.[57]

In addition to animism, fairy cults have been linked with 'shamanism',[58] with Wilby arguing that the frequent appearance of animal familiar spirits in British witch trials ought to be understood in 'shamanic' terms.[59] As Hutton has noted, 'shamanism' is a scholarly construct inspired by ritual behaviours first encountered in Siberia that has become 'one of the phenomena against which modern western civilisation has defined itself'.[60] However, most

---

[55] Ostling, 'Introduction', pp. 19–20.
[56] Hunt, 'Pagan Animism', pp. 143–44.
[57] Hunt, 'Pagan Animism', p. 145.
[58] Ostling, 'Introduction', pp. 26–32.
[59] Wilby, *Cunning Folk*, pp. 123–64.   [60] Hutton, *Shamans*, pp. vii–viii.

accounts of shamanism are dominated by the idea that shamans make contact with the spirit world in an altered state of consciousness, sometimes assuming the behaviours of animals. Shamanism thus differs from 'paganism' as conventionally understood in the Western world as the offering of sacrifice to deities who may or may not choose to communicate with the worshipper. The idea that shamanism is older – and more basic – than later religious developments is widespread in anthropological scholarship, and scholars frequently identify the earliest evidence of Palaeolithic religion as 'shamanic' in character.[61] Like all conclusions that can be drawn from archaeological evidence alone, in the absence of written sources, identifications that draw on comparisons with contemporary indigenous societies are inevitably tenuous.

Hutton has been critical of Miranda Aldhouse-Green's efforts to associate Iron Age and Romano-British religious practices with shamanism, on account of the absence of any clear definition of the term.[62] Aldhouse-Green drew on stories of shape-shifting druids in medieval Irish literature as potential evidence for people assuming the identities of animals in ritual trances.[63] John Creighton has even suggested that apparent therianthropic images (people transforming into animals) also appear on Iron Age coins, which he argued often feature imagery emerging from trance states.[64] Britain's Iron Age coins certainly bear imagery that is bafflingly strange, and which challenges the idea that British religion was anything like its

[61] Hutton, *Pagan Britain*, pp. 15–16.
[62] Hutton, *Pagan Britain*, p. 434 n.205.
[63] Green, *Exploring the World of the Druids*, p. 127.
[64] Creighton, *Coins and Power*, pp. 45, 47.

Roman counterpart. If such imagery is not evidence of 'shamanism', it nevertheless suggests a perception of the divine bound up with the animal world. Jane Webster notes the existence of some portrayals of Epona simply as a mare accompanied by a foal, suggesting that the 'goddess of horses' was perhaps once a horse herself, a zoomorphic representation of the equine as divine who became anthropomorphised under Roman influence.[65]

The anthropologist Roald Knutsen's confidence that 'a shaman is unmistakably represented' by the therianthropic 'chicken man' featured in a fourth-century mosaic at Brading, Isle of Wight is just one example of the tendency to see a kind of Iron Age 'shamanism' surviving in Roman Britain.[66] This proposal requires us, of course, to assume that shamans existed in Iron Age Britain to begin with. Aldhouse-Green has suggested that a man interred near a Bronze Age barrow at Deal in Kent in the first century BCE might have been a shaman, owing to his separation from other burials and the presence of a bronze crown similar to ritual crowns later used in Roman Britain.[67] Antlers discovered at some fourth-century Romano-British temple sites, such as Maiden Castle, have been connected to the worship of horned deities,[68] but the wearing of these antlers in religious ceremonies is another possible interpretation – leading to inevitable comparison with shamanic practices of therianthropic performance. A bronze figurine of a

---

[65] Webster, 'A Dirty Window', p. 140.
[66] Knutsen, *Tengu*, p. 52. On alleged shamanism in Roman Britain see Aldhouse-Green, *Sacred Britannia*, pp. 141–48.
[67] Aldhouse-Green, *Sacred Britannia*, p. 23.
[68] De la Bédoyère, *Gods with Thunderbolts*, p. 197.

dog with a human face from the fourth-century shrine at Lydney, Gloucestershire, has similarly been put forward as possible evidence of shamanic beliefs in the ability of humans to transform into animals.[69]

While the Brittonic names of gods worshipped in Roman Britain are usually taken as an indication that these gods were survivals from Iron Age Britain,[70] this need not necessarily be the case. We cannot even be certain that the deities and spirits of Iron Age Britain had names at all. Furthermore, there is no reason why those deities invented at need in Roman Britain would not have been given names in the local language, making them seem like immemorial native cults when they may have been creations of the Roman era. One example of a Roman phenomenon that scholars may be erroneously reading back onto the Iron Age is the deification of rivers. All of the evidence we have of riverine deities, such as sculptures of the Thames and Tyne as bearded gods and an inscription identifying Verbeia (goddess of the River Wharfe), is Roman. Scholars have sometimes assumed that the personal names of deities lie behind the names of rivers, such as the putative goddess Sabrina, patron of the Severn.[71] Yet the exact opposite is also possible: that Iron Age Britons did not deify rivers as named characters at all, and the Roman conquerors confected deities like Verbeia from the hydronyms, not vice versa.

Stephen Yeates, whose interpretations of Roman and post-Roman religion in the Cotswolds are controversial (but thought-provoking nonetheless), has suggested that

[69] Aldhouse-Green, *Sacred Britannia*, p. 96.
[70] Aldhouse-Green, *Sacred Britannia*, p. 225.
[71] Yeates, *Tribe of Witches*, pp. 31–33.

deities whose names were associated with territories were not so much the gods *of* that territory, but the deified landscape itself.[72] Similarly, Martin Henig has suggested that the cult of the nymphs in Roman Britain perpetuated the veneration of bodies of water in Iron Age Britain.[73] Yet rather than deifying bodies of water by association with a named deity, it is equally possible that rivers in general were, for Iron Age people, a place of contact with an otherworld of spirits, and that *interpretatio Romana* made sense of animistic practices through the veneration of gods and goddesses named after the river who were essentially Roman creations. If animism is alien to the thought-world of Christianity, it was also alien to the thought-world of sophisticated Romans of the first century BCE. In some cases, such as the River Churn at Cirencester, the river seems to have been identified with a genius.[74] We cannot be sure of the extent or depth of *interpretatio Romana* in taking an entirely alien religious landscape of animism, 'shamanism' and veneration of aniconic and nameless spirits and turning it into something comprehensible in Roman terms. Yet in such a thoroughgoing process of reinterpretation, as in the translation of one language into another, loose ends will be left: aspects of the pre-existing religious landscape not easily conformable to the patterns imposed on it by the demands of Roman cultural transformation.

It is even possible that the Britons (or some of them) were forced by Roman hegemony into a position similar to the Japanese in the mid-nineteenth century,

---

[72] Yeates, *Tribe of Witches*, pp. 28–29.
[73] Henig, *Religion in Roman Britain*, pp. 45–46.
[74] Yeates, *Tribe of Witches*, p. 51.

compelled to invent the very concept of religion (which did not exist in their society) when Japan was forcibly opened to the world by the United States.[75] Certainly the Roman legal distinction of *religio* (the authorised rites) and *superstitio* (rites considered immoral and disgusting, like human sacrifice) would have been a novelty to Iron Age Britons.[76] Jane Webster has suggested that 'religion' should not be thought of as a 'discrete category of human experience' in the Iron Age, but rather as 'largely embedded within, and inseparable from, the world of the everyday'.[77] The otherness of Iron Age religion is suggested by the occasional failure of Romano-British iconography of the gods to conform to the anthropomorphic conventions of Roman art at all, such as a small bronze figurine from Cambridgeshire that apparently depicts the god Erriapus as a 'phytanthropic' tree trunk with a human head.[78]

Webster notes that 'much of our understanding of Iron Age deity worship has been obtained by squinting back at the past through a window provided by Roman sculpture, epigraphy and texts',[79] and she challenges the idea that Iron Age religion can be reconstructed from Roman-era evidence, arguing that the colonial influence of Rome radically transformed British religion. Britain's Iron Age gods were in all likelihood 'highly localised, and possibly multi-functional, "deities of place"'.[80] Since there is

[75] Josephson, *Invention of Religion in Japan*, pp. 1–21.
[76] On Roman definitions of *superstitio* as unacceptable religion see Beard et al., *Religions of Rome*, 1: 215–19.
[77] Webster, 'A Dirty Window', p. 121.
[78] De la Bédoyère, *Gods with Thunderbolts*, p. 48.
[79] Webster, 'A Dirty Window', p. 121.
[80] Webster, 'A Dirty Window', p. 134.

'not a single firmly dated Iron Age example of figured, freestanding deity imagery from Britain itself',[81] it is reasonable to speculate that the Roman conquest may have been the first time Iron Age gods were realised anthropomorphically, because they were subject to iconographic representation.[82] The lack of images could also be down to the perishable nature of the wood in which these effigies were carved, however.[83]

On the other hand, Charles Thomas has observed that the religion of Iron Age Britain may have resembled an earlier stratum of Roman religion, 'partly maintained in a background of private sprites and godlings', with the result that Iron Age British religion may not have been all that different from Roman popular religion, even if it differed markedly from the official cults.[84] As Chapter 2 will explore, educated Romans like Ovid and Varro were well aware of an archaic, 'animistic' substratum to Roman religion, and it is possible that some Romans recognised in British religion an older version of themselves. We know very little about the everyday practice of Iron Age religion, although the deposition of metalwork in bodies of water by Iron Age people, apparently for religious purposes, is well attested. The older view that Iron Age Britain was strangely devoid of sacred sites has been challenged by the suggestion that hillforts were in fact the site of seasonal ceremonies[85] – which, if true, would go some way towards explaining why Romano-Britons of the fourth-century 'pagan revival' gravitated towards hillforts as sacred sites.

[81] Webster, 'A Dirty Window', p. 133.
[82] Webster, 'A Dirty Window', pp. 138–39.
[83] Aldhouse-Green, *Sacred Britannia*, pp. 39–40.
[84] Thomas, *Celtic Britain*, p. 26. [85] Hutton, *Pagan Britain*, p. 212.

What seems certain is that Iron Age religion was extremely diverse, ranging from worship at temples (such as at Harlow in Essex, Wanborough in Surrey and Hayling Island in Hampshire) to worship in purely natural settings.[86] The discovery of Iron Age features beneath some later Roman temples, most of them 'water shrines', is suggestive of continuity in at least one aspect of pre-Roman British religion.[87] The location of the temple at Dean Hall near Newnham-on-Severn (apparently the successor to an Iron Age site) within site of a bend in the River Severn where the force of the Severn Bore could be seen to full advantage supports a circumstantial case for some sort of personification or worship of the river as a deity.[88]

There is an ongoing debate about the extent to which Britain was ever truly 'Romanised' throughout the Roman occupation,[89] but the archaeological and numismatic evidence suggests that in the century or so before the Claudian conquest Romanisation was already underway in late Iron Age Britain. The Lexden Tumulus in Essex, excavated in 1924, revealed the burial of a late Iron Age chieftain full of Roman objects and even a portrait medallion of the Emperor Augustus.[90] Similarly, the coins of British rulers such as Verica, Tincomarus and Cunobelinus display Roman religious and state symbolism such as eagles, winged Victories and augurs, with Cunobelinus even appearing in a Roman cavalry

[86] De la Bédoyère, *Gods with Thunderbolts*, pp. 113–14.
[87] Jones and Mattingly, *Atlas of Roman Britain*, pp. 290–95.
[88] Jones and Mattingly, *Atlas of Roman Britain*, p. 294.
[89] See for example Russell and Laycock, *UnRoman Britain*.
[90] Foster, *Lexden Tumulus*, pp. 91–92.

helmet on one issue.[91] Coins of the Romanised king of the Atrebates and Regini, Verica, portrayed the head of Medusa, sphinxes and even a Roman-style pedimented temple,[92] while coinage surely reached the summit of *Romanitas* in Hertfordshire and Essex under King Cunobelinus. Centaurs, capricorns, Pegasuses, griffins, a club-wielding Hercules and even the eastern deity Jupiter Ammon all feature on the coins of this king who seems to have been the first to style himself 'king of the Britons'.[93]

Iron Age British coins were not straightforward copies of Roman issues, and they displayed considerable skill, not only in the quality of engraving that went into the dies (perhaps by foreign craftsmen) but also in the deployment of Classical imagery. It is even possible that the identification between Mars and the British god Camulos (patron of Cunobelinus' capital Camulodunum at Colchester, whose name his coins bore) had already been made before the Claudian invasion, judging from the appearance of an armed and mounted figure on some of the Iron Age king's coins alongside the legend *CAMV*. However, as almost our sole source of evidence for late Iron Age visual culture, it is impossible to judge the extent to which the imagery on these coins was religious, purely political or a mixture of both. There is certainly insufficient evidence from Iron Age Britain to indicate one way or the other whether animistic spirits or practices associated with 'shamanism' survived into Roman Britain and beyond. The idea that belief in godlings represents a prehistoric substratum of

---

[91] Cottam et al., *Ancient British Coins*, p. 45.
[92] Cottam et al., *Ancient British Coins*, pp. 74–75.
[93] Cottam et al., *Ancient British Coins*, pp. 138–41.

religious belief pre-dating both anthropomorphic polytheism and monotheism remains an attractive one, but nevertheless a purely speculative suggestion. Both 'shamanism' and 'animism' are concepts that are rather too easy to apply to widely divergent eras and societies, raising the suspicion that they may be fuzzy, ill-defined terms of limited historiographical usefulness. Furthermore, it is important to note that prehistoric religion was not the only possible source for ideas of therianthropy or animal transformation in later popular religion and folklore. Classical literature, patristic commentary and the Bible itself are replete with examples of such transformations, which will be explored further in Chapter 4 below.

One or Many, Male or Female?

The folklorist Simon Young has argued that a fundamental feature of the fairies is that they are social spirits, forming a parallel society mirroring that of human beings.[94] This is not to say that all fairies are *sociable*, however; as Katharine Briggs observed in her still influential classification of the fairy world, fairies can be divided into both the 'trooping' and the solitary types.[95] Yet even the solitary fairies, like the brownie, are social beings. They are part of the fairy world, even if they do not (like the trooping fairies) form part of a fairy court. The fairies are, generally speaking, beings of the indefinite article; they are not a single being manifesting in different forms, at different times, to different people, but rather a class of beings containing many individuals.

---

[94] Young, *The Boggart*, p. 100. [95] Briggs, 'English Fairies', p. 270.

One or Many, Male or Female?

The plurality of Britain's godlings is one manifestation of a much wider phenomenon. Daniel Hraste and Krešimir Vuković associate 'fluctuation between plural and singular' with woodland godlings in particular, pointing to the examples of Faunus/the fauns and Silvanus/the silvani in the Latin tradition, and comparing it with Vedic tradition where groups of deities are common.[96] However, groups of godlings were clearly more common in the Latin tradition than the example of the fauns and silvani; the nymphs, the Parcae, the Lares and the Penates are all obvious examples. In the same way, in early modern British folklore 'Puck' or 'Robin Goodfellow' was sometimes presented as a specific character (as in Shakespeare's *A Midsummer Night's Dream*) and sometimes as a class of being (pucks), just as in Lithuanian folklore Velnias (the god of the underworld) is simultaneously one being and also a class of beings.[97]

Similar ambiguities between singular and plural can be found in the religions of Roman Britain. The goddess Sulis Minerva may have been connected with the Matres Suleviae, known from inscriptions at Bath, Cirencester and Binchester, who were probably versions of the widely portrayed Deae Matres.[98] It is possible that the Suleviae represented an alternative understanding of Sulis, not as a single deity but as a group of beings – a reminder that the Romans both imposed their own religious ideas on Britain and, in all likelihood, privileged some understandings of deities over others. The prevalence of triadism

[96] Hraste and Vuković, 'Rudra-Shiva and Silvanus-Faunus', pp. 109–10.
[97] Vėlius, *Chtoniškasis*, p. 140.
[98] De la Bédoyère, *Gods with Thunderbolts*, p. 72; Aldhouse-Green, *Sacred Britannia*, pp. 83, 106–7.

in Romano-British religious art, where deities appear in threes, has traditionally been interpreted in light of the apparent sacredness of the number three. Yet the number three in ancient art as far back as the Egyptians was also a simple representation of the idea of plurality itself and stood for any unspecified number higher than two.[99] A relief recovered from the shrine of Coventina at Carrawburgh depicts three nymphs, all of whom hold up jars in their left hands while water pours out of a jar in their right (Plate 2). The relief has been variously interpreted as a triplication of Coventina and a representation of Coventina and two nymph attendants,[100] but it is also possible that it represents an alternative understanding of Coventina (the Coventinae?) as a plural rather than a singular being.

Likewise, on Hadrian's Wall a group of beings called the Veteres were sometimes named as a group and sometimes as a singular being, variously spelled Veter, Hvitris, Hueeteris, Vheteris and Votris, and sometimes conflated with the obscure god Mogons. Judging from the crudely carved altars honouring them, the Veteres were the object of private cults among ordinary soldiers, but whether the Veteres were native spirits or imported Germanic beings remains unclear. The only other reference to them comes from Thistleton, Rutland, where a dedication was made by a woman with a probable Germanic name, Mocuxsoma.[101] Whatever their origin, however, the lack of a standardised spelling for the Veteres suggests that they arose from a non-literate oral culture in which

---

[99] Curry, 'Commentary on the *Orphic Argonautica*', p. 81 n.6.
[100] De la Bédoyère, *Gods with Thunderbolts*, pp. 166–67.
[101] De la Bédoyère, *Gods with Thunderbolts*, p. 160.

their nature was ambiguous, extending even to ambiguity about whether the Veteres/Veter were many or one.

If Sulis was not only ambiguous with regard to her number as both the singular Sulis and the plural Suleviae, Bath's patron deity was also ambiguous with regard to gender. The name Sulis may be cognate with Latin *sol* ('sun'), in which case it was probably grammatically masculine in the British language as it was in Latin. One possible interpretation of the bearded, gorgon-like face surrounded by rays on the pediment of the temple of Sulis is that he represents the sun – Sulis in his male aspect, as it were.[102] Similarly, in one portrayal of the Mother Goddesses from Cirencester one of the figures appears to be male, suggesting the gender of these figures was not entirely stable.[103] Alaric Hall has shown that in Anglo-Saxon England elves were also beings of ambiguous gender,[104] while as late as the fifteenth century one of the male leaders of Thomas Cheyne's rebellion called himself 'the Queen of the Fairies', suggesting that godlings continued to defy social norms of gender identity.[105]

The fact remains, however, that evidence for plural groups of godlings in Roman Britain does not amount to evidence that people in Roman (or pre-Roman) Britain believed in a parallel society of godlings of the kind we encounter in medieval texts. No stories or myths survive to accompany images of triple Deae Matres, Genii Cucullati or nymphs, if indeed there were ever narrative myths associated with these figures. Perhaps the closest thing to a society of godlings in Romano-British art – or,

[102] Cousins, *The Sanctuary at Bath*, p. 80.
[103] Aldhouse-Green, *Sacred Britannia*, p. 107.
[104] Hall, *Elves*, pp. 157–66.   [105] Green, *Elf Queens*, p. 22.

at least, a miscellaneous collection of godlings coming together for a purpose – is the Bacchic *thiasos*, most memorably portrayed on the great silver dish of the Mildenhall Treasure; this is the ecstatic retinue of Dionysus or Bacchus, consisting of an assortment of fauns, satyrs, nymphs, maenads, pans and silvani. However, in medieval texts the society of godlings seems to be dependent on the existence of an otherworld they inhabit, which could mean that the otherworld came first, and its inhabitants later. If this is the case, then the fairy otherworld may be an artefact of Christianisation – the consignment of godlings to the underworld by demonising clerics, where those godlings stubbornly refused to become devils but formed a society of their own, interacting with the human world and mimicking the heavenly communion of saints. Whether anything like this really occurred is impossible to judge, but there is no clear evidence that belief in a 'social supernatural' can be pushed back as far as the Roman period in Britain.

Godlings, Hags and Witches

While witches are almost invariably human beings in modern folklore, as late as the early modern period the distinction between the human witch and the non-human hag was by no means a clear one.[106] Famously, the so-called witches of Shakespeare's *Macbeth* were apparently perceived by contemporaries as something more like fairies.[107] The absence of a clear distinction between

---

[106] Green, 'Refighting Carlo Ginzburg's *Night Battles*', pp. 382–85.
[107] Avarvarei, 'Shakespeare's Weird Sisters', pp. 107–17.

fairies and witches in sixteenth-century England and Lowland Scotland was a situation traceable to Anglo-Saxon belief. The Old English word *hæg* (the ancestor of 'hag') referred not to witches in the later sense of evil people using supernatural power to harm others, but to night-riding supernatural warrior women.[108] These supernatural women were by no means unique to Anglo-Saxon or even Germanic belief, but can be found in British sources too. In around 700 the anonymous Breton or Welsh author of a life of St Samson of Dol recounted how the sixth-century St Samson once had to pass through a Welsh forest on a journey from Ynys Bŷr (Caldey Island) to his father's home somewhere in South Wales. Samson was accompanied by a young deacon. Suddenly, the two men heard a terrifying voice and the deacon fled, encountering a *theomacha* (literally a 'God fighter') who pinned him to the ground with a three-pronged spear. Samson found the *theomacha* fleeing the scene; she was 'shaggy and grey-haired, already an old woman, cloaked in her robes, holding a three-pronged hunting spear in her hand, and flitting fast through the vast forests and pursuing the fleeing [deacon] in a straight line'.

When Samson demanded to know who the supernatural woman was, she replied that she was the last of her kind left in the forest, which she was unable to leave now that her husband was dead. Samson asked the *theomacha* to restore his companion to health but she said she could do nothing, so Samson ordered her to die, and she did so.[109] The trident she wields surely identifies

---

[108] Hutton, *The Witch*, p. 160.
[109] Marzella, '*Hirsuta et cornuta*', pp. 221–29.

the *theomacha* as a nereid, who were sometimes depicted bearing tridents in Roman art.[110] This is consistent with a pattern of survival of aquatic deities that will be further explored in Chapter 3; the nereid's appearance in a forest nowhere near the sea is no stranger than the transformation of nymphs into nereids in medieval Greece or the transformation of the god Neptune into the French *lutins*.[111] The title of *theomacha* by which she is identified may be a reference to Ephesians 6:12 in the New Testament, 'For we wrestle not against flesh and blood, but against principalities, against powers, against the rulers of the darkness of this world, against spiritual wickedness in high places'. Christianisation had opened up a spiritual war between Christ, his angels and his faithful against the powers who formerly commanded the allegiance of the people, and thus the nereid/*theomacha* appears armed as if for battle.

While the *theomacha* does not seem to be human (since St Samson introduces himself to her as a human being), she has a family and is subject to old age. The woman has certain characteristics of a witch: her old age, her description as a *maligna mulier* ('evil woman') and the word *theomacha* itself. In his commentary on the Acts of the Apostles, Bede connected the phrase *deo repugnare* ('to rebel against God') with a class of beings called *theomachoi*, and in the Vulgate the verb *repugnare* is directly linked to witchcraft in 1 Samuel 15:23: *quoniam quasi peccatum ariolandi est repugnare* ('For rebellion is as the sin of witchcraft', according to the Authorised

---

[110] Mylonopoulos, 'Odysseus with a Trident?', p. 189.
[111] Larson, *Greek Nymphs*, p. 62.

Version). Furthermore, the *theomacha* is said to be one of nine sisters. This is a characteristic that ties her to the Parcae, the Deae Matres and other triadic deities, since the number nine is three times three and therefore an intensification of the number three (a triad within a triad, as it were).

St Samson's *theomacha* might be linked with the Welsh word *gwyddon*, which has various meanings, including 'giantess', 'female monster', 'hag', 'witch', 'sorceress', 'giant', 'monster', 'wizard', 'sorcerer', 'woodland deity', 'satyr' and 'nymph'. The word may be derived either from *gwŷdd* ('wood') or *gŵydd* ('wild').[112] Of course, we have no way of knowing what Breton word the author of St Samson's life might have used for the *theomacha*, but the triadism of her status as one of nine sisters invites comparison not only with the Parcae and Deae Matres of Roman belief but also with the 'wyrd sisters' of medieval Scottish belief, the Norns of Norse mythology,[113] and the various supernatural women of Anglo-Saxon belief such as the *hægtessan* and *burgrunan*. These monstrous female beings appear to be the common ancestors of elements of both fairy lore and witch lore, even if witch lore would go on to project their characteristics onto human agents in subsequent centuries. The question of whether the idea of human witchcraft itself originated as a form of euhemerisation – the attempt to portray deities as powerful humans – lies beyond the scope of this study.

---

[112] *GPC*, s.v. 'gwiddon, gwiddan, gwyddon, gwyddan', accessed 14 October 2021.
[113] Young, *Magic in Merlin's Realm*, p. 193.

Spirits of the Waters

Some of the strongest evidence for the persistence of pre-Christian practices in Britain from the early medieval period onwards is associated with water sources such as wells, springs, rivers and lakes. In the same way that bodies of water such as rivers and lakes often retain very ancient names because they are fixed points of reference in the landscape, so wells and springs will remain significant for any people occupying a landscape, as crucial sources of fresh water. Settlements may come and go, and the significance of other landscape features may change over time, but in a landscape where there are limited sources of fresh water there is unlikely to be a break in the use of wells and springs.[114] As Simon Young has observed, Britain's fairies are primarily to be found near running water or wells, or near impressive rocky crags.[115]

In the same way that mountains were particularly sacred to the ancient Galicians, so springs and bodies of water seem to have been particularly significant in Britain, since no other set of natural features is as persistently associated with the sacred in the archaeological evidence, in folklore, and in textual sources. The archaeological evidence for the ritual significance of bodies of water in Iron Age Britain has already been mentioned; even the Romans seem to have wistfully regarded sacred springs as relics of an ancient religious past,[116] and many were discovered or developed anew in the Roman period. Whether the Romans began ritual activity at the site of

---

[114] Dowden, *European Paganism*, pp. 39–59.
[115] Young, *The Boggart*, p. 106.
[116] Rattue, *The Living Stream*, pp. 27–28.

Bath or simply took it over remains a question actively debated by archaeologists,[117] but we know that many wells and springs were located close to late Roman villas and were probably developed by landowners as sacred sites, likely dedicated to the nymphs. A fifth of Roman wells identified by James Rattue were associated with villas, leading him to suggest that they may have been created as a consciously nostalgic act of archaic religiosity.[118]

Rattue identified thirty-eight known holy wells in Britain of Roman origin, along with a further sixteen wells at Roman sites that may have been holy wells, and a further five wells traditionally said to be Roman.[119] At Bromham in Bedfordshire, Little Dean in Gloucestershire and Litton Cheney in Dorset the archaeology has confirmed local folklore that identified wells as Roman,[120] although it is more likely that such traditions bore witness to the unrecorded speculations of antiquaries transmitted into folklore rather than immemorial tradition. While no trace of most shrines of local godlings survives, the simple shrine of Coventina at Carrawburgh on Hadrian's Wall is an exception. The boggy conditions at the site preserved the well and its precinct, which consisted only of a paved area with a semi-circular bench and a votive altar.[121]

There is an established tradition of archaeologists interpreting votive deposits of metalwork in bodies of water as offerings to an otherworld whose interface with our reality

---

[117] Aldhouse-Green, *Sacred Britannia*, pp. 111–14.
[118] Rattue, *The Living Stream*, p. 31.
[119] Rattue, *The Living Stream*, pp. 29–30.
[120] Rattue, *The Living Stream*, p. 32.
[121] De la Bédoyère, *Gods with Thunderbolts*, p. 121.

was water and marsh.[122] While this interpretation is not uncontested, the deliberate deposition of metalwork in bodies of water is a thread of continuity between the ritual (and presumably religious) practices of Iron Age, Roman and post-Roman Britain, and apparent ritual deposits of post-Roman metalwork have been recovered from the rivers Avon, Cherwell, Kennet, Lea, Nene, Thames, Way and Witham.[123] The River Witham, in particular, witnessed continuity in depositions near causeways that connected medieval monasteries to the river but which may have existed as early as the Iron Age. However, as Hutton has noted, no written source survives to explain *why* weapons continued to be deposited in the Witham in the Middle Ages.[124] However, while the deposition of metalwork in rivers, pools and lakes was a thread of continuity between the Iron Age, Roman and post-Roman periods, the deposition of offerings (especially coins) in springs may have been introduced by the Romans, as the well-known near total absence of pre-Roman coins from the spring at Bath suggests.[125] Whether this also means that a cult of godlings associated with springs was brought in by the Romans is impossible to judge, however.

Rattue argued that wells and springs were among the last sites of pre-Christian religious observance in Britain to undergo Christianisation, on the grounds that patterns of dedications to saints suggest that Christianisation generally occurred after the Norman Conquest.[126] The overt

---

[122] Hutton, *Pagan Britain*, pp. 182–88.
[123] Semple, *Perceptions of the Prehistoric*, pp. 72–73.
[124] Hutton, *Pagan Britain*, p. 360.
[125] Sauer, 'Sacred Springs and a Pervasive Roman Ritual', pp. 51–55.
[126] Rattue, *The Living Stream*, p. 71.

and ostentatious Christianisation of wells and springs in the late Middle Ages and subsequently, especially in Cornwall and Brittany, may be an eloquent testimony in itself to the problematic status of these sites before the decision was taken to tie them explicitly to the saints. However, archaeological evidence of the continuity of particular wells and springs as sacred sites in the *longue durée* is scarce; only at Leyton Low in Essex has a well yielded clear evidence of pre-Christian votive offerings followed by offerings from the Christian era.[127] Something that is difficult to ascertain is whether ancient people accorded particular significance to specific water sources in certain locations, or whether they were inclined to venerate any well or spring. If the latter was true, it might explain why it is unusual to find a great concentration of votive deposits in one particular water source, because the veneration of wells and springs was highly diffuse.

There are good reasons to think that belief in a chthonic otherworld whose name can be inferred from Gaulish inscriptions as **Andedubno* (the Welsh *Annwn*) was a feature of Romano-British religion, even if such beliefs are neither epigraphically attested nor described by Roman authors. In 1983 a Gallo-Roman lead tablet was discovered at Larzac in France, featuring an apparent ancestral Gaulish cognate for *Annwn*, *antumnos*, in the phrase *ponne antumnos nepon / nes liciatia neosuode / neia uodercos nepon* (tentatively translated by Pierre-Yves Lambert as 'If she is in the underworld, or enchanted by the thread, if she is [still] visible ...').[128] Lambert traces *Annwn* to a hypothetical British word **Andedubno*, 'the

---

[127] Hutton, *Pagan Britain*, p. 359. [128] Lambert, *Langue gauloise*, p. 173.

world below'.[129] Perhaps the British underworld was sufficiently similar, in the minds of Romans and Romanised Britons, to be elided entirely with Classical ideas of the underworld. However, the absence of epigraphic evidence for the worship of chthonic deities in Roman Britain is unsurprising, given the standard ancient practice of making offerings to the gods of the underworld in hollows in the ground rather than on altars elevated towards the heavens.[130] A chalk figurine found buried in a deep shaft at Upper Deal in Kent might even represent an underworld deity.[131] On the whole, however, the material nature of Roman veneration of underworld deities lends itself to the loss of archaeological evidence, although it should be noted that Roman coins and other votive offerings are often found at prehistoric monuments such as barrows.[132] The re-use of underground grain silos for votive offerings also suggests worship of chthonic deities in Roman Britain.[133]

If, as Salisbury has argued, Christianisation was finally accomplished by associating natural features formally linked to deities with saints, or by blessing and re-consecrating them,[134] a question arises as to why godlings survived at all. When it came to the sacred mountains of Galicia, Salisbury suggested that the saints who ruled the mountains in place of the old gods may have been less reassuring; after all, the protection of the people from rockfalls, landslides and falling trees now depended

---

[129] Lambert, *Langue gauloise*, p. 155.   [130] Hitch et al., 'Introduction', p. 2.
[131] Aldhouse-Green, *Sacred Britannia*, pp. 208–9.
[132] Semple, *Perceptions of the Prehistoric*, p. 84.
[133] Aldhouse-Green, *Sacred Britannia*, p. 148.
[134] Salisbury, *Iberian Popular Religion*, pp. 231–40.

on the holiness of the saint and his or her relationship with God, not on rituals of placation of the god.[135] There was thus a potential space in which godlings could continue to exist; a spiritual place, in other words, that God and the saints could not reach which involved the propitiation of spirits to protect against random fate. Overt acts of Christianisation such as the blessing of springs may not have been so much for the benefit of the peasantry as for the benefit of the church, since they 'establish[ed] a theoretical construct that permitted peasant worship to satisfy official requirements of religious uniformity'.[136] In other words, and somewhat cynically interpreted, blessings of water sources provided 'plausible deniability' for clergy who could now convince themselves and others that ongoing popular religious practices were, in fact, Christian.

The evidence of Anglo-Saxon charters suggests that a being called *puca* (and its diminutive form *pucel*) was associated with springs, and a more sinister entity, *scucca*, was associated with barrows.[137] While the root meaning of *puca* was connected with fear, and may be indicative of the demonisation of spirits connected with wells and springs, the use of the less threatening diminutive form *pucel* in connection with some water sources is suggestive of subsequent 'undemonisation', where a previously fearful being was minimised or mocked. Aldhelm glossed *puca* with the Latin diminutive *larbula* (*larvula*), meaning 'little ghost/spirit'.[138] Perhaps early efforts at the demonisation of godlings associated with wells and

---

[135] Salisbury, *Iberian Popular Religion*, pp. 232–33.
[136] Salisbury, *Iberian Popular Religion*, p. 240.
[137] Semple, *Perceptions of the Prehistoric*, pp. 180, 187.
[138] Napier (ed.), *Old English Glosses*, p. 191.

springs occurred, but were unsuccessful. The influential encyclopaedist Isidore of Seville explicitly identified nymphs as 'goddesses of the waters' (*deas aquarum*) and 'spirits of the springs' (*numina lympharum*).[139]

The *Canons of Edgar*, from the early eleventh century, are among the first in England to forbid well-worship and other forms of veneration of the natural world: 'We forbid well-worship (*wilweorþunga*), and necromancy (*licwiglunga*), and witchcrafts (*hwata*), and *galdra*, and man-worship (*manweorðunga*), and those errors that men practise in various sorceries (*gewiglungum*) ... and also about many other trees and stones'.[140] One story that may offer some insight into what Anglo-Saxon *wilweorþunga* may have involved can be found in the twelfth-century *Liber Eliensis*, a compilation of material on the history of the abbey of Ely. When William the Conqueror's army was besieging the English warrior Hereward the Wake at Ely in 1070, the Normans resorted to magic in an attempt to dislodge the English. The Normans brought 'an old witch' (*anus illa venefica*) to their headquarters at Brandon, who they hoped could defeat the English with her enchantments. Hereward, however, disguised himself as an English peasant and went to Brandon, where he observed what the old woman did at night:

Getting up in the middle of the night, she withdrew to the springs of water, which flowed out nearby in the eastern part of the same house; [Hereward] followed her secretly when

[139] Isidore, *Etymologies* 8.11.96.
[140] Fowler (ed.), *Wulfstan's Canons of Edgar*, p. 4: ... *forbeode wilweorþunga, and licwiglunga, and hwata, and galdra, and manweorðunga, and þa gemearr ðe man drifð on mistlicum gewiglungum ... and eac on oðrum mistlicum treowum and on stanum.*

she went out and began to try her incantations. And he heard answers, I do not know of whom, from the guardian of the springs (*a custode fontium*); these I scarcely know. [Hereward] wanted to kill her, but questions unheard delayed him.[141]

Later, when the woman was set on a high wooden gantry to curse Ely, Hereward and his men set light to it and caused the enchantress's downfall. However, the incident at Brandon suggests the woman was seeking to divine the future with the help of a water-dwelling spirit, here identified only as 'the guardian of the springs'. It is unclear whether the woman was consulting a spirit associated with a specific spring in Brandon, or whether the spring was simply a domestic water source and the woman claimed the power to summon a spirit from any body of water. Unfortunately, we do not know enough about Anglo-Saxon beliefs about water spirits. However, the story offers an insight into the possible alliance between water-dwelling spirits and magical practitioners.

For Pierre Gallais, the frequent association between fairies and fountains in medieval literature and folklore was down to the primal characteristics of water sources themselves, as living sources of refreshment, revitalisation and magic.[142] Stephen Yeates, meanwhile, has argued that the concept of the presiding spirit of a water source may have survived into the early

---

[141] Blake (ed.), *Liber Eliensis*, pp. 182–83: *Que consurgens media nocte, ad fontes aquarum, que iuxta in parte orientali eiusdem domus decurrunt, secessit, quam ille egressam clam sequebatur, sua carmina attemptare concepit. Audivit namque responsa nescio que inquirere a custode fontium, illi haut cognito; voluit eam perimere, sed inaudite ipsius interrogationes sui conanimis moras preveniunt.*

[142] Gallais, *La fée à la fontaine*, pp. 5–9.

medieval period.[143] These, however, are not the only possible interpretations of the apparent survival of 'well worship' into the medieval period. Rather than being associated with specific supernatural personalities and presiding spirits, it is possible that *wilweorþunga* represented a specific kind of divinatory practice that involved summoning the spirits present in any water source. Even when wells became associated with saints, it seems that their association with godlings was not always entirely extinguished. John Aubrey recorded that 'Near St. Clements at Oxford, was a spring (stopt up since the warres) where St. Edmund [of Canterbury] did sometimes meet & converse with an Angel or Nymph: as Numa Pompilius did with Egeria'.[144] The cult of the nymph of St Edmund's Well may lie behind an official condemnation of pilgrimages to the well by the bishop of Lincoln in 1290.[145] Efforts to explicitly Christianise wells continued into the late Middle Ages, and the well sacred to the goddess Arnemetia at Buxton in Derbyshire did not receive its dedication to St Anne until the fifteenth century (Plate 3).[146]

Aubrey's uncertainty about the identity of the 'Angel or Nymph' whom St Edmund of Abingdon met at an Oxford well evokes the angel that used to agitate the waters of the Pool of Bethesda in John 5:4: 'For an angel went down at a certain season into the pool, and troubled the water: whosoever then first after the troubling of the water stepped in was made whole of whatsoever disease he had'. It is easy to see how this passage could have been

---

[143] Yeates, *Tribe of Witches*, p. 160.   [144] Aubrey, *Remaines*, p. 34.
[145] Gunton, *History of the Church of Peterburgh*, pp. 227, 341–42.
[146] Rattue, *The Living Stream*, p. 81.

deployed to legitimate the veneration of beings associated with sacred water sources, and there can be little doubt that the cult of water sources was part of medieval Christianity. While it may be true that the frequent association between wells and the martyrdom of virgin saints – often by decapitation – was a relic or reimagining of a pre-existing pagan cult of the severed head,[147] the virgin saints associated with water sources could equally be interpreted as Christianised nymphs or fairies. In one case, at Woolpit in Suffolk, a site that emerged as a holy well dedicated to the Virgin Mary in the thirteenth century was also the scene of a celebrated fairy narrative (the discovery of the 'Green Children' of Woolpit) in the twelfth. The well is set in a ditch at the edge of the village which may be one and the same as the *fossa* in which reapers discovered a boy and girl with green skin, accidental visitors from an underground otherworld.[148] If Gallais is correct that the archetypal supernatural encounter at the well or spring was with a fairy, then encounter with saints in similar locations could represent sanitised reinterpretations of fairy lore.[149] The green girl of Woolpit, on this interpretation (who outlives her brother) perhaps re-emerges as the Virgin Mary.

Conclusion

Godlings are beings that are difficult to define – to the point that their elusiveness may even be considered one of their distinctive characteristics. Nevertheless, the idea

---

[147] Dowden, *European Paganism*, pp. 49–50.
[148] Young, *Suffolk Fairylore*, p. 40.
[149] Purkiss, *Troublesome Things*, pp. 65–66.

that there were lesser, older, chthonic and earthbound deities was familiar to the Romans, who attempted to distinguish between higher and lesser deities. The religious landscape that the Romans encountered when they invaded and occupied Britain remains elusive, but they brought with them an understanding of deities that they may have imposed on very different forms of belief – perhaps containing elements of 'animism' and 'shamanism', although these terms are problematic. Britain's 'small gods' are characterised by their resilience, their adaptability, and their continued existence in popular religion across the *longue durée* even if their identities fluctuated. Across all eras, British godlings are generally:

1. Non-human
2. Chthonic
3. Ambiguous as to species, gender and number
4. Associated with abstract concepts of fate and destiny

It is possible that these kinds of beliefs date back to prehistory and originate within animism or shamanistic practices; it is also possible that they were introduced to Roman Britain for the first time. However, godlings seem to be persistently connected with the idea of human or non-human supernatural or magical women. Furthermore, the connection between godlings and water sources is especially strong in Britain. However, it is time to move from the general to the particular, and to examine in detail the earliest set of Britain's godlings about whom we have any meaningful information: the 'small gods' of Roman Britain.

2

Menagerie of the Divine

Godlings in Roman Britain

~

The religions of Roman Britain are the best attested expressions of pre-Christian religion from any era of British history. While prehistoric monuments bear mute witness to the tremendous importance of ritual activity for the societies that built them, we know virtually nothing of the details of the belief systems of those societies. In much the same way, the pre-Christian religions of Anglo-Saxons and Scandinavians that succeeded the Romans have left little trace in the archaeological or historical records. It is in Roman Britain, for the first time, that we meet gods and godlings face to face, since the Romans brought an epigraphic tradition that recorded the names of deities, as well as representational art on a monumental scale. Substantial temples, shrines and altars of stone replaced the elusive remains of Iron Age religion, making it possible for us to reconstruct the spaces in which some Romano-British religious activities took place. And, perhaps most importantly of all, Britain became part of a religious world (the Roman Empire) that has left behind an abundant literary record – even if that literary record often contains little information on Britain itself.

In spite of all this, the true nature of religion in Roman Britain remains frustratingly elusive. The problem faced by the historian of religion in Roman Britain is not a lack of evidence in and of itself, but the absence of a suitable context in which to interpret the evidence available. As Guy de la Bédoyère has observed, the evidence 'reveals the abundantly unpredictable panorama of human religious perspective, experience and expression', yet without the cultural context of belief, reliable reconstruction of Romano-British religion is tremendously difficult.[1] In one sense, the gods and godlings of Roman Britain are familiar, often conforming to standard Roman patterns of iconography or going under the names of familiar Roman deities. But we are also confronted, again and again, with evidence that Romano-British religion was a multi-layered phenomenon involving the apparent reinterpretation of pre-Roman Iron Age divinities, the importation of gods from elsewhere in the empire, and even the deliberate invention of new gods and cults. Just as it is impossible to speak of a single 'Romano-British religion', so it is impossible to regard the entire period between the Claudian invasion and the introduction of Christianity as a period of uniform belief. In the four centuries of Roman rule, Romano-British religions had their phases of rise and decline, many of which are only partially visible to us, such as the 'pagan revival' of the late fourth century.

In addition to being aware of the limitations of the evidence of Romano-British religion for reconstructing belief, it is important to be mindful of the vast amount of evidence for religion in Roman Britain that, in all likelihood, has not survived. For example, the discovery of a wooden cult image of a deity at Twyford, Buckinghamshire, in 2021 – the first of its kind to

---

[1] De la Bédoyère, *Gods with Thunderbolts*, p. 13.

survive – hints at an entire lost world of Romano-British religious imagery in wood, which no doubt comprised many or most images of the more minor godlings.[2] While we know the Romans suppressed druidism and the practice of human sacrifice in Britain, it is likely that many other religious practices from the Iron Age simply continued alongside more materially sophisticated cults, just as Iron Age roundhouses survived into the Roman period as the dwellings of ordinary people. Worship in sacred groves or at water sources has, by its very nature, left little in the archaeological record; and the people who commissioned epigraphic inscriptions in Roman Britain were, by definition, likely to be wealthier, more Romanised and literate. They are thus scarcely a representative sample of Roman Britain's population as a whole. There is a great deal we do not understand about Romano-British religion, and the further we move out from the more conventional cults practiced in urban centres, the more our ignorance deepens. For example, we have little idea why temples and shrines were sometimes established on prehistoric sites, and whether this may represent some form of ancestor worship unattested in the historical or epigraphic record,[3] or alternatively a 'Celtic revival' involving the re-establishment of native styles and the re-use of long-dormant sacred sites.[4] Furthermore, the epigraphic evidence clusters in certain areas that were the focus of both intense monumentalising activity and

[2] 'Wooden Roman Figure Found at Twyford during HS2 dig', *BBC News*, 13 January 2022, bbc.co.uk/news/uk-england-beds-bucks-herts-59972275, accessed 16 April 2022.
[3] Semple, *Perceptions of the Prehistoric*, p. 99.
[4] Jones, *End of Roman Britain*, p. 178.

intense archaeological activity in later ages, such as the military sites of Hadrian's Wall.[5]

By their very nature, as lesser divine beings, the godlings of Roman Britain are less likely to be visible in the archaeological record. In a sense, every deity of the native people was a mere local godling in comparison with the mighty gods of the Roman pantheon, yet the Romans (and perhaps the Britons as well) seem to have decided early on to equate British with Roman deities through the process of *interpretatio Romana*. Local gods such as Mars Camulus and Apollo Cunomaglus thus acquired the lustre of Olympians, if that was how their devotees chose to interpret their cults; and yet it is clear that deities identified with Roman counterparts, such as Sulis Minerva, nevertheless preserved the character of godlings rather than their more exalted Roman alter egos; Sulis's primary function was always to preside over the hot springs at Bath, and there is little evidence she was worshipped anywhere else. As we have seen in Chapter 1 above, *deus* and *dea* were words with a wide range of meaning in the Roman world, and inscriptions rarely distinguished between different ranks of divine beings in the same way as poets or grammarians. The word *numen*, for example, appears in Britain only in dedications to the divinity of the emperor (*numen Augusti*) or the imperial house (*numinibus Augustorum*), with the sole exception of a votive leaf inscribed *Numen Volcani* ('the spirit of Vulcan') found near Barkway[6] – which, given Vulcan's status as an Olympian, seems a somewhat anomalous use of the term.

---

[5] De la Bédoyère, *Gods with Thunderbolts*, p. 15.
[6] *RIB* 220, romaninscriptionsofbritain.org/inscriptions/220, accessed 10 October 2021.

The traditional taxonomy of the deities of Roman Britain has generally categorised them according to their relationship to official Roman religion; thus Barri Jones and David Mattingly, for instance, divided the gods into deities of landscape features (presumed to be of local origin), gods paired with Roman gods in *interpretatio Romana* and imported 'foreign' gods from other provinces of the empire.[7] This taxonomy can prove somewhat limiting, however. For one thing, there is no reason to assume that gods of landscape features were always native deities surviving from the Iron Age, rather than characters invented at need. Furthermore, there is no good reason to believe that the pairing of British with Roman theonyms always meant that a native deity was being exalted to the status of a god of the official Roman pantheon. The Roman name might have served simply as a gloss on the British god's name for some potential worshippers, or vice versa. Furthermore, the designation of some gods as 'foreign' is of only limited usefulness, since the Roman occupation of Britain endured for four centuries; in that time, while some cults failed, other imported gods from elsewhere in the empire seem to have been entirely enculturated into Britain (such as the Deae Matres, if they were of Germanic origin as sometimes suggested – and not to mention the God of the Christians).

While there may well be no 'right' way to divide up and analyse the deities of Roman Britain, the focus of this chapter is on deities that seem to have been the subject of veneration as lesser gods and goddesses in Roman Britain,

---

[7] Jones and Mattingly, *Atlas of Roman Britain*, p. 264.

either because they belonged to a category of lesser gods in Roman religion (such as the nymphs, archaic nature gods like Faunus and spirits such as genii and lares), or because they seem to have been native gods who did not fit comfortably into the categories of Roman religion (even if a superficial attempt was made to pair them with a Roman god), or because they were represented in ways that fell outside the norms of official Roman religion and were the objects of unofficial and popular rather than official cults. While the Roman Empire's pantheon was seemingly infinite at the time of the Claudian invasion of Britain, promiscuously absorbing the gods of many peoples, an 'implicit hierarchy' nevertheless existed within it.[8] This chapter is concerned with the 'small gods' of Roman Britain: figures who, by their very nature, might be considered *numina* rather than gods proper. These deities have sometimes been ignored in Roman Britain because there is little epigraphic evidence for their cults. For example, the god Bacchus, in spite of frequent appearances in mosaics in Roman Britain, appears in no inscription and has therefore been neglected as an important deity in the province because he was not a god of public cult but of 'personal fulfilment'.[9]

Interpretatio Romana

The practice of *interpretatio Romana* – the identification of native deities with gods of the Roman pantheon – is best known from Julius Caesar's accounts of Gaul and

---

[8] De la Bédoyère, *Gods with Thunderbolts*, p. 31.
[9] Henig, '*Ita intellexit*', p. 161.

Britain and Tacitus' account of Germanic tribes. Caesar and Tacitus presumed that the 'pantheons' of barbarians could usually be slotted into the Roman pantheon, at least as a convenient literary device, with barbarian gods taking on the classic functions of deities such as Jupiter, Mars, Apollo and Ceres. So great was Caesar's confidence in his interpretation that he did not even bother to record the names of the deities of the Gauls and Britons – leaving scholars to guess at the correct identification of Gaulish Mercury, for example.[10] The attempt to understand a culture by assimilating it to the familiar patterns of another rests on large assumptions about the similarity of cultures and ignores the possibility that one ancestral religion might differ very greatly from another in form as well as in substance. If we assume the existence of an Olympian-style pantheon, led by a thunder god, with gendered deities assigned distinct personalities and functions, we are already under the spell of Rome.

As we have seen in Chapter 1, it is far from certain that the deities of Iron Age Britain were anything like the leading gods of the Romans of the first century CE, although they might have been quite similar to the archaic rustic godlings of the Latins. It may be a mistake to view *interpretatio Romana* as something deliberate and planned; De la Bédoyère viewed it as a natural result of the encounter between a literate and a non-literate society, and the need for the literate to label what they found.[11] There is no evidence of official pressure to pair the names of local deities

---

[10] On *interpretatio Romana* see Ando, 'Interpretatio Romana', pp. 51–65.
[11] De la Bédoyère, *Gods with Thunderbolts*, p. 45.

with those of Roman gods,[12] and Webster has suggested it was primarily a military phenomenon.[13] *Interpretatio Romana* was far from universal, and some local gods (such as Viridius at Ancaster in Lincolnshire and Abandinus at Godmanchester in Cambridgeshire) do not seem to have been paired with a Roman deity. Furthermore, deities such as the Deae Matres, the Veteres, Coventina and Epona were never paired with a Roman analogue.[14] While the pairing of the names of Roman deities with Brittonic words has usually been interpreted as a form of double naming, with the Brittonic word as the name of a native god, it is by no means certain that this was always the case. In a handful of cases we have evidence of the pre-existence of native gods before the Claudian invasion (like Camulus), but other 'names' sound very much like epithets rather than distinct personalities. Apollo Cunomaglus, for example, simply means 'Apollo, lord of hounds' while words paired with Mars like Belatucadrus ('the fair slayer') and Cocidius ('the red one') may make more sense as epithets than as divine personalities.

There is no good reason to assume that every deity worshipped under a Brittonic 'name' in Roman Britain was a native god whose identity stretched back into the mists of time. It is just as likely that some (or even most) of these deities were confected during the Roman period, perhaps with deliberately 'British-sounding' names.[15] The name of the god Antenociticus (or Anociticus),

---

[12] Hutton, *Pagan Britain*, p. 246.
[13] Webster, 'A Dirty Window', pp. 137–38.
[14] Webster, 'A Dirty Window', p. 137.
[15] Aldhouse-Green, *Sacred Britannia*, p. 220.

worshipped at Benwell on Hadrian's Wall, echoes both the Roman names Anicetus and Antoninus, and may simply have been invented.[16] Similarly, Martin Henig has argued that the goddess Brigantia was not a native goddess but rather a deity confected at need in the reign of the Emperor Septimius Severus, rather like the personification of Britannia invented by the Roman invaders under Claudius. The cult of Brigantia, on this view, was 'a focus for loyalty in northern Britain during a period in which the island was being divided into two provinces'. The iconography of the cult of Brigantia had eastern characteristics (suggesting an origin in the Severan period, when eastern cults were heavily promoted) and some dedicators of altars to Brigantia seemed unclear about her nature, with Marcus Cocceius Nigrinus dedicating an altar to *Dea Nympha Brigantia* ('the goddess-nymph Brigantia') near Brampton early in the third century.[17]

On another interpretation, Brigantia was originally the predecessor of the personification Britannia, with the result that Brigantia and Britannia were interchangeable figures.[18] Although we have epigraphic evidence of the worship of Brigantia only from northern Britain, place-name evidence suggests that she was much more widely venerated.[19] She may also have had a lost male consort or analogue, judging from the Welsh word *brenin* ('king'), whose likely root is **brigantinos*. While

---

[16] De la Bédoyère, *Gods with Thunderbolts*, p. 152.
[17] Henig, '*Ita intellexit*', p. 161.
[18] Hewitt, 'Britannia', *ODNB* (online edition), doi.org/10.1093/ref:odnb/68196, accessed 18 October 2021.
[19] *RIB* 623, 627, 628, 630, 1053, 1131, 2066, 2091, romaninscriptionsofbritain.org, accessed 17 October 2021.

the Iron Age kings of the Britons before the Roman conquest styled themselves *rigon*, cognate with Latin *rex*, by the early Middle Ages the Old Welsh word *rhi* usually had the sense of a subordinate ruler, while *brenin* had come to mean a king exercising sovereignty. If Brigantia had a male consort he may have been the king himself, who obtained sovereignty through a symbolic or ritual marriage with a goddess of the land. Twelfth- and thirteenth-century Welsh poetry described kings as *gŵr priod Prydain*, 'the husband of Britain', and *priodor Prydain*, 'the rightful possessor of Britain', suggesting that rites of sovereignty involving a divine marriage may have persisted in some form in the post-Roman world, if only rhetorically as a dim memory of former practices.[20] None of this, however, is incompatible with the idea that Brigantia was a Roman creation.

We know so little about pre-Roman Iron Age religion that we cannot assume many of the spirits worshipped by Iron Age Britons had names at all. If much religion in Iron Age Britain (especially beyond the Gallo-Belgic- and Roman-influenced southeast) was indeed 'animistic' in nature, there may have been no need for the differentiation of divine personalities from the features of the natural world they inhabited. Just as the sixteenth-century Polish commentator on Baltic paganism Jan Łasicki made the mistake of identifying Kirnis as the Lithuanian god of cherry trees when *kirnis* just means 'cherry tree' in Lithuanian,[21] so the Romans in Britain

---

[20] Charles-Edwards, *Wales and the Britons*, pp. 324–28.
[21] Young (ed.), *Pagans in the Early Modern Baltic*, p. 141.

(and the Romanised Britons of subsequent generations) may have imposed Roman conceptual categories on an alien religion in a more or less clumsy fashion. Webster observes that religious syncretism is sometimes portrayed as a sympathetic phenomenon, but it was in reality a form of Roman 'cultural arrogance' that imposed Roman religious concepts on native religion.[22] However, Webster suggests that some of the deities of Roman Britain are best understood as 'creole gods' – composite figures that were neither native nor Roman, but came about as a result of resistance to the imposition of Roman religious categories. Thus the horse goddess Epona may have been a creole deity, replacing earlier zoomorphic understandings of the divine horse but rejecting identification with any Roman or Greek analogue. Epona was thus a new creation of popular religion, 'an adaptive *alternative* to a dominant belief system'.[23]

The Nymphs

The cult of nymphs was a borrowing from Greek religion that was thoroughly integrated in Roman popular religion by the time of the Claudian invasion of Britain. The nymphs were, in essence, spirits of the waters, and a total of sixteen surviving inscriptions from Roman Britain mention nymphs. In some cases the nymph is named, such as the nymph Neine who was the recipient of a dedication by a mother and daughter at Greta Bridge, County

---

[22] Webster, 'A Dirty Window', p. 138.
[23] Webster, 'A Dirty Window', p. 141.

Durham,[24] and the nymph Coventina at Carrawburgh on Hadrian's Wall.[25] At Chester an altar was dedicated 'to the nymphs and fountains' (*nymphis et fontibus*), reflecting the usual identification of nymphs as water spirits.[26] At Castleford, West Yorkshire, two heads were crudely incised on a piece of stone with the misspelt legend *nympis* ('to the nymphs'), providing likely evidence of a cult of the nymphs among those without the resources to commission professionally made altars and inscriptions.[27] In other cases, however, the nymphs were unnamed; Martin Henig interprets such locations as the result of an anxiety to ensure that 'every divine power received its due', and nymphs presided over bodies of water as genii presided over land.[28]

Shrines associated with springs have usually been identified as nymphaea, such as at Chepstow beside the Wye and at Horseland on the banks of the Avon.[29] The 'nymph room' at Lullingstone is a particularly interesting example of a domestic nymphaeum (Plate 4).[30] In the second century a sunken room that may have served originally as a grain store was converted into a nymphaeum, with a

[24] *RIB* 744, romaninscriptionsofbritain.org/inscriptions/744, accessed 26 January 2022.
[25] *RIB* 1526, romaninscriptionsofbritain.org/inscriptions/1526, accessed 26 January 2022; *RIB* 1527, romaninscriptionsofbritain.org/inscriptions/1527, accessed 26 January 2022.
[26] *RIB* 460, romaninscriptionsofbritain.org/inscriptions/460, accessed 26 January 2022.
[27] *RIB* 3189, romaninscriptionsofbritain.org/inscriptions/3189, accessed 26 January 2022.
[28] Henig, *Religion in Roman Britain*, p. 31.
[29] Yeates, *Tribe of Witches*, pp. 36, 45.
[30] Henig, *Religion in Roman Britain*, p. 162.

well dug in the floor and a niche featuring three painted nymphs (perhaps representing the tutelary spirits of the River Darent) which had its own external access. This suggests that people from the locality may have used the room as a shrine, and could enter without passing through the villa. Similar shrine rooms with external access have been identified at St Albans and at Great Witcombe, Gloucestershire.[31] Nymphs were typically represented as naked or semi-naked young women reclining against water jars from which a stream of water is flowing, for example, at Carrawburgh and in a mosaic recovered from Brantingham in East Yorkshire, where nymphs occupy the corners of a mosaic at whose centre appears Tyche, the Greek goddess of chance.[32]

While nymphs were usually thought of as water spirits, however, this was not always the case. One particularly strange inscription from Westerwood near Cumbernauld Airport, *Silvanis et Quadriviis Caelestibus* ('to the celestial Silvanae and Quadriviae') applies an apparently inappropriate heavenly epithet to the earthbound wood nymphs and spirits of the crossroads. One possible interpretation is that *caelestis* is here an allusion to the goddess Brigantia, sometimes called Caelestis Brigantia (paired with the Syrian goddess Caelestis), with whom the Silvanae and Quadriviae were here implicitly identified.[33] Furthermore, while nymphs might seem to be highly localised deities, this was not always the case. The

[31] De la Bédoyère, *Gods with Thunderbolts*, p. 134.
[32] Liversedge et al., 'Brantingham Roman Villa', pp. 90–99.
[33] Aldhouse-Green, *Sacred Britannia*, p. 76; *RIB* 3504, romaninscriptionsofbritain.org/inscriptions/3504, accessed 17 October 2021.

nymph Coventina, venerated at Carrawburgh and often linked uniquely to that specific location on Hadrian's Wall under the implicit assumption that she was a native spirit,[34] was actually venerated at Narbonne in France and in north-western Spain.[35]

Nymph-cults in Britain sometimes had a visionary or vatic dimension, judging from an inscription on an altar from Risingham, Northumberland: 'Forewarned by a dream, the soldier bade her who is married to Fabius to set up this altar to the Nymphs who are to be worshipped' (*Somnio praemonitus miles hanc ponere iussit aram quae Fabio nupta est Nymphis venerandis*).[36] Evidence of a similar kind of ecstatic, charismatic religion based on dreams comes from the shrine at Lydney, where an inscription mentions an 'interpreter of dreams'.[37] While 'nympholepsy' (the idea of a nymph taking control of a person in a dream or trance state) was part of Greek religion it was regarded with suspicion by the Romans, who associated visions of nymphs in fountains with madness.[38] However, the Risingham inscription is perhaps an indication that such misgivings had less prominence at the edge of empire. While Romano-British religion in the archaeological record can often appear highly pragmatic and transactional, there was clearly also a more mystical dimension to religious rites, even outside of the formal mystery religions themselves.

[34] Aldhouse-Green, *Sacred Britannia*, p. 116.
[35] Hutton, *Pagan Britain*, p. 246.
[36] RIB 1228, romaninscriptionsofbritain.org/inscriptions/1228, accessed 19 December 2021; De la Bédoyère, *Gods with Thunderbolts*, p. 161.
[37] De la Bédoyère, *Gods with Thunderbolts*, p. 199.
[38] Larson, *Greek Nymphs*, pp. 61–62.

Goddesses of Destiny

Deities of destiny exist in many cultures and hover on the line between personifications of mysterious forces (fate, destiny, fortune) and personal beings to be invoked in order to ensure good fortune or to avert misfortune. Often personified as female, goddesses of destiny and abundance are often without an accompanying narrative framework, with the result that we cannot be sure they always represent the same characters or the same set of concepts.[39] For example, the idea of divine mothers, often portrayed in triplicate, was widespread in Roman Britain both among native Britons and immigrants from elsewhere in the empire. However, the Matres were given a number of different titles in inscriptions, suggesting the existence of local variants, while other titles such as Ollototae ('of all peoples') or Tramarinae ('from overseas') were deliberately vague and all-encompassing.[40] It is even possible that some versions of the Matres, such as the Matres Suleviae, were a way of making sense of local spirits (the deity Sulis?) within the framework of the cult of the Mothers. The cult of the Matres seems to have been particularly popular with soldiers (perhaps from Germany) and is well evidenced on Hadrian's Wall, but the cult of the Matres also took hold in a civilian context in the Cotswolds.[41]

While many inscriptions to the Deae Matres survive, there are only two surviving dedications to the Parcae from Roman Britain, testifying to the existence of a more

---

[39] Hutton, *Pagan Britain*, pp. 237–38.
[40] De la Bédoyère, *Gods with Thunderbolts*, p. 31.
[41] Hutton, *Pagan Britain*, pp. 238–39.

explicit cult of the Fates.[42] P. C. Van der Horst argued that the Parcae originated as personifications of the words (*fata*) pronounced by the gods, but came to take on the characteristics of godlings in their own right.[43] However, the cult of the Parcae as godlings was not standard Roman practice. Michel Christol and Michel Janon identified dedicatory inscriptions to the Parcae (as opposed to non-cultic mentions of the Parcae) in funeral inscriptions as distinctively 'Celtic', with examples surviving only from Celtic-speaking areas of the empire such as Celtiberia and Gaul.[44] Aldhouse-Green has suggested a link between the Deae Matres and the Parcae, based on the triadism of the representation of both groups of goddesses. At Nuits-Saint-Georges in Burgundy the Mothers appear in the guise of a young, a middle-aged and an elderly woman, suggesting a cult associated with 'the inexorability of time',[45] and Julio Mangas Manjarrés has argued for syncretism between the Parcae and Matres in Celtiberian regions of Roman Iberia.[46] On another interpretation, however, belief in three supernatural women who determine fate is a feature of Indo-European mythology rather than anything particularly Celtic. A popular story in Lithuanian folklore, for example, features a mother or father overhearing three women talking outside the window before, during

---

[42] *RIB* 247, romaninscriptionsofbritain.org/inscriptions/247, accessed 14 January 2022; *RIB* 953, romaninscriptionsofbritain.org/inscriptions/953, accessed 14 January 2022.
[43] Van der Horst, 'Fatum, Tria Fata', 217.
[44] Christol and Janon, 'Révision d'inscriptions de Nîmes', p. 264.
[45] Aldhouse-Green, *Sacred Britannia*, pp. 153–54.
[46] Manjarrés, 'El ara de las *Parcae* de *Termes*', pp. 331–61.

or after the birth of a child, who decide the child's fate. These are the Laimės, the goddesses of fate.[47] While they may reward and bring good fortune, the Laimės are also causes of plague.[48]

Whether veneration of the Parcae and the Deae Matres was a way of coming to terms with fate or an attempt to seek divine intervention to avert or redirect it is something on which we can only speculate. However, in a deviant burial of the late third century excavated at Kimmeridge in Dorset a group of elderly women were buried with their skulls placed by their feet and the lower jaws removed from the skulls (perhaps an attempt to silence their speech), along with a spindle whorl (symbol of the Parcae) beside each body. As Hutton has noted, the burial can be interpreted either as a way of honouring a group of weavers or as a posthumous punishment of women suspected of harmful magic of some kind.[49] That these human women were in some way identified with the Parcae is suggested by the spindle whorls. Had they in some way taken the role of the Parcae, speaking people's fates and thus causing harm? Or had they invoked the Parcae in an effort to change people's fates?

The Deae Matres and the Parcae were just two groups of godlings within the religious world of Roman Britain who dealt with fate and fortune. An altar from Maryport in Cumbria was dedicated to 'the Genius of the place, to Fortune the Home-Bringer, to Eternal Rome, and to Good Fate' (*Genio loci/Fortun[ae] Reduci/Romae Aetern[ae]/*

---

[47] Greimas, *Of Gods and Men*, pp. 112–13.
[48] Greimas, *Of Gods and Men*, p. 149.
[49] Hutton, *Pagan Britain*, p. 266.

et Fato Bono). It is difficult to be sure of the extent to which 'the good Fate' was considered an abstraction or a personified spiritual being by the dedicator of this altar. Personifications of this kind were also fluid; Fortuna, for example, was sometimes portrayed as a world ruler, sometimes assimilated to Nemesis, sometimes identified with Ceres and sometimes made a companion of the personified god Bonus Eventus.[50]

Personifications of abstract concepts were often portrayed as female in the Roman world,[51] but the boundary between personification and deification is sometimes a vague one. For example, the figure of Britannia was a female personification of the island of Britain apparently invented by the Romans, and while there is no evidence of a cult of Britannia herself (unlike the goddess Roma), the genius of the land of Britain was worshipped at Auchendavy – suggesting that the conceptualisation of Britain as a single cohesive whole had an impact on religious practice.[52] Once personification occurs, it is always possible that deification and a cult may follow at any future time, perhaps long after the intent of the original personification has been forgotten. It is possible that the goddess Brigantia, for example, began as a bare personification of what is now northern England, the territory of the Brigantes. Over time, however, she became the object of a genuine cult.[53]

---

[50] Henig, *Religion in Roman Britain*, p. 161.
[51] Aldhouse-Green, *Sacred Britannia*, p. 66.
[52] *RIB* 2175, romaninscriptionsofbritain.org/inscriptions/2175, accessed 10 October 2021.
[53] Aldhouse-Green, *Sacred Britannia*, pp. 75–76.

Whether a genuine cult would emerge around an invented or confected deity was, of course, unpredictable, and it is likely that many such personifications were unsuccessful as a focus of cult. The sudden creation of the figure of 'Saint Javelin' (a figure of a female saint, in the style of an Orthodox icon, holding a FGM-148 anti-tank weapon) in the early days of Russia's 2022 invasion of Ukraine is a contemporary example of the phenomenon of the creation of a deity (or in this case an imaginary saint) at need;[54] at the time of writing, however, it remains to be seen whether 'Saint Javelin' will remain simply a meme, marketing ploy and symbol of Ukrainian resistance, or whether she will eventually become the focus of an ironic or even serious religious cult.

The Victories (winged female figures) were common subjects for sculpture in Roman Britain, but there is little sign that these personifications (while technically godlings) had a genuine cult as personal beings.[55] The fate and revenge goddess Nemesis, on the other hand, had a cult in the amphitheatres at Chester and Caerleon,[56] and an apparent depiction of Nemesis holding a pair of shears in order to cut the thread of life appears on an altar in Gresford church near Wrexham found in 1908. Edward

---

[54] Debusmann, Bernd, 'How "Saint Javelin" raised over $1 million for Ukraine', *BBC News*, 10 March 2022, bbc.co.uk/news/world-us-canada-60700906, accessed 28 March 2022.
[55] De la Bédoyère, *Gods with Thunderbolts*, p. 166.
[56] Henig, *Religion in Roman Britain*, pp. 152–53; *RIB* 3149, romaninscriptionsofbritain.org/inscriptions/3149, accessed 30 December 2021; *RIB* 323, romaninscriptionsofbritain.org/inscriptions/323, accessed 30 December 2021. An altar dedicated to Nemesis (*RIB* 2065) was also recovered from an unknown site on Hadrian's Wall (romaninscriptionsofbritain.org/inscriptions/2065, accessed 30 December 2021).

Hubbard interpreted this figure as Atropos or her Roman equivalent, Morta.[57] However, although Aulus Gellius quoted a line from the Old Latin poet Livius Andronicus that suggests Morta was once treated as an individual figure,[58] by the period of the Roman occupation of Britain the Parcae were invariably venerated and mentioned in inscriptions as a triad. Nemesis, therefore, is a far more likely identification for the Gresford figure than Morta. In 2018 a worn sculptural relief found at Calne, Wiltshire (and perhaps from a mausoleum), was restored and identified by Martin Henig as a depiction of the three Parcae holding the thread of life between them (Plate 5). The Calne relief is the first and so far only figurative depiction of the Parcae found in Britain.[59]

Another female deity of good fortune venerated in Roman Britain was Fortuna or Abundantia, who was worshipped at Lydney alongside the god Nodens.[60] The nature of worship at Lydney seems to have been linked to the fact that the temple site had previously been used for mining, as shown by the deposition of votive offerings of miniature picks and the offering of libations directly into the ground. If the name Nodens derived from the Proto-Indo-European stem *neud- ('to acquire possession of'), then the god may have presided over the mine and became linked with storms, flooded mines and life. Nodens was thus a god of wealth and health, and an ideal consort for Fortuna or Abundantia.[61]

[57] Hubbard, *Buildings of Wales*, p. 173.
[58] Gellius, *Noctes Atticae* 3.16.10–11.
[59] 'Calne Fates Sculpture', Wiltshire Museum, wiltshiremuseum.org.uk/?artwork=calne-fates-sculpture, accessed 10 April 2022.
[60] Yeates, *Tribe of Witches*, p. 23.
[61] Yeates, *Tribe of Witches*, p. 95.

One of the strangest of all votive inscriptions from Roman Britain was found at Benwell in 1751: an altar dedicated 'to the three *lamiae*' (*lamiis tribus*), which is unique in the Classical world.[62] As Matthias Egeler has observed, 'the dedication to the "three lamiae" and the character of the contemporary lamia in literary sources seem entirely irreconcilable', since Lamia was primarily a child-killing demon 'associated with death, with the devouring of her victims, and with sexuality or obscenity'.[63] The demonic nature of the lamiae is not, in and of itself, a reason they would not have been venerated; the placation of threatening beings is, after all, traditional grounds for veneration. However, the presence of an altar to the *lamiae tres* in a fort at Benwell is puzzling both because we might expect dedications to martial deities (and the *lamiae* have no martial associations) and because lamiae do not appear in threes in Classical myth. Much later, in sixth-century Spain, Martin of Braga identified lamiae as river spirits, and Ken Dowden suggested a link with the Latin word *lama* meaning 'boggy ground'.[64] However, it is difficult to project a sixth-century understanding of lamiae back onto the third century. Emma Wilby, on the other hand, associates lamiae and other cannibalistic spirits with the lingering survival of shamanism.[65]

Stamatios Zochios has interpreted Benwell's *lamiis tribus* in the light of the *morrígna* of early medieval Ireland, a trio of supernatural women associated with battle, fate

---

[62] *RIB* 1331, romaninscriptionsofbritain.org/inscriptions/1331, accessed 18 January 2022.
[63] Egeler, 'A Note on the Dedication *lamiis tribus*', 16.
[64] Dowden, *European Paganism*, pp. 41–42.
[65] Wilby, 'Burchard's *strigae*', pp. 18–49.

and death: Morrigan, Macha and Badb.[66] While a cult of battlefield goddesses would seem suitable for the military context of the fort at Benwell, any connection between these *lamiae tres* and figures from medieval Ireland must be speculative, resting as it does on large assumptions about pan-Celtic mythology and continuity of beliefs between the third century and the early Middle Ages. Egeler's argument that a Gallo-Roman dedication to *Cassi[b]odua* (reconstructed as Gaulish *Cathubodua*) shows that entities like the Bodbs of medieval Ireland were venerated in the Gallo-Roman world is somewhat thin.[67] While it may be too much to identify the *lamiae tres* with specific beings attested in later folkloric and mythological traditions, therefore, the application of triadism in the dedication does suggest that, in this one instance, lamiae were added to a broad category of female godlings of destiny, retribution and chance who were usually represented triadically in a British context.

The Lares and Penates

As elsewhere in the Roman Empire, domestic shrines to the Lares and Penates were common in Roman Britain, with small bronze figures of these godlings often forming part of local museum collections dedicated to Roman Britain. Martin Henig has interpreted votive deposits found under the floors of houses as offerings to the Lares, and indeed draws attention to the close relationship between the Lares and Manes (spirits of the dead),

---

[66] Zochios, 'Lamia', p. 26.
[67] Egeler, 'A Note on the Dedication *lamiis tribus*', pp. 18–20.

who were embodied by ancestral busts and portraits. At Lullingstone, offerings of sheep bones were found in association with ancestral busts. Henig also notes that the Lares, in the form of *lares compitales*, were deities of the countryside as well, suggesting that a figure found in a hoard at Felmingham, Norfolk, may represent such a rural spirit.[68] The epigraphical evidence for cults of the Lares and Penates is more meagre, however; a single altar is known from York dedicated to the Penates, specifically 'To Jupiter Best and Greatest, to the gods and goddesses of hospitality and to the Penates'.[69] It seems reasonable to conclude, therefore, that the cult of the Lares and Penates in Roman Britain was largely a private and domestic affair, without written records or the need for inscriptions.

Evidence for a more unusual expression of the cult of the Lares, integrated into indigenous belief, may survive at Maryport, Cumbria, in the form of the 'serpent stone', which may have begun life as an altar but was later carved into a phallic shape. The stone features on one side a long serpent along its full height while the other side features a head with characteristic 'British' features wearing a torc, above what were once two snakes and some fish.[70] Although it takes a strongly British cultural form, the Maryport image is morphologically similar to Campanian images where a lar or genius appears between two snakes, and the Romans seem to have entertained the idea that a lar or genius could manifest itself in the

---

[68] Henig, *Religion in Roman Britain*, p. 158.
[69] *RIB* 649, romaninscriptionsofbritain.org/inscriptions/649, accessed 26 January 2022.
[70] Breeze, *Maryport*, pp. 80–81.

form of a snake in order to receive offerings.[71] It remains unclear whether the Maryport serpent stone represents a syncretism of British and Campanian beliefs or reflects native beliefs that we simply do not understand, although the idea of snakes consuming sacred offerings is found in more than one Indo-European culture.[72]

Faunus, Silvanus and Bacchic Cults

In November 1979 a metal detectorist, Arthur Brooks, was using his metal detector without the landowner's permission on an area of ground being cleared for the construction of an industrial estate on the outskirts of the Norfolk town of Thetford (a place called Gallows Hill). Late in the afternoon, as the light was failing, he came across metal objects and hastily excavated them. The Thetford Treasure, which has been variously interpreted as a jeweller's stash of second-hand silver and a cult treasure, eventually found its way to the British Museum in May 1980 – but not before the find site had been built over and the archaeological context eliminated. While less visually spectacular than the Mildenhall or Hoxne treasures from the same region, the assemblage contains some of the most interesting evidence for late Romano-British cultic activity. Among the silver items in the hoard were thirty-three spoons (Plate 6), twelve of which bore enigmatic inscriptions naming the god Faunus – a surprising find in Roman Britain, since there is no other evidence of a cult of Faunus in the province (and, indeed, little evidence

---

[71] Flower, *Dancing Lares*, pp. 63–70.
[72] Young (ed.), *Pagans in the Early Modern Baltic*, p. 26.

for a cult of Faunus anywhere in the empire at the time). Although Faunus was an ancient Latin deity, belonging to 'a deep and basic stratum of religious belief that can be paralleled in almost any ancient rural community',[73] the cult of Faunus largely disappeared from view in Rome after the first century BCE, and the Thetford cult is the only one attested anywhere in the later empire.[74]

As we saw in Chapter 1 above, Faunus was an example of a godling who failed to conform to later Roman perceptions of how a god should behave, and was ambiguous in terms of number, and even gender. Late pagans like Macrobius (writing around 430) were much preoccupied with archaic pagan religion,[75] perhaps in the hope that paganism might regain its vitality by returning to its roots – or simply because Rome's last pagans, aware that their belief system was in decline, were drawn to nostalgia for a pristine, archaic Roman paganism. However, Macrobius endorsed the euhemerism of earlier Classical authors like Varro when it came to the figures of Faunus and his father Picus, envisaging them purely as deified early kings of Latium – puzzlingly, given the extensive deployment of euhemerism in the kind of Christian anti-polytheistic polemic Macrobius was apparently trying to counter.[76] There was a tension here, perhaps, between the duty to respect the authority of earlier authors and the campaign to revive paganism in Macrobius' intellectual circle. A Christian anti-pagan poem apparently composed in the

---

[73] Johns, 'Faunus at Thetford', p. 94.
[74] De la Bédoyère, *Gods with Thunderbolts*, p. 214; Dorcey, *Cult of Silvanus*, p. 34.
[75] Cameron, *Last Pagans*, p. 515.   [76] Cameron, *Last Pagans*, p. 624.

year 394, the *Carmen contra paganos*, attacked and mocked the pagan consul Virius Nicomachus Flavianus (334–394) for his worship of fauns and nymphs (along with Bellona, Neptune, Pan and Vulcan). However, Alan Cameron has argued that the Christian author of the *Carmen* selected fauns and nymphs because they were mocked by Cicero and Prudentius.[77]

In addition to being linked to wild places, Faunus had an association with nightmares and buried treasure.[78] He also occasionally performed the role of an oracle, and was known as Fatuus or Fatuclus, 'the speaking one'.[79] This oracular characteristic linked Faunus with the nymphs as *fatuae*, or speakers of human fates, and thereby with the Parcae.[80] In Ovid's *Fasti*, King Numa responds to a poor harvest by going to an ancient wood, 'sacred to the god of Maenalus' (*Maenalio sacra ... deo*) – which would normally refer to Pan, but here signifies Faunus, since Numa sacrifices two ewes to Faunus and to sleep. Numa then spreads their fleeces on the ground and sleeps in the wood for a number of days, abstaining from sexual intercourse and from meat, as well as the wearing of jewellery. He twice sprinkles his head with water from a spring, and twice wears beech leaves on his head, while narcotics seem to be involved in Numa's rituals of sleep ('Night came, her calm brow wreathed with poppies').[81] Numa then experiences 'dark dreams' (*nigra somna*), including a visit from Faunus, who places his hoof on the fleece and instructs

---

[77] Cameron, *Last Pagans*, p. 283.
[78] Rose, 'Faunus', p. 432; Dorcey, *Cult of Silvanus*, pp. 33–40.
[79] Dorcey, *Cult of Silvanus*, p. 35 n.9.
[80] Varro, *De lingua Latina* 6.55.
[81] Ovid, *Fasti* 4.661.

Numa on the sacrifice required to secure a better harvest. However, Numa struggles to understand the god's commands and it is his wife, the nymph Egeria, herself a godling and 'most dear to the grove' (*nemori gratissima*), who interprets Faunus' instructions.[82]

In the early Roman cult Faunus was paired with an even more obscure goddess, Fauna, who was either his sister, daughter or consort; *Bona Dea*, 'the good goddess', was a euphemism used in order to conceal her true name of Fauna or Fatua.[83] While Varro derived the names of Faunus, Fauna and the fauns from *fari* ('to speak') and the gerund *fando*,[84] Macrobius derived Fauna's name from *faveo* ('I favour/nurture') on account of her role as a nurturer of nature. Faunus was also linked with the god Saturn, since Saturn was his grandfather, and one of the spoons from Thetford bears the inscription *Deo fauni Saternio*, perhaps suggesting that the rites at Thetford were celebrated on 5 December (the Faunalia) and thus close to Saturnalia.[85]

Faunus and fauns were often identified with Pan or the satyrs in the Renaissance, and it is possible that something similar happened in the ancient world[86] – in which case a cult of Faunus could be linked with the interest in the Bacchic/Dionysian/Orphic *thiasos* (ecstatic retinue) in late Roman Britain, a scene which features on a number of mosaics as well as on the great dish of the Mildenhall Treasure (found less than twenty miles from the Thetford Treasure (Plate 7)). The satyr on a golden belt buckle

[82] Ovid, *Fasti* 4.649–72.
[83] Hraste and Vuković, 'Rudra-Shiva and Silvanus-Faunus', p. 108.
[84] Varro, *De lingua Latina* 7.36.
[85] Henig, *Religion in Roman Britain*, p. 213.
[86] Johns, 'Faunus at Thetford', p. 94.

found with the Thetford Treasure might then be interpreted as Faunus himself (Plate 8). Dorothy Watts interpreted the Thetford treasure as the cult silver of 'a cult ... of a Bacchic type popular in the fourth century, especially as a counter-influence to Christianity'.[87] However, De la Bédoyère evinced scepticism about the actual existence of Orphic and Bacchic cults in Britain, pointing to the purely aesthetic appeal of the *thiasos* for mosaic designs (and indeed for a circular dish), as a collection of figures that could be viewed from any angle. In the absence of direct evidence of the worship of Bacchus or Orpheus in Roman Britain, it is always possible to interpret this kind of imagery as sophisticated cultural allusions and figures of speech – and perhaps even as Christian allegories.[88] Furthermore, we usually have no idea what was painted on the walls of rooms whose mosaic floors featured Bacchic themes, thus making it impossible to reach any considered judgement about the true purpose of such spaces.[89]

It would be surprising enough if the Thetford Treasure were only evidence for a late Roman cult of Faunus, but it seems that the cult also had a native element. On the Thetford spoons Faunus is called by epithets in the Brittonic language: Andicrose, Ausecus, Blotugus, Cranus (or Granus), Medigenus and Narius.[90]

---

[87] Watts, *Christians and Pagans*, p. 147. See also Watts, 'Thetford Treasure', pp. 55–68.
[88] Some twelfth-century scholars regarded Orpheus as a type of Christ, and it is conceivable that such ideas had their roots earlier in Christian history (Friedman, 'Eurydice', p. 24).
[89] De la Bédoyère, *Gods with Thunderbolts*, pp. 202–7.
[90] Hassall and Tomlin, 'Roman Britain in 1980', p. 390. These entities are clearly identified as deities by the addition of *dei*, and appear sometimes coupled with Faunus and sometimes separately.

Some of these names have been speculatively interpreted; Cranus might correspond to modern Welsh *crand*, 'grand', and Medigenus might mean 'mead-giver',[91] or 'mead-begotten'[92] – the latter, perhaps, an indication that ritual intoxication was part of the Faunus cult.[93] Ausecus could mean 'long-eared' or 'prick-eared',[94] and Blotugus 'bringer of blossom' or 'bringer of corn'.[95] Johns identified these British words as names of deities and suggested the Thetford cult was engaging in *interpretatio Romana* by pairing native deities with Faunus, while M. W. C. Hassall speculated they were 'native woodland and/or agricultural spirits'. In Hassall's view, the Thetford Faunus cult was therefore the earliest evidence for such spirits in the 'Celtic' world, although 'scenes of curious figures harvesting grapes, or of diminutive hooded figures engaged in conflict' appear on pottery from Roman Colchester.[96] On this interpretation Andicrose, Ausecus, Blotugus, Cranus, Medigenus and Narius are the direct ancestors of the fairies: 'British fauns', perhaps analogous to the Dusii reported by Augustine as the fauns of the Gauls. However, it is considerably more likely that the words are simply epithets of the god, applied in a

---

[91] De la Bédoyère, *Gods with Thunderbolts*, pp. 213–14. Cranus/Granus might also be linked with Apollo Grannus, a god worshipped in the Roman Rhineland (Hassall and Tomlin, 'Roman Britain in 1980', p. 391 n.98). Johns ('Faunus at Thetford', p. 98) links the name Cranus to treasure.
[92] Johns, 'Faunus at Thetford', p. 98.
[93] De la Bédoyère, *Real Lives of Roman Britain*, p. 179.
[94] Henig, '*Ita intellexit*', p. 166.
[95] Johns, 'Faunus at Thetford', p. 98.
[96] Hassall and Tomlin, 'Roman Britain in 1980', p. 390 n.94.

bilingual context where people were speaking both Latin and Brittonic.[97]

In their analysis of the Thetford treasure, Catherine Johns and Timothy Potter concluded that a group in eastern Britain was attempting a self-conscious revival (or invention) of the cult of Faunus,[98] a phenomenon attested elsewhere in Britain for other cults at a time when the Roman Empire was entering a period of spiritual searching, apparently dissatisfied with state religion. The fourth century saw the decay of temples in urban areas and the rise of Christianity, but in rural areas of Britain new temples were built, sometimes dedicated to obscure local gods.[99] Self-conscious revival is certainly suggested by the paradoxical nature of the cult at Thetford, which honoured the most Roman of gods, who was intimately associated with Latium and the city of Rome itself, in the British language.

Watts argued that the Thetford treasure was a cult treasure, perhaps kept at a temple, which was donated by or belonged to a number of lapsed Christians. Items bearing the names Agrestius, Auspicius, Ingenuus, Persevera, Primigenia and Silviola bore Christian imagery such as fish and specifically Christian phrases: *uti felix* ('use happily') and *vir bone vivas* ('o man, live well!'). Most strikingly of all, Spoon 69 bears the inscription *Silviola vivas* ('Silviola, may you live') followed by a cross. According to Watts' hypothesis, the revival of the cult of Faunus

[97] Henig, '*Ita intellexit*', p. 166. Mattingly (*An Imperial Possession*, p. 484) suggests that there is some uncertainty as to whether the names on the Faunus spoons refer to deities or to members of the cult.
[98] Johns and Potter, *The Thetford Treasure*, p. 49.
[99] De la Bédoyère, *Gods with Thunderbolts*, pp. 191–202.

occurred under Julian (360–363) and may have continued until Theodosius' decree closing temples in 391.[100] Watts suggested that the cult may seem so odd because there was a break in knowledge of pagan rites in fourth-century Britain as a result of the early success of Christianity; paganism thus needed to be invented afresh, as it were.[101] If the Thetford cult was inspired by Ovid's account of the worship of Faunus, it may have been aimed at ensuring good harvests through a mystery cult involving the ingestion of narcotics, followed by visionary dreams of the god. However, Faunus still seems a rather strange choice for a cult focussed on good harvests and visionary dreams, since Faunus was a god who threatened the harvest (requiring appeasement) and, as a god of the wild, was inimical to cultivation.[102] Furthermore, an incubation cult focussed on visionary dreams in honour of a god associated with nightmares seems counter-intuitive, to say the least. One possibility is that the Thetford cult of Faunus was expiatory in character, as that of the *lamiae tres* at Benwell may have been – seeking to avert the destructive energy of a dangerous being. Alternatively, the cult could be seen as a transgressive esoteric sect, deliberately honouring a dangerous god – an interpretation perhaps borne out by the appearance of magical names on rings in the Thetford Treasure, which may or may not be connected with the Faunus assemblage.

Given that Roman religion identified Faunus with Pan, the significance of Pan within the Eleusinian Mysteries

---

[100] Watts, *Christians and Pagans*, p. 147.
[101] Watts, *Christians and Pagans*, p. 149.
[102] Dorcey, *Cult of Silvanus*, p. 38.

of Dionysus provides one possible framework for understanding the nature of the Thetford mystery cult, which could have been an enculturated 'British' version of a Dionysian cult. Pan and Dionysus always enjoyed a close relationship,[103] and the Orphic hymn to Pan was apparently part of the rites of Eleusis. The hymn plays on the pun of Pan's name with the Greek word *pan* ('all'), portraying Pan as a cosmic deity whose composite human/animal nature served as a symbolic microcosm of all reality.[104] However, there is no evidence that Roman participants in Orphic and Dionysian mystery cults ever replaced Pan's name with that of Faunus – and clearly, Pan's cosmic dimension was potentially diminished by the use of a Latin name. Martin Henig has offered an alternative interpretation, associating Faunus' oracular function with a sacred grove and suggesting a link with the deity Mars Rigonemetus ('Mars, King of the Grove'), who was honoured with an inscription at Nettleham, near Lincoln, by a man named Quintus Neratius Proxsimus, who was probably a Samnite or of Samnite descent. At the sacred grove of Tiora in Samnite territory, oracles were delivered in a grove by a sacred woodpecker identified both with Mars and with the archaic Latin god Picus ('woodpecker'), the supposed father of Faunus,[105] and the idea of oracular birds can be found throughout Europe; in Lithuanian folklore, for example, the cuckoo serves as an oracular bird and a personification of the Fates.[106] That Picus was involved in the Faunus cult at Thetford is

[103] Robichaud, *Pan*, p. 19.
[104] Robichaud, *Pan*, pp. 41–43.
[105] Henig, *Religion in Roman Britain*, p. 35.
[106] Greimas, *Of Gods and Men*, pp. 116–18.

suggested by the appearance of two woodpeckers on one of the rings in the hoard.[107]

The interest of the Thetford Treasure deepens even further when we consider that it was found close to an important Iron Age religious site at Fison Way. The 'antiquarian' revival of Iron Age cults, sometimes after an interval of centuries, seems to have been a feature of religion in fourth-century Britain – perhaps a cultural consequence of a crisis of religious identity induced by the rapid rise of Christianity and the pagan revival under Julian.[108] The rather murky circumstances of the treasure's discovery by treasure-hunters meant that its archaeological context could not be investigated any further, but it is possible that no archaeological evidence would have been found anyway. Faunus was a god of groves as much as a god of temples, and if there was a sacred grove at Gallows Hill, it is unlikely that anything would survive in the archaeological record. The major Iron Age religious site at Fison Way, which was apparently dismantled in the aftermath of the Boudiccan Revolt, featured what may have been an 'artificial oak grove', based on discoveries of post-holes and a copper alloy votive oak leaf.[109] It is also possible that the members of the Faunus cult knew that Gallows Hill had been an ancient sacred site, but knew no more about its true nature than we do.

A notable feature of the spoons in the Thetford Treasure is that the human beings mentioned on them

---

[107] Johns, 'Faunus at Thetford', p. 103.
[108] Jones, *End of Roman Britain*, p. 178.
[109] Smith, 'Differentiated Use of Constructed Sacred Space', vol. 1, pp. 118–20.

have names so appropriate to the cult of Faunus (or of the fauns) that they were probably new names or nicknames assumed by devotees. These include Agrestius ('rustic') and Silviola ('little forest-dweller').[110] Henig saw these names as *signa*, 'religious names appropriate to the cult';[111] perhaps the desire of devotees was to spiritually join the ecstatic retinue or *thiasos* of the god, becoming assimilated to godlings like nymphs and satyrs. For Watts, the Thetford Treasure is 'conclusive' evidence of the decline of Christianity and persistence of paganism in Britain at the end of the fourth century, while the people who honoured Faunus were 'lapsed Christians'.[112] However, this interpretation risks imposing our perceptions of religion on the Romano-Britons. Henig has drawn attention to the religious creativity of the Roman world, where, 'provided that traditional practices were not challenged ... every man was free to define the nature of the gods as he wished'.[113] While Christianity, in theory, stood against such an approach, in reality fourth-century Christianity was marked by syncretism as well, especially in Britain.

Some evidence indicates that syncretism in the province did cross the ultimate religious Rubicon by honouring Christ as a pagan god. Henig has argued that the Chi Rho motif in a mosaic at Frampton, which appears in an entirely pagan context, is best explained as the result

[110] Hassall and Tomlin, 'Roman Britain in 1980', 390 n.95. The word *silvicola* is used by Virgil for the nymph Dryope, who bears a son for Faunus named Tarquitus (*Aeneid* 10.551).
[111] Henig, '*Ita intellexit*', p. 166.
[112] Watts, *Christians and Pagans*, p. 225.
[113] Henig, '*Ita intellexit*', p. 159.

of this kind of syncretism. Just as the *Historia Augusta* reported that the Emperor Severus Alexander had images in his domestic shrine of Apollonius of Tyana, Abraham, Orpheus, Alexander the Great and Christ, so some people in Roman Britain may have understood Christ as an illuminator of mysteries and one god among many. A signet ring discovered at Silchester bears an image of Venus but a distinctively Christian legend, *Seniciane vivas in Deo*, 'Senicianus, may you live in God', while curse tablets from Bath suggest that Christians visited the shrine of Sulis, and the 'votive feathers' deposited as part of Christian worship at Water Newton in the Nene Valley directly mirrored pagan practice.[114]

Magic provided another possible context for syncretism, and it is noteworthy that one of the rings in the Thetford assemblage depicted the chicken-headed god Iao and another bore the magical words *Abrasax Sabaoth*.[115] If the members of the Thetford *collegium* had these kinds of occult interests, which often bore little relationship to confessional allegiance, invocations of the god Faunus could be reinterpreted as part of some sort of magical or esoteric practice. Just as some Christians today see Freemasonry as compatible with their faith, so it is possible to imagine that some people in late Roman Britain might have considered the public adoption of Christianity to be compatible with continued membership of mystery cults, which did not involve public worship or the maintenance of temples – the kind of activities outlawed by the edicts of Christian emperors. It is even

[114] Henig, '*Ita intellexit*', p. 164.
[115] Henig, *Religion in Roman Britain*, p. 178.

possible that clubs and *collegia* originating as mystery cults continued as vestigial dining societies out of habit, or out of aristocratic concern for the maintenance of tradition, with the ritual paraphernalia remaining in use but losing its sacred significance. Perhaps the last people to use the Thetford treasure were nominal Christians for whom these items were primarily heirlooms.

Just as the novel saviour-god Antinous was equated with Pan in the reign of Hadrian,[116] and the late Roman poet Nonnus presented Dionysus as a kind of 'polytheistic Christ',[117] is it possible that the Thetford cult could have equated Christ with Faunus? This is perhaps the most extreme interpretation possible for the apparent syncretism evident in the Thetford assemblage, but the continuation of a faun cult alongside Christian allegiance is another possibility. Henig points to the presence of items such as wine strainers as evidence that the Thetford cult of Faunus was a private cult focussed on feasting,[118] but if the Thetford devotees were indeed inspired by the presence of a disused and decayed Iron Age religious site in the landscape, and identified its tutelary spirit with Faunus, this suggests a high degree of learned and sophisticated *interpretatio Romana*. However, as Guy de la Bédoyère has noted, the presence of splendid treasures such as those buried at Mildenhall, Hoxne and Thetford is at odds with the absence of evidence for a culture of lavish villas in East Anglia; the most opulent villas of the period are found in Gloucestershire.[119] The social and material

---

[116] Henig, '*Ita intellexit*', p. 160.
[117] Shorrock, *Myth of Paganism*, p. 80.
[118] Henig, '*Ita intellexit*', p. 166.
[119] De la Bédoyère, *Gods with Thunderbolts*, p. 115.

context of East Anglia's late Roman Bacchic cults remains obscure, therefore, and it is unclear whether these items should be associated with villas, temples or cult banqueting houses of some kind.

Christians showed an interest in Faunus elsewhere in the fourth-century empire that might shed some light on the Thetford cult. Benjamin Garstad has shown that a doctrine found in the fourth-century *Clementine Recognitions*, that good and evil come in pairs, is likely to have inspired a short euhemeristic Christian narrative that re-imagined Zeus-Picus and Faunus-Hermes as magicians who posed as gods and, in the case of Faunus-Hermes, came to rule Egypt through magic arts.[120] Dating from the fourth century, and perhaps the work of a mysterious historian named Bruttius (or Bouttios),[121] the Faunus-Hermes narrative imagined Faunus-Hermes as the 'evil twin' of Joseph, who also ruled Egypt but in doing so brought honour to the true God instead of promoting idolatry.[122] Garstad showed that the author drew on popular Christian Hellenistic romances about the life of Joseph; but in addition to the contrast between Hermes and Joseph, the most distinctive feature of the narrative is the identification of Hermes and Faunus, which at first sight makes little sense, but probably originated from a desire to identify the Egyptian Hermes with an Italian god of magic for a specifically Roman audience. At the very least, the Faunus-Hermes narrative is evidence for a revival of interest in Faunus among fourth-century Romans, if only

---

[120] Garstad, 'Joseph as a Model for Faunus-Hermes', pp. 514–20.
[121] Van Hoof and Van Nuffelen (eds.), *Fragmentary Latin Histories*, pp. 250–61.
[122] Garstad, 'Joseph as a Model for Faunus-Hermes', p. 509.

to reject him. It is easy to imagine Romans disillusioned with eastern mystery cults attempting to invent an 'indigenous' cult of their own, based on the ancient oracular god Faunus as the Latin equivalent of Hermes. Such a religious development may provide the background to both the anti-pagan Faunus-Hermes narrative and the Thetford cult.

One possible assemblage of cult items that may be comparable to the Thetford Treasure is detritus from a sacred feast found in the Drapers' Gardens well in London, which has been dated to no earlier than 375. In addition to vessels and tableware, the apparent ritual deposition included the partially articulated remains of a juvenile red deer,[123] perhaps suggesting a feast in honour of Silvanus or some other hunting god. However, whereas as at Thetford the probable context of the burial of the cult objects was in a jeweller's collection of scrap metal, at Drapers' Gardens the deposition of the items seems to have been part of the cult's rites. That Silvanus, like Faunus at Thetford, was worshipped by *collegia* of devoted worshippers is evidenced by a ring from Wendens Ambo, Essex, with the inscription Col[legium] Dei Sil[vani], 'the college of the god Silvanus'.[124]

While Faunus was an obscure god in the late Roman world, Silvanus (with whom Faunus was sometimes identified[125]) was much more popular. Silvanus, unlike Faunus, is attested epigraphically in Britain, and there was even a 'guild of Silvanians' (either devotees of

---

[123] Gerrard, 'Wells and Belief Systems', pp. 551–72.
[124] Henig, *Religion in Roman Britain*, p. 154.
[125] Dorcey, *Cult of Silvanus*, p. 34.

Silvanus, or hunters, or both) at Corbridge, while at Housesteads on Hadrian's Wall, Silvanus was conflated with Cocidius and Mars. At the fort of Lavatris on Scargill Moor he was conflated with Vinotonus, presumably a local deity.[126] Silvanus was sometimes identified with the hammer-wielding Gaulish god Sucellus, perhaps worshipped at the temple at Farley Heath as a composite of Taranis, Sucellus, Silvanus and Dis Pater (although the principal hunter god worshipped in Roman Britain seems to have been Apollo Cunomaglus ('hound lord'), who was represented accompanied by a stag, dog and hare[127]).[128]

Silvanus was a god of the grove,[129] and Yeates has argued that sacred groves or *nemetoi* in Roman Britain can be identified by the presence of linear ditch systems in areas known to have been wooded, and that (in the West Country at least) these were sites of worship of a hunter god. Furthermore, among the Dobunni of the West Country, the hunter god became conflated with Orpheus as lord of the animals, resulting in a number of representations in mosaics of 'a figure, playing a Lyre and wearing a Phrygian cap, in a central roundel accompanied by two animals, one of which is a dog'.[130] Yeates suggested that *nemetoi* represented a kind of deification of the wooded landscape,[131] or indeed of trees themselves. As we have seen in Chapter 1 above, the presence of animism of this kind in the Roman world is unsupported by the evidence,

---

[126] De la Bédoyère, *Gods with Thunderbolts*, pp. 161–62.
[127] Yeates, *Tribe of Witches*, pp. 110–11.
[128] Goodchild, 'The Farley Heath Sceptre', pp. 83–85.
[129] Henig, *Religion in Roman Britain*, p. 41.
[130] Yeates, *Tribe of Witches*, p. 113.
[131] Yeates, *Tribe of Witches*, p. 115.

but the possibility of an animistic strand in native British religion is possible, and it is not altogether clear why worship in a *nemeton* should always be associated with hunting cults. It is also possible that worship in groves reflected an older stratum of religious practice in Roman religion originally linked with forms of animism, and it may be a mistake to link the *nemeton* with specific deities.

It is tempting to view the cult of Faunus at Thetford as a Romano-British precursor of later fairy belief,[132] given the parallels between Faunus and medieval folkloric beings: his association with untamed nature, oracles, buried treasure, and nightmares, as well as the possible expiatory character of his cult – and even a name linked by Roman authors to the speaking of fate. The way in which the god's devotees adopted cultic names suggests a desire to enter into a supernatural world by joining the god's ecstatic retinue, rather like later ideas of mortals journeying into fairyland. In the words of Charles Thomas, the Faunus cult could be taken by some as evidence that 'the "Old Faith" ... never wholly vanished, but grumbled away stubbornly in the background of post-Roman and medieval Christianity'.[133] Furthermore, the very name Gallows Hill is suggestive; pre-Christian sacred places were sometimes demonised by being turned into 'killing places' in the Anglo-Saxon period, meaning that an association with judicial executions sometimes preserved a trace of former pagan significance.[134] Johns characterised the Thetford cult as the absorption of Faunus into

---

[132] Young, *Suffolk Fairylore*, pp. 19–23.
[133] Thomas, *Celtic Britain*, p. 57.
[134] Semple, *Perceptions of the Prehistoric*, pp. 190, 194.

Celtic religious belief,[135] and this seems to have survived: a folk belief in fauns as abductors of children could be found in Brittany in the thirteenth century.[136] The existence of the Thetford cult raises the question of whether faun cults were more widely spread in late Roman Britain and Gaul than the one discovered by chance in Norfolk. It is conceivable that these otherwise unrecorded faun cults formed the background to the demonisation of the fauns of Gaul (under the name of *dusii*) in the writings of Augustine. The difficulty is not, as Angana Moitra suggests, in understanding how Greek and Roman ideas were culturally translated into the 'Celtic' world,[137] but how they survived in the Christianised insular world of post-Roman and early medieval Britain. The continuity or otherwise of belief in fauns and other godlings in that world will be explored in detail in Chapters 3 and 4 below, but it is important to view the Thetford Faunus cult in context; while unusual, it also formed part of a continuum of Bacchic cults and can be linked plausibly with *collegia* in honour of Silvanus, a deity routinely confused with Faunus, and other 'gods of the grove'.

Genii Loci

The genius was the Roman godling *par excellence*, divine in the sense that a genius might be offered worship, yet also emphatically a lesser being than a god. The genius of a person was even imagined to be mortal, barring the

---

[135] Johns, 'Faunus at Thetford', p. 102.
[136] Purkiss, *Troublesome Things*, pp. 53–56.
[137] Moitra, 'From Graeco-Roman Underworld to the Celtic Otherworld', p. 92.

exceptional circumstances of an individual's elevation to divine honours after death. But genii could also be tied to places and inanimate objects; almost anything could have a genius.[138] Although Ralph Häussler has argued soldiers in Roman Britain attempted to reconcile local deities with the concept of the genius loci,[139] the majority of surviving dedications to genii loci (or to the genius of a particular military unit) are generic. It is most likely that *Genio [huius] loci* ('to the genius of this place') was simply a conventional formula which conceals no knowledge of specific 'land spirits' connected with a place, rather like the famous Athenian dedication 'To the unknown god' mentioned in Acts 27:23.[140] Occasionally dedicators were a little more specific, like an altar dedicated 'to the genius of York',[141] or more global, like Marcus Cocceius Firmus' dedication 'to the genius of the land of Britain' at Auchendavy.[142] Occasionally evidence survives for rural shrines to genii loci, such as at Tockenham in Wiltshire; here a shrine of the genius loci (whose cult image may be preserved in the wall of the church) may have been associated with a sacred spring, judging from the discovery of an elaborately carved fountain spout in the shape of a fish in a nearby pool.[143]

---

[138] De la Bédoyère, *Gods with Thunderbolts*, p. 162.
[139] Häussler, 'La religion en Bretagne', p. 491.
[140] De la Bédoyère, *Gods with Thunderbolts*, p. 163.
[141] *RIB* 657, romaninscriptionsofbritain.org/inscriptions/657, accessed 10 October 2021.
[142] *RIB* 2175, romaninscriptionsofbritain.org/inscriptions/2175, accessed 10 October 2021.
[143] Harding and Lewis, 'Archaeological Investigations at Tockenham', p. 35.

Yeates has suggested that the *genius Eboraci* ('genius of York') was in effect the *tyche* (good fortune) of the city, perhaps worshipped in the municipal basilica and represented wearing a mural crown.[144] A sculpture of such a municipal genius survives from Cirencester.[145] Yeates goes on to the argue that, in some cases, a genius or tyche went on to be reimagined as the mythical ancestor of a post-Roman people group; thus Glywys, the legendary founder of the Welsh kingdom of Glywysyng, may originally have been the *genius Glevensis* (genius of Gloucester).[146] Yet while the character of Glywys may well be linked with Gloucester and the *civitas* of which it was the capital, it is scarcely necessary to hypothesise the existence of a distinct supernatural being to account for the name. The back-formation of the names of legendary founders from existing place names was common in medieval Europe, and if Welsh speakers needed an imaginary founder figure for Gloucester, his name might well have been Glywys.

While the Roman genius was usually portrayed wearing a toga drawn over his head and holding a cornucopia, alternative iconographies of genii developed in the northern provinces. The so-called *genii cucullati* are three diminutive male figures dressed in a *cucullus* (the type of all-over hooded cloak popular in Britain and the northern provinces of the empire) who appear in a number of religious contexts in Germany and Britain (Plate 9). The term *genii cucullati* is a descriptive one assigned by

---

[144] Yeates, *Tribe of Witches*, p. 62.
[145] Yeates, *Tribe of Witches*, p. 74.
[146] Yeates, *Tribe of Witches*, pp. 158–59.

archaeologists, since we do not know what these beings were called. In Britain, surviving representations of the *genii cucullati* are confined to Hadrian's Wall and the Cotswolds, and in the Cotswolds they tend to appear in association with a mother goddess identified by Stephen Yeates as Cuda (from an inscription to Cuda ploughed up at Daglingworth, Gloucestershire, in 1951). The name of the goddess Cuda may be linked to the British word for pigeon, and also seems to be the root of 'Cotswolds'.

Stephen Yeates was sceptical that the *genii cucullati* 'belonged to the world of dwarfs and goblins', preferring instead to see them as analogous to the three mythical brothers of the goddess Danu in Irish legend.[147] It is important to note that in ancient sculpture, figures often appeared as diminutive to denote their status relative to other characters – not because they were imagined as diminutive in reality – so there is no good reason to link the *genii cucullati* with dwarfs. All we can say with certainty is that they were considered somehow junior or subordinate to the goddess with whom they appear. Aldhouse-Green considered them to be a distinctly British expression of the genius, combined with the British reverence for the number three.[148] However, the *genii cucullati* may also have been a transference of Roman imagery to a more familiar cultural context; like Roman genii, the heads of the *genii cucullati* were covered, albeit by the familiar *birrus Britannicus* rather than the unfamiliar toga.

---

[147] Yeates, *Tribe of Witches*, pp. 12–17.
[148] Aldhouse-Green, *Sacred Britannia*, p. 58.

Conclusion

The religions of Roman Britain were exceptionally diverse and often highly localised, and more questions than answers remain about this intriguing period in Britain's religious history. Romano-British religion was characterised by its creativity, including a capacity and willingness to confect and create deities as they were needed. Popular religion in Roman Britain is usually readily distinguishable from the official and military cults of the emperor and the imperial house, which took an overt and conventional form in the provinces. Popular religion, by contrast, was characterised by its eccentricity and willingness to recombine deities and religious concepts in new formations, often taken from all over the empire. While popular religion in Roman Britain may have contained ancient native elements dating from the Iron Age, this is not something that can be established as fact, and it is more helpful to approach Romano-British religion as a phenomenon in its own right without excessive speculation on a 'Celtic' past. While it is possible to debate the extent to which Britain was ever Romanised, it seems unlikely that no religious beliefs or cults were entirely untouched by Roman influence, and the surviving evidence strongly suggests that syncretism prevailed.

The fourth-century pagan resurgence associated with the Emperor Julian was an important moment in the development of Romano-British popular religion, involving a 'romanticised' revival of worship in the countryside and at places in the natural landscape, as well as at Iron Age and other prehistoric sacred sites. De la Bédoyère has argued that the resistance to Christianity that provoked the pagan revival of the fourth century was motivated not so much by religion, but by 'its link with tradition and also with established patterns of power and influence'.[149] However, what is curious about fourth-century religion is that it did not involve what we might expect – a determined attempt to maintain Roman civic religion in the face of advancing Christianity. Instead, the fourth-century revival seems to have been an internal renaissance within Romano-British paganism, shifting its focus to the countryside, to features of the natural world and to the prehistoric sacred landscape.

The enigmatic Thetford Treasure, with its ambiguous relationship to Christianity, provides an intriguing glimpse of how cults of godlings may have survived in a Christianised environment at the end of Roman Britain. But it is speculation to suppose that the Thetford Faunus cult represents the beginning of a popular British Christianity in which minor deities and spirits could survive under the Christian God. As we shall see in the following chapters, it is likely that godlings in early medieval Britain were predominantly textual creations from the works of the Church Fathers that passed into folklore, and it is possible that virtually no continuity existed between the religion of Roman Britain and the folklore of the early medieval societies that succeeded it. On the other hand, the dominant theme of religion in Roman Britain was its creativity and adaptability to change, which allowed it to survive the incorporation of native British religion into Roman religion; the changing religious preferences of emperors and evolving religious fashions.

---

[149] De la Bédoyère, *Gods with Thunderbolts*, p. 191.

Conclusion

In one important respect, the religion of Roman Britain did survive – as British Christianity.

The question of whether the minor deities of Roman Britain managed to survive the coming of Christianity in some form, to emerge again in the Middle Ages, is almost impossible to answer. Yet it is important, as I shall argue in Chapter 3 below, that early medieval folkloric traditions developed against a cultural background and amid the wreckage of a material culture inherited from the Romans and Romano-Britons. Thus, for example, the importance of the underworld and trooping and dancing godlings in medieval folklore recalls the *thiasos* – the dancing procession of godlings portrayed so often in Roman art from Britain in connection with Orpheus and Bacchus. Any historical connection between the two remains tantalisingly beyond the reach of the evidence available to us, but the Romano-British background may have conditioned not only which beings re-emerged in medieval Britain, but also which beings did not. For example, in spite of their frequent appearances in medieval art and learned writing, medieval folklore did not people the British landscape with griffins and centaurs. It is unlikely that the godlings of Roman Britain vanished without a trace, and whether or not they came directly from Roman Britain, medieval Britain's godlings certainly derived in one way or another from the legacy of Rome.

3

The Nymph and the Cross

Godlings and Christianisation

Sometime in the sixth century, when the British writer Gildas denounced the sins of his fellow countrymen (which in his view had left the Britons a fractured people, vulnerable to attack by invaders), he took the opportunity to mention some of his people's historic sins. These included the idolatry of their ancestors, everywhere visible among the ruins of decaying Roman cities:

> I therefore omit those ancient errors, common to all nations, by which before the coming of Christ in the flesh the whole human race was being held in bondage; nor do I enumerate the truly diabolical monstrosities of my native country, almost surpassing those of Egypt in number, of which we behold some, of ugly features, to this day within or without their deserted walls, stiff with fierce visage as was the custom. Neither do I, by name, inveigh against the mountains, valleys or rivers, once destructive, but now suitable for the use of man, upon which divine honour was then heaped by the people in their blindness.[1]

---

[1] Williams (ed.), *Gildae De Excidio Britanniae*, pp. 16–17: *Igitur omittens priscos illos communesque cum omnibus gentibus errores, quibus ante adventum Christi in carne omne humanum genus obligabatur astrictum, nec enumaerans patriae portenta ipsa diabolica paene numero Aegyptiaca vincentia, quorum nonnulla liniamentis adhuc deformibus intra vel extra deserta moenia solito mores rigentia torvis vultibus intuemur, neque nominatum inclamitans montes ipsos aut colles vel fluvios olim exitiabiles, nunc vero humanis usibus utiles, quibus divinus honor a caeco tunc populo cumulabatur.*

At the time Gildas was writing, it is likely that Romano-British religion had been extinct in any organised form (centred on shrines and temples), for well over a century. Only indelible monuments, like a still visible figure of Minerva cut into the side of a quarry outside the gates of Roman Chester (Plate 10), could yet be seen. But it seems unlikely that everyone in sixth-century Britain would have agreed with Gildas that mountains, valleys and rivers no longer received divine honours from anyone. The fact that Gildas could think that such things lay entirely in the past is revealing in itself, showing that it was possible for someone who belonged to the island's educated Latinate elite to ignore popular religion. It is also revealing that Gildas made a distinction between the urban idolatry of Roman Britain and the worship of nature. While Roman monuments decayed and were gradually hidden from view by the undergrowth, Britain's landscape remained a constant throughout the turbulent period when Gildas wrote.

This chapter is an attempt to investigate what may have happened to Britain's godlings in the period of the island's conversion to Christianity – those 'small gods' of nature and everyday life that, to a learned cleric like Gildas, may have been unworthy of notice. Popular accounts of the origins of folklore often portray folkloric beings as the lucky survivors of a thoroughgoing conversion to Christianity which stamped out pre-Christian belief. This is a view grounded in earlier scholarship; for example, Gordon Laing argued that the cult of the Lares survived in modern Italy.[2] The reality, as this chapter will argue, is a great deal more complex, and it is important

---

[2] Laing, *Survivals of Roman Religion*, p. 18.

to set aside cultural assumptions about both Christianity and folklore in order to make progress in understanding how Britain's folkloric beings may have emerged from the post-Roman world.

Michael Ostling's characterisation of godlings as animistic survivals excluded by Christianity suggests that conflict with Christianity is an inevitable part of belief in folkloric beings.[3] But it does not follow from the non-Christian character of godlings that they are always pre-Christian survivals, and this chapter will suggest some processes by which folkloric beings having nothing directly to do with Christianity can come into being within a Christian society. Furthermore, the relationship between Christianity and belief in godlings was not always and not solely marked by conflict. The godlings of early medieval Britain are best understood not as 'pagan survivals' but as artefacts of Christianisation. As Lisa Bitel has noted of the people of early medieval Ireland, they were neither pagans nor Christians in a sense that we might readily recognise, but rather 'dwellers on a land constantly revised to accommodate religion and the supernatural' who remained open to the possibility of non-Christian otherworlds and their inhabitants.[4] The same was surely true of the peoples of early medieval Britain, albeit Britain's landscape featured the wreckage of the Roman world as well as the monuments of prehistoric cultures.

The major challenge of studying the origins of folkloric beings in post-Roman Britain – or indeed any aspect of post-Roman Britain – is the dearth of evidence. While this chapter analyses the evidence available, therefore, it also

---

[3] Ostling, 'Introduction', pp. 4–11.   [4] Bitel, 'Secrets of the *Síd*', p. 98.

adopts a comparative approach, drawing on the insights of anthropologists studying Christianisation within modern societies as well as our knowledge of other European societies that converted to Christianity at a later date than the peoples of early medieval Britain. The chapter applies interpretative models of Christianisation to the societies of late Roman, post-Roman and early medieval Britain in the hope of understanding – by comparison with other cultures – the shifts in religious belief and practice that may have taken place in the fourth, fifth and sixth centuries, producing the familiar folkloric beings of medieval and early modern Britain.

The Christianisation of Britain was a long process, occurring in one form or another over the space of six hundred years, between the early fourth century and the 970s. For historiographical reasons, it is rarely studied as a single process; the Christianisation of Roman Britain has traditionally been considered separately from the conversion of the Anglo-Saxons, while the Christianisation of Scandinavian pagans in Britain in the tenth century may be treated as different again.[5] From an Anglocentric point of view, the conversion of Roman Britain and the conversion of the Anglo-Saxons is characterised by a rupture of two centuries, while the conversion of the Vikings was a coda to the triumph of Christianity in early medieval England. Yet as soon as we set aside this Anglocentric approach to view the island of Britain as a whole, it becomes clear that neither Christianity nor Christian missionary activity ever went away. There were Christian missionaries from Roman Britain, Christian missionaries in post-Roman

---

[5] Petts, *Pagan and Christian*, p. 13.

Britain and early medieval Wales and missionaries in Anglo-Saxon England from Rome, Francia and Ireland. Even if the Christian mission suffered major setbacks, such as the apparent dominance of Germanic paganism in Anglo-Saxon areas in the fifth and sixth centuries and the Viking invasions of the ninth, in a study of belief ranging across the whole island of Great Britain there is no good reason to treat Christianisation as anything other than a single (albeit halting and complex) process.

Treating Christianisation as a single process is important because ongoing Christianisation is one of the few clear threads that unites the Roman, post-Roman and early medieval periods in British history. While it is undeniable that the British church failed – in contrast to its Gaulish counterpart – to play a key role in the transition from Roman rule to a coherent post-Roman polity, the British church in some form nevertheless survived the chaotic and disruptive fifth and sixth centuries, and it is highly likely it was the sole Roman institution to do so. In the early medieval world ideals of *Romanitas* were closely entwined with Christianity.[6] When early Christian missionaries in Anglo-Saxon England re-used Roman remains they may have been making a conscious point about the continuity of the Christian faith in Britain from the Romans to the missionary Roman church at Canterbury. It is also important to note that for early medieval people, the Roman past was the familiar past – in contrast to a prehistoric past that was much harder to process and understand.[7] However, the re-use

---

[6] On *Romanitas* in Anglo-Saxon England see Hawkes, 'Anglo-Saxon Romanitas', pp. 19–36.
[7] Semple, *Perceptions of the Prehistoric*, pp. 190–91.

of Roman remains, and an emphasis on continuity with the Roman past, glossed over the possibility that Roman Britain was never an entirely Christianised society, and embracing *Romanitas* meant embracing the remains of paganism as well as the Roman Christianity that triumphed over it.

Although scholars remain very much divided on the nature of relations between people groups in post-Roman Britain, there has been a steady drift in the scholarship away from the picture of conflict, displacement and even genocide portrayed by Bede and Gildas, towards a greater emphasis on the continuity between late Roman and early medieval Britain. For example, on the basis of the appearance of British names in early medieval documents, Stephen Yeates has proposed 'stable communal development into the fifth and sixth centuries AD' in the territory of the Dobunni (later Hwicce) in the West Country,[8] a people group who apparently bore a British name (**Hywych*) and may have preserved their church organisation throughout the fifth and sixth centuries.[9] Yeates has argued that the folk-names of people groups in the West Country are often of Roman or pre-Roman origin, suggesting that later Anglo-Saxon territorial units reflected pre-existing identities, and were perhaps even built around memories of cults of pre-Christian territorial spirits that helped define identities.[10] While this is highly speculative, Stephen Rippon, Chris Smart and Ben Pears have emphasised the continuities between

---

[8] Yeates, *Tribe of Witches*, p. 59.
[9] Coates, 'The Name of the Hwicce', pp. 51–61; Bassett, 'How the West Was Won', pp. 107–18.
[10] Yeates, *Tribe of Witches*, p. 89.

Iron Age, Roman and early medieval land boundaries in Britain, often down to the level of individual fields.[11]

Much of the archaeological evidence of conflict in post-Roman Britain, such as the re-use of Iron Age hill-forts and the construction of giant earthworks, appears to be associated with conflict between different British groups rather than conflict between Britons and Germanic settlers,[12] and some historians are now prepared to see the transition from post-Roman Britain to early England as a process of cultural assimilation, in a context of urban collapse and population decline, rather than brutal conquest. Yet while there remains little agreement among scholars on the level of violence and upheaval involved in the birth of England, it is clear that these events involved a complex two-way cultural exchange. In the area of folkloric belief, the complexity is such that the origins of British folklore are better treated as a holistic whole-island historical problem rather than along potentially contentious ethno-cultural lines.

An Interpretative Model: Demonisation, Undemonisation and Re-Personification

The word 'Christianisation' is often used by scholars in two different but overlapping ways: to refer to the transformation of a society from a pagan to a Christian one, and to describe a process of turning pagan sacred sites, festivals and ritual practices Christian. Yet it is possible to turn a

---

[11] See Rippon et al., *The Fields of Britannia*; Rippon, *Territoriality and the Early Medieval Landscape*.

[12] Laycock, *Britannia the Failed State*, pp. 135–68.

society Christian without giving new Christian meanings to its sacred sites, festivals and ritual practices. Instead, Christianisation of a society might leave those features of life alone, on the basis that they have little to do with religious adherence, or it might replace them altogether with unrelated Christian sites, events and rites. To presume that there was a 'turning Christian' of pre-Christian religious aspects of life is therefore to come to the issue of Christianisation already loaded with assumptions. Furthermore, the idea that Christianisation was a mere 're-badging' of pagan figures or festivals, a cultural veneer on top of paganism or a camouflaging of pagan belief[13] is an outdated trope rooted not in the evidence of history or archaeology but in the religious polemic of the Reformation, which portrayed Catholicism as little more than re-badged paganism in order to discredit it.[14]

Christianity and the church are not the same thing, yet there is a danger of scholars of Christianisation assuming that Christianisation is to be identified with the exercise of authority by the institutional church. Yet the establishment of the church in a society and its Christianisation are not entirely coterminous processes. At a certain point, the creation of a distinctive popular Christianity within a culture becomes an organic and self-sustaining process only indirectly related to the institutional church, and frequently giving rise to beliefs and practices that the church may well condemn or view with suspicion. It is a paradox of Christianisation that the more successful it is, the

---

[13] De la Bédoyère, *Gods with Thunderbolts*, p. 239; Hutton, *Queens of the Wild*, p. 36.
[14] Parish, 'Magic and Priestcraft', pp. 393–425.

less control the church will ultimately exercise over its development – which may explain why some nations (such as Ireland and Greece) that were thoroughly Christianised at an early date have the most vibrant popular Christianities. It is against this background of popular Christianity that godlings of the early Middle Ages can be considered artefacts of Christianisation: they were not, perhaps, part of the official outlook of the church and its officials, but they were part of the outlook of ordinary Christians, and therefore linked with popular Christianity.

Another potential trap for the historian of Christianisation is to assume excessive intentionality in the imitation or replacement of a feature of one religion with another. Martin Henig has argued persuasively that Christian standing crosses in Britain were in some sense a development from the Roman Jupiter column or votive column, which stood at the heart of religious enclosures in the same way that Roman columns stood at the heart of the Romano-British *civitas*.[15] Yet it does not follow from this that the standing cross is a *Christianisation* of the Roman municipal sacred column, because such monuments may already have been thought of as Christian if they were still standing in the early medieval period. Their pagan imagery might already have been removed, that imagery might already have been Christianised in some way or some early medieval people simply assumed that everything Roman was somehow linked with Christianity, forgetting that the Roman empire had ever been pagan at all.

Joel Robbins has argued persuasively against the concept of 'crypto-religion': an interpretation of Christianity

---

[15] Henig, '*Murum civitatis*', pp. 11–28.

by anthropologists as a mere cultural overlay in societies where ancestral spirits remain important. Syncretism, as 'crypto-religion', is to be understood as a worldview that permits people to continue venerating the spirits of their ancestral religion under the cover of various forms of Christianity. For Robbins, however, this reading misses the mark; instead, people in Christianised societies 'continue to believe in the reality and power of the spiritual beings who were at the center of their traditional religion, but at the same time demonize them and enlist God as their ally in a struggle to defeat them'.[16] What results is the 'ontological preservation' of pre-Christian spirits through a rhetoric of opposition.

Anthropological studies of the interplay of Christianity and traditional religion in contemporary societies now inform scholarship on the Christianisation of the ancient world. Aldhouse-Green, for example, compares Roman Britain to the Bahia region of Brazil, where Amerindian religion, Catholicism and Yoruba religion have become fused to the extent that 'it is hard to identify which – if any – has dominance'.[17] Yet the use of anthropological analyses undertaken in colonial and post-colonial environments in an attempt to understand ancient societies is problematic.[18] David Frankfurter has argued that Christianity actively preserved godlings as part of the cosmology and experience of believers, since these 'liminal and chaotic' spirits frequently possessed believers at the shrines of the saints. The advent of Christianity brought

---

[16] Robbins, 'Crypto-Religion', 421.
[17] Aldhouse-Green, *Sacred Britannia*, p. 230.
[18] For a discussion of these issues see Petts, *Pagan and Christian*, pp. 73–77.

a 'reorganisation' of the pantheon, but it certainly did not eliminate those beings whose status had already been ambivalent in the pagan world. The reorganisation 'marginalized spirits associated with the landscape, ancestors, or divination' but it did not eliminate them. The old spirits became the foil to the new religion and were crucial to the formation and preservation of its identity, just as women manifesting signs of possession at the Catholic shrine of Kudagama in Sri Lanka claim to be possessed by Hindu gods and thereby cement Catholic identity over against Hinduism.[19]

It has long been recognised that spirit possession in Christianity is an ambivalent phenomenon, associated as much with prophecy and the performance of conflict as it is with the eventual expulsion of the possessing spirits by God or a saint.[20] In the twelfth century Gerald of Wales encountered a British example of this kind of ambiguous possession in Meilyr of Caerleon, a man with the ability to see and converse with demons in the form of tiny huntsmen, who revealed to him people's secret sins, and errors in books. Meilyr's possession clearly brought him certain benefits and gave him the reputation of a seer, although Meilyr would sometimes ask for St John's Gospel to be placed in his lap to dispel the demons and give him some relief.[21]

Robbins's confidence that pre-Christian spirits are ontologically preserved by the process of demonisation may not be altogether justified; 'onomastic preservation',

---

[19] Frankfurter, 'Where the Spirits Dwell', pp. 27–46.
[20] Young, *History of Exorcism*, pp. 20–21.
[21] Gerald of Wales, *Journey through Wales*, pp. 116–20.

the idea that the names of spirits are preserved even if their original identities and functions are lost, may be nearer the mark. But his emphasis on the importance of demonisation of former deities appears to be borne out by the linguistic evidence from early medieval Britain and France, where demonisation seems to have been a vehicle of preservation for godlings as well as a means of eradicating them. Furthermore, the prevalence of euphemistic titles for godlings, especially in Welsh, could be interpreted as a result of the demonisation process – either because official demonisation made people reluctant to name godlings or because resistance to demonisation encouraged people to confect new godlings hidden beneath euphemistic titles: 'the good people', 'the fair folk', 'the blessing of the mothers' and so on. This linguistic evidence will be explored in detail in Chapter 4 below.

The Bible supplies its own commentary on paganism – specifically, the pagan religions that surrounded the ancient Israelites – and Christian missionaries rooted in the Scriptures perceived ancestral religions through this biblical lens.[22] This means that we cannot necessarily depend on Christian accounts of pagan practices as reliable, since Christian commentators were often attempting to assimilate local practices to patterns of expectation based on biblical narratives about idolatry. However, it is possible that this focus on biblical models of idolatry also caused some missionaries to overlook local practices that did not clearly correspond to anything that appeared in Scripture. However, it is important to bear in mind that the authors of the New Testament belonged to a Hellenistic world

[22] Petts, *Pagan and Christian*, pp. 77–79.

that shared a widely accepted common conceptual language of demonology rooted in Neoplatonic philosophy, which influenced the Jewish as well as the Greek and Roman worlds.[23] When it came to godlings, Christianity and Graeco-Roman paganism were not so much diametrically opposed cosmologies as different interpretations of the same set of beings.

Demonisation might be preceded by demotion, whereby formerly powerful deities were relegated to the status of godlings without any share in the celestial sovereignty assumed by the Christian God. Demotion was a strategy deployed by Christian authors keen to discredit the gods of the pagans as unworthy of worship; thus it was rare for medieval commentators on the pagans of the Baltic, for example, to characterise their religion as a worship of gods, preferring terms like *numina*.[24] Clearly, demonisation is not necessary for existing godlings, who are already unimpressive entities in pagan belief, and it was perhaps the absence of the need for demotion that made it harder to demonise beings such as fauns and nymphs. Furthermore, insofar as some godlings already resembled the demons denounced by the church, it was arguably almost impossible to demonise them anyway. And in some cultures there were beings so different from the 'demonisable' godlings of Greece and Rome – such as Ireland's *áes síde* – that they were not usually identified with demons, and could at best be sidelined by the church and portrayed as part of an obsolete past.[25]

[23] Luck, *Arcana Mundi*, pp. 209–10.
[24] Young (ed.), *Pagans in the Early Modern Baltic*, p. 15.
[25] Bitel, 'Secrets of the *Síd*', pp. 79–82.

An Interpretative Model

In one sense all pre-Christian spirits underwent demotion, under the church's insistence that *omnes dii gentium daemonia* ('all the gods of the nations are demons', Psalm 96:5), but the Bible's emphasis on the evils of idolatry may have made it harder to impress the evil of pre-Christian beings that were not the objects of overt cultic veneration and sacrifice. Martin of Braga argued that in the ignorance that followed the repopulation of the world after the Flood, people began to worship nature; it was then that demons appeared to people on hilltops and at springs, demanding sacrifice and worship. Demons thus deluded nature-worshippers into demonolatry.[26]

Related to the phenomenon of demotion was that of substitution, where formerly appealing supernatural beings were replaced by frightening and unpleasant ones. The traces of such a process can be found in modern Greek folklore, for example, where the formerly beautiful nymphs and nereids now have many of the characteristics of the lamia, stealing children, causing illness and luring unwary travellers to their deaths.[27] Diane Purkiss has suggested that the origin of medieval fairies could be sought in the 'nursery bogies' of the ancient world, such as Lamia and Mormo;[28] and while this is unlikely to be true in any straightforward way, it is nevertheless the case that Christian missionaries seeking to demonise benevolent supernatural beings had to speak the cultural language of the cultures in which they operated. Writing about beliefs current around Arles in the twelfth century,

---

[26] Filotas, *Pagan Survivals*, pp. 82–84.
[27] Larson, *Greek Nymphs*, pp. 61–64.
[28] Purkiss, *Troublesome Things*, pp. 11–31.

Gervase of Tilbury reported that lamiae were 'said to be women, who in the night break into houses in a momentary leap, and look into vessels, baskets, bowls, drinking vessels and jars, drag infants from their cradles, light lamps, and afflict many sleeping people'.[29] The deliberate substitution or conflation of lamiae with nymphs and other classes of supernatural women in the Christian era is one possible explanation for the appearance of the medieval trope of the child-stealing fairy. Evil godlings already existed in the ancient world, and it was surely easier for missionaries to convince people that godlings formerly thought good were bad than to convince people to set the godlings aside altogether.

Demonisation of both gods and godlings was often followed, eventually, by processes of 'undemonisation' that saw missionary efforts undermined by folklore. The nymphs and nereids of Byzantine and early modern Greece were not always monstrous beings of horror; people venerated 'the Fair One of the Mountains' or queen of the nereids, while the fourteenth-century preacher Joseph Bryennios blamed the success of the Ottomans on superstitious practices of the Greeks such as relying on the nymphs for divination.[30] Similarly, Jeffrey Burton Russell documented the process by which the devil steadily became a figure of fun in western European folklore throughout the Middle Ages, to the point that the devil of folklore is arguably a character rather different from

---

[29] Gervase of Tilbury, *Otia imperialia* 3.85: *lamiae dicuntur esse mulieres, quae noctu domos momentaneo discursu penetrant, dolia vel et cofinos, catinos, cantharos et ollas perscrutantur, infantes ex cunis extrahunt, luminaria accendunt, et nonnunquam dormientes affligunt.*

[30] Larson, *Greek Nymphs*, pp. 63–64.

the devil of theology.[31] Ecclesiastical denunciation, ironically, could have had the effect of preserving the names of supernatural beings and reinforcing the fact that such beings might be considered powerful. It was only a matter of time, therefore, before some people took it upon themselves to invoke such beings or reinstate them as objects of veneration. Beings of limitless cosmic evil are rarely encountered in folklore, perhaps because they make for unsatisfying storytelling.

Just as Reginald Scot's *Discoverie of Witchcraft* (intended as a denunciation of magic) ironically became a source text for magicians in the sixteenth century,[32] so it is not difficult to imagine the preaching of early medieval missionaries creating and reinforcing new demonologies as well as discouraging interest in godlings. Salisbury argued that the dualism of the Iberian heretic Priscillian was 'influenced by tales of spirits that lived in the dark woods and storm-swept peaks of Galicia', causing him to incorporate a traditional demonology derived from popular religion into his demonology.[33] In other words, his entire theology came to be determined, in part, by the influence of folklore, just as the witchfinders of seventeenth-century England were as much under the sway of folklore as of theology.[34] As Ostling puts it, 'the fairies are products of their problematization, created by Christian attempts at expulsion'.[35]

Not only can denunciation keep spiritual beings alive, however: repeated denunciation could have had the effect

---

[31] Russell, *Lucifer*, pp. 259–61.   [32] Davies, *Popular Magic*, pp. 124–25.
[33] Salisbury, *Iberian Popular Religion*, p. 196.
[34] Oldridge, *The Devil in Tudor and Stuart England*, pp. 178–80.
[35] Ostling, 'Introduction', p. 19.

of making such beings seem less fearful over time, or even comical. Demonised figures persistently re-emerge as folkloric beings distinct from the devil and demons of Christian belief because there is a narrative mismatch between these characters and Christianity's figures of supreme evil. Thus the Lithuanian chthonic god Velnias, whose very name has come to be the Lithuanian word for the devil, is nevertheless a distinct character from the Christian devil because Velnias sometimes assists the poor and the oppressed.[36] Similarly, the Welsh Annwn is an underworld that, while ostensibly hell, is clearly distinct from the Christian place of damnation (see Chapter 4 below). As Coree Newman has shown, the possibility of morally ambivalent, penitent and even holy demons was accepted by some theologians – with the consequence that the category of 'demon' was a more ambiguous one for many of the faithful than many preachers would have liked, and a dualistic view of good angels and evil demons did not always prevail.[37] Indeed, it may be helpful to draw a distinction between demons and devils; 'demon' was not a word with exclusively negative connotations, even in the Middle Ages, while the devils were demons who overtly served Satan.

Demonisation was only ever partially successful, owing to the diversity of strategies adopted by Christian commentators on the pagan gods. For example, euhemerisation (the theory that the gods had once been human beings whom demons had tempted people to worship as gods) served an important evangelistic purpose in

---

[36] Vėlius, *Chtoniškasis*, pp. 201–3.
[37] Newman, 'The Good, the Bad and the Unholy', pp. 103–22.

An Interpretative Model

the northern world because it allowed veneration of the ancestors to continue without the contamination of idolatrous worship.[38] Yet if euhemerisation worked for the gods, it could also be applied to godlings, and stories of euhemerised gods and godlings reimagined as human heroes became a space in which the gods could – to some extent – survive or revive.[39] Advocates of euhemerisation theory such as Isidore of Seville sought to portray the gods as mere human beings, and pagan worship as the misguided outcome of what were originally good impulses to venerate the mighty dead.[40] According to Alberic of London, writing in the twelfth century, some of the gods were originally nothing more than poetic names given to activities – Ceres to agriculture, Bacchus to viticulture and so on – that superstitious people came to personify and worship as gods.[41]

Even if the demonisation of a god or godling was successful, there was always the possibility that a new folkloric being might emerge through a process of 're-personification', whereby an abstract force once associated with a deity came to be personified anew. As Barbara Newman has shown, personification was an ongoing process throughout the Middle Ages that created fully autonomous culturally constructed beings capable of agency within the collective cultural imagination, and Ronald Hutton has shown the full extent to which a being originating as a personification, such as Mother Earth, could rise to a quasi-goddess-like status even within the

---

[38] Filotas, *Pagan Survivals*, pp. 82–84. [39] Hall, *Elves*, pp. 50–51.
[40] See Isidore, *Etymologies* 8.11.5 (p. 184).
[41] Bode (ed.), *Scriptores rerum mythicarum*, vol. 1, pp. 171–72.

Christian world.[42] 'Re-personification', however, refers specifically to the revival or re-emergence of a personification where an abstract quality has been stripped of personal characteristics. The figure of 'Lady Luck' among gamblers, who resembles the medieval personification of Fortuna but can hardly be identified with her, is one modern example; or 'Fumsup', a First World War mascot figure (a personification of good luck) sometimes venerated with religious fervour in the trenches.[43] Yet no-one would argue seriously that 'Lady Luck' or 'Fumsup' represent the emergence of suppressed cults of pagan deities of fortune; they are, rather, re-personified figures who do much the same job. Further afield, the Mexican cult of Santa Muerte represents the worship of a personification of death, ultimately derived from but not necessarily identical with the Aztec death goddess Mictēcacihuātl; and Santa Muerte now has her own identity and function, distinct from her Aztec antecedent.[44]

The linguistic evidence suggests that the word 'fairy' may be a product of such 're-personification'. The earliest uses of the word in Old French (*faé*) and medieval Latin (*fatata*) are adjectival, with the sense of 'fated' or 'enchanted', and therefore it is impossible to say that the *fées* are simply the diminished Fatae or Parcae. In its earliest sense as a noun, *fée* referred to someone with the ability to enchant; only later did it come to refer to a supernatural being or class of supernatural beings.[45]

---

[42] Hutton, *Queens of the Wild*, pp. 41–74.
[43] Davies, *Supernatural War*, pp. 165–67.
[44] Kingsbury and Chesnut, 'Syncretic Santa Muerte', doi.org/10.3390/rel12030220, accessed 29 November 2021.
[45] Williams, 'Semantics of the Word *Fairy*', pp. 457–78.

An Interpretative Model

In France at least, where the word *fée* arose, it seems that beings fulfilling some of the functions of the pre-Christian Parcae re-emerged after Christianisation, but as re-personifications of the concept of fate rather than as straightforward survivals of the Fatae/Parcae. When a godling in a Christianised society is associated with a universal and perennial concept – such as death, good fortune or fate – it is questionable whether a 'pagan survivalist' hypothesis is needed to explain the existence of such a being. The cultural conditions established by earlier pre-Christian cults may be more important in determining the development of such godlings than actual cultural memory of the specific identities of pre-Christian deities.

In the same way that the cult of a saint may leave behind cultural, religious, onomastic and linguistic detritus, even after the saint has long since ceased to be venerated,[46] so extinguished pre-Christian cults leave all these kinds of detritus behind them. The observation that folkloric beings are in some way constructed from the detritus of pre-Christian religion does not make them 'pagan' (and still less 'pagan survivals'), because they are new characters, brought into being under Christian hegemony, and often without verifiable historical or cultic links with their predecessors. Yet the form taken by the godlings of a Christian society will be shaped by the cultural conditions of that society: conditions established, in part, by the religions that preceded Christianity in that region.

---

[46] For an example, see the cult of the English saint Edmund in Ireland (Young, *Athassel Priory*, p. 155).

Understanding Christianisation and Syncretism

The historical interpretation of societies at an early stage of Christian conversion is persistently hampered by some scholars' attachment to the idea that the introduction of Christianity (and of the church's representatives) invariably resulted in the imposition of a radically exclusivist religious outlook. On this interpretation, if any religious syncretism occurred it was thanks to the inventiveness of the laity in temporarily resisting the relentless homogenising power of the church. Historians' tendency to see the church's agenda as one of wholesale religious replacement is no doubt influenced by the colonial role of the church in Africa, Asia and the Americas in recent centuries, where the church brought with it not only the Christian faith but also the intellectual legacy of the Enlightenment, imposing 'western' ways of thinking on indigenous peoples. The colonial missionary project was not only to introduce Christianity but also to eradicate 'superstition'; it was not enough for indigenous peoples to come to Christ – they also needed to reject the cult of the ancestors, witch doctors, pre-Christian rituals and whatever else the missionaries deemed unacceptable.[47]

However much the church's complicity in colonialism may inform our present-day views of it, it is a mistake to back-project the heavy-handed culturally homogenising agenda of nineteenth- and twentieth-century colonial missionaries on late antique and early medieval Europe, in a

---

[47] Young, *Witchcraft and the Modern Roman Catholic Church*, p. 41.

'Spanish-Inquisition-style mindset'.[48] Christian mission has its own history and has undergone its own evolution over time, and the exact processes by which missionaries reconciled pagan cultures to Christianity in the early Middle Ages can rarely be studied in detail. The scarcity of the evidence means that we cannot afford to burden ourselves with preconceptions about the compromises Christian missionaries were and were not willing to make with pre-Christian cultures. In medieval Iceland, for example, a prohibition on pagan sacrifice was accompanied by acceptance that people might continue pagan practices in private, and Adam of Bremen noted that Norse Christians continued to engage in rites honouring pagan gods. During the eighth-century conversion of Germany, the popes expressed concern about the validity of baptisms performed by priests who were also officiants in pagan cults.[49]

As David Kling has noted, paganism was decentralised and non-hierarchical in its organisation,[50] and the persistence of pagan rites in ostensibly converted societies may have been, in part, owing to the fact that Christianity and paganism did not compete for the same space in people's lives. While the church was concerned with matters of identity, eternal salvation and sacred authority, the spontaneous cults of the gods continued to mark the ritual and natural year. As long ago as 1926, F. M. Powicke eloquently described the complex relationship between Christian and pre-Christian religion in late antiquity and the early Middle Ages:

[48] De la Bédoyère, *Gods with Thunderbolts*, p. 205.
[49] Filotas, *Pagan Survivals*, p. 72.
[50] Kling, *A History of Christian Conversion*, p. 104.

The history of the Church is the record of the gradual and mutual adaptation of Christianity and paganism to each other. The complete victory of the former has always been a remote vision ... as the Christian faith penetrated the society of the Roman world, it fell under the influence both of rustic traditions and of a variegated paganism which shaded off into those philosophical and mystical refinements so dear to the theologian ... From the first the Church was the victim as well as the victor, and as it absorbed the peoples of the Mediterranean in the west and spread eastwards into Persia and India, its spiritual life was shot through and through with the glittering fancies, the antinomianism, the morbid extravagances and the endless subtleties of men. It tried to purify a great sluice into which all the religions, every kind of philosophy, every remedy for the troubles and ennui of life had passed. And from this ordeal it passed on to cope with the mental and spiritual traditions of the great northern peoples. If we imagine that the Church was able to work on a *tabula rasa*, we cannot understand the development either of its theology, its ritual, or its religious experience.[51]

More recently, David Petts has been critical of the persistence of a dominant narrative of 'hegemonic conversion' in discussions of the conversion and Christianisation of Europe, which portray conversion and Christianisation as invariably top-down processes led and directed by the powerful.[52] Likewise, Petts rejects 'essentialist' models of both Christianity and paganism that assume that Christianity and paganism were excessively simple and mutually exclusive opposites. Instead, it is more accurate (albeit tautological) to

[51] Powicke, 'The Christian Life', pp. 31–32
[52] Petts, *Pagan and Christian*, p. 29.

say that 'Christianity is what people who say they are Christians do'.[53]

Late antique and early medieval Christian mission engaged, in practice, in a process of negotiation with pre-Christian beliefs and practices – openly suppressing some, overtly Christianising others, and tacitly tolerating others still. Iconoclasts who defaced and destroyed major pagan sites may not have bothered with the cults of the nymphs and fauns, and the nymphs endured, even in Greece itself.[54] On the other hand, an early Christian baptistery at Chedworth in Gloucestershire may originally have been a nymphaeum.[55] This transformation may have had more to do with the re-use of a convenient water source than with the deliberate eradication of the cult of the nymphs, although the scratching of the Chi Rho symbol on slabs around the nymphaeum might suggest a determined attempt to Christianise it.[56] Yet godlings like the nymphs were unofficial and did not have large shrines, priesthoods or sacred texts, and the transmission of traditions about them was oral and popular in character. Furthermore, they continued to serve the same functions under the new faith as they had under the old.[57] The language of 'survival' is therefore problematic as applied to godlings within a Christian society, because it carries with it the assumption that Christianity *replaces*, as a matter of course, every aspect of pre-Christian belief

[53] Petts, *Pagan and Christian*, pp. 33–35.
[54] On nymphs in modern Greece see Purkiss, *Troublesome Things*, pp. 45–46.
[55] Perring, *The Roman House in Britain*, p. 182; Yeates, *Tribe of Witches*, p. 54
[56] Aldhouse-Green, *Sacred Britannia*, p. 191.
[57] Purkiss, *Troublesome Things*, p. 52.

and practice. Yet just as Christianity did not immediately replace pre-Christian rites of betrothal, marriage, burial or commemoration of the dead in most European societies,[58] so it did not entirely replace godlings.

The prevalence or intensity of belief in folkloric beings in a Christian society should not and cannot be taken as an indication of the depth or sincerity of that society's Christianisation, because belief in godlings has historically co-existed with Christianity with minimal conflict in many European Christian societies. This does not mean the church embraced or accepted such beliefs; but they were more often ridiculed than formally condemned or suppressed – much as they continue to be ridiculed in contemporary secular societies, while few would suggest steps should be taken to actively suppress belief in fairies.[59] At times, medieval authors even portrayed the fairies as Christians,[60] and it was not until the fifteenth century that belief in fairies was routinely treated as heretical in England.[61]

Writing in the 1930s about the Christianisation of Greece, Campbell Bonner observed that 'The last battles were not merely against the worship of the great Olympians, but also against Isis, Sarapis, Mithra, Asklepios, against stubborn village cults of godlings and heroes, against astrology and black magic'.[62] However, this approach assumes that Christian missionaries always considered these elements of Christian culture worth fighting. In the early stages of its conversion, a society is often only as Christianised as it needs to be. Lithuania,

---

[58] Petts, *Pagan and Christian*, pp. 38–40.   [59] Green, *Elf Queens*, p. 48.
[60] Green, *Elf Queens*, p. 62.   [61] Green, *Elf Queens*, p. 20.
[62] Bonner, 'Some Phases of Religious Feeling', pp. 139–40.

which underwent the process of conversion later than any other country in Europe, provides a useful and comparatively well-evidenced example. The baptism of Lithuania in 1387 involved the sprinkling of large groups of Lithuanians with holy water by a priest wielding an aspergillum, and everyone in each cohort received the same baptismal name. The Polish priests who were supposed to be instructing the people did not know the Lithuanian language, and therefore the Lithuanians departed baptised, but almost entirely uninstructed in the Christian faith.[63] Furthermore, there were not enough priests to establish a functioning parish structure in Lithuania, and the work of converting the Lithuanians took many centuries and involved annual missions to heavily forested and inaccessible settlements that continued into the eighteenth century.

Nevertheless, the Lithuanians seem to have accepted early on the supremacy of the Christian God. When a Czech missionary visited a few years after the formal baptism, he found that the people were baptised but were worshipping trees in groves; yet when he began to cut the sacred groves down, local women complained to the Christian ruler, Grand Duke Vytautas, that the groves were where they communicated with God.[64] The idea that Samogitians were honouring the Christian God (or their understanding of him) in groves is not altogether unlikely, given the paucity of clergy and churches. Similarly, in the mid-sixteenth century the barely Christian Samogitians asserted that their highest god was 'Aukštėjas Visgaljsis',

---

[63] Young (ed.), *Pagans in the Early Modern Baltic*, p. 47.
[64] Young (ed.), *Pagans in the Early Modern Baltic*, p. 13.

'the highest almighty', which was probably a reference to the Christian God rather than the name or title of a Baltic deity.[65] One possible interpretation of the slow rate of Lithuania's Christianisation is that the structure of Baltic religion, which was essentially an animistic cult of spirits associated with trees, fire, snakes and other features of the natural world, was perfectly suited to syncretism. The higher Lithuanian gods, deprived of sovereignty and displaced by the Christian God, soon dwindled; but it was more difficult to displace the sovereignty of the little gods of nature, simply because their sphere was not that of the 'highest almighty' of the Christians. Furthermore, from a political point of view Lithuania only needed to meet the minimal requirements of conversion so that its rulers could be considered part of Christendom; the thorough Christianisation of Lithuania's rural pagans was not an urgent matter, because pagan peasants presented no threat.

In the 1970s the Norwegian scholar Fridjof Birkeli identified three 'stages of conversion' of a society, which have proved influential in framing interpretation of the Christianisation of late antique and medieval Europe. According to Birkeli, an 'infiltration' phase in which a pagan society has extensive passive contact with Christianity is followed by mission, when missionaries actively introduce Christianity. At this stage a formal conversion event may occur, such as mass baptisms. The third phase, 'institution', involves the establishment of the organisational structures of the Christian church.[66]

---

[65] Young (ed.), *Pagans in the Early Modern Baltic*, p. 141.
[66] For a summary of Birkeli's scheme see Hoggett, *Archaeology of the East Anglian Conversion*, p. 15.

Timothy Insoll added an additional phase of 'identification', which is when a population begins to assimilate Christianity into its worldview and aligns itself with the new faith, followed by a final displacement of the old religion.[67] Yet it is difficult to assess the extent and speed of the Christianisation of any society. What constituted acceptable Christian behaviour changed over time, thereby allowing those who failed to meet the required standards at any time to be labelled as 'pagan'.[68]

Hutton has observed that debates about Christianisation can lead to 'endless, and irreconcilable, arguments over the extent of the survival of the essence of a religion when the people who professed it have been formally converted to another'.[69] However, the relationship between Christianisation and the persistence of godlings in a Christian society may be an indirect one; where godlings persist, it is not so much because they have 'survived' the Christianisation process but because they have either sidestepped it – as beings unworthy of much attention from the church until the late Middle Ages – or because they were confected anew within Christian societies from the detritus of former cults. Early medieval Christianity sometimes lacked the resources, the capacity and, in some cases, the will to control every aspect of people's lives, provided certain basic requirements were met. The presence of Christianity should not be seen, therefore, as a threat in and of itself to the development of beliefs about folkloric beings.

[67] Insoll, 'Introduction', pp. 1–32.
[68] Baronas, 'Christians in Late Pagan, and Pagans in Early Christian Lithuania', p. 53.
[69] Hutton, *Pagan Britain*, p. viii.

Related to the temptation to view medieval Christianity as more effective in imposing its exclusivist outlook than it really was is the temptation to see 'pagans under the bed': the presence of pagans and paganism where there is no convincing evidence of pagan survival in any meaningful sense. Emma Wilby, for example, has written of the 'surviving bedrock of pre-Christian animism' in early modern Britain.[70] In Wilby's view, this 'bedrock' emerged once more into view after the Reformation's assault on the paraphernalia of Catholicism that had been 'superimposed' on pre-existing pagan beliefs and festivals.

Wilby's interpretation implicitly gives a privileged status, for no apparent reason, to hypothetical prehistoric animistic beliefs as more likely to survive and re-emerge than any others. The term 'bedrock' is a very loaded one, suggesting certain beliefs and ritual responses to nature are fundamental to human beings, and suggesting an ahistorical approach to the history of religion that shades into cultural anthropology. Wilby's analysis also implies an active and conscious occlusion of pre-Christian belief by Christianity – or, in her words, 'homogenization'. Yet the evidence for any concerted attempt to stamp out belief in folkloric beings – and, indeed, any concerted attempt to replace it with something else – is largely lacking in Britain, where such beliefs rarely receive a mention in the proceedings of the ecclesiastical courts. When they do receive notice, it is only at the very end of the Middle Ages.

There is always a danger of seeing paganism where we want to see it. Both Della Hooke and Stephen Yeates have suggested that the felling of a nut-tree at Longney

---

[70] Wilby, *Cunning-Folk*, p. 17.

in Gloucestershire by Bishop Wulfstan of Worcester in the reign of Edward the Confessor might represent the elimination of a sacred tree comparable to St Boniface's felling of the oak of Donar at Gaesmere in 772.[71] While there are accounts of wondrous trees in early medieval Britain, such as Nennius' ash tree that bears apples, there are no accounts of the worship of trees or the felling of sacred trees, as we often find elsewhere in pagan northern Europe. However, a handful of place names seem to bear witness to significant trees,[72] and the tradition that it was unlucky to break a branch of the ash tree that grew by a well close to the tomb of St Bertram at Ilam, Staffordshire, is reminiscent of Irish traditions of fairy trees.[73]

When the thegn Elsi invited Bishop Wulfstan to consecrate a newly built church at Longney, Wulfstan found his work obstructed by a troublesome nut-tree in the churchyard:

Besides, there was in the churchyard a nut-tree, shady with wide-spreading branches. This tree, by the luxuriant width of its branches, denied light to the church.[74] Having been taken there by the one who invited him, the bishop ordered it to be cut down. [Elsi] agreed that if nature had denied the space, he would have supplied the work; yet not because he had given it; it entertained with games. For that man was accustomed, especially on summer days, to amuse himself with dice or feasting, or to induce laughter by other games. In this he not only

---

[71] Hooke, *Trees in Anglo-Saxon England*, p. 36; Yeates, *Tribe of Witches*, p. 122.
[72] Yeates, *Tribe of Witches*, p. 122.
[73] Hooke, *Trees in Anglo-Saxon England*, p. 103. On modern folklore of fairy trees in England see Young, 'In Search of England's Fairy Trees', pp. 16–21.
[74] Literally 'envied the church's light'.

did not humbly obey, but even stubbornly contradicted the bishop – so much so that, as he afterwards admitted, he was mad with impudence to the point that he preferred the church not to be dedicated rather than the tree be cut down. Then the saint, somewhat perturbed by this shamelessness, hurled a missile of cursing at the tree, by which it was wounded. Within a short while it became sterile and lacked fruit, and dried up from the roots. The owner was enraged by this infertility, so that what he had owned with envy, he now desired with grace; wearied by the tree's sterility, he ordered it to be cut down.[75]

It is far from clear from this account that the nut-tree at Longney had any sacred significance, although if it was so large the tree was presumably of great age. St Wulfstan's cursing of the tree is obviously based on Christ's cursing of the fig tree (Mark 11:12–14); if the tree had been an object of worship, we might expect William of Malmesbury to mention it, and we might expect Wulfstan to cut the tree down in a gesture of confrontation with idolatry. Instead, the Longney nut-tree is simply a convenient shady spot for games in the summer months, while nuts were a metaphor for trifling pursuits. The England of Edward the

---

[75] Darlington (ed.), *Vita Wulfstani*, pp. 40–41: *Preter hec erat in cimiterio arbor nucea, patulis frondibus umbrosa; que lascivia ramorum amplitudine, diem invidebat ecclesie. Eam invitatore asscito, iussit abscidi episcopus. Congrueret enim, ut si spacium negasset natura, ipse suppleret industria; ne dum quod illa dederat; ille suis occuparet ludibriis. Solebat enim vir ille sub eadem arbore presertim estivis diebus, aleis vel epulis vacare; vel aliis ludis hilaritatem allicere. Qua non solum non humiliter paruit; sed etiam pertinaciter contradixit. Tamque ut postea confessus est, erat impudentis amentie; ut mallet ecclesiam non dedicari, quam arborem abscidi. Tum vero sanctus non nichil hac protervia motus; maledictionis iaculum in arborem intorsit. Quo illo vulnerata; paulatim sterilescens et fructu caruit, et radicitus exaruit. Qua infecunditate, ita possessorem exacerbavit; ut quam possederat cum invidia, desideraverat cum gratia; sterilitate pertesus abscidi iuberet.*

Confessor was, broadly speaking, as Christian a country as the England of Edward III, and William's miracle story is not about idolatry but about commitment to the church and obedience to a bishop's commands.

Christianisation and Godlings in Late Roman Britain

The extent of Christianity's success in Britain before the withdrawal of Roman authority in the early years of the fifth century is a classic problem in the historiography of Roman Britain, with scholars divided between those who believe Christianity was a dynamic force and those who perceive it as an anaemic elite allegiance to the dominant imperial cult that was sustained only by Roman rule.[76] What is clear, however, is that the archaeology of Christianity in Roman Britain testifies to some eccentric features that may reveal a particular approach to Christianisation in the fourth century. For example, the votive feathers bearing the Christian Chi Rho emblem found with a collection of altar silver at Water Newton, Cambridgeshire in 1975 appear to be a direct borrowing of Romano-Celtic votive practice, suggesting that the British church 'was tending to absorb current pagan usage rather than to confront and destroy it',[77] or even that the Christianity of the Water Newton treasure represented 'a kind of "half-way house" between paganism and Christianity'.[78] One of the votive feathers even

---

[76] For a discussion of this debate see Hutton, *Pagan Britain*, pp. 276–83.
[77] Frend, 'Pagans, Christians, and the "Barbarian Conspiracy"', p. 122.
[78] Aldhouse-Green, *Sacred Britannia*, p. 185.

bore a legend recording that a woman called Anicilla had fulfilled a vow, suggesting that people were making vows to Christ in much the same way as to pagan deities.[79]

Similarly, the Mildenhall Treasure contains Christian items, some perhaps associated with the celebration of the eucharist, in spite of the intensely Bacchic imagery of other objects such as the great dish, suggesting that elite British Christians were comfortable with the co-existence of Christian and pagan imagery. The remarkable mosaics at Hinton St Mary, Dorset, which feature an apparent portrait of Christ as well as a depiction of Bellerophon slaying the Chimera, likewise suggest a relaxed Christian attitude both to the use of mythological imagery and to the figurative representation of Christ himself, which was rare at that time in the western church.[80] At Frampton, Dorset a mosaic bearing a large Chi Rho monogram also featured a head of Neptune,[81] and Dominic Perring has argued that the Frampton mosaics represent a form of heterodox Gnostic or Orphic Christianity.[82] It is possible that the philosophical tendencies of late Roman paganism, which was open to the idea of the gods as embodiments of abstract concepts, helped allow the survival of pagan imagery in Christian contexts, because artistic portrayals of the gods were perceived as posing no threat to the new faith. Archaeological evidence of heteropraxy is not evidence of heterodoxy, however,[83] and the textual

---

[79] De la Bédoyère, *Gods with Thunderbolts*, p. 183.
[80] Frend, 'Pagans, Christians, and the "Barbarian Conspiracy"', pp. 122–23.
[81] Aldhouse-Green, *Sacred Britannia*, p. 187.
[82] Perring, '"Gnosticism" in Fourth-Century Britain', pp. 97–127.
[83] Petts, *Pagan and Christian*, p. 27.

evidence suggests that the fourth-century British church was stridently orthodox and resisted Arianism.[84]

Another striking example of British Christian eccentricity is the fourth-century situation at Lullingstone in Kent, where a house church in a villa was built above a domestic nymphaeum in the mid-fourth century. The nymphaeum was renovated while the house church was apparently in use – suggesting simultaneous pagan and pre-Christian worship in the same building.[85] While one possible interpretation of this is the need for Christians to tolerate a resurgence of pagan cult under the emperor Julian, it is also possible that the nature of the lower shrine as a nymphaeum rendered it less threatening, from a Christian point of view, than a shrine to one of the Olympian gods. Hutton has compared the continuing practice of depositing coins at pre-Christian sacred sites into the fifth century to later practices of Christians leaving out food for the fairies.[86] Similarly, even though the Orthodox church in early modern Russia consistently elided nature spirits with the realm of the demonic in the early modern period, people continued to offer prayers to *Leshii* ('masters of the forest') and *Vodyanye* ('masters of the water') at forest margins and bodies of water.[87]

The adoption of Christianity alone may not have been enough, on its own, to eliminate popular ritual practices; at least one self-confessed Christian, after all, wrote a plea to Sulis Minerva on a curse tablet before casting it into the sacred spring at Bath,[88] while a small shrine

---

[84] Frend, 'Pagans, Christians, and the "Barbarian Conspiracy"', pp. 121–22.
[85] Hutton, *Pagan Britain*, p. 278.   [86] Hutton, *Pagan Britain*, p. 281.
[87] Antonov, 'Between Fallen Angels and Nature Spirits', pp. 136–39.
[88] Hutton, *Pagan Britain*, p. 282.

containing the stone head of a pagan idol co-existed with Christian mosaics at a house in Caerwent.[89] Some high-status burials in the early Christian cemetery at Poundbury, Dorset, were adorned with small mausolea decorated with painted plaster, suggesting that pagan burial customs died hard – and even, perhaps, that there was some sort of continuation of the Parentalia in which people dined at the tombs of the dead.[90] It is noteworthy that much 'iconoclasm' in late Roman Britain consisted not of the haphazard defacing or smashing of statues, but the careful decapitation and burial or concealment of statues, such as a beheaded figure of Fortuna concealed in a flue inside a bathhouse. In line with the significance ascribed to the head in Iron Age British culture, these acts of decapitation have been interpreted as an attempt to end an image's power.[91]

But it is possible that the beheading of statues was not iconoclasm at all, and the purpose of the careful removal of heads from cult statues was to re-use them as part of Christian images. This suggestion has been made concerning the undamaged head of a statue of Mercury at Uley, which may have been re-used as an image of Christ when the temple was converted into a church – enduring, it seems, into the mid-Anglo-Saxon period.[92] The early fifth-century Hoxne Treasure, which is adorned with Christian symbolism, apparently bears the same name, Aurelius Ursicinus, who appears as the dedicator of a statue of the god Nodens found at Cockersand Moss

---

[89] Aldhouse-Green, *Sacred Britannia*, p. 184.
[90] Aldhouse-Green, *Sacred Britannia*, p. 194.
[91] Aldhouse-Green, *Sacred Britannia*, p. 222.
[92] Aldhouse-Green, *Sacred Britannia*, pp. 192–93.

in Lancashire.[93] While there is some evidence of iconoclasm in Britain, especially directed against the cult of Mithras, it cannot be clearly associated with Christians. Rather than a destruction of pagan sites, Christopher Snyder suggests that temples simply fell into disuse at the end of the fourth century, with the 'traditional sanctity' of some sites, such as at Nettleton and Uley, being recognised by the church.[94]

The interpretation of this sort of archaeological evidence is difficult. Christian artefacts were not necessarily owned or deposited by Christians, nor pagan artefacts by pagans, and objects buried in the ground were often already old, perhaps representing obsolete belief systems for the people who deposited them. Yet the archaeological evidence is also a reminder of the complexity of the relationships thrown up by the conversion event. The Christian writings we have from the fourth-century Roman world were, on the whole, the product of zealous Christians and not those who converted reluctantly or for personal advantage. When the leading Sussex Catholic Sir Thomas Gage converted to the Church of England in 1715 he made provision for the continuation of a Catholic chapel funded by his family.[95] His conversion was therefore an ambivalent act – a personal choice that advantaged him (in this case, it allowed him to take up a seat in the House of Lords), but did not reflect on his family's historic commitment to Roman Catholicism. It is not difficult to imagine many wealthy Romano-Britons of the fourth century adopting a similar attitude towards Christianity, in an attempt to

---

[93] De la Bédoyère, *Gods with Thunderbolts*, p. 199.
[94] Snyder, *Age of Tyrants*, pp. 236–37.
[95] Glickman, *The English Catholic Community*, pp. 58–59.

balance the political need for conversion with traditions of veneration of ancestral gods.

The sort of tolerance and assimilation of the pagan past that emerges from the archaeological record for fourth-century Britain does not mean the British church was unorthodox; it may simply have adopted a distinctive approach to Christianisation, perhaps because its leaders were less zealous against the relics of paganism, or even because the character of late Romano-British paganism seemed unthreatening to early British Christians. The opposite interpretation is also possible, however: paganism was so strong in Britain that Christians were compelled to engage in a certain degree of tolerance and mimicry of pagan practice in order to make any headway at all. Dorothy Watts argued that Christianity's hold was not strong in rural areas of Roman Britain, and 'the latent paganism of the Romano-Britons laid them open, first, to the pagan revival sponsored by Julian, and then to internal dissension, heresy and, for many, reversion to the old religions, when left to their own devices following the Roman withdrawal'.[96]

However, the idea that Christianity failed to make headway in rural and more remote areas of Britain is rendered problematic by the apparent survival of Roman Christian learning in Wales – a part of the island scarcely at the heart of the Roman province – which can no longer be explained purely by the replanting of Christianity in western Britain by Irish missionaries.[97] Indeed, the extraordinary success of the conversion of Ireland in the fifth century, which

---

[96] Watts, *Christians and Pagans*, p. 224.
[97] Lapidge, 'Latin Learning in Dark Ages Wales', pp. 91–107.

produced a powerhouse of Christian learning and evangelism that made a major contribution to the conversion of northern Europe, sits uneasily with the picture of a lukewarm and unsuccessful missionary project in late Roman and post-Roman Britain. Indeed, it is possible that the success of the Christianisation of Ireland created a loop of 'recursive Christianisation' in the fifth-century Irish Sea world in which Irish raiders and settlers reinforced the Christianity of western areas of Britain, in contrast to the paganising influence of Germanic settlers in eastern Britain. Higham suggested that the emigration of Britons to Armorica (and of high-status Britons to more westerly parts of Britain) brought with it 'a high degree of literacy and of intellectual vigour', which produced a renewed Christianity capable of re-planting the faith in the wreckage of the Romano-British institutional church.[98]

Christianity seems to have made faster early progress in Britain than it did in northern Gaul,[99] but in the late fourth century Victricius, bishop of Rouen (c. 390–410), spearheaded an aggressive campaign of Christianisation on the other side of the English Channel. Victricius visited Britain briefly in around 396 to meet with the island's bishops, but as far as we know there was no charismatic evangelistic figure working in Britain comparable to Victricius or Martin of Tours (or Patrick in Ireland) who presided over the process of Christianisation, and this could explain why British Christianity seemed to be in retreat in the late fourth century.[100]

[98] Higham, *Rome, Britain and the Anglo-Saxons*, p. 100.
[99] Frend, 'Pagans, Christians, and the "Barbarian Conspiracy"', p. 121.
[100] Frend, 'Pagans, Christians, and the "Barbarian Conspiracy"', pp. 125–26.

As we saw in Chapter 2, there is evidence that there was enthusiasm in Britain for the pagan revival under Julian, yet this occurred before the specifically anti-pagan legislation of Theodosius I and the closure of temples in the 390s. However, the presence of heresy in Britain is evidence for the vitality of the Christian faith there rather than for the shallowness of Christian commitment, since heresy in the ancient world usually represented an informed rejection of orthodoxy rather than a failure to understand it. Furthermore, while those post-Roman Britons who came under Germanic cultural and linguistic influence in the east and south of Britain seem to have adopted Germanic paganism, evidence for the post-Roman continuity or recrudescence of a specifically *Romano-British* paganism is lacking or equivocal.

During his excavation of Maiden Castle in the 1930s Sir Mortimer Wheeler uncovered a crude circular stone hut of the late fourth century that succeeded the older Roman temple. This makeshift temple contained the marble base for a statuary group that Wheeler identified as representing the goddess Diana (but which Henig later identified as Bacchus) and a bronze pedestal for a small votive figurine.[101] At Camerton in Somerset, William Wedlake found a small stone seated figure in a building from around 380, alongside a re-used column which had been repurposed as a pedestal for the figure, suggesting that pagans as well as Christians were making use of the materials of decaying Roman buildings as spolia.[102] Similarly, although the

---

[101] Wheeler, *Maiden Castle*, p. 135; Henig, 'The Maiden Castle "Diana"', pp. 160–62.
[102] Wedlake, *Exacavations at Camerton*, pp. 66, 214.

shrine of Apollo at Nettleton Shrub, Gloucestershire, was closed in around 330 and perhaps used for Christian worship, when the main temple building became a homestead in around 370 a makeshift shrine was constructed where pagan worship resumed, albeit briefly.[103]

Watts has likewise pointed to the apparent desecration and abandonment of some lead baptismal tanks in late fourth-century Britain as evidence for the decline of Christianity, with the deposition of some tanks in wells indicating 'perhaps even a rededication of some of them to some Celtic water spirit'. Items decorated with Christian symbols were deposited at watery sites and in pits, suggesting either a deliberate de-Christianisation of these items or simply that Christians continued to follow ritual practices of deposition similar to their non-Christian neighbours.[104] Similarly, some early Christian cemeteries were apparently abandoned (at Icklingham in Suffolk, Nettleton in Gloucestershire and Ashton in Rutland), while some house churches (such as that at Lullingstone) clearly failed to grow into larger churches.[105] The impact of the Julianic resurgence of paganism on Christianity in Britain may have been considerable, but it is also possible it had an impact on how Christianity reasserted itself after Julian's death in 363. In the aftermath of the revival, were Christians more or less open to expressions of religious syncretism? It is possible that post-Julianic Christianity was more tentative, and more accommodating, than the first flush of Christianity in Britain.

---

[103] Wedlake, *Excavation of the Shrine of Apollo*, p. xix.
[104] Hutton, *Pagan Britain*, p. 279.
[105] Watts, *Christians and Pagans*, pp. 224–25.

Few (if any) examples of late pagan resurgence can certainly be dated to the period after the end of Roman authority in Britain. Evidence of re-paving with Roman fragments and considerable wear from foot traffic suggests that the hot spring at Bath remained in use in some form in the fifth and sixth centuries, but we can know little about the spring's religious significance (if any) during this period. A single penannular brooch was deposited, discarded or lost in the spring in the sixth century,[106] but the earliest attested post-Roman name for Bath, Aquamania, excises the name of the goddess by whom Bath was known in Roman times.[107] Offerings of coins at the nymph Coventina's well in Northumberland continued up to the end of the fourth century, after the official suppression of pagan cult and apparently after the nearby Mithraeum was destroyed.[108] A single fifth-century sword was deposited in the water in a crumbling bathhouse at Feltwell in Norfolk,[109] but it is difficult to know how to interpret these post-Roman acts of deposition. Petts has suggested that, while continuity or survival of cults is too much to claim, 'certain sites loomed large in ritual memory' such as the River Witham, where ancient practices of deposition of weaponry resumed after a hiatus between the fifth and seventh centuries.[110] Similarly, attempts to argue that a fifth- and sixth-century roundhouse at Cadbury Congresbury was a possible temple were based on little

---

[106] Petts, *Pagan and Christian*, p. 94.
[107] Davenport, *Medieval Bath*, pp. 19, 24.
[108] *Gods with Thunderbolts* (2002), p. 193.
[109] Semple, *Perceptions of the Prehistoric*, p. 83.
[110] Petts, *Pagan and Christian*, pp. 94–95.

more than an absence of evidence for domestic occupation and the discovery of some copper alloy leaves.[111]

Overall, there is no concrete evidence of pagan cults practised by post-Roman Britons into the fifth and sixth centuries, and Philip Rahtz and Lorna Watts caution against assuming a clear dichotomy between Christianity and paganism in this period, and they also remind us that the archaeological evidence may sometimes bear witness to entirely lost forms of religious belief and practice that have left no other trace.[112] For example, Christian post-Roman British leaders were sometimes buried in tumuli or under cairns, in spite of the pagan associations of those forms of burial; yet whether this is evidence of pagan-Christian syncretism or simply local variations of custom we may never be able to know.[113] Even if the church in post-Roman Britain suffered some sort of institutional collapse, this need not be equated with the decline of Christianity. Some centuries later, the widespread collapse of episcopal succession in eastern and northern England in the late ninth century, along with the extensive destruction of monasteries, did not lead to a decline in Christian allegiance or Christian conversions to Norse paganism in the Danelaw, whose rulers in fact *adopted* Christianity during the period. On the other hand, Christianity had been established in England for centuries before the settlement of pagan Vikings. In post-Roman Britain, by contrast, in most places Christianity probably had fairly shallow roots of only a few decades before the withdrawal of Roman authority.

[111] Dark, *Britain and the End of the Roman Empire*, p. 121.
[112] Rahtz and Watts, 'Pagans Hill Revisited', p. 366.
[113] Higham, *Rome, Britain and the Anglo-Saxons*, pp. 102–3.

If British communities in the south, east and northeast of Britain were indeed absorbed into a Germanic cultural and linguistic sphere in the fifth and sixth centuries, we can presume that at least some of them underwent a process of de-Christianisation, abandoning Christianity in favour of Germanic cults.[114] There is no known archaeological evidence for any process of *interpretatio Germanica*, by which the still-familiar gods of barely Christianised or unchristianised post-Roman Britons came to be reinterpreted as Germanic gods within a dominant Germanic cultural framework – although we must surely presume that something like this did indeed occur. Stuart Laycock has noted the close correspondence of Anglo-Saxon deities in the English days of the week to the functions of the gods of the Roman week, perhaps preserving a trace of some religious rapprochement between Romano-Britons and pagan Anglo-Saxons. The name Saturday, in particular, suggests the preservation of a memory of the Roman god Saturn within the Anglo-Saxon community, since Saturn was the only Roman god in the days of the week not replaced by a Germanic cognate being.[115] Similarly, Yeates has suggested that the hunter god Cunomaglus may have come to be identified with Woden, the hunter of the souls of the dead, with some of the earthworks

[114] On the possibility that British Christianity survived in early Anglo-Saxon England see Meens, 'Background to Augustine's Mission', pp. 5–17.
[115] Laycock, *Britannia the Failed State*, pp. 202–3. Thus the English days of the week apparently identify Tīw (Tuesday) with Mars (*dies Martis*), Woden (Wednesday) with Mercury (*dies Mercurii*), Thunor (Thursday) with Jupiter (*dies Iovis*), and Frig (Friday) with Venus (*dies Veneris*).

marking out the old *nemetoi* or sacred groves becoming Grim's Ditches.[116] However, such an interpretation need not presume the controversial idea of religious contact between Romano-British and Anglo-Saxon pagans; the surviving grove-like shrines in the landscape may simply have been sufficiently similar to Germanic shrines to Woden that the religious idea was suggested by the landscape itself.

St Patrick, writing at some point in the fifth century about his youth in what was probably post-Roman western Britain, noted that 'I did not know the true God' (*Deum enim verum ignorabam*) in spite of being the son of a deacon and the grandson of a priest. One reason Patrick believed God had allowed him to be captured by Irish pirates, along with his companions, was that 'we had not been obedient to our priests, who counselled us on our salvation' (*sacerdotibus nostris non oboedientes fuimus, qui nos nostram salutem admonebant*), a comment that reveals his community was supplied with clergy.[117] However, while Patrick gives us the sole autobiographical account of education and upbringing in post-Roman fifth-century Britain, it is difficult to interpret his words. Patrick followed the conventions of Christian spiritual autobiography in exaggerating his spiritual ignorance before he received his divine calling, and therefore we cannot be certain if Patrick and his friends' 'disobedience' was youthful high spirits, doctrinal dissension or attachment to pagan cults. Yet there is no hint in Patrick's *Confessio* that he encountered paganism anywhere but among the Irish.

---

[116] Yeates, *Tribe of Witches*, p. 116.
[117] Bieler (ed.), *Libri epistolarum Sancti Patricii*, pp. 56–57.

There is no reason to suppose that the withdrawal of Roman authority at the start of the fifth century would have weakened the position of Christianity in Britain. It might even have strengthened it, enhancing the status of bishops and clergy as community leaders in the absence of formally appointed Roman governors and magistrates. In the seventh century the Christian Anglo-Saxons were in awe of Christian *Romanitas*, and therefore keen to re-use Roman sites in order to emphasise their continuity with the Christians of the fourth century.[118] Similarly, the early medieval Britons were preoccupied with their own *Romanitas*, even continuing to date inscriptions by the consulships of Eastern Roman emperors.[119] In the minds of some elite Britons, it seems that they never left the empire or ceased to be its citizens,[120] and it therefore seems unlikely that the Britons would have wanted to be seen as anything less than as Christian as the emperor himself.

The apparent universality of Christianity among the Britons by the sixth century, compared with the insecure position of Romano-British Christianity at the start of the fifth century, is one of the puzzles of post-Roman British history. However, James Gerrard's suggestion that Britons came to identify with Christianity in order to differentiate themselves from the pagan Germanic invaders and settlers is a plausible one,[121] and it is easy to imagine the imperially sponsored Christian faith becoming the centre of efforts at self-conscious *Romanitas* in a Britain rapidly losing touch with the Roman world.

---

[118] Semple, *Perceptions of the Prehistoric*, pp. 132–36.
[119] Charles-Edwards, *Wales and the Britons*, pp. 234–38.
[120] Charles-Edwards, *Wales and the Britons*, p. 241.
[121] Gerrard, *Ruin of Roman Britain*, p. 273.

Perhaps the blessing of bishops lent legitimacy to the local tyrants and warlords described by Gildas;[122] in Nicholas Higham's view, 'Christianity offered the nascent British dynasties an institutional dimension to their control over local society'.[123] Furthermore, in the face of attacks from the pagan Irish, Picts and Germanic peoples, it is easy to imagine that Christianity became part of a new identity that defined the 'civilised' Britons against the dangerous 'other' of barbarians. Post-Roman Britons may well have been practicing Christianity somewhat differently from their late Roman predecessors, but texts like the *Life* of St Germanus of Auxerre, who visited the British church in around 429, leave little doubt that Christianity was the dominant religious note in post-Roman Britain for at least half a century after 410.[124] As we have seen, when he wrote in the sixth century Gildas seemed certain that paganism belonged to Britain's past.

The Evidence of Penitentials

Penitentials were pastoral manuals describing sins and assigning suitable penances for them, for the guidance of confessors. A number of penitentials from early medieval Britain survive, mostly from an Anglo-Saxon context, and they frequently mention practices deemed idolatrous. However, the penitentials rarely gave much information about the forbidden beliefs and practices they enumerated, and it is difficult to be certain of the extent to which the content of penitentials derived from their specific

---

[122] Jahner et al. (eds.), *Medieval Historical Writing*, p. 27.
[123] Higham, *Rome, Britain and the Anglo-Saxons*, p. 99.
[124] Barrett, 'Saint Germanus', pp. 197–217.

cultural context, or from a textual 'penitential tradition' in which scribes uncritically copied sins from penitentials produced in other regions. The penitential tradition in Gaul, Iberia and Italy can be traced back to the sixth century; although some British penitential material of this period survives, it makes no mention of idolatry,[125] but this is probably due to the incompleteness of the evidence rather than the fact that idolatry was not deemed a problem in sixth-century Britain. In the absence of strong episcopal or royal authority, coherent campaigns for the enforcement of Christian orthopraxy were much more difficult to undertake in post-Roman Britain.

By contrast, Anglo-Saxon penitentials do target idolatry associated with the ongoing cults of Germanic gods, although the nature of such pagan practices remains enigmatic. For example, the seventh-century *Penitential of Theodore* assigns a year's penance to those who sacrifice to demons 'in trivial matters', but ten years to one who sacrifices 'in serious matters'. There is no indication of what might make a sacrifice (or its purpose) trivial or serious,[126] but perhaps something like a distinction between blood sacrifice and spontaneous libations is meant, with 'trivial' sacrifices including offerings of grain or beer for good fortune. There was a considerable degree of consistency in the ways bishops in Gaul and Iberia viewed the idolatry of the *rustici* (country people), and they persistently denounced the worship of stones, wells and trees.[127] In spite of Gildas' indications to the contrary, it is hard to imagine that the embattled Christian post-Roman Britain of the fifth and

---

[125] McNeill and Gamer (eds.), *Medieval Handbooks of Penance*, pp. 169–78.
[126] McNeill and Gamer (eds.), *Medieval Handbooks of Penance*, p. 198.
[127] Filotas, *Pagan Survivals*, pp. 91–94.

The Evidence of Penitentials

sixth centuries was any different. The Continental material therefore serves as a useful comparative tool in understanding how religious practices in post-Roman Britain might have developed, even if we have little evidence for them – although it is important, of course, not to place too much weight on what happened in other regions.

Bernadette Filotas identified the main deities honoured in late antique and early medieval Gaul and Iberia, where most of the evidence comes from, as Jupiter (albeit usually under a regional identity rather than the Roman Jupiter Capitolinus),[128] Mercury (who sometimes ended up being replaced by the Archangel Michael),[129] Minerva[130] and various manifestations of Diana.[131] It is the early medieval cult of Diana that has attracted the greatest scholarly attention, owing to its apparent association with the earliest hints of European beliefs about witchcraft.[132] In addition to these greater deities, however, there were also ongoing cults of the Parcae,[133] satyrs and *pilosi*,[134] and aquatic godlings identified with Neptune and Orcus, as well as the mysterious figure Geniscus who may have been linked with the genius.[135] Furthermore, there were some entities that preachers claimed people believed in and feared but did not worship or placate, such as *lamiae, mavones* (perhaps linked to the *di manes*,

---

[128] Filotas, *Pagan Survivals*, pp. 70–72.
[129] Filotas, *Pagan Survivals*, pp. 72–73.
[130] Filotas, *Pagan Survivals*, pp. 73–74.
[131] Filotas, *Pagan Survivals*, pp. 74–76.
[132] For an overview of this subject see Hutton, 'The Wild Hunt', pp. 161–78; Hutton, *Queens of the Wild*, pp. 110–42.
[133] Filotas, *Pagan Survivals*, pp. 76–78.
[134] Filotas, *Pagan Survivals*, p. 78.
[135] Filotas, *Pagan Survivals*, pp. 78–79.

the spirits of the dead), *silvaticae* (forest-dwelling spirits perhaps comparable to the *theomacha* encountered by St Samson of Dol), *dusioli* and *aquaticae*.[136]

Dusioli is a diminutive of *Dusii*, a class of spirit mentioned in many late antique and early medieval sources, who were supposedly godlings found in Gaul. However, the origins of the Dusii seem to be literary rather than folkloric in nature, since they were mentioned by Augustine in his *City of God* and subsequently accepted by other authors on Augustine's authority. Yet no evidence independent of the literary tradition exists to confirm that the Dusii were really beings the Gauls believed in. Augustine's Dusii are essentially Gaulish fauns, whose characteristic is sexual rampancy:

> One often hears talk, whose good faith ought not to be doubted, since it is confirmed by a number of people who know from their own or others' experience, that Silvani and Pans, commonly called incubi, have often appeared to women as wicked men, trying to sleep with them and succeeding. These same demons, whom the Gauls name Dusii, are relentlessly committed to this defilement, attempting and achieving so many things of such a kind that to deny it would seem brazen. Based on this, I dare not risk a definitive statement as to whether there might be some spirits, aerial in substance (for this substance, when it is set in motion by a fan, is perceived as sensation within the body and as touch), who take bodily form and even experience this sexual desire, so that, by any means they can, they mingle with women sensually. But that the holy angels of God in no way fell in like manner during that era – that I would believe.[137]

---

[136] Filotas, *Pagan Survivals*, pp. 80–82.
[137] Augustine, *De civitate Dei* 15.23 (PL 41.468): *Et quoniam creberrima fama est multique se expertos vel ab eis, qui experti essent, de quorum fide*

Although Xavier Delamarre sees in the name *dusii* a Gaulish word for a divine being,[138] Lambert notes that the prefix *dus-* has the meaning of 'evil',[139] so *dusii* might simply mean 'evil ones': a Christianised description of a class of folkloric beings rather than their name. This would explain the apparent lack of any word in the languages of Britain or France clearly derived from *dusii* (although Breton *duz*, 'evil spirit', is a possible exception).[140] It is a distinct possibility that the Dusii originated solely as a textual tradition; the Dusii seem to have arrived in England in the writings of Bede, who reported that the Dusii were incubi who seduced women.[141]

The term 'folkloresque' has been coined in recent years to describe the simulation of something like popular belief in contemporary popular culture.[142] While the context was clearly different, the concept of the 'folkloresque' may be one way to understand the problem of the Dusii, who are widely reported by late antique and

> *dubitandum non esset, audisse confirmant, Silvanos et Panes, quos vulgo incubos vocant, inprobos saepe extitisse mulieribus et earum appetisse ac peregisse concubitum; et quosdam daemones, quos Dusios Galli nuncupant, adsidue hanc inmunditiam et temptare et efficere, plures talesque adseverant, ut hoc negare inpudentiae videatur: non hinc aliquid audeo definire, utrum aliqui spiritus elemento aerio corporati (nam hoc elementum etiam cum agitatur flabello sensu corporis tactuque sentitur) possint hanc etiam pati libidinem, ut, quo modo possunt, sentientibus feminis misceantur. Dei tamen angelos sanctos nullo modo illo tempore sic labi potuisse crediderim.*

[138] Delamarre, *Dictionnaire de la langue gauloise*, p. 158
[139] Lambert, *Langue gauloise*, p. 169.
[140] Dowden, *European Paganism*, p. 306 n.57. Dowden also notes potential cognates deriving from a common Indo-European ancestor in Lithuanian *dvasia* ('breath, spirit') and *dusuoti* ('to breathe').
[141] Bede, *In Lucae evangelium expositio* (PL 92.438B).
[142] On the modern folkloresque see Foster and Tolbert (eds.), *The Folkloresque*.

early medieval authors while there is little independent evidence that the Dusii really were folkloric beings venerated in Gaul or elsewhere. If the Dusii were a purely textual construction, then we may be dealing with a kind of patristic folkloresque of the early Christian centuries, where Christian authors exchanged information about the beliefs of pagans which in fact bore no relation to actual belief. Of course, just as with the modern folkloresque, it is possible that the Dusii *did* become folkloric beings in the true sense as a consequence of their transmission into folklore from a textual tradition.

The Dusii represent a cautionary tale that should alert us to the possibility that not all beings who found their way into the lists of early medieval preachers and confessors were really believed in by the people; some were almost entirely literary constructions. Furthermore, if the real meaning of the Gaulish word *dus-* is simply 'evil', it is possible that *dusii* is not a name but a demonised description that subsequently became a name, 'the evil ones'. William Sayers has suggested a similar origin for the word 'puck' and its many cognates in Celtic, Germanic and even Baltic languages. According to this interpretation, a term derived ultimately from an Indo-European root **bheug-*, meaning 'to be frightened of', came to refer to supernatural beings in the aftermath of Christianisation as the church encouraged people to react to godlings of the former belief system with terror and fear.[143]

While comparisons can be made between Britain and the wider European context of the effect of Christianisation on godlings, there are also differences. In Britain, as

[143] Sayers, 'Puck and the Bogymen', pp. 52–56.

we shall see, there was a strong tradition of frightening supernatural women (seemingly among both Britons and Anglo-Saxons), apparently representing the Parcae and the related or identical *burgrunan*, as well as the similar *hægtessan*. The Continental penitential tradition, by contrast, portrays the Parcae as diminutive beings who make their way into people's houses and eat with tiny knives. A tenth- or eleventh-century Frankish penitential assigned two years' penance to those 'who have prepared a table of the Parcae in their household' (*qui mensam praeparaverit in famulatu parcarum*).[144] No such domesticated tradition of the Parcae or similar divine women survives in the evidence from pre-Conquest Britain. It was only after the Norman Conquest, as I shall argue in Chapter 5 below, that Continental demonologies began to have a significant impact on the way in which the English (and Britain's other peoples) perceived folkloric beings.

Anglo-Saxon Pagans in a Roman Landscape

While the evidence for the persistence of open pagan cults among the Britons into the fifth and sixth centuries is equivocal, imported Germanic paganism came to dominate large parts of Britain in the fifth and sixth centuries. Even where Germanic settlers may have encountered a landscape inhabited by British Christians or largely devoid of people, that landscape was still filled with the detritus of pagan Roman worship, and such encounters with the ruins of a former world had a profound cultural influence

---

[144] Schmitz (ed.), *Bussbücher*, vol. 1, p. 460.

on Anglo-Saxon folklore and beliefs that will be discussed in Chapter 4 below. The landscape of post-Roman Britain was littered with substantial material remains of well-built structures such as villas, bathhouses, mausolea, temples and – presumably – late Roman churches.

While the re-use and adaptation of such structures may have begun early,[145] it was not until the seventh century that it intensified, at 'a time when elite or aristocratic families began to assert their power more widely in the landscape and when the new Christian Church was also establishing its visible presence and its place within secular elite ideologies'.[146] Many of the Roman sites re-used in the early Middle Ages were formerly sacred sites, but it does not follow from this that any continuity of awareness of their sacredness existed in later centuries. In post-imperial Italy and Gaul, pagan religion was kept alive on country estates where a conservative patrician landowning class sometimes shared the religious sympathies of country people, but it is difficult to imagine dead gods worshipped on rotting altars in fields and storehouses (denounced by Maximus of Turin) in Britain.[147] The landed patrician class that survived (to some extent) under Frankish, Visigothic and Ostrogothic rule on the Continent ceased to exist in Britain, being replaced by a warrior aristocracy that (judging from the evidence of post-Roman inscribed stones) was apparently firmly wedded to Christianity.

It is by no means certain that early medieval people re-using Roman structures in Britain would have had any

---

[145] Semple, *Perceptions of the Prehistoric*, p. 98.
[146] Semple, *Perceptions of the Prehistoric*, p. 6.
[147] Filotas, *Pagan Survivals*, p. 85.

clear idea of the original purposes of those buildings, and there is no need to invoke an unsupported hypothesis of ongoing sacrality in order to explain the re-use, adaptation and exploitation of prominent landmarks located at key points in the landscape. Roman sites such as temples were often used for early medieval burials, as were prehistoric features such as long barrows, but it is unclear whether much more can be read into this than a desire to bury the dead close to striking landmarks.[148] A late Roman temple at Lamyatt Beacon in Somerset seems to have endured into the fifth century but was then carefully dismantled; however, a cemetery of east-west oriented burials continued on the site into the eighth century, but it is difficult to interpret this.[149] The temple site might have been adapted into a Christian oratory, and even if it was not, it is difficult for us to know what significance Romano-British temple sites had for post-Roman Britons. Even if temples were not repurposed as Christian shrines of some kind, people may have erroneously *thought* they had Christian significance – such is the power of forgetting. Whatever the truth, it is not possible for us to project our knowledge of what Romano-British temples were back onto the people of the post-Roman past.

There is some evidence that places whose Old English names incorporated the word *hearg* (meaning 'temple') were sites of Romano-British shrines, such as at Woodeaton in Oxfordshire, Waden Hill in Wiltshire and Thurtaston in Cheshire,[150] but there are a number

---

[148] Semple, *Perceptions of the Prehistoric*, pp. 13–14; Yeates, *Tribe of Witches*, p. 130.
[149] De la Bédoyère, *Gods with Thunderbolts*, pp. 227–28.
[150] Semple, *Perceptions of the Prehistoric*, pp. 76–77.

of different ways to interpret this. It is possible, for example, that some standing Romano-British temples were adapted for re-use as shrines to the Anglo-Saxon gods because they were convenient standing buildings, and thus gave their name to the locality; but this need not imply any knowledge of their former Roman use. At Egleton in Rutland the roof of a small Roman temple collapsed at some point in the sixth century, sealing in a sixth-century burial and smashing an ox skull that was probably hanging in the rafters at the time – which suggests some continued significance as a cult site or the continued presence of antique votive offerings.[151] Equally, it is possible that *hearg* names were inspired by the stories Anglo-Saxon people told about their landscape, imagining that any imposing old building had been a temple to long-forgotten gods – or even that such names were given by Christian missionaries of the seventh century, who knew from their books or their own experience of Rome that the Romans built temples. The idea that *hearg* names indicate popular memory of a pagan Roman sacred site that survived both the late Roman decommissioning of pagan shrines and the cultural transformations of Anglo-Saxon England is perhaps the least likely of all possible explanations.

Pope Gregory I's well-known instruction to the missionary Mellitus in 601 not to destroy England's temples but to cleanse them of idols and turn them into churches has caused historians and archaeologists to puzzle over

---

[151] Brown, 'A Middle Iron Age Enclosure', p. 93. In the fifth century Maximus of Turin decried 'the heads of animals fixed along boundary lines' (*pecudum capita adfixa liminibus*) as a relic of paganism (quoted in Filotas, *Pagan Survivals*, p. 85).

the apparent absence of Anglo-Saxon temples from the archaeological record. On the one hand, it is possible that Gregory was simply projecting a Roman (or Old Testament–derived) norm on remote Britain, not knowing that the Anglo-Saxons rarely worshipped in enclosed shrines and temples.[152] On the other hand, it is possible the Anglo-Saxons re-purposed some Roman temples and it was these that were the subject of Gregory's letter.[153]

St Pancras' church in Canterbury, built from Roman bricks, is one possible example of a Roman shrine taken over by English pagan worship which was re-purposed as a church.[154] The ruined Stone Chapel near Faversham (Plate 11), which still retains the intact walls of a Romano-British temple within its ground plan, is another example where the tantalising possibility that the building was originally a pagan cult site for the Anglo-Saxons presents itself. The idea that the temple of Mercury at Uley, Gloucestershire, was turned into an early medieval church is well established, and based in part on the discovery of seventh-century window glass on the site, but in this case the site seems to have remained continuously Christian after its Roman or post-Roman conversion.[155] Another site where Anglo-Saxon pagan religious activity at a Romano-British site may be evidenced in the archaeology is Pagans Hill near Chew Stoke in Somerset, the location of an octagonal third-century Romano-British temple. Here a glass jar and metal pail were deposited

---

[152] Filotas, *Pagan Survivals*, pp. 89–90.
[153] Chaney, *Cult of Kingship*, pp. 74–75.
[154] Thomas, *Christianity in Roman Britain*, pp. 171–73. On the letter to Mellitus see Demacopoulos, 'Gregory the Great', pp. 353–69.
[155] Rahtz and Watts, 'Pagans Hill Revisited', p. 337.

in a well in the seventh century, suggesting some sort of revived interest in the site.[156]

In 2018 a much-worn jet pendant depicting the head of Medusa, of a kind often found in Roman graves, was found in a seventh-century Anglo-Saxon burial (alongside a chatelaine of that period) near Houghton in Huntingdonshire. One possibility is that the pendant was a treasured heirloom, perhaps even from the Roman period, or an accidental find in the landscape that came to be treasured by a seventh-century individual.[157] In Roman burials, the head of Medusa served as a protective amulet to ward off evil; and it is noteworthy that Old English was not lacking in words for 'mythological female shapers of fate'.[158] The Furies, who like Medusa were portrayed with snakes as hair,[159] were later glossed in Old English by the word *burgrunan*,[160] perhaps from Old English *beorgan* ('to save'), suggesting a belief in formidable supernatural female figures who nevertheless played a protective function. The Houghton pendant could thus be archaeological evidence of complementarity in beliefs over the cultural chasm that separated Roman Britain from Anglo-Saxon England, even if it is not evidence of any kind of continuity. Some fifth- and sixth-century burials in Norfolk make use of Roman building materials, as if 'mourners were engaged in the conscious creation of individual narratives about people and place using old places and antique things'.[161]

---

[156] Rahtz and Watts, 'Pagans Hill Revisited', pp. 363–66. See also Rahtz and Harris, 'The Temple Well', pp. 15–51.
[157] Hilts, 'A Landscape Revealed', pp. 21–22.
[158] Hall, *Elves*, p. 86.   [159] Isidore, *Etymologiae* 8.11.95.
[160] Hall, *Elves*, p. 85 n.41.
[161] Semple, *Perceptions of the Prehistoric*, pp. 47–48.

PLATE 1 A Roman relief of dancing godlings, Peterborough Cathedral

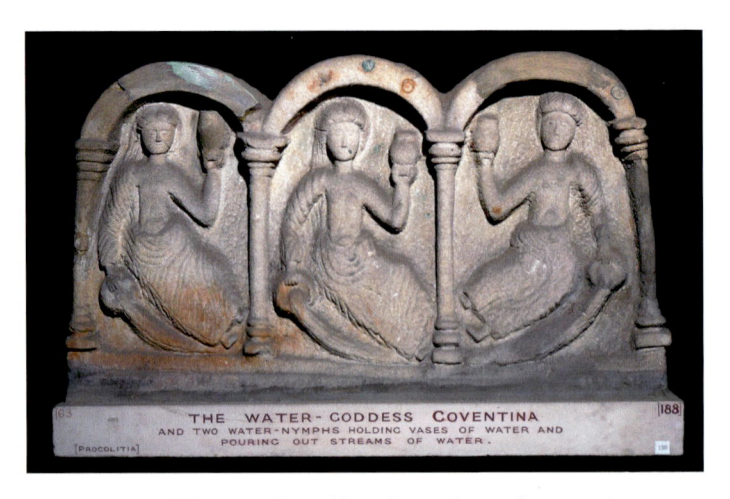

PLATE 2 The nymph-goddess Coventina and companions, Carrawburgh

PLATE 3 St Anne's Well, Buxton

PLATE 4 Three nymphs in the 'nymph room', Lullingstone

PLATE 5 A Roman relief of the Parcae, Calne

PLATE 6 Spoons from the Thetford treasure bearing a mixture of pagan and Christian symbolism

PLATE 7 A satyr on a gold belt buckle from the Thetford treasure

PLATE 8 The Bacchic *thiasos* on the Great Dish of the Mildenhall Treasure

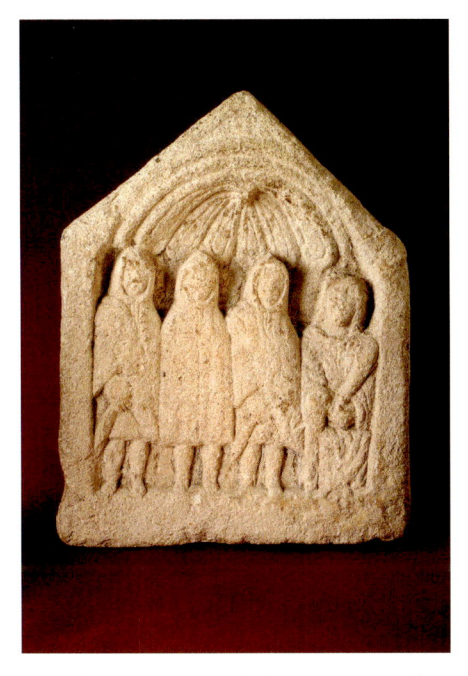

PLATE 9 A Mother Goddess with the Genii Cucullati, Cirencester

PLATE 10 A figure of Minerva carved into the side of a quarry, Chester

PLATE 11 Stone chapel, near Faversham

PLATE 12 Medieval satyrs

PLATE 13 A woodwose on the font, Waldringfield

PLATE 14 The stoke-hole of a Roman hypocaust, Richborough

PLATE 15 Anglo-Saxon-era lead amulet bearing the runic legend 'the dwarf is dead', found near Fakenham

PLATE 16 The conception of Merlin by an incubus

PLATE 17 A reconstructed nymphaeum, Vindolanda Roman fort

PLATE 18 Robin Goodfellow as Pan or Faunus (1639)

PLATE 19 A faun surrounded by fairies (1840)

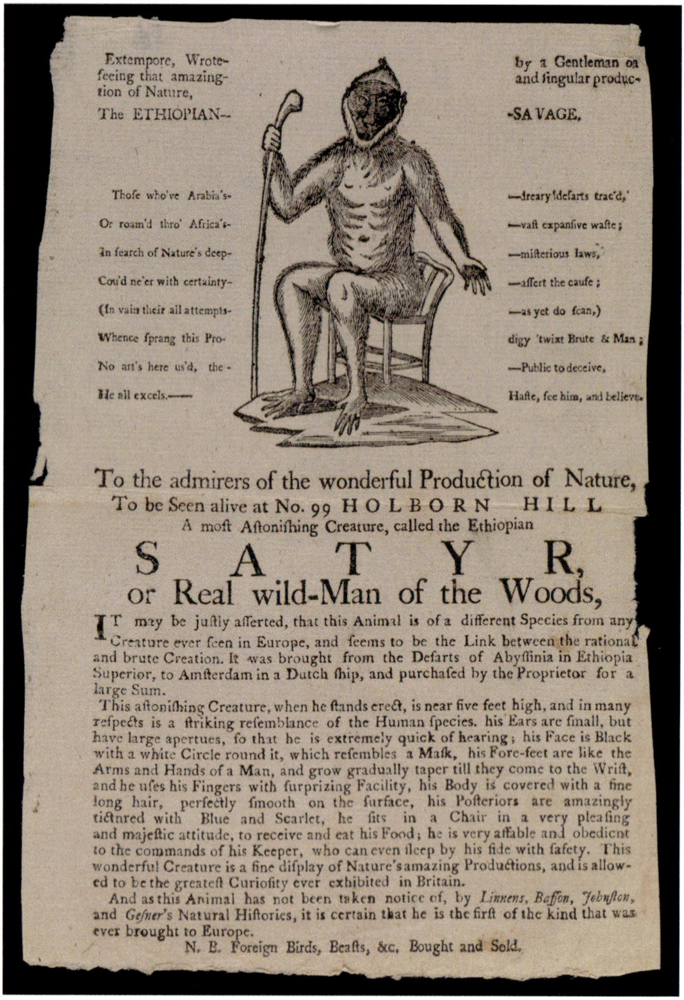

Extempore, Wrote- by a Gentleman on
ſeeing that amazing- and ſingular production of Nature,
The ETHIOPIAN- -SAVAGE.

Thoſe who've Arabia's- —dreary deſarts trac'd,
Or roam'd thro' Africa's- —vaſt expanſive waſte;
In ſearch of Nature's deep- —miſterious laws,
Cou'd ne'er with certainty- —aſſert the cauſe;
(In vain their all attempts- —as yet do ſcan,)
Whence ſprang this Pro- digy 'twixt Brute & Man;
No art's here us'd, the- —Public to deceive,
He all excels.—— Haſte, ſee him, and believe.

To the admirers of the wonderful Production of Nature,
To be Seen alive at No. 99 HOLBORN HILL
A moſt Aſtoniſhing Creature, called the Ethiopian

S A T Y R,
or Real wild-Man of the Woods,

IT may be juſtly aſſerted, that this Animal is of a different Species from any Creature ever ſeen in Europe, and ſeems to be the Link between the rational and brute Creation. It was brought from the Deſarts of Abyſſinia in Ethiopia Superior, to Amſterdam in a Dutch ſhip, and purchaſed by the Proprietor for a large Sum.

This aſtoniſhing Creature, when he ſtands erect, is near five feet high, and in many reſpects is a ſtriking reſemblance of the Human ſpecies. his Ears are ſmall, but have large apertues, ſo that he is extremely quick of hearing; his Face is Black with a white Circle round it, which reſembles a Maſk, his Fore-feet are like the Arms and Hands of a Man, and grow gradually taper till they come to the Wriſt, and he uſes his Fingers with ſurprizing Facility, his Body is covered with a fine long hair, perfectly ſmooth on the ſurface, his Poſteriors are amazingly tictnred with Blue and Scarlet, he ſits in a Chair in a very pleaſing and majeſtic attitude, to receive and eat his Food; he is very affable and obedient to the commands of his Keeper, who can even ſleep by his ſide with ſafety. This wonderful Creature is a fine diſplay of Nature's amazing Productions, and is allowed to be the greateſt Curioſity ever exhibited in Britain.

And as this Animal has not been taken notice of, by *Linnens, Baffon, Johnſton,* and *Geſner's* Natural Hiſtories, it is certain that he is the firſt of the kind that was ever brought to Europe.

N. B. Foreign Birds, Beaſts, &c. Bought and Sold.

PLATE 20 An early modern handbill advertising 'the Ethiopian Satyr, or Real wild-Man of the Woods'

Conclusion

The evidence of archaeology and a few sparse texts offer little indication of how the process of Christianisation affected the veneration of godlings in post-Roman times, but by comparison with other societies that are better evidenced, it seems likely that the 'mountains, valleys or rivers' that Gildas claimed had been forsaken as sites of worship continued to be sacred to some people in the years after the withdrawal of Roman authority. In addition, it is likely that some descendants of Romano-Britons underwent a process of inculturation into Germanic paganism in those parts of the island dominated by Anglo-Saxon culture. There is no reason to assume that Christianisation meant the extinction of Britain's godlings, which were an inheritance of Romano-British religion, but they may well have undergone transformation as a result of the demonisation of Christian missionaries. Demonisation serves to preserve folkloric beings but also reorganises their position in the cosmos, and has an impact on the language used to describe them even when popular belief 'undemonises', recovers or reinvents them. Exactly how that process of recovery and reconstruction may have occurred in early medieval Britain is the subject of the next chapter.

4

Furies, Elves and Giants

Godlings in Early Medieval Britain

Early medieval Britain, from the withdrawal of Roman authority at the beginning of the fourth century to the Norman Conquest in the eleventh, was a society of great diversity and complexity. From the fifth century, the descendants of Romano-Britons co-existed in many areas with Germanic settlers and it is likely that many descendants of Romano-Britons became 'anglicised' from the sixth century onwards.[1] With the settlers and their cultural influence came the Old English language as well as Germanic paganism, while the Britons remained Christian. In British areas the Latin language was gradually abandoned, as the Welsh, Cumbric and Cornish languages (descendants of the British language) became established in the 'Old North', Wales, the Isle of Man and Britain's southwestern peninsula, respectively. In addition, a Brittonic-speaking community was established in Armorica in north-western Gaul, which would become Brittany. Meanwhile the far north-western coast of Britain (as well as parts of Wales) was settled by migrants from Ireland who brought the Gaelic language.

[1] For overviews of current thinking on post-Roman Britain see Oosthuizen, *Emergence of the English*, pp. 1–18; Hutton, *Pagan Britain*, pp. 294–97. Stephen Rippon's recent study of the Kingdom of Essex, *Territoriality and the Early Medieval Landscape*, lays particular stress on the survival of inland British communities even in the easternmost areas of southern Britain (pp. 171–226).

The extent to which the languages of early medieval Britain can be matched to people groups remains an active subject of historical debate. All that can be said with certainty is that five main linguistic groups existed in the turbulent island: speakers of Brittonic languages, speakers of Old English, speakers of Gaelic, speakers of Pictish and learned speakers of Latin. By 600 the conversion of the English to Christianity was underway, which brought English culture within the sphere of Latin (the language of the church), although the English showed a preference for writing in the vernacular over Latin. By the middle of the seventh century Christianity, the Latin language and a common tradition of Christian learning had become shared features of the societies and kingdoms of Britain. While it is possible to emphasise the major differences between cultures in early medieval Britain they also had much in common, and a rigid delineation of Anglo-Saxons and Britons as cultural groups is unhelpful. This chapter will therefore examine what we know of beliefs about godlings and otherworlders circulating among both Britons and Anglo-Saxons in the early medieval world.

As one recent writer on the monstrous in Anglo-Saxon England has noted, the Anglo-Saxons had no concept of a supernatural world in the way modern people might understand it, as a different realm of being.[2] The same, of course, can be said of the Britons. Folkloric beings might inhabit a different part of the physical world from humans (such as hills, mounds, caves or bodies of water), and time might even pass differently in their realm, but modern ideas of supernatural beings existing on another 'plane of

---

[2] Flight, *Basilisks and Beowulf*, pp. 27–29.

existence' or 'another dimension' would probably have meant nothing to early medieval people. Supernatural beings were as real to them as the ordinary wild and domesticated animals they saw every day, or indeed strange creatures and peoples reported by travellers.

Different languages had different words for these beings, and it is clear that the Germanic settlers imported some beings, such as elves, who were conceptually different from the folkloric beings of the Britons – but there was also a great deal of commonality in perceptions of godlings. Furthermore, the use of the Latin language by the learned (mostly monks and clerics) anchored early medieval British societies to wider traditions of European learning and to the Roman past. When Anglo-Saxons or Britons writing in Latin chose words for supernatural beings they were not simply engaging in a thoughtless or haphazard process of *interpretatio Latina*, but were undertaking a complex process of cross-cultural evaluation of religious and quasi-religious concepts. This chapter will show that the interpretation of folkloric beings in early medieval Britain was governed by cultural change (which sometimes resulted in the introduction of entirely new beings, such as elves), the influence of learned commentary (which might include clerical demonisation) and continuity from the Roman and post-Roman eras.

The Influence of Learned Traditions

The old idea that folklore exists as a pure oral tradition, which was still often accepted by folklorists up to the later twentieth century, has now been abandoned in favour of a recognition that oral folklore exists in constant dialogue with other media – most notably, in the modern era, with print.[3] However, just as modern folklore interacts with print, so the folklore of the era before printing interacted with learned written commentary, and both influenced and was written by what learned individuals committed to writing. In the same way that folklorists have come to understand the importance of print to the survival of folklore in the modern era, so learned commentary interacted with folklore in the Middle Ages. Any attempt to consider the folkloric concepts current in a medieval Christian nation is futile without studying them against the background of biblical and Classical learning present in that society. While the list of monsters in *Beowulf*, for example, provides valuable information on Anglo-Saxon folklore, it would be misguided indeed to consider it apart from the interpretative framework within which the author of *Beowulf* situated the existence of monsters: namely, the biblical story of Cain:

For a long while the unblest creature [Grendel] had inhabited the territory of a species of water-monsters (*fifelcynnes*) since the Creator had proscribed him along with the stock of Cain. The everlasting Lord avenged that murderous act by which he slew Abel. He enjoyed no benefit from that violent assault, for God the Ordainer exiled him for that crime far away from humankind. From him all misbegotten things were born – ogres (*eotenas*) and elves (*ylfe*) and hellishly deformed beings (*orcneas*) such as the giants who fought for a long time against God; for that he paid them their due.[4]

---

[3] Fontes, *Folklore and Literature*, pp. 4–5.
[4] Bradley (ed.), *Anglo-Saxon Poetry*, p. 414.

The elaboration of biblical mythology in order to account for supernatural beings was by no means unique to the Christian Anglo-Saxons. In medieval Ireland, Cain was said to have fathered a siren named Ambia who had intercourse with a trout, giving birth to both Fomoir (the ancestor of the Fomorians) and Becnait (the ancestor of the leprechauns).[5] Rationalisations of monsters and folkloric beings in relation to the punishment of Cain (Genesis 4), the interbreeding of a race of giants with human women (Genesis 6), the curse placed by Noah on the race of Ham (Genesis 9) or the fall of some of the angels were just as important as pre-Christian mythologies in accounting for folkloric beings (if indeed those original mythologies were remembered at all in Christianised societies). As I argued in Chapter 3 above, the prevalence or intensity of belief in folkloric beings in a Christian society should not be taken as an indication of the depth of that society's Christianisation, since the mistaken view that folklore is somehow incompatible (or only partially incompatible) with Christianity arises from misconceptions about the nature of medieval Christianity. The church often demonised folkloric beings, and it may have eliminated the pre-Christian myths that accounted for their existence; but popular Christianity seldom stamped out belief in godlings themselves, instead reinterpreting these beings for a Christian world.

Understanding the extent, the quality and the sources of biblical and Classical learning at a given point in

---

[5] Bisagni, *'Leprechaun'*, p. 78.

time is a key step towards understanding how and why supernatural beings were interpreted at that time. Just as Christianisation was a continuous process in Britain between the fourth and seventh centuries, so Christian learning was (to a greater or lesser extent) a persistent feature of this period. The surviving writings of Gildas, Patrick, Pelagius and Faustus of Riez testify to the presence of Christian learning in Roman and post-Roman Britain, which continued to be a learned, literate and Latinate society (at least for some) after 410.[6]

However, in contrast to Anglo-Saxon England, vanishingly few texts and manuscripts from post-Roman Britain and early medieval Wales survive (largely owing to a combination of Irish, Viking, English and internecine depredations against Welsh monasteries), and our evidence for literacy and post-Roman British Latinity is derived primarily from the inscribed stones set up (mainly as cenotaphs) in western and south-western Britain. Biblical quotations in the writings of the sixth-century author Gildas that correspond to no known version of the Latin Bible that preceded Jerome's Vulgate suggest the possibility that post-Roman Britain had its own distinct Latin Bible.[7] While Welsh learning was probably influenced by Irish teachers, there are also hints that Latin learning in early medieval Wales was very archaic indeed, perhaps stretching back to the fifth century and providing a link with the Christian culture of late Roman Britain.[8]

---

[6] Lapidge, 'Latin Learning', pp. 91–107.
[7] Lapidge, 'Latin Learning', p. 92.
[8] Lapidge, 'Latin Learning', p. 102.

The Brittonic Linguistic and Onomastic Evidence

While the English language came to dominate southern and eastern Britain within what was apparently a remarkably short period of time in the fifth and sixth centuries, a Brittonic- and Latin-speaking population endured in western and northern Britain throughout the early Middle Ages. The Welsh, Cornish and Breton languages survived into the later Middle Ages and beyond, producing a rich literature that was one of the earliest vernacular literatures in Europe. Although the native spoken Latin of the Romano-Britons seems to have died out by the eighth century (meaning that Britain did not develop its own distinct Romance language), Anthony Harvey has shown that Latin 'enjoyed a surprisingly deep and tenacious hold on early medieval Celtic Britain' and profoundly affected the vocabulary of the Welsh language.[9] We might, therefore, expect the Brittonic languages to preserve religious and folkloric concepts carried over from Roman Britain, just as Welsh legends seem to have preserved half-remembered Roman history. These are notions that need to be treated with caution, however, being mindful of the centuries of interaction between Welsh, English and Latin.

The romantic idea of the Welsh language and medieval Welsh literature as arks preserving pristine knowledge of pre-Roman 'Celtic' culture and religion must be set aside, just as the idea that Irish medieval literature

---

[9] Harvey, 'Cambro-Romance?', p. 179. On the Latin language in medieval Wales see also Charles-Edwards, *Wales and the Britons*, pp. 625–50; Russell, '"Go and Look in the Latin Books"', pp. 213–46.

records Iron Age culture has largely been set aside by scholars of medieval Ireland. Contemporary scholarship on the Irish literature of the marvellous emphasises, instead, the extent to which learned authors drew syncretistically on traces of pre-Christian belief in order to fashion a literature for Ireland that gave it a place in universal Christian history and European religious culture.[10] Ben Guy has drawn attention to the difference between the common frame of reference provided by 'culturally specific knowledge' in Welsh traditional histories (such as the names of characters) and the literary works in which that knowledge was deployed. We ought not to imagine 'a common pool of culturally specific historical and literary knowledge that was transmitted principally by an official class of trained poets, whose learning was mostly communicated orally'. This is the myth of the bardic tradition, transmitting ancient pre-Christian mythology in medieval Wales. While a common cultural frame of reference did exist, its sources were diverse (including written works and sources from outside Wales) and literature drew on the framework 'freely and idiosyncratically'.[11] For example, it would be wrong to assume (just because they apparently take the form of mnemonics suitable for oral transmission and contain no trace of the notoriously unreliable Geoffrey of Monmouth) that the *Trioedd Ynys Prydein* ('Triads of the Island of Britain'), first attested in the thirteenth century, are of immemorial antiquity.[12]

[10] Bitel, 'Secrets of the *Síd*', pp. 80–81.
[11] Guy, 'Constantine, Helena, Maximus', pp. 382–83.
[12] Guy, 'Constantine, Helena, Maximus', p. 384.

However, names of legendary Welsh figures ending in *-on* are likely to be of ancient origin. These include Mabon (cognate with Gaulish Maponos), Modron (cognate with Gaulish Matrona), Gofannon (cognate with Gaulish Gobannos) and Rhiannon (cognate with Gaulish Rigina).[13] Yet, as Guy notes for the names of Roman historical figures like Constantine, Magnus Maximus and Helena, the mere preservation of a name in a pseudo-genealogy need not indicate actual knowledge of the character who lay behind it or the stories associated with them.[14] The medieval Welsh stories known as *The Mabinogion* are works of fiction woven from the fabric of popular story rather than unproblematic witnesses to the nature of medieval Welsh folklore, and attempts to extract information about the nature of ancient cults from *The Mabinogion* are misguided. As Ken Dark has observed, apart from the general significance of springs, severed heads and the number three, it is perilous to attempt to relate any specific details of these medieval stories to archaeology.[15] In the same way that a character in modern fiction called Peter should not be taken as evidence for the cult of St Peter the apostle, so the behaviour of fictional characters who bear names derived from pagan gods may not be evidence for the characters of those deities.

There is no way to establish whether Modron descends from the Gaulish/British Matrona or the Classical Latin Matrona, but it is worth noting that no inscriptions survive from Roman Britain to the goddess Matrona or

---

[13] Lambert, *Langue gauloise*, p. 29.
[14] Guy, 'Constantine, Helena, Maximus', p. 389.
[15] Dark, *Civitas to Kingdom*, p. 117. For a less cautious approach see Yeates, *Tribe of Witches*, p. 159.

referring to the Deae Matres as *Matronae* (although a tablet from Vindolanda bears an apparent reference to the Roman festival of Matronalia on 1 March[16]). It is possible that Modron is a cambricisation not of the name of a deity but of the Latin word *matrona*, 'the lady', as an elliptical or euphemistic way of referring to some unknown supernatural being. Furthermore, the fact that Modron appears as an individual character in Welsh literature and not as a triad suggests that, if there was ever a connection with the Deae Matres, it has been lost.

It is not possible to say with any certainty, therefore, that the folkloric beings of Welsh legend are the gods of Roman and pre-Roman Britain. Yet on the other hand, the idea that Welsh fairy beliefs are a medieval importation from England, 'displacing earlier and historically obscure traditions',[17] is decidedly unlikely. Indeed, as I shall argue in Chapter 5 below, quite the opposite is more likely to be the case: 'British' beliefs about godlings influenced England after the Norman Conquest. There is no reason to suppose that Welsh fairy beliefs are not part of the continuum of belief in an underground community of supernatural beings found across northern Europe, from Ireland to Scandinavia. While one word, *ellyll*, is perhaps a borrowing of English 'elf',[18] a striking feature of Welsh

---

[16] *RIB Tab. Vindol.* 581, romaninscriptionsofbritain.org/inscriptions/TabVindol581, accessed 15 October 2021.
[17] Suggett, 'The Fair Folk', p. 138.
[18] Andrea Bargan's argument that *ellyll* represents a separate Celtic expression of a proto- or pre-Indo-European word seems unlikely, given the geographical proximity of the Welsh language to English, its history of borrowing and the absence of cognates of *ellyll* in other Celtic languages (Bargan, 'The Probable Old Germanic Origin of Romanian *iele*', 16).

terms for folkloric beings is the *absence* of borrowing, from English, Irish or Latin, and a decided preference for euphemistic terms. While a word exists in Welsh cognate with Latin *fata* (*ffawd*), it was never personified by analogy with French *fée* and its Romance cognates, and thus never became a term for folkloric beings.

Instead, the best known and most widely used Welsh term for the nation's folkloric beings is perhaps *tylwyth teg*, 'the good folk', first attested in the fourteenth century in a poem of Dafydd ap Gwilym,[19] and later in William Salesbury's Welsh-English dictionary (1547).[20] Other later terms such as *plant* ('children'), *plant annwn* ('children of the underworld'), *gwragedd annwyl* ('dear women') and *anweledig* ('hidden ones') are similarly euphemistic and elliptical. A few Welsh words for otherworldly beings are borrowings from other languages: *coblyn*, a borrowing of Middle French *gobelin* (probably via English 'goblin') was known to Salesbury in 1547,[21] while *ellyll*, a possible borrowing from Old English *ælf*, is attested in Welsh from the fourteenth century.[22] A word shared across the Brittonic languages is a borrowing of the Latin *spiritus*, yielding Welsh *anysbryd/ysbryd*, Breton *spered* and Cornish *spyrys* (the last being the origin of Anglo-Cornish 'spriggan'). The universality of *spiritus*-derivatives across all the Brittonic languages suggests an early borrowing from Latin, perhaps influenced by Christian demonology; aside from references to the Holy Spirit, most occurrences of the word *spiritus*

[19] Ap Gwilym, *Fifty Poems*, p. 248.
[20] Salesbury, *Dictionary*, sig. R.i[v].
[21] Salesbury, *Dictionary*, sig. J.iii[r].
[22] *GPC*, s.v. 'ellyll', accessed 15 October 2021.

in the Latin Vulgate New Testament refer to a *spiritus immundus* ('unclean spirit') being cast out in exorcism.

Another term of some antiquity may be the old Welsh word for nightmare, *gwyll* (the modern Welsh word for a nightmare or incubus, *hunllef*, seems to be a borrowing from Old English with the suffix *-ælf*[23]). Salesbury recorded *gwyll* as 'Nyght mare' in 1547.[24] *Gwyll* literally means 'dusk' or 'darkness' but has the meaning in modern Welsh of 'manes, the spirits of the dead, shades, ghosts, sprites, hobgoblins; night-prowlers, night-thieves, vagabonds'[25]. However, another word *gwyll* (a variant spelling of *gwyllt*) has the meaning 'wild',[26] lending an ambiguity to any use of *gwyll* as a word that conjures both darkness and wildness – in much the same way the Latin word *incubus* alludes both to the terrors of the night and to an aspect of the nature god Faunus.

One of the most interesting Welsh euphemisms for the fairies, from a historical point of view, is *bendith y mamau*, 'the blessing of the mothers', a phrase found especially in South Wales, because it might suggest a memory of the Deae Matres.[27] The euphemism was first identified by the Protestant preacher John Penry in 1587:

> our swarmes of south saiers, and enchanters ... will not stick openly, to profese that they walke, on Tuesdaies, and Thursdaies at nights, with the fairies, of whom they brag themselves to have their knowlege. These sonnes of Belial, who shuld die the death, Levit. 20.6. have stroken such an astonishing

[23] *GPC*, s.v. 'hunlle, hunllef', accessed 14 October 2021.
[24] Salesbury, *Dictionary*, sig. G.ii^v
[25] *GPC*, s.v. 'gwyllon, gwyllion', accessed 14 October 2021.
[26] *GPC*, s.v. 'gwyllt, gwyll', accessed 24 October 2021.
[27] MacKillop, *Dictionary of Celtic Mythology*, p. 40.

reverence of the fairies, into the harts of our silly people, that they dare not name them, without honor. We cal them *bendith û mamme*, that is, such as have deserved their mothers blessing. Now our people, wil never utter, *bendith û mamme*, but they wil saie, *bendith û mamme û dhûn*, that is, their mothers blessing (which they account the greatest felicity that any creature can be capeable of) light upon them,[28] as though they were not to be named without reverence.[29]

The idea that the name of the *bendith y mamau* could derive from the pre-Christian cult of the Deae Matres is not new,[30] and it is lent some support by Breton folklore where the fairies were sometimes spoken of as 'our good mothers the fairies' or 'the good ladies'.[31] Furthermore, the indirectness of *bendith y mamau*, which does not call the fairies mothers but implies that they are personifications of speech uttered by the mothers, mirrors the origin of the French word *fée* as a re-personification of the fate-bearing speech of the Parcae. However, Penry himself interpreted the 'mothers' as the mothers of people who dared to speak of the fairies, who invoked a maternal blessing every time they mentioned them. Any association of this interesting euphemism with the Parcae or Deae Matres must therefore remain speculative.

One apparently ancient class of words used to refer to supernatural beings, in both the Brittonic languages and in English, derives from the Indo-European root **bheug-*, with the meaning 'to flee in fear, be frightened of'. This

[28] Penry mistranslates the phrase 'Bendith y mamau y ddyn', whose actual meaning is 'The blessing of the mothers to man'.
[29] Penry, *Treatise*, p. 46.
[30] Huws, *Y Tylwyth Teg*, pp. 5–6.
[31] Sébillot, *Traditions et Superstitions*, vol. 1, p. 74.

yields Welsh *bwg*, Old English *puca*, Middle English *pouke* and early modern English *puck*, as well as a range of dialect words for frightening beings from *bug* to *boggart*. *Pouke* would go on to become the standard word for a fairy in southern England in the later Middle Ages, prior to the introduction of French *fée*.[32] The origins and transmission of these cognates has been hotly debated, since *puck*-related words can be found widely spread throughout Germanic and Scandinavian languages, as well as in Finnish and the Baltic languages. Linguists have been divided over whether Celtic languages transmitted a loan to Germanic languages, or vice versa.[33] Most recently, William Sayers has argued that Germanic speakers in Britain encountered Britons already using a word so familiar to them that the semantics of the two terms merged, rendering moot the question of which language was more influential on the other.[34]

Gwyddon, derived (as noted above) either from *gwŷdd* ('wood') or *gŵydd* ('wild'), is a Welsh word that has been applied to many supernatural beings (giantess, female monster, hag, witch, sorceress, giant, monster, wizard, sorcerer, woodland deity, satyr, nymph), but it is without a Latin cognate.[35] Iolo Morganwg's suggestion that the word had something to do with druids writing on wood seems unlikely,[36] and the word may have had the original sense of 'a woodland dweller' or 'a dweller in

---

[32] Harte, 'Fairy Barrows', p. 68.
[33] Young, *The Boggart*, pp. 27-30.
[34] Sayers, 'Puck and the Bogymen', p. 54.
[35] *GPC*, s.v. 'gwiddon, gwiddan, gwyddon, gwyddan', accessed 14 October 2021.
[36] Charnell-White, *Bardic Circles*, p. 245.

the wild'. Pierre-Yves Lambert proposes Gaulish *uidu-* ('wood') as cognate with Welsh *gwŷdd*,[37] but whether a Brittonic ancestor of *gwyddon* was applied by the Britons to godlings we cannot know. The earliest attested Welsh word that can be translated as 'nymph' was *chwyfleian* (lit. 'wandering prophetess'), from the thirteenth century;[38] the direct borrowing from Greek and Latin, *nymff*, is not attested until the sixteenth century.[39]

As we saw in Chapter 1 above, the Welsh word for the fairy realm, *Annwn* or *Annwfn* (lit. 'the underworld') is undoubtedly of great antiquity. However, the use of an ancient term for fairyland in medieval Welsh does not necessarily mean the *Annwn* of medieval Welsh literature is the mythological successor of a mythical otherworld realm of the ancient Britons. In the same way that the word 'hell' was adopted from Anglo-Saxon paganism to refer to the place of damnation in Christian belief, so it is highly likely that *Annwn*, the name of the underworld of the pagan ancient Britons, was borrowed by early Christian missionaries. Unlike 'hell', however, which has retained its exclusively infernal connotations, Annwn may have undergone a process of 'undemonisation' in the centuries between its adoption into British Christian culture and the emergence of Welsh mythological literature.

That the Annwn of folklore is not quite the same place as the hell of Christian belief (Welsh *uffern*, from Latin *inferna*) may owe something to the ambiguity of a term

---

[37] Lambert, *Langue gauloise*, p. 203.
[38] *GPC*, s.v. 'chwyfleian, chwimleian, chwimbleian, chwibleian', accessed 15 October 2021.
[39] *GPC*, s.v. 'nymff', accessed 15 October 2021.

that simply means 'the world below'. As we have seen, a belief that godlings lived beneath the earth is common across north-western Europe, but British belief also had distinctive features. Patrick Sims-Williams has shown that while the Irish *síd* is apparently equivalent to the Welsh Annwn, the two are rather different because Annwn is a single realm that can be reached through multiple points of access. By contrast, the Irish *síde* (mounds leading to underground dominions) are individual realms, and there is no single king of the otherworld in Irish tradition.[40] Two references in medieval Welsh literature to *Kaer Sidi* ('the castle of the Síd') can probably be set aside as hibernicising borrowings rather than evidence of a close relationship between the Irish and Welsh otherworlds,[41] and they may have nothing to do with the *síd* at all.[42]

Annwn can thus refer to both a spiritual realm and to a dwelling of the godlings beneath the earth, accessed via hills and mounds, in much the same way as someone speaking English might use a phrase like 'the great beyond' to mean death, the afterlife, or even a remote geographical region. Annwn in its current usage, therefore, is likely to have more to do with a process of demonisation and undemonisation than with mythological survival from a remote period of antiquity. The suggestion that the name of Arawn, the king of Annwn, might derive from the Rhineland god Arubianus (identified in inscriptions

---

[40] Sims-Williams, *Irish Influence*, pp. 58–59.
[41] Sims-Williams, *Irish Influence*, pp. 67–68.
[42] *GPC*, s.v. 'sidydd' gives the likely meaning of *Caer Sidi* or *Caer Sidydd* as 'castle of the zodiac', perhaps linked to Latin *sidera* ('stars') (accessed 15 October 2021).

with Jupiter) should be treated with caution.[43] Arubianus is attested only in the Rhineland area, and while other Rhineland deities were certainly imported to Britain in the Roman period, there is no evidence of this god in Britain whatsoever. On the other hand, there is also barely any evidence for the popular Gaulish god Lugus in Britain, and Lugus emerges in the Welsh legendary tradition as Lleu.[44] Yet as noted in Chapter 2, the epigraphic evidence for the deities worshipped in late Roman Britain is inevitably incomplete, reflecting only the devotional interests of those able to afford to erect an altar or other inscription.

In Welsh tradition Arawn undergoes replacement by the hero Gwynn ap Nudd as king of Annwn (and later king of the fairies), who is the son of Nudd (later Lludd) Llaw Ereint, a figure whose name apparently derives from the god Nodens, venerated at Lydney. J. R. R. Tolkien suggested that the *Lyd-* element in the place name Lydney derived from the Welsh Lludd, the medieval descendant of the god Nodens once worshipped there.[45] However, the Anglo-Saxon place-name forms *Lidaneg* and *Ledanei* suggest Lydney may be named after a man called Lida rather than the god, in spite of the fortuitous similarity between Lydney and Lludd.[46] Yeates, however, has suggested that the place name Nustles (recorded as *Nothehalles* in 1565), which refers to the specific land on which the temple of Nodens is located, could be derived from the name of the god.[47] By analogy with Bolivian miners

[43] Steiner (ed.), *Codex inscriptionum*, vol. 3, p. 228.
[44] Lambert, *Langue gauloise*, p. 30.
[45] Scull and Hammond (eds.), *The J. R. R. Tolkien Companion*, p. 161.
[46] Mills (ed.), *Dictionary of English Place-Names*, p. 218.
[47] Yeates, *Tribe of Witches*, p. 94.

who make offerings to the devil and a bountiful earth mother, Yeates speculated that the cult at Lydney was a dual cult of Nodens and Abundantia, perhaps surviving Christianisation in some respect.[48] It is noteworthy that the thirteenth-century theologian William of Auvergne paired the fairy king Hellequin with 'Lady Abundance' (*dame Habunde*),[49] suggesting that the pairing of an underworld deity with Abundantia may have been a feature of Roman popular religion that survived into the Middle Ages.

The names Nodens and Nudd/Lludd are also cognate with that of the Irish god Núadu, although it cannot be presumed from this that the figures are also mythologically cognate. All that can be said with certainty is that Nodens/Nudd/Núadu are linguistically connected, perhaps by a common ancestor.[50] Núadu might have been planted in Ireland by settlers from late Roman Britain, and then re-introduced from Irish literature in the form of Nudd Llaw Ereint long after Nodens was forgotten in Britain; alternatively, both Nodens and Núadu developed in prehistoric times from a deity common to Britain and Ireland, and the later importation of the name of a deity formerly worshipped in Britain is no more than accidental. Either way, the case of Nodens/Nudd/Núadu shows how little faith can be placed in theonyms alone as a guide to mythology or belief. On the other hand, it is not impossible that the pairing of a king of fairyland or of the underworld with a female deity representing abundance did indeed survive into later ages.

[48] Yeates, *Tribe of Witches*, p. 101.
[49] Green, 'Refighting Carlo Ginzburg's Night Battles', p. 393.
[50] Sims-Williams, *Irish Influence*, p. 10.

Fauns, Woodwoses and the Origins of Male Fairies

The reappearance of fauns (or, under their English name, woodwoses) in early medieval Britain is one of the most striking examples of biblical and patristic influence on popular belief. The Vulgate Bible was the most widely read and copied text in medieval Britain, with the result that Jerome's translation choices heavily influenced the ways in which medieval Christians perceived the world, including folkloric beings. The Latin translation of the Bible that preceded Jerome, the *Vetus Latina*, translated the Hebrew word *se'irim* (a kind of demon) as *daemonia*,[51] but Jerome selected the obscure Latin term *pilosi* for Isaiah 13:21 and Isaiah 34:14, later translated as 'satyrs' in the Authorised Version:

> But wild beasts of the desert shall lie there; and their houses shall be full of doleful creatures; and owls shall dwell there, and satyrs (*pilosi*) shall dance there.
>
> The wild beasts of the desert shall also meet with the wild beasts of the island, and the satyr (*pilosus*) shall cry to his fellow; the screech owl also shall rest there, and find for herself a place of rest.

In his *Commentary on Isaiah* Jerome added 'and the *pilosi* will dance there, or the incubi or satyrs or certain men of the woods (*silvestres quosdam homines*), which many call *Fauni ficarii* or understand to be a kind of demons'.[52]

---

[51] Sabatier (ed.), *Bibliorum Sacrorum versiones antiquae*, vol. 2, p. 542: *Sed requiescent ibi bestiae, et replebuntur domus sonitu; et accubabunt ibi sirenae, et daemonia saltabunt ibi* (Isaiah 13:21).

[52] Jerome, *Ad Isaiam* 13.21 (PL 24.159): *et pilosi saltabunt ibi, vel Incubones vel satyros vel silvestres quosdam homines, quos nonnulli Faunos ficarios vocant aut daemonum genera intellegunt.*

While the phrase 'fig fauns' has been interpreted as a euphemistic reference to the rampant fauns' habit of penetrating the anus (*ficus* in Latin slang),[53] T. P. Wiseman suggested the term may refer instead to fig trees that marked the beginning and end of the run of the young men known as *luperci* at the Roman festival of the Lupercalia, anciently associated with the god Faunus.[54] Jerome used the term directly in his translation of Jeremiah 50:39: *Propterea habitabunt dracones cum faunis ficariis, et habitabunt in ea struthiones* ('Therefore the wild beasts of the desert with the wild beasts of the islands shall dwell there, and the owls shall dwell therein', according to the Authorised Version).

Although the *pilosi* appear first in the Vulgate, Wiseman argued that they can be traced in archaic Latin art to a much earlier period. On one mirror of the late fourth or early third century BCE, Incubo, Inuus and Ephialtes appear as distinct characters in a wedding chamber, with Incubo and Ephialtes portrayed as hairy all over: *pilosi*.[55] By the fourth century CE, however, the characters of Faunus, Incubo and Ephialtes (and even Pan) were conflated, and Jerome's translation and commentary suggest that the term *pilosi* could be applied indiscriminately to fauns, satyrs, incubi, panitae and other godlings of the untamed wild, the *silvestres homines*. In Jerome's *Life of St Paul*, an incubus encountered by St Anthony confesses that he is one of those worshipped by pagans as fauns, satyrs and incubi.[56]

---

[53] Dempsey, *Inventing the Renaissance Putto*, p. 137.
[54] Wiseman, *Unwritten Rome*, pp. 64–65.
[55] Wiseman, *Unwritten Rome*, pp. 65–69.
[56] Jerome, *Vita Sancti Pauli*, PL 73, pp. 112–13.

An authority equal to Jerome in the Latin west, Augustine, reported that 'Silvani and fauns, who are commonly called incubi, often misbehaved towards women and succeeded in accomplishing their lustful desires to sleep with them'.[57] While Augustine's identification of incubi with fauns was nothing new, and the sexual behaviour of the fauns was well known, the idea that the name *incubus* had a specifically sexual meaning (as opposed to a being associated with the phenomenon of sleep paralysis) seems to have been an original attempt at demonisation by Augustine, and it was to prove highly successful.[58]

Jerome and Augustine's demonology passed into the highly influential encyclopaedic work of Isidore of Seville – an author whose work we know was present in post-Roman Britain, even if no manuscripts survive. An inscribed stone at Llanllyr House in Ceredigion bears the obscure word *tesquitus* (meaning 'waste-plot', 'hermitage' or 'monastery'), derived from the word *tesqua* which is known in Britain only from Isidore's *Etymologies*, composed in the early seventh century.[59] The *Etymologies* was the encyclopaedic work *par excellence* of early medieval Christian Europe, providing a helpful digest of Classical learning, and the inscription from Llanllyr is good evidence that Isidore was known in at least one early medieval Welsh monastery. Paraphrasing Jerome's *Commentary on Isaiah*, Isidore provided a description of the 'fig fauns':

---

[57] Augustine, *De civitate Dei* 3:548–49 (*PL* 41:468): *Silvanos et Faunos, quos vulgo Incubos vocant, improbos saepe extitisse mulieribus, et earum appetisse ac peregisse concubitum.*
[58] Green, *Elf Queens*, p. 78.
[59] Ryan, 'Isidore amongst the Islands', p. 424.

The Satyrs are little people with hooked noses; they have horns on their foreheads, and feet like goats' – the kind of creature that Saint Anthony saw in the wilderness ... There are also said to be a kind of wild men (*silvestres homines*), whom some call Fauns of the fig.[60]

Elsewhere, Isidore explained the nature of the fauns in relation to their supposed etymology, an explanation largely derived from Varro's *De lingua Latina* ('On the Latin language'):

Fauns (*faunus*) were so called from 'speaking' (*fando*, gerund of *fari*) or after the term φωνη ('vocal sound') because by voice, not by signs, they seemed to show what was to come – for they were consulted by pagans in sacred groves, and gave responses to them not with signs, but with their voices.[61]

The *pilosi*, according to Isidore, 'are called *Panitae* in Greek, and "incubuses" (*incubus*) in Latin, or Inui, from copulating (*inire*) indiscriminately with animals'.[62] Isidore thus attempted to associate two main characteristics with fauns: the bestial behaviour of the *silvestres homines* and the traditional prophetic or vatic function of Faunus. However, the bestial and the prophetic need not be perceived as antithetical. The figures of Myrddin Wyllt and Lailoken in Welsh and Scottish legend, who are driven mad by the horror of battle and flee to the

---

[60] Isidore, *Etymologiae* 11.3.21–22: *Satyri homunciones sunt aduncis naribus; cornua in frontibus, et caprarum pedibus similes, qualem in solitudine Antonius sanctus vidit ... Dicuntur quidam et silvestres homines, quos nonnulli Faunos ficarios vocant.*
[61] Isidore, *Etymologiae* 8.11.87, paraphrasing Varro, *De lingua Latina* 7.36.
[62] Isidore, *Etymologiae* 8.11.103.

woods, are cases in point. Myrddin and Lailoken go mad and live as wild men, but these *silvestres homines* also acquire magical powers.[63] The Welsh word *gwyddon*, which can refer to both a woodland deity and a wizard, hints at a world of British belief in which the line between the divine and the bestial was a porous one. In one version of the story of St Samson and the *theomacha* (discussed in Chapter 1), who may well embody how early Welsh people imagined a *gwyddon*, the *theomacha* is horned (*cornuta*) – perhaps a simple scribal mistranscription of *canuta* ('grey-haired'), or alternatively a more telling indication of beliefs about therianthropic forest-dwelling godlings.[64]

Anglo-Saxon scholars had the same access to Isidore's *Etymologies* as learned Britons,[65] but they also seem to have had access to other Classical sources – some of them now lost, such as the Roman poet Lucan's *Orpheus*, quoted by Aldhelm and paraphrased in the *Liber monstrorum de diversis generibus* ('The book of monsters of various kinds'), probably composed in the kingdom of Wessex in the late seventh or early eighth century. The *Liber monstrorum*'s information on fauns comes from Lucan:

For the forest dwelling *Fauni* are so-called from their speech; from their head to their bellybutton they have the appearance of a man. But their heads, with curved horns on their noses, give them away and their lower part, consisting of their feet and legs, is formed in the shape of a stag. And the poet Lucan

---

[63] Thomas, 'The Celtic Wild Man Tradition', pp. 27–42.
[64] Marzella, '*Hirsuta et cornuta*', p. 228.
[65] Ryan, 'Isidore amongst the Islands', pp. 438–50.

sang that these same creatures, with innumerable other types of beasts, were led by song to the lyre of Orpheus, according to the opinions of the Greeks.[66]

One possible source for the surviving manuscript of Lucan's *Orpheus* used by Aldhelm and the author of the *Liber monstrorum* was the library of Glastonbury Abbey in Somerset, an abbey with both post-Roman traditions and strong links to Ireland which was the source of the manuscript tradition of Isidore's *Etymologies* in England.[67]

Where Aristotle observed that anyone without the need for human society 'must be either a beast or a god',[68] British tradition may have elided the bestial and the divine. Whether this can be interpreted as a legacy of ancient veneration of therianthropic beings or 'shamanic' practices in which people 'became' animals is impossible to know, but it is just as likely that the idea was inspired by the Bible. The madness of Nebuchadnezzar in Daniel 4:31–37 sees the king 'driven from men, and [he] did eat grass as oxen, and his body was wet with the dew of heaven, till his hairs were grown like eagles' feathers, and his nails like birds' claws'. The purpose of the king's transformation into a wild man is illumination, however, and on his return to sanity Nebuchadnezzar comes to knowledge of God, and Nebuchadnezzar's royal splendour is greater than before.

---

[66] *Liber monstrorum* 1.5, quoted in Pollard, '"Lucan" and "Aethicus Ister"', p. 9: *Fauni enim siluicolae, qui sicut a fando nuncupati sunt; a capite usque ad umbilicum hominis speciem habent; capita autem curuata naribus cornua dissimulant et inferior pars duorum pedum et femorum in caprarum forma depingitur. Quos poeta Lucanus, secundum opinionem Graecorum, ad Orphei liram, cum innumerosis ferarum generibus, cantu deductos cecinit.*

[67] Herren, 'Transmission and Reception', p. 90.

[68] Aristotle, *Politics* 1 (1253a 27–29).

The 'man of the woods' was therefore an ambivalent figure, cursed with madness but also rewarded with wisdom. An example of a positive portrayal of a faun in Christian iconography can be found on the tympanum of St Paul-de-Varax in Burgundy, where St Anthony encounters a faun accompanied by the inscription 'the abbot was seeking Paul and the faun taught' (*abbas querebat Paulum faunusque docebat*). This image was interpreted by Kirk Ambrose as evidence of Christian admiration for the almost-human.[69]

The depth of influence of patristic commentary on the roots of Irish folklore has been emphasised by Jacopo Bisagni and Angana Moitra. Bisagni argues that the ultimate origin of the Irish word *lupracán* ('leprechaun') was the Roman Luperci, the young men who dressed in animal skins in February and ran in the Lupercalia. Patristic tradition from Augustine onwards associated the Luperci with actual transformation from men into wolves, by passing through water, which was further developed in early Irish texts of *computus* (commentaries on the church calendar) into the idea that the Luperci represented an actual race of monsters. Owing to the importance of water to the transformation of the Luperci, the *lupracáin* became water-sprites and, later, the leprechauns of modern Irish folklore.[70] Similarly, Angana Moitra has argued that the figure of Midir in Irish legend derived in part from Dis/Pluto, the Roman god of the underworld, via Classical influence on Irish learning.[71] If Bisagni's and Moitra's analyses of Irish legend are correct, then the case for investigating

---

[69] Ambrose, *The Marvellous and the Monstrous*, pp. 34–37.
[70] Bisagni, '*Leprechaun*', pp. 78–83.
[71] Moitra, 'From Graeco-Roman Underworld to the Celtic Otherworld', pp. 93–104.

Classical-patristic origins for folkloric beings in both Britain and Ireland before reaching any conclusions about pre-Christian or prehistoric origins is a strong one.

While Old English sometimes received loanwords from Latin, there was also a strong tendency to coin new Old English terms glossing the perceived meaning of the Latin term. Ælfric of Eynsham's tenth-century glossary gives *unfæle men* ('evil men'), *wudewasan* ('woodwoses') and *unfæle wihtu* ('evil people') as glosses of *satiri, vel fauni, vel sehni* (sic. for *sileni*), *vel fauni ficarii*.[72] While *unfæle men/wihtu* can be set aside as euphemisms, the Old English word *wuduwasa* directly translates *homo silvestris*, and in later portrayals of woodwoses in medieval art they are both *pilosi* (hairy from head to toe) and apparently behave like incubi (portrayed as pursuing women). When John Wycliffe came to translate Isaiah 13:21 in the 1380s he gave *wodewoosis* for *pilosi*,[73] and the incident of the 'wild man of Orford', recounted by Ralph of Coggeshall (and discussed in Chapter 5 below) is evidence that woodwoses were a potential experiential reality for medieval English people as well as a mythological, heraldic or decorative conceit.[74]

Furthermore, Anglo-Saxon commentators glossed the Old English word *mære* with *incuba, satyrus* and *pilosus*, a puzzling juxtaposition of feminine terms with the distinctly masculine *satyrus* and *pilosus*. Alaric Hall has argued that Isidore and Jerome's elision of incubi, satyrs and *pilosi* provides an explanation for the gloss, since a *mære* was a female spirit of nightmare essentially equivalent to

---

[72] Wright, *Volume of Vocabularies*, p. 17.
[73] Sayers, 'Middle English *wodewose*', p. 12.
[74] Ralph of Coggeshall, *Chronicon*, pp. 117–18.

an *incuba* or *succuba*, female demons linked to the Classical *lamiae* or *empousai*, who feed on men while enticing them with sex.[75] The glossing of *mære* with *satyrus* and *pilosus* is evidence of the extent of the strength of the identification of incubi, satyrs, fauns and *pilosi*, which could even cross gender boundaries.[76] Caroline Batten goes somewhat further, however, to argue that a pre-existing Anglo-Saxon concept of a sexually predatory supernatural female being was so strong that *incubus* always became *incuba* in Old English glosses, and the Latin words *satyrus* and *pilosus* acquired feminine meanings.[77] For Batten, the *mære* is essentially unstable as to gender, 'the female form of a masculine sexual assailant'.[78]

Bede asserted that sexually predatory supernatural beings appeared in both male and female form in his commentary on St Luke's Gospel: 'Whether appearing to men in female form, or to women in male dress (which demons the Gauls call Dusii), by an unspeakable miracle incorporeal spirits contrive to seek and desire to sleep with a human body'.[79] Bede went on to recount the deliverance of a nun molested by an incubus, whose touch resulted in ulcers on her body; a belief in health problems resulting from demonic touch seems to have been a peculiarly English preoccupation.[80] Yet Bede's use of the term *Dusii* is unilluminating,

---

[75] Egeler, 'A Note on the Dedication *lamiis tribus*', p. 16.
[76] Hall, 'The Evidence for Maran', pp. 301–8.
[77] Batten, 'Dark Riders', p. 357. [78] Batten, 'Dark Riders', p. 359.
[79] Bede, *In Lucae evangelium expositio* (PL 92.438B): *quando vel viris in specie feminea, vel in virili habitu feminis apparentes, quos daemones Galli Dusios vocant, infando miraculo spiritus incorporei corporis humani concubitum petere se ac patrare confingunt.*
[80] Raiswell and Dendle, 'Demon Possession', pp. 741–72.

representing only deference to the authority of Augustine. We have no indication of what Old English name Bede might have used for an incuba/incubus, but *mære* and *wuduwasa* are possibilities. A single eleventh-century Old English charm survives that appears to be intended against (or for) people who sleep with a devil.[81] If the woodwose was indeed the male insular inheritor of the characteristics of the *pilosi*, who stand in the Vulgate for the whole panoply of male Classical rustic therianthropic godlings (fauns, satyrs, incubi, Sileni, Silvani, Panitae and so on) then it is conceivable that the idea of the woodwose hovers behind some Anglo-Saxon accounts of incubi.

While much of the learned knowledge of fauns and *pilosi* in medieval Britain seems to have been transmitted via Jerome and Isidore (and, in Aldhelm's case, via Lucan), there was also a parallel tradition of commentary on satyrs (and, by implication, fauns) as *naturalia* – phenomena of the natural world, rather than godlings or supernatural beings. According to the second-century *Physiologus*, whose text formed the basis of most medieval bestiaries,[82] satyrs were non-supernatural monsters living in Ethiopia. Since the *Physiologus* omitted to mention that satyrs had hooves, satyrs in bestiaries had horns and tails (and sometimes only tails), but were often without hooves (Plate 12).[83] This may go some way towards explaining why the woodwose of medieval art differs

---

[81] Hutton, *Queens of Wild*, p. 78.
[82] Gorla, 'Some Remarks', pp. 145–67.
[83] See British Library, MS Royal 12 C XIX, fol. 15v; Aberdeen University Library MS 24, fol. 13r (the Aberdeen Bestiary); Morgan Library MS M.81, fol. 20v (the Worksop Bestiary). For hooved satyrs see British Library, MS Harley 3244, fol. 41v.

so markedly from the fauns and satyrs of the Classical world. The medieval woodwose is generally without either hooves or horns and is usually a man completely covered in hair, bearing a club. However, depictions of woodwoses with hooves can be seen on the church fonts at Waldringfield and Nacton in Suffolk, serving as a reminder of the ultimate origin of woodwoses as fauns (Plate 13).[84]

Elves

Since 'elf' emerged as the standard Middle English word for a fairy (until the adoption of French *fée* in the late Middle Ages), the idea that the Anglo-Saxon *ylfen* were the ancestors of later fairies is understandably attractive. However, the evidence regarding the function and place of elves in Anglo-Saxon society remains somewhat obscure, in spite of exhaustive analysis by Alaric Hall. Anglo-Saxon elves were human-like, otherworldly, but not monstrous, and presented a risk to humans through their practice of a kind of magic known as *ælfsiden*. Elves also embodied a specific beauty – *ælfscyne* – which, in spite of the fact that elves were usually conceptualised as male, was of a seductive feminine kind.[85] Indeed, the word *ælf* itself may refer to physical appearance, since its Proto-Germanic antecedent could well be cognate with Latin *albus* ('white'), perhaps with the original meaning of 'white/shining ones'.[86]

---

[84] Ellis, 'The Wodewose', pp. 287–93; Simon Knott, pers. comm., 8 November 2021.
[85] Hall, *Elves*, pp. 173–75. [86] Hall, *Elves*, pp. 54–56.

Medieval elves lived under the earth or in wild places, formed an alternative society with a king or queen, dwelt in a specific otherworldly realm and were sometimes diminutive in stature or monstrous in appearance. We are lacking the evidence that Anglo-Saxon elves had these characteristics – although absence of evidence is not, of course, evidence of absence.[87] I shall argue in Chapter 5 below that the medieval elves (who were eventually renamed fairies) were composite beings who acquired the characteristics of a broad range of British and Anglo-Saxon early medieval supernatural beings, but it remains the case that Anglo-Saxon elf-lore was probably more extensive than the surviving evidence suggests, especially if it was comparable to the more richly evidenced Norse elf-lore. However, separating the original elf-lore of the Anglo-Saxons from elements that may have been introduced by Norse settlers in the ninth century is difficult, and by the end of the Anglo-Saxon era it is likely that elf-lore in some regions was already a composite of Anglo-Saxon and Norse belief. A trace of this can be found in the persistence of 'elf' as the name for a fairy into the late Middle Ages in northern and eastern England.[88]

Like the *aos sí* of Ireland and Scotland, the word *ælf* often defied translation and glossing in Anglo-Saxon England – an indication, in and of itself, that the concept of *ælf* did not correspond in any straightforward way to readily available Classical or biblical analogues. Elves were never identified with fauns, presumably because they lacked any of the fauns' connotations of monstrous

---

[87] Hutton, *Queens of the Wild*, pp. 74–75.
[88] Harte, 'Fairy Barrows', p. 68.

therianthropy, although elves were sometimes identified as demons. As we have seen, elves joined other monstrous beings in *Beowulf* as the offspring of the sin of Cain, while the Mercian Royal Prayerbook (*c.* 800) featured an exorcism of *satanae diabulus ælfae* ('devil of Satan, of an *elf*').[89] However, unlike some of its Germanic cognates in other cultures, the Old English word *ælf* never became a functional synonym for a demon (even if elves were sometimes seen as demonic), and elves thus never underwent an entirely successful 'pejoration'.[90]

Hall has emphasised the evolution and transformation of belief in elves over time, arguing that the concept of female elves probably came late, in the eleventh century. Unlike the untranslatable male elves, female elves were glossed in Latin with *nympha* and various related Latin words.[91] However, in spite of the later ascendancy of the word 'elf' in Middle English, elves were just one among many classes of folkloric beings in early medieval England, and their greatest achievement may well have been to pass on their name as a generic term for a human-like supernatural being. The extent to which the elves of the later Middle Ages resembled the elves of Anglo-Saxon belief remains an open question, and the process by which 'elf' became the generic term for fairies in much of medieval England until the late fourteenth century, rather than some other term, remains obscure. While Norse cultural influence in the Danelaw is one possible explanation, it must count as one of the most significant unanswered questions in the development of Britain's godlings.

[89] Hall, *Elves*, pp. 71–72. [90] Hall, *Elves*, p. 73.
[91] Hall, *Elves*, pp. 78–83.

Female Godlings in Early Medieval Britain

As we have seen in Chapter 1, there is evidence that belief in frightening and warlike female godlings was current among Britons from as early as the seventh century, perhaps signified by the Welsh word *gwyddon* and associated with the number nine (three times three).[92] And as we have seen in Chapter 2, the cults of the Parcae and Deae Matres were present in Roman Britain. The Parcae are the subject of another part of the section in Isidore's *Etymologies* dealing with godlings, where Isidore again partially paraphrases Varro:[93]

And [the pagans] say that Fate [*Fatum*] is whatever the gods say, or whatever Jupiter says. Therefore the name *fatum* is from 'saying' (*fari*, 3rd person *fatur*), that is, from speaking. Except for the fact that this word is now usually understood in another context, toward which I do not wish to incline people's hearts (*Quod nisi hoc nomen iam in alia re soleret intellegi, quo corda hominum nolumus inclinare*), we can with reason speak of 'fate' as from 'saying' ... Pagans imagine that there are three Fates – with the distaff, with the spindle, and with fingers spinning a thread from the wool – on account of the three tenses ... They were called *Parcae* (*Parca*) κατ' ἀντίφρασιν ('by opposition of sense') because they scarcely spare (*parcere*) anyone. People claimed there were three: one who would lay the initial warp of a person's life; the second, who would weave it; and the third, who would cut it short ...[94]

Isidore's reluctance to engage with the understanding of *fatum* in his own time is suggestive; was Isidore reluctant to discuss folkloric understandings of the Fates

---

[92] Marzella, '*Hirsuta et cornuta*', p. 227.
[93] Varro, *De lingua Latina* 6.52.   [94] Isidore, *Etymologiae* 8.11.90–93.

that would eventually evolve into fairy lore? Perhaps in an effort to dissuade people from trying to placate the Parcae, Isidore argues that their name (based on his etymology derived from *parcere*) is a euphemistic one, because in reality the Fates spare no-one.[95] Here, perhaps, is a hint of a new understanding of the Parcae and Deae Matres as exclusively threatening beings rather than deities of fortune.

British beliefs about frightening supernatural female beings may have survived from the Roman period (as we have seen, at least one altar was set up to *lamiae*), but they can also be explained in terms of imported Germanic beliefs, the influence of authors such as Isidore, and even the influence of Frankish penitentials which, uncritically copied, brought Frankish ideas of popular religion into Britain in the Christian era. Old English authors were certainly aware of the Parcae, albeit apparently from Classical literary sources. Aldhelm's Latin riddles displayed the extent of his Classical learning, including a riddle on the spindle that referenced the Parcae:

I was born in the forest, green on a leafy bough, but fortune changed my condition in due course, since I move my rounded shape twirling through the smooth-spun thread; from this is made the royal covering of a robe. No hero (anywhere) is girded by a belt as long as mine [i.e. the distaff]. They say that the Parcae decree the fates of men through me.[96]

---

[95] Isidore, *Etymologiae* 8.11.100.
[96] Lapidge and Rosier, *Aldhelm*, p. 79: *In saltu nascor ramosa fronde virescens,/Sed fortuna meum mutaverunt ordine fatum,/Dum verbo per collum teretem vertigine molam:/Ex quo conficitur regalis stragula pepli./ Tam longa nullus zona praecingitur heros./Per me fata virum dicunt decernere Parcas;/Frigora dura viros sternant, ni forte resistam.*

The Old English word for fate was *wyrd*, yet the personification of *wyrd* as the three 'weird sisters' is only attested in the later Middle Ages in lowland Scotland, and may have been influenced by the Norse tradition of the Norns.[97] However, the Anglo-Saxons had an established literary tradition of conceptualising non-personified fates in triplicity: the 'three fates' of illness, old age and military conflict which could determine an individual's destiny.[98] Furthermore, Herbert Merritt argued that the Old English word used to gloss the Latin Parcae, *burgrunan*, may have originated as an attempt to express Isidore's etymology of the Parcae from *parcere*. The *burg-* element, on this view, derives from Old English *beorgan*, 'to spare'.[99] If this is correct, then it is evidence that the Parcae did, indeed, continue to have significance in early medieval Britain – even if that significance probably derived from their role in Isidore's *Etymologies*. It is conceivable that the Parcae underwent 're-personification' in Anglo-Saxon England, aided by the existence of similar supernatural women such as *hægtessan* in Germanic culture, and that the *burgrunan* were godlings fashioned at need in Christian England in order to provide an Anglo-Saxon equivalent to the Parcae.

A hint that something like this may have occurred can be found in a story from Winchester recounted by the French monk Lantfred in the tenth or eleventh century. According to Lantfred, early in July 971 (a few days before the translation of St Swithun from his grave to the Old Minster on 15 July) an unnamed man approached

---

[97] Shamas, 'We Three', p. 17.
[98] Anderson, *Folk Taxonomies*, pp. 310–11.
[99] Merritt, 'Conceivable Clues', pp. 197–98.

the River Itchen at noon close to the walls of Winchester in order to check on his mules. The man fell asleep and, when he awoke and began on his way he noticed two women on the riverbank:

[He] saw not far in front of him two female creatures – not decked out in any finery nor covered up with any clothing, but rather naked to their foul skin and terrifying with their swarthy hair, blackened with faces like Tisiphone and armed with hellish wickedness and poison – who were sitting on the bank of the river, as if they were two of the three Furies.

The 'undressed Ethiopians' demanded to speak to the man but he ran away. The women closely pursued him, while threatening:

'Why, fool, do you flee? Where, doomed man, are you going? You shall not, as you imagine, escape from us unscathed after having scorned our conversation. In no way shall you evade the danger of our savagery. Although you dismiss our commands, swift flight shall not liberate you. You shall on no account get away from here unharmed, given that you have intentionally disregarded the purport of our disquisition'.

The man prayed in desperation to God as they drew close to the city, but just as he thought he was getting away from the two 'raven-like females', a third made her appearance:

[A] third one of immense height approached who stood like a tower over the others, and who moreover was different from the others in being of a shining white colour and being decently clad in snowy-white garments. She, however, relying on deception, was hiding behind a hill next to the road along which the man was intending to go, so that she might capture him if he escaped unharmed from the dark ones.

The third woman chastised her dark-skinned sisters for chasing noisily after the man, and instead lay in wait for him on the crest of the hill: 'Remaining stationary on the crest of the aforesaid hill, she folded over the sleeve of her tunic three times into a plait; lifting it up with a mighty commotion and striving to strike him with the total effort of her strength'. God protected the man from her strike, but the man's side was nevertheless struck by the wind from the woman's sleeve. The three women threw themselves into the Itchen, but the man was paralysed by the blast from the supernatural garment.[100]

Michael Lapidge has identified the three women of Lantfred's account as *hægtessan*, the term by which *Furiae* are often glossed in Anglo-Saxon texts.[101] Furthermore, one Old English spell against 'sudden stitch' (which may be the ailment that afflicts the man in his side) promises to turn back the attacks of *hægtessan*.[102] On the other hand, Lantfred does not explicitly identify the women as Furies (they are said to be *like* Furies), and Francesco Marzella has noted that Old English sources often linked unfamiliar supernatural beings with familiar characters from Classical mythology in order to better explain them to learned readers.[103] The role played by a knotted garment in the story is highly suggestive of a link with the Parcae (or, in Old English terms, the *burgrunan*), especially since the supernatural women appear to represent and personify inexorable fate; there is, after all, no reason for them to pursue and attack the unfortunate man

---

[100] Lapidge, *Cult of St Swithun*, pp. 275–77.
[101] Lapidge, *Cult of St Swithun*, p. 275 n.118.
[102] Niles, 'Pagan Survivals and Popular Belief', p. 130.
[103] Marzella, '*Hirsuta et cornuta*', p. 225 n.18.

apart from their role as the enforcers of the fates of men. Furthermore, while two of the women are portrayed as hideous, the third does not seem to be ugly. It is possible that the *burgrunan* and *hægtessan* have become conflated in this story, as a result of the demonisation of both sets of beings; although the beautiful appearance of the third supernatural woman suggests that the process of demonisation was by no means complete.

The association between the Parcae and witchcraft – specifically acts involving tying and binding – was discussed in Chapter 2 above. In Old English the association between *hægtessan* and witchcraft is borne out not only by the meaning of the modern English descendant of the word, 'hag'; as we have seen, *hægtessan* were also associated with sudden stitch, the sort of unexplained illness and misfortune often blamed on witches in pre-modern societies. Furthermore, in the Leiden Glossary the Old English *hægtisse* seems to have become confused with **Hecatissa*, an otherwise unattested Latin neologism that seems to mean 'associated with Hecate'.[104] This is strongly suggestive of a false etymology for *hægtisse* current among learned Anglo-Saxon scholars which linked the term to the name of the Greek goddess of witchcraft. The cultural association between *hægtessan* and witchcraft further strengthens the idea that the *hægtessan*/Furies were conflated with the *burgrunan*/Parcae, since it was the Parcae who were linked above all to the tying and untying of destinies.

The curious term *Modraniht* ('night of the mothers') used by Bede for the night of 25 December in pagan England has been advanced as possible evidence for the

---

[104] Herren, 'Transmission and Reception', p. 99.

survival of the cult of the Deae Matres in early England, which was still remembered by Bede in the eighth century.[105] However, Bede himself believed that the name stemmed from rituals performed by human mothers on that night. Bede may well have been wrong, but if he was it remains unclear whether the divine mothers honoured on 25 December by the pagan Anglo-Saxons were goddesses adopted from Roman Britain (who were themselves probable Germanic imports in the Roman era), or Germanic goddesses brought to England in the Anglo-Saxon era. There is not much other evidence for Anglo-Saxon veneration of divine mothers, but there is also not much evidence for Anglo-Saxon pre-Christian religion *tout court*.

Ronald Hutton has compared Lantfred's story of the Furies/Parcae with Byrhtferth of Ramsey's account of the foundation of Evesham Abbey in his late tenth-century *Life of St Egwin*, which likewise features three mysterious supernatural women – but this time Christianised rather than demonised.[106] The events described by Byrhtferth supposedly took place in 701, when a swineherd named Eof (the source of the name *Eofeshamme*) in the service of St Egwin, bishop of Worcester, lost a piglet and went looking for it in dense woodland:

He saw miraculously, as is said, a certain virgin standing with two others singing, and holding a most beautiful book in her hand. But the one who stood in the middle was so beautiful, as

---

[105] Parker, *Winters in the World*, p. 69; Meaney, 'Bede and Anglo-Saxon Paganism', pp. 1–29.
[106] Hutton, 'Making of the Early Modern British Fairy Tradition', p. 1140.

if her beauty alone excelled all the other virgins. Indeed, she was also so much more beautiful than that radiance of the sphere of the sun, more splendid than lilies, ruddier than roses – so that on account of her beauty he did not dare look, but having called back the piglet he returned home.[107]

The swineherd went to Egwin, fell at the bishop's feet and told Egwin of his vision. The bishop, impressed by the swineherd's humility and apparent truthfulness, went himself to witness the same thing (Byrhtferth has Egwin speak in the first person):

Arriving in the morning, and with the dawn light of the following day shining, I rose quickly and with bare feet I proceeded with three companions to the place of which Eof had spoken to me. And since I was close at hand, I perceived at a distance how far off it stood, that I might come to know more surely the thing revealed to the servant, and related to me by him. Having seen, I returned concerned to the place, quietly contemplating with me the sacred psalms, while earnestly imploring the holy Mother of God, that those who were spoken of might deign to show themselves to me. I prostrated myself there in prayer, while I prayed for a long time with groans, that she would take pity on my many sins and show me the thing revealed. But rising quietly from prayer, behold close to where I stood appeared three holy virgins, one of whom was more sublime than the others, having a cross and book in her hand, whiter than the splendour of snow, and more graceful than the flower

---

[107] British Library, Cotton MS Nero E 1, fol. 28v: *Vidit quod dici miraculose quandam virginem stantem cum aliis duabus psallentem, et librum in manu perpulchrum tenentem. Erat autem tam speciosa quae in meditullio stabat, uti solum species excelleret omnis omnium virginum. Verum etiam ut ipsi in summae pulchrior erat quam iubar solaris globi, splendidior liliis, rubicundior rosis; quam per pulchritudine non audebat respicere, sed vocata porcella domi redit.*

of the rose. Having seen these things, I considered quietly that it could have been the holy perpetual Mary the Mother of God whom I saw. Then she, having lifted up her hand, signed me with the blessing of the holy cross, and vanished.[108]

Alaric Hall has shown that the use of the Old English word *ælfscyne* reveals that elves were associated with exceptional female beauty in Anglo-Saxon England,[109] and the implication of Egwin's admission that he 'considered quietly that it could have been the holy perpetual Mary the Mother of God whom I saw' is that it was not immediately obvious to the bishop that he was experiencing a vision of the Virgin Mary. It is possible, therefore, that Egwin considered and dismissed the possibility that the women were folkloric beings – especially since they appeared in a wild place and in a group of three, like the Furies/Parcae in Lantfred's narrative of the miracles of St Swithun; Byrhtferth's narrative never makes clear who the other two women are, although later versions

---

[108] British Library, Cotton MS Nero E 1, fol. 29r: *Mane adveniente, et illuscente aurorae sequentis diei, surrexi concite et discalciatis pedibus, perrexi cum tribus sociis ad locum de quo mihi dixerat Eoves. Cumque comminus essem, percipiens eminus sistere quoadusque certius scirem rem servo demonstratam, et mihi ab eo relata. Revolui sollicitos visus hinc inde, mecum tacitus ruminans psalmos sacros, dum enixius obsecrans sanctamque eius genitricem, ut pandere mihi dignarentur quae dicta sunt. Prostravi me in orationibus ibique, diu dum oravi cum gemitibus, ut meis perplurimis delictis miseresceret et rem ostensam demonstraret. Surgens autem tacite ab oratione, ecce penes quo steti apparunt tres sacrae virgines, quae una erat sublimior ceteris, crucem habens et librum in manibus, niveo splendore candidior, et roseo flore venustior. His perspectis, cogitavi tacitus quod sancta Dei genitrix perpetua Maria potuisset esse quam cernebam. Tum illa elevata manu consignavit me benedictione sanctae crucis, et evanuit.* For a slightly variant version of the story (which makes Eof a shepherd rather than a swineherd) see D'Achery and Mabillon (eds.), *Acta Sanctorum*, p. 319
[109] Hall, *Elves*, pp. 88–94.

identify them as angels. On the other hand, Byrhtferth stresses the beauty of the book held by the most beautiful of the women, along with a cross, and has her perform a specifically Christian gesture by signing Egwin with the cross. A book was a specifically Christian object in early medieval England, and not one likely to have been associated with elves. On the other hand, in Roman art the Parcae are sometimes depicted with scrolls, such as on a third-century sarcophagus depicting the myth of Prometheus in Rome's Capitoline Museum, where Atropos/Morta sits reading a scroll.[110]

Yeates interpreted Eof's encounter as a meeting with the Dobunnic mother goddesses, and argued that it preserves evidence that the local genii of people groups had to be individually reimagined in Christian terms and incorporated into a Christian story as part of the process of Christianisation.[111] This rather fanciful interpretation rests on a number of problematic assumptions – not least the idea that the *Hwicce* of the eighth century were still worshipping Romano-British mother goddesses. All things considered, it is unlikely that the vision of Eof and Egwin was an encounter with non-Christian folkloric beings reinterpreted in a Christian form, not least because Byrhtferth was recording it nearly two centuries after the event. Hall notes that there is no evidence for a feminine form of the word *ælf* (*ælfen*) until the early eleventh century,[112] and it is possible that no concept of female elves existed in England until the late Anglo-Saxon period (just

---

[110] Van der Horst, 'Fatum, Tria Fata', p. 219.
[111] Yeates, *Tribe of Witches*, p. 156.
[112] Hall, *Elves*, p. 87.

as female elves do not make an appearance in medieval Norse literature). Neither in the eighth nor in the tenth century was someone likely to have perceived elves as Eof perceived the three women in the wood on the future site of Evesham Abbey, and Anglo-Saxon England had no tradition of encountering elves in threes.

The triplicity of the divine women is suggestive of a different order of being, perhaps the Parcae or Deae Matres who seem to have become the *burgrunan* of Anglo-Saxon England. Yeates has noted that Evesham lies historically in the Forest of Arden, a name that may be cognate with the Ardennes in France, where the goddess Arduinna was worshipped as a form of the goddess Diana and associated with a boar. Yeates therefore suggests that the vision of Eof may be linked to a dim memory of a mother goddess connected with pigs,[113] but this also seems a rather thin basis on which to make a connection with pre-Christian cults. There is no direct evidence of which goddess was worshipped in the Forest of Arden, and no evidence that she was worshipped in triple form.

On the other hand, visionary experiences of the Virgin Mary were not common in the western church in the eighth or tenth centuries; Byrhtferth may simply have been reaching for appropriate imagery and alighting almost inadvertently on pre-Christian ideas of nymphs and dryads in the absence of an agreed cultural iconography of Marian visions. Christian hagiographers inherited from the ancient world the narrative motif of an animal on the loose leading a founder to the site of a future structure or settlement; the wildness of woodland accentuated

[113] Yeates, *Tribe of Witches*, pp. 26–27.

the transition from wilderness to monastic settlement and cultivation. As Sarah Semple has noted, the 'liminal ruinous qualities [of wild places] and associations with perhaps exile, despair, and terror rendered them ideal locales at which to stage a narrative of spiritual battle and triumph'.[114]

Perhaps for the same reasons, wild animals were sometimes involved in foundation stories of this kind. The ninth-century Westphalian saint Meinulf, for example, built a church on the spot where his swineherd (again searching for a lost pig) saw deer strangely circling around a mysterious light.[115] Similarly, the Scottish king David I famously built Holyrood Abbey on the spot where he had a vision of the cross between the antlers of a hart in 1127.[116] It may be that Evesham's dedication to the Virgin Mary inspired Byrhtferth to have Eof and Egwin see Mary in the woods, but woodland visions in and of themselves were a hagiographical commonplace.

While Eof and Egwin's vision may be best understood as the literary device of a hagiographer, questions remain: why does the Virgin Mary appear with two companions, and who are these women? Angels did not appear in female form in the Middle Ages, even if they were sometimes represented with characteristics of feminine beauty,[117] and the other two figures seen by Eof and Egwin are unambiguously female. Unless

---

[114] Semple, *Perceptions of the Prehistoric*, p. 138.
[115] Surius, *De probatis sanctorum historiis*, vol. 5, p. 585.
[116] Anderson, *History of the Abbey and Palace of Holyrood*, pp. 4–5.
[117] Gorgievski, *Face to Face with Angels*, p. 113.

Byrhtferth considered it somehow unfitting for the Virgin to appear without attendants – which seems unlikely, given the absence of a tradition of female angels – the triplicity of the vision does seem to hark back, consciously or unconsciously, to pre-Christian triads of supernatural women.

Such a mixing of Christian and non-Christian elements can be found in a late twelfth-century life of Hereward the Wake, the English rebel against Norman rule. Recounting events that took place in 1070, the *Gesta Herewardi* tells how Hereward and his men became lost in the forest of Bromswold after plundering the abbey of Peterborough – an apparent punishment from St Peter, who had appeared to Hereward in a dream as an angry old man brandishing a key. Hereward's men escaped from the forest only when they followed a gigantic white wolf, and strange lights 'like those which are commonly called nymph-lights' (*velut illae quae vulgus appellant candela nympharum*) appeared on the soldiers' lances to light their way.[118] The wolf guided the men to the outskirts of Stamford before disappearing. The mention of *nymphae* in the story – even if only indirectly – suggests one possible interpretation of the white wolf as a fairy beast; certainly it is far from clear from the text that the wolf was sent by a relenting St Peter. Instead, the wolf may be intended to evoke English national identity by reminding the reader of the animal that rescued St Edmund's head from the clutches of the pagan Danes in the ninth century.[119]

---

[118] Hardy and Martin (eds.), *Gesta Herwardi*, vol. 1, p. 396.
[119] Young, *Peterborough Folklore*, p. 28.

Pygmy Otherworlders

In Isidore's *Etymologies* the existence of diminutive peoples in India called pygmies is discussed immediately after the *fauni ficarii*,[120] and learned individuals in early medieval Britain would have been well aware of foreign races of diminutive peoples from authors such as Pliny the Elder. The *coraniaid* ('dwarfs') who invade Britain in the medieval Welsh tale *Lludd and Llefelys* come from Asia, and seem to derive from the *naturalia* tradition of commentary on pygmies. However, the boundary between supernatural otherworlders and the monstrous denizens of unimaginably remote lands was a porous one in early medieval Britain and Ireland. Rachel Bromwich has suggested that the *coraniaid* may be equivalent to the Irish Tuatha Dé Danaan, the ancient invaders of the island who become the ancestors of the *sídhe*.[121] Since the Tuatha Dé are not of diminutive stature this seems unlikely, but an early medieval Irish gloss mentioned *lupracáin* (leprechauns) in a discussion of Indian pygmies.[122] The *lupracáin*, in contrast to the Tuatha Dé, were represented as diminutive beings; the term was even used to gloss Latin *nanus* ('dwarf').[123]

The diminutive size persistently (but not consistently) attributed to the fairies of medieval belief was often attributed by early folklorists to their demotion from a former status as deities, but this is by no means the only possible explanation of diminutive stature. The smallness of the fairies – and indeed their wild fluctuations in size – may

---

[120] Isidore, *Etymologiae* 11.3.26.
[121] Bromwich (ed.), *Trioedd Ynys Prydain*, p. 92.
[122] Bisagni, '*Leprechaun*', p. 66.   [123] Bisagni, '*Leprechaun*', p. 62.

simply render them other, uncanny and monstrous. Alternatively, the smallness of the fairies was inspired by the little hills and underground chambers they were supposed to inhabit; or the smallness of fairies was inspired by reports of pygmies in medieval writings on *naturalia*. One, all or none of these explanations may be true, but what is clear is that there is no one satisfactory or obvious explanation for the small size of medieval and early modern fairies.

In the Welsh tale, the diminutive *coraniaid* are in possession of magically acute hearing. Given that a fourteenth-century Welsh text glossed satyrs as *correit*, it is possible that the *coraniaid*'s Asian origin could have been inspired by geographical works that reported satyrs among the monsters at the edges of the world – and even that the *coraniaid*'s acute hearing was inspired by the satyrs' large goat-like ears. However, *Lludd and Llefelys* contains no physical description of what the *coraniaid* actually look like, so it is impossible to link them with fauns and satyrs. Scholars have long been puzzled as to why the invaders of *Lludd and Llefelys* are the *coraniaid* and not the Romans. However, we know that surviving Roman archaeology was interpreted in eighteenth- and nineteenth-century folklore as the work of dwarfs and fairies as well as giants, and it is possible that such traditions stretched into the more distant past. In Herefordshire and Worcestershire Roman coins found in the soil at sites like Kenchester were sometimes identified as 'fairy money' or 'pennies from heaven', and were believed to magically disappear.[124]

[124] Jones, 'Pucks and Lights', p. 37.

In 1879 William Hiley Bathurst noted that the temple complex at Lydney Park first excavated by his father in 1805 'was long known popularly by the name of Dwarfs' Hill, from the notion that the buildings were the work of fairies, always supposed to be a diminutive people'.[125] This name for the site could have been inspired by Lydney's hypocaust, since a hypocaust (with its miniature arches as stoke-holes) might give the impression of a dwelling constructed by tiny people (Plate 14). Furthermore, some votive offerings at Roman shrines and temples were miniature models, such as the miniature spears recovered from shrines at Neighbridge, Lydney and Uley in Gloucestershire and Woodeaton in Oxfordshire,[126] and it is possible to imagine such objects (like prehistoric arrowheads and spearheads) being misidentified as evidence of the former existence of diminutive peoples. If the *coraniaid* do represent a dim folkloric memory of the Romans, the folkloric interpretation of Roman archaeological remains such as hypocausts and miniature votive offerings might explain why the Romans are imagined as pygmies in this medieval Welsh tale. If the *coraniaid* are the Romans, however, they have little to do with fairy lore.

The pygmy king described by Walter Map (1130–c. 1210) in the story of King Herla in Map's *De nugis curialium* ('On trifles of courtiers') is clearly and unambiguously a faun, suggesting that there was conflation between pygmies and fauns/satyrs in some traditions:

---

[125] Hiley Bathurst, *Roman Antiquities*, p. 3.
[126] Yeates, *Tribe of Witches*, p. 19; Aldhouse-Green, *Sacred Britannia*, pp. 130–31, 136.

a pygmy in respect of his low stature, not above that of a monkey ... and might be described in the same terms as Pan; his visage was fiery red, his head huge; he had a long red beard reaching to his chest, which was gaily attired in a spotted fawn's skin: his belly was hairy and his legs declined into goats' hoofs.[127]

On the other hand, the pygmies encountered by the young Eliodorus on a riverbank in Gerald of Wales' *Journey through Wales* are described as *homunculi* or *pygmaei* but are not otherwise identified as monstrous,[128] suggesting that more than one tradition existed of imagining pygmies. For Gerald, pygmies were simply people of diminutive stature.

In addition to these Latin sources, evidence for the reception of the learned tradition of commentary on monstrous *naturalia* in Welsh language and culture can be found in a fourteenth-century Welsh translation of the *Elucidarium* of Honorius of Autun, in the *Book of the Anchorite of Llanddewibrefi* (1346). The text includes a section from a supposed letter of Prester John describing the strange creatures living in his kingdom, including *fauni* and *satiri*,[129] rendered into Middle Welsh as *choriuti* and *correit*.[130] While *choriuti* may be an attempt to render Kouretes or Korybantes (the dancing attendants of Cybele who were conflated with the satyrs by Strabo),[131]

---

[127] Map, *De nugis* 1.11: *qui pigmeus videbatur modicitate stature, que non excedebat simiam ... vir qualis describi posset Pan, ardenti facie, capite maximo, barba rubente prolixa pectus contingente, nebride preclarum stellata, cui venter hispidus et crura pedes in caprinos degenerabant.*
[128] Gerald of Wales, *Opera*, vol. 6, pp. 75–76.
[129] Morris-Jones and Rhys (eds.), *Elucidarium*, p. 239.
[130] Jones and Rhys (eds.), *Elucidarium*, p. 165.
[131] Edmonds, *Redefining Ancient Orphism*, p. 364.

correit corresponds with modern Welsh *cor*, which derives from Proto-Celtic **korso-* or even from Latin *curtus* ('short', but with an additional sense of 'mutilated' or 'deformed').[132] Although it is no longer applied to a class of supernatural being in Welsh, in Breton *korriganez* (Cornish *korrigan*) is one of the two main terms used for fairies (along with *boudig*, which is simply a diminutive of *boud* ('being'), meaning 'little being').[133] All of this suggests that the learned tradition of commentary on satyrs, fauns and pygmies interacted with popular folklore in Brittonic-speaking regions, not only in the creation of stories like those of Eliodorus and Herla but also in the naming of folkloric beings.

The Britons were not alone in their belief in diminutive supernatural beings. Belief in dwarfs seems to have been characteristic of Germanic belief, although here (as elsewhere) Norse culture supplies the richest evidence. In Norse mythology, the dwarfs were 'associated with the dead, with battle, with wisdom, with craftsmanship, with the supernatural, and even to some extent with the elves'.[134] Among the few mentions of dwarfs in Old English sources are references in charms that treat dwarfs as a source of threat and disease. Scholars remain divided on the meaning of the enigmatic charm *wið dweorh* ('against a dwarf'), but the discovery of a possible holed lead amulet near Fakenham, Norfolk, in 2015 bearing the runic inscription 'the dwarf is dead' (which can be dated tentatively to the mid-eighth century) may be a

---

[132] *GPC*, s.v. 'cor', accessed 15 October 2021.
[133] MacKillop, *Dictionary of Celtic Mythology*, pp. 50, 289.
[134] Lindow, *Norse Mythology*, p. 100.

survival of countermagical measures against these entities (Plate 15).[135] While Anglo-Saxon belief in dwarfs has generally been compared with Norse analogues, a potential link with the British tradition of *coraniaid* and the later Welsh identification of satyrs with dwarf-like beings should not be ruled out. On the other hand, Anglo-Saxon dwarfs tend to appear in a medical context (in contrast to the pygmy peoples of Welsh tradition), and interpretation is complicated by the fact that *dweorh* was an Old English term for a spider, making it conceivable that some of these charms were directed against spiders.[136]

Work of Giants

Medieval knowledge of Roman Britain was limited, and interwoven with legend. Yet the physical remains of the Roman province were available to medieval observers as they are to us. Geoffrey of Monmouth's assertion that King Bladud, the legendary founder of Bath, dedicated the sacred spring to Minerva may derive from inscriptions recording the goddess's name in the city's Roman ruins; how else, except by a lucky guess, could Geoffrey have discerned the identity of Bath's patron deity?[137] The idea that any folkloric tradition linking Bath with Minerva survived in oral tradition to the twelfth century is fantastically unlikely. However, the likelihood that

---

[135] Arthur, '*Charms*', *Liturgies and Secret Rites*, pp. 84–86; Hines, 'Practical Runic Literacy', pp. 36–40; NMS-63179C, Portable Antiquities Scheme, finds.org.uk/database/artefacts/record/id/751600, accessed 19 April 2022.
[136] Gay, 'Anglo-Saxon Metrical Charm 3', pp. 174–77.
[137] Geoffrey of Monmouth (trans. Wright), *Historia Regum*, p. 41.

Geoffrey was already relying on Roman epigraphy as evidence for Bath's history is a reminder that antiquarian information of a rudimentary nature already existed in medieval Britain.

The most persistent early medieval idea about the origins of Britain's Roman remains, however, was that they were the work of giants. The Old English word *gigant* (from *gigas*) was even borrowed from Latin, along with *orc* (from *orcus*), a word for a monster. Old English already had a number of non-Latin words for gigantic supernatural beings such as *eóten*, *ent* and *þyrs*.[138] *Gigant* was, in all likelihood, a borrowing from the Vulgate where Genesis 6 describes the race of giants that lived before the Flood, and denoted these beings specifically because they differed from an *eóten*, *ent* or *þyrs*. Orcus, on the other hand, was originally the name of a god, sometimes conceptualised as a distinct god and sometimes as a Roman equivalent to Pluto or Hades. According to Varro, Orcus was simply another manifestation of Jupiter 'in his lowest capacity, which is joined to the earth' (*infimus, qui est coniunctus terrae*), and one and the same as Dis Pater: a kind of chthonic Jupiter, in other words. However, Varro may have confused an archaic name for Jupiter, *Diespiter*, with *Dis Pater*.[139] Orcus was also a synonym for the realm of hell, both before and after Christianisation, and this seems a more likely origin for the Anglo-Saxon figure.[140] The word *orc* did not pass into medieval or modern English, although its Italian and French cognates *orco* and *ogre* were borrowed back

---

[138] Hall, *Elves*, p. 73.   [139] Varro, *De lingua Latina* 5.66.
[140] Bernstein, *Formation of Hell*, p. 63.

into English in the sixteenth and eighteenth centuries.[141] The original word *orc* then re-entered modern English via the fiction of J. R. R. Tolkien.

While the Anglo-Saxons clearly had their own traditions of chthonic monsters, their need to borrow words from Latin suggests that existing vocabulary was insufficient to describe their folklore of gigantic beings. There is a good deal of evidence that such folklore was linked with Roman remains. When the Anglo-Saxon author of *The Ruin* described the crumbling remains of the sacred spring and baths of Sulis as *enta geweorc* ('the work of giants'), he or she was using a standard literary phrase that recurs throughout Old English literature, but which may speak to an older folkloric trope.[142] The author of *The Ruin* understood that the monumental remains of the Roman city of Bath had been built by human beings, but later folklore suggests that this was not the perception of all ordinary people. In twentieth-century Sussex, local folklore spoke of 'one of the Romans' buried in a golden coffin beneath the Long Man of Wilmington, with the implication that the Long Man was somehow a representation of a Roman giant.[143]

Semple has argued that whereas dragons were associated with barrows in Anglo-Saxon England and fens with the monstrous *þyrs*, *enta* (giants) were repeatedly associated with *ceastra* (urban settlements) and with worked stones and other objects.[144] In the sixteenth century William Camden

---

[141] *OED*, s.vv. 'ogre, *n.*', 'orc, *n.2*'.
[142] Anderson, *Folk Taxonomies*, pp. 274–75.
[143] Grinsell, *Folklore of Prehistoric Sites*, p. 127.
[144] Semple, *Perceptions of the Prehistoric*, pp. 179–80.

recorded that at Silchester (the site of the Roman town of Calleva Atrebatum) 'are commonly dug up British tiles, and great plenty of Roman Coins, which they call Onion-pennies, from one Onion whom they foolishly fancy to have been a Giant, and an inhabitant of this city'. A portion of the ruins then still standing at Silchester was known as 'Onion's Hole', although curiously Camden found that 'Onion's Hole' was more suitable for a dwarf than a giant: 'For by the rubbish and ruins the earth is grown so high, that I could scarce thrust my self through a passage which they call *Onion's hole*, tho' I stoop'd very low'.[145] While Thomas Hearne, visiting Silchester in 1714, thought that 'Onion' represented a misreading of legends on coins of the emperor Constantine,[146] John Alfred Kempe traced the name to an alternative name for Silchester in the Ravenna Cosmography, Ard-onion, which he interpreted as Ardal Einion, 'the region of Einion'.[147]

'Onion' was in fact the obscure English hero Unwen, who (as 'Onewyn') appears as one of the 'strong champions' (*athlete fortissimi*) mentioned in the fourteenth-century *Fasciculus morum* (a preachers' handbook) as an inhabitant of *elvenlond*.[148] Unwen first appears in the Old English poem *Widsith*, where he is said to be the son of Eastgota (Ostrogotha), the eponymous ancestor of the Ostrogoths. A document known as the *Gesta Unwini* ('The Deeds of Unwen') is now lost.[149] However, by the eighteenth century Onion may have been imagined as a fairy of

[145] Camden, *Britannia*, pp. 125–26.
[146] Higgins, *Under Another Sky*, pp. 63–64.
[147] Mann, 'Silchester', pp. 45–46.
[148] Wenzel (ed.), *Fasciculus Morum*, pp. 578–79.
[149] Green, *Elf Queens*, pp. 158–59.

some kind, since according to Hearne he was said to have thrown a rock called the 'Imp Stone' from Silchester to Silchester Common.[150] Onion/Unwen was a Germanic figure in origin, and it is unclear how he became associated with the Roman ruins at Silchester, but the stories encountered by Camden and Hearne at least suggest that some attempt was made to give identities to the 'giants' credited with Roman monuments.

Once again, it is possible that the connection between heroes and fairyland derives from Isidore, who traced the etymology of the Greek word 'hero' to a belief that heroes live in the air and are 'men of the air' (*aerius*).[151] The idea of heroes as 'men of the air' recalls the idea, frequently expressed by medieval theologians, that fairies are spirits of the air.[152] Another named giant hero was Ghyst, identified by William Worcestre in the fifteenth century with Ghyston Cliff, a natural rock formation containing caves that presumably inspired stories of giants. Worcestre identified Ghyst as the founder of a nearby hillfort, which was built by 'Saracens or Jews':

> The hillfort upon the high ground not a quarter of a mile distant from Ghyston Cliff, as it is called by the common people, was founded there before the time of William the Conqueror by the Saracens or Jews, by a certain Ghyst, a giant portrayed on the ground.[153]

---

[150] Higgins, *Under Another Sky*, p. 64.   [151] Isidore, *Etymologiae* 8.11.98.
[152] Green, *Elf Queens*, p. 89.
[153] Worcestre, *Topography of Medieval Bristol*, pp. 34–35: *Castellum super altitudinem terre non distans per quartam partem miliaris de Ghyston cliff, ut dicitur a vulgaribus plebeis, ibidem fore Fundatum ante tempus Willelmi Conquestoris per Saracenos vel Judeos per quondam Ghyst gigantem in terra portraiatum.*

Worcestre's reference to 'the common people' suggests he may have been somewhat sceptical of the giant Ghyst who, like the 'Saracens and Jews', was little more than a cipher to represent an imagined other in order to account for otherwise inexplicable human-made features in the landscape. The persistent tendency to associate Roman remains with giants in folklore extended even to 'Robin of Risingham', a representation of a hunter god at Risingham, Northumberland, which came to be associated with Robin Hood. Robin, in this case, was imagined as a giant whose brother lived at Woodburn.[154] In reality, it is possible the figure represents the god Cocidius in his guide as a hunter.[155]

Conclusion

By the eleventh century it is possible to discern five main strands in British belief in folkloric beings, across the various linguistic and cultural communities:

1 Belief in 'men of the woods' (woodwoses or fauns) gifted with prophetic powers
2 Belief in elves (although it remains unclear exactly what elves were)
3 Belief in supernatural women, often in a triad, governing the fates of human beings
4 Belief in diminutive otherworlders, sometimes living beneath the earth in a subterranean kingdom
5 Belief in heroes who have somehow become supernatural beings

---

[154] 'Third Country Meeting', p. 313.
[155] De la Bédoyère, *Gods with Thunderbolts*, p. 164.

Conclusion

To these five features of early medieval British folk belief can be added the evident continuance of some sort of veneration and communication with the tutelary spirits of water sources, discussed in Chapters 1 and 3 above. With the exception of belief in elves, which is somewhat meagrely attested in literary sources, all of these beliefs correspond to learned discussions emerging from commentary on the Bible, the church fathers and *naturalia* (marvels of the natural world). This is not to say that folklore did not exist apart from learned commentary, or that it was entirely created by it; but the influence of authors such as Isidore of Seville and Jerome on perceptions of godlings is evident, and in some cases beliefs that had died out (such as in the Parcae) may have been re-introduced through the influence of learned clerics.

Reconstructing early medieval Welsh beliefs about folkloric beings is hampered by the prevalence of euphemistic and vague terms for godlings in the Welsh language, while a complex and problematic process of glossing the names of Roman godlings into Old English occurred in the Christianised Anglo-Saxon community. However, the evidence suggests that no class of beings readily identifiable with the elves and fairies of later medieval belief existed in Britain before the Norman Conquest. The elves and fairies of later medieval belief were, then, in all likelihood a synthesis of the natures and functions of various classes of godlings of early medieval Britain. It is to that 'fairy synthesis', which created fairies as we know them, that we shall now turn.

5

The Fairy Synthesis

Godlings in Later Medieval Britain

~

In the summer of 1499 a church court sitting at Ixworth, Suffolk, interrogated the Clerk family from the village of Great Ashfield, who were accused of claiming to heal people by superstitious means. Marion, the daughter of John and Agnes Clerk, declared she had powers of healing, prophecy and treasure-finding 'from God and the Blessed Virgin and the gracious fairies (*les Gracyous Fayry*)'. Marion described the fairies as 'little people who gave her information whenever she wanted it', and said that they did not believe in the Trinity, but only in God the Father. The fairies had shown her God, and introduced her to the Archangel Gabriel and St Stephen. Marion's mother Agnes confessed that, as a child, she had spoken with the elves (*les Elvys*), but they twisted her head and neck. An old man healed her, and prophesied that she would have a daughter with healing powers.[1]

The case of the Clerks of Great Ashfield is a rare example of belief in fairies being mentioned in a church court. While the non-literary evidence of fairy belief in Britain before 1500 has been extensively scrutinised by scholars seeking the origins of the literary fairies of medieval Romance, it is rather meagre. Sermons, theological

---

[1] Harper-Bill (ed.), *Register of John Morton*, pp. 215–16.

The Fairy Synthesis

treatises, bishops' ordinances, hagiographies, chronicles and proceedings of ecclesiastical trials give us occasional glimpses of a world of belief that was clearly widespread, but rarely impinged on the elite world that produced written records.[2] However, the case of the Clerks shows late medieval fairy belief in a more or less fully formed state. The fairies are known interchangeably as fairies and elves, and incorporated (however clumsily) into a Christian folk-cosmology. They are diminutive in stature, and associated with healing, prophecy and treasure-finding. Yet they are also a source of illness and danger.

In Chapter 4 above I identified five strands of belief that came together, probably only after the Norman Conquest, to create what would become the kind of fairy belief we see in this late medieval case. Those strands included belief in 'men of the woods' gifted with prophetic powers, a triad of supernatural women governing human fates, diminutive otherworld communities living beneath the earth, heroes who were transformed into supernatural beings, and the enigmatic elves. The post-Conquest evidence suggests that the term 'elves' came to be generally applied to a class of beings that acquired some or all of these characteristics, with elves becoming a 'greedy concept' that devoured other distinctive supernatural beliefs. However, the Old English word *pūca* maintained a strong hold in the south and south-west of England, judging from the evidence of place names, while *ælf* predominated in the old Danelaw of eastern and northern England. As we have seen, *pūca* (and its diminutive form

---

[2] For a summary of spiritual beings of ambiguous character mentioned in medieval English sources see Gray, *Simple Forms*, pp. 30–31.

pūcel) was a term often associated with springs,[3] while 'fay' and 'fairy' were late medieval arrivals – and clearly still interchangeable with 'elf' in Suffolk at the end of the fifteenth century.

This chapter examines the evolution of the fairies in medieval Britain after the Norman conquest, considering ecclesiastical interest in fairy belief, changing attitudes to 'British' culture in the Norman era, the evolution of English elves into fairies and the significance of Latin terms used for fairies such as *faunus*, *nympha* and *incubus*. The chapter explores the fashioning of a fairy otherworld and assesses what we may be able to learn from medieval 'folklore' recorded as anecdotes by medieval chroniclers and other writers. Finally, the chapter tackles the relationship between medieval imaginative literature and fairy belief. The chapter concludes that medieval fairy lore was a composite construction distinctive to its time, fashioned from the wreckage of earlier belief systems – albeit some of that wreckage went back a very long way indeed. However, much must be inferred about the circumstances and reasons for the synthesis of modern fairies, since the synthesis is not directly visible in the sources.[4]

Medieval Fairies

Richard Firth Green has drawn attention not only to the increasing identification of fairy belief as heresy (or apostasy) in the later Middle Ages but also to the ways in which demonologists engaged in 'restricting

---

[3] Semple, *Perceptions of the Prehistoric*, p. 180.
[4] Hutton, 'Making of the Early Modern British Fairy Tradition', p. 1141.

and redefining [the] semantic field' of a diverse range of terms hitherto used to refer to fairies.[5] This diversity of terminology arose, at least in part, on account of people's penchant for euphemism when it came to avoiding direct mention of capricious beings they feared.[6] In Hutton's view, the chief reason for the variety of terms used was sheer uncertainty about what these beings were: medieval writers 'struggled both to create a meaningful category within which to group them and a language for the beings described'.[7] Green bemoans 'the tendency of scholars to reduce the scattered traces of disparate and localized folk motifs to a single homogenized generality',[8] particularly their reluctance to recognise the diversity of fairy beliefs and the possibility that supernatural beings were manifestations of fairy belief. The Clerk case, for example, is suggestive of popular elision of angels, saints and fairies. It would be equally reductive, of course, to assume that *all* otherwise uncategorisable medieval supernatural encounters should be interpreted as part of fairy lore, but the sheer flexibility of fairy lore means that a fairy explanation is often a good place to start.

Theologians were invariably ready to class fairies as demons, but in contrast to late antiquity and the early medieval period, when there was a conscious effort to demonise all spiritual beings who could not be classed as angels of God, the later medieval classification of morally ambiguous spiritual entities as demons occurred 'as it

[5] Green, 'Refighting Carlo Ginzburg's Night Battles', p. 387.
[6] Green, 'Refighting Carlo Ginzburg's Night Battles', p. 388.
[7] Hutton, *Queens of the Wild*, p. 77.
[8] Green, 'Refighting Carlo Ginzburg's Night Battles', p. 392.

The Fairy Synthesis

were by elimination'.[9] Furthermore, as we have seen the very word 'demon' contained within it an ambiguity of meaning, potentially referring not only to 'unclean spirits' under the dominion of Satan in hell, but also to the daemons of the philosophers, those spirits who inhabited the sphere of the moon and were trapped between heaven and earth. When medieval authors gave an account of fairy beliefs their formulaic denunciations of these beings as demons were somewhat undermined by the curiosity they displayed about fairy activities and the way in which they portrayed godlings as fairly unthreatening neighbours of human beings.[10]

While the supernatural was ever present in the late medieval world, it was also often present as a rather mundane reality. For example, rites of exorcism were deployed in medieval England against toothache or as forms of domestic and agricultural pest control, but rarely for their original purpose of liberating demoniacs from the power of the devil.[11] In the same way, what little evidence we have for popular fairy belief suggests that the threats and opportunities represented by the fairy realm were a mundane part of life, and this may be one reason fairy belief was rarely reported until the late Middle Ages. In England and Wales, heightened awareness of the threat of heresy prompted by the rise of Lollardy may have made the ecclesiastical authorities more sensitive to potential threats posed to orthodoxy by fairy belief. However, fairy belief was usually connected with popular

---

[9] Cameron, *Enchanted Europe*, p. 42.
[10] Cameron, *Enchanted Europe*, pp. 43–44.
[11] Young, *History of Exorcism*, p. 61.

magic, which medieval English church courts tended to deal with quite leniently.[12] Only one other case that came before an ecclesiastical court in medieval England involved fairy belief – that of Alice Hancock, who 'professed to heal children touched or harmed by spirits of the air, which the vulgar call "feyry".'[13]

There is little evidence that fairy belief, in and of itself, was of any real interest to medieval church courts in England and Wales. Because people did not worship fairies, belief in fairies was seldom classed as idolatry or apostasy. Instead, fairy belief became a subject of judicial interest only when it led to 'superstitious' practices such as magical healing (whether by the power of the fairies, or from harm caused by fairies) and quasi-religious claims such as those made by Agnes Clerk on behalf of her daughter Marion. Agnes portrayed Marion as a saint, echoing claims made by Joan of Arc earlier in the century.[14] Just as for Joan the distinction between fairies and saints seems to have been fluid (Joan described hanging garlands in honour of the Virgin Mary on the 'fairy tree' at Domrémy),[15] so such distinctions mattered little in the Clerks' popular Christianity. For the Clerks, the fairies were benevolent and powerful beings whom they effortlessly bracketed with religious figures who were similarly benevolent and powerful, creating the heterodox Trinity of 'God and the Blessed Virgin and the gracious fairies'.

---

[12] Parish, *Superstition and Magic*, p. 16.
[13] Harper-Bill (ed.), *Register of John Morton*, p. 215: *quod ipsa profitetur se sanare pueros tactos vel lesos a spiritibus aeris, quos vulgus 'feyry' appellant.*
[14] Warner, *Joan of Arc*, pp. 94–101.
[15] Purkiss, *Troublesome Things*, pp. 65–66. On the 'fairy tree' of Domrémy see Maraschi, 'Tree of the Bourlémonts', pp. 21–32.

The fourteenth-century Dominican friar John Bromyard referred to 'certain deluded women who believe themselves taken off by a certain race and led to certain beautiful and unknown places',[16] and Marion Clerk's apparent conflation of archangels with fairies shows that 'her account has become entangled with Christian machinery'.[17] While it is easy to dismiss such beliefs as the ignorance of the imperfectly catechised peasants of medieval England, the portrayal of the saints in medieval saints' lives did not always differ substantially from beliefs about the fairies. Like the fairies, saints could be capricious, vengeful and arbiters of rough spiritual justice, and popular saints with no official recognition were often the objects of unauthorised cults. It is not difficult to see how some medieval people struggled to see very much difference between saints and fairies; the Clerks were only caught out in their unorthodoxy when they turned up at their local church with a branch of holly given to them by the fairies, and asked the curate to bless it together with other greenery on Palm Sunday.[18]

The Norman Cultural Revolution

While England's new Norman rulers after 1066 preserved many Anglo-Saxon institutions of local and national government, the cultural transformation of the kingdom was far-reaching and profound. In addition to the replacement of both the secular and ecclesiastical Anglo-Saxon elites by a new 'Norman' elite, the

---

[16] Quoted in Green, *Elf Queens*, p. 20.   [17] Green, *Elf Queens*, p. 20.
[18] Harper-Bill (ed.), *Register of John Morton*, p. 216.

Norman French language supplanted Old English as the language of power. Similarly, Latin replaced Old English almost entirely as the language of learning, where hitherto there had been a thriving culture of vernacular learning alongside Latin in the pre-Conquest monasteries. However, while the Norman Conquest resulted in the incorporation of England into an extended Anglo-Norman realm on both sides of the English Channel, there were also more complex cultural transformations underway. Around a third of the knights who fought alongside William I at Hastings were not Normans but Bretons, and many Breton nobles and knights received English lands from the Conqueror. Bretons who settled in Devon and Cornwall and on the edge of Wales found themselves in contact with Cornish- and Welsh-speaking populations, at a time when the Brittonic languages were probably mutually comprehensible.[19]

It is possible that the strong Breton contingent in the Norman forces was one reason Norman writers became particularly interested in 'British' history. Anne Lawrence-Mathers has argued that Geoffrey of Monmouth – who may have had Welsh or Cornish connections – became so successful as a confabulator of pseudo-histories because 'the Anglo-Norman realm was in need of a new narrative to replace Bede's account of the Anglo-Saxons'.[20] Rather than claiming that the Normans were descended from the ancient Britons, however, Geoffrey produced the supernatural narrative of Merlin, who according to

---

[19] Brett et al., *Brittany and the Atlantic Archipelago*, pp. 292–337.
[20] Lawrence-Mathers, *True History*, p. 22. On Geoffrey's possible Cornish connections see Padel, 'Geoffrey of Monmouth', pp. 1–28.

Geoffrey prophesied the arrival of the Normans.[21] For Orderic Vitalis, the Norman Conquest was a punishment of those 'foreigners' (the English) who had invaded the land of Britain, and the restoration of Britain to its original inhabitants.[22] While it is easy to dismiss narratives like this as cynical propaganda calculated to justify the Conquest and its subjugation and dispossession of the English, the advancement of such claims had important cultural consequences in the cultural valorisation of 'British' narratives in post-Conquest England.

Victoria Flood, drawing attention to the way in which writers associated with the contested lands between England and Wales seemed particularly preoccupied with stories of spirits, has argued that such tales may be 'a coded Welsh oppositional discourse remediated in the courtly writings of Normanized clerics with a cultural investment in tales of Wales and the border'.[23] For Flood, Geoffrey of Monmouth established a precedent with the story of the conception of Merlin for narratives in which incubi appeared at critical moments of political change and violent transition. On this interpretation, far from being a sign of Normanisation through the adoption of 'British' legends to replace the ousted Anglo-Saxon culture, the incubus tales recorded by Gerald of Wales and Walter Map should be seen as 'geopolitically rooted within a [Welsh] milieu hostile to Normanization',[24] where the incubus was a portent of catastrophic change.

[21] Lawrence-Mathers, *True History*, pp. 73-74.
[22] Lawrence-Mathers, *True History*, p. 76.
[23] Flood, 'Political Prodigies', p. 23.
[24] Flood, 'Political Prodigies', p. 43.

Normans were already in contact with Breton literature at the time of the Conquest, which seems to have intensified interest in an imagined 'British' past which would give birth, in time, to the phenomenon of Arthurian romance.[25] Breton *lais*, written in or translated at first into French, came eventually to be imitated even in the vernacular of Middle English – such as the early vernacular fairy romance *Sir Orfeo* (c. 1330), which A. J. Bliss argued was based on the lost Breton *lai* of Orpheus.[26] Hutton has made the case for a synthesis of native English elves, Norman/Breton-imported fays and 'diverse human-like creatures' into a single coherent category of beings in the late thirteenth and early fourteenth centuries.[27] It seems likely he is broadly correct in this, although Hutton rather neglects the possibility that Norman and Breton ideas about supernatural beings and realms interacted with pre-existing Welsh and Cornish cultural themes. In the same way that, as we have seen, Romans and Romano-Britons confected at need the figures of new gods and godlings in the period of Roman occupation, so when changed cultural circumstances mean that gods and godlings are no longer required they may be merged into other categories of being.

This process of merging or conflation presents one possible interpretation of the emergence of the fairies as a single class of being in the late Middle Ages. Thus Hutton notes the way in which the imported French word 'goblin', which arrived in the fourteenth century,

---

[25] Fulton (ed.), *Companion to Arthurian Literature*, p. 79.
[26] Bliss (ed.), *Sir Orfeo*, pp. xxxi–xxxiii.
[27] Hutton, 'Making of the Early Modern British Fairy Tradition', pp. 1141–42.

came to refer to any nocturnal or malevolent spirit, merging the pre-existing figures of the puck and bug (and perhaps even the night-mare).[28] While direct evidence is lacking, it is likely that the period between 1066 and 1330 saw a degradation (or, to use a less loaded term, a simplification) of the lore of godlings in England, driven by Norman cultural influence and the preferential value placed on 'British' understandings of the island's history. Exactly how these elite cultural influences permeated the daily lives of ordinary people is something we largely have to guess at, since most of the evidence for medieval English fairy belief post-dates 1300. Those who did mention belief in godlings belonged to the Anglo-Norman elite, and the extent to which their reports reflect popular belief will always be questionable, even if they offer us the occasional glimpse of Britain's godlings. However, on the basis of later fairy belief it is clear that major changes in popular understandings of supernatural beings were underway in the centuries between 1066 and 1300.

From Elves to Fairies

The terms 'elf', 'elves' and 'elvendom' continued to be used in medieval English until the borrowing of the French words *fée* and *féerie* into English in the fourteenth century (as 'fay' and 'faerie') – and indeed 'elf' continued to be used as a synonym for 'fairy' even after the widespread adoption of the French term. By the early modern period 'faerie' (properly the realm of the fays, or the state of fay enchantment) had become conflated with 'fay' to

---

[28] Hutton, 'Making of the Early Modern British Fairy Tradition', p. 1142.

produce the word 'fairy'.[29] However, the late appearance of 'fairy' in English is of fairly slight importance given that Norman French remained England's foremost literary language until the fourteenth century, while Latin was the language of scholarly communication. Fairies thus existed in England from the twelfth century, even if not in the English language. By around 1190 the Latin term *fatalitas* was in use in British Latin sources to mean 'a fairy nature', while *fatatus* (first attested in around 1212) had the sense of 'haunted', along with *fata* or *fada* for 'fairy' in Gervase of Tilbury's *Otia imperialia*.[30] Meanwhile, *fadus* had the sense of a male witch or warlock.[31]

However, the ultimate origins of these words are not to be found in learned medieval Latin but in the vernacular Romance languages, from which learned Latin re-adopted them in the twelfth century. According to Noel Williams,

> The accepted etymology ... would seem to be derived from Latin *fatum* = 'thing said.' This gave *fata* = 'fate,' a neuter plural which, it is supposed, was misinterpreted in the Dark Ages as feminine singular, *fata* = 'female fate, goddess,' ... This identification firstly gives a noun *fai, fae, fay*, referring to an individual female with supernatural powers.[32]

This etymology seems to imply a process whereby the ones who determined fates by their utterance (such as the Parcae) were no longer named, perhaps on account of

---

[29] Harte, 'Fairy Barrows and Cunning Folk', p. 68.
[30] Gervase of Tilbury, *Otia imperialia* 3.87.
[31] On the earliest instances of fairy vocabulary in British medieval Latin see *RMLWL*, p. 186.
[32] Williams, 'Semantics of the Word "Fairy"', pp. 462–63.

sensitivities created by Christianisation. The use of the synecdoche *fata* to stand for the Parcae was already established in antiquity,[33] but it may be that, in the aftermath of the demonisation of the Parcae in the early Middle Ages, the utterances (*fata*) of the Parcae came to stand for the Parcae themselves as a kind of euphemism – only for the *fata* of the Parcae to be re-personified as new characters. Van der Horst, as we saw in Chapter 2 above, argued that this was how the Parcae themselves originally came into being, as personifications of the utterances of the gods. The *fata* of the Parcae were their binding words, and the Parcae were thus beings inseparable from magic, as well as beings associated with the underworld.

While the term 'elf' was used as an English synonym for *fée/fata* throughout much of the Middle Ages, it is by no means clear that the elves of medieval England bore much relation to the elves of Anglo-Saxon England. I have argued elsewhere that in seventeenth-century England, 'witchcraft' became a 'greedy concept' that swallowed up a broader range of magical crimes because the finer distinctions of earlier ages were no longer important.[34] Something similar may have occurred in post-Conquest England, as the former distinctions between supernatural beings such as *hægtessan*, *burgrunan*, *mæran* and *ylfen* became blurred. Thus neither the 'hag' nor the 'nightmare' survived as clearly defined beings ontologically distinct from elves/fairies in medieval and early modern England. In the late twelfth century, the priest Layamon was among the first to identify the magical inhabitants of

---

[33] See, for example, Statius, *Thebaid* 1.173–74.
[34] Young, *Magic as a Political Crime*, p. 186.

Avalon (who raised the young King Arthur) as *alven*, thus establishing 'elf' as a gloss of *fée* but eliding the distinction between the *fées* as supernatural creatures and human beings as enchanted (or enchanter) *fées*.[35]

Laurence Harf-Lancner argued that it was only when the two concepts of eroticism and destiny were brought together that the medieval fairy truly came into being.[36] When Burchard of Worms placed a clause denouncing belief in *silvatici* (supernatural woodland women who seduced men) between two clauses denouncing rites propitiating the Parcae, he seems to have been making an early connection between godlings as erotic and destiny-determining beings.[37] On this interpretation, late medieval fairy belief formed a single category of beings from the Parcae (or their vestigial, re-personified successors the *fata*) and lamia-like creatures that preyed on men sexually and stole children. While the elision of these types of supernatural creatures into a single order of being has merit as a hypothesis for the evolution of the female fairy, it does little to explain the appearance of male fairies and it is likely that the process of evolution (and the variety of supernatural beings elided into the fairy category) was more complex than this.

From Fauns to Fairies

One of the major challenges of dealing with medieval Latin accounts of folkloric beings is the tendency of many authors to use classicising terminology, thus both

---

[35] Hutton, 'Making of the Early Modern British Fairy Tradition', p. 1141.
[36] Harf-Lancner, *Les fées au moyen âge*, pp. 17–25.
[37] Filotas, *Pagan Survivals*, p. 81.

The Fairy Synthesis

concealing the names these beings were given in the vernacular and conceptually obfuscating how these beings functioned as cultural artefacts – since the use of Classical terms immediately links them with beings of Classical mythology rather than the vernacular folklore of the time. On one interpretation, when authors called folkloric beings *fauni* or *nymphae* (which are often taken by modern translators as meaning 'male fairy' and 'female fairy'), they were simply reaching for the closest equivalents in the Classical tradition – especially if learned authors were squeamish of the eccentricity of folklore, and preferred to squeeze it into the straitjacket of Classical mythology. Just as when Julius Caesar decided that the principal god of the Gauls was equivalent to Mercury and left that god's true name unspoken, so learned medieval *interpretatio Romana* drew a veil over the true identities of the beings hidden behind fauns and nymphs.

Yet this is not the only possible interpretation of such 'classicising'. Latin was a language of medieval Britain: a language in which people thought as well as wrote, entwined with the vernacular in a relationship of mutual exchange of vocabulary. Latin was a language of literature as well as learned commentary, and the words *faunus* and *nympha* were living terms with specific contemporary meanings, not just evocations of a vanished Classical world. While examples of purely literary classicisation of fairies as nymphs and fauns certainly occurred in medieval literature,[38] both *faunus* and *nympha* were versatile words that were used in a number of different ways. *Faunus* could cover any being from disturbingly therianthropic denizens of the

---
[38] Green, *Elf Queens*, p. 198.

wild to fairly unthreatening household spirits, while a *nympha* might be a supremely beautiful supernatural female or a hideous threatening denizen of pools or ponds. In 1483 an English-Latin wordbook suggested *lamia* as a Latin equivalent for 'elfe', suggesting that elvish child-stealing and harm were foremost in the writer's mind.[39]

As we saw in Chapter 4 above, in the Anglo-Saxon period Ælfric glossed *fauni* as *wudewasan*, and the phenomenon of identifying fauns as woodwoses was not confined to England. In the tenth-century Latin epic *Waltherius* about the Visigothic king Walter of Aquitaine, one of Walter's enemies puns on his name (Walter = *Wald herr*, 'lord of the forest') by comparing him to a *faunus*.[40] This suggests that in Germany, as in England, *fauni* were associated with wild men of the woods. When Wycliffe came to translate the Vulgate's *fauni ficarii* in Jeremiah 50:39 he opted for 'fonned woode theves', but with variant readings of 'woodwoses' and 'fonnyd woode wosys' in some manuscripts.[41] In doing so he drew on a long tradition of linking fauns with woodwoses, discussed in Chapter 4 above.

In his twelfth-century penitential, the Norman-born bishop of Exeter Bartholomew Iscanus (d. 1184) prescribed fifteen days' penance for 'Anyone who throws into a granary or storehouse a bow, or any such thing, for the devils, which they call "fauns" (*faunos*) to play with, to bring more [grain]'.[42] Bartholomew's text derived

---

[39] Wade, *Fairies in Medieval Romance*, p. 4.
[40] Green, *Elf Queens*, pp. 5–6.
[41] Forshall and Madden (eds.), *Holy Bible*, vol. 3, p. 461.
[42] Wright and Halliwell-Phillipps (eds.), *Reliquiae Antiquae*, vol. 1, p. 286: *Qui in horreum vel cellarium arcum vel aliquod tale projecerit, unde diaboli ludere debeant quos faunos vocant, ut plus afferant.*

from Burchard of Worms, who asked penitents 'Did you make little children's bows and children's shoes and throw them into your pantry and storehouse for the *satyri* and *pilosi* to play with there, so that they would bring you other people's goods and enrich you as a result?'[43] The penance of a mere ten days assigned to this offence suggests that the *satyri* and *pilosi* were not perceived as especially threatening beings, perhaps comparable to the German *schrätlein* or the Lithuanian *barstukai* – small, male, hairy and bearded spirits who took up residence in domestic dwellings. On another interpretation, however, the *satyri* and *pilosi* were the ghosts of dead children, who were often buried under the floor of the home if they died in infancy, since miniature weapons have been found in children's graves.[44]

Bartholomew Iscanus diverged from Burchard by using the word *fauni* in his penitential instead of *satyri* or *pilosi*. Since (as we saw in Chapter 4 above) these terms were essentially equivalent, this may be no more than an insignificant preference for one synonym over another. We cannot know what vernacular terms lay behind Bartholomew's *fauni*, or even if this belief really was shared between early medieval Germany and twelfth-century Devon and Cornwall. However, the twelfth-century diocese of Exeter covered a territory containing speakers of both English and Cornish. Bartholomew's mention of bows might call to mind the Anglo-Saxon belief in elf-shot, but on the other hand there was no tradition of glossing elves as *fauni* in Old English, and the

---

[43] Quoted in Filotas, *Pagan Survivals*, p. 78.
[44] Filotas, *Pagans Survivals*, p. 78 n.62.

phenomenon of elf attacks was much more sinister than what Bartholomew seems to be describing. The withdrawal of fauns to granaries and their diminution into small, childlike beings in the twelfth century might be compared with the way in which, centuries later, the stable and the bread oven became the last refuge of the fairies in parts of rural England in the twentieth century.[45] If Bartholomew was describing a real practice rather than simply following a textual tradition of Continental penitentials, then his fauns might be linked to Gervase of Tilbury's portunes (who inhabit farm buildings) and follets (who display playful behaviour), and even to the story of Malekin told by Ralph of Coggeshall – all of which will be discussed further below.

Richard Firth Green has shown convincingly that the word *incubus*, in most medieval contexts, was the standard word for a fairy rather than the specifically demonological term it later became.[46] As we have seen, *incubus* was essentially a synonym for *faunus* as far as Isidore of Seville and the Church Fathers were concerned. Until the elaboration of a theory of demonic artificial insemination by Thomas Aquinas,[47] an embodied spirit that was capable of intercourse with men or women was, by definition, a member of that intermediate class of beings between the purely spiritual fallen angels and human beings – and therefore a fairy. Indeed, in some medieval accounts of incubi the incubus is called a *faunus* – such as in the story of a young woman of Dunwich molested by 'one of those called fauns and incubi' (*unus ... eorum quos faunos*

---

[45] Young, *Suffolk Fairylore*, p. 98.
[46] Green, *Elf Queens*, p. 79.   [47] Green, *Elf Queens*, p. 59.

dicunt et incubos) who appeared in the form of a handsome young man who showered her with gifts.[48] M. R. James, the translator of Thomas of Monmouth's text, translated *faunos* as 'fairies', perhaps because he was aware of Roman authors' identification of Faunus with Fatuclus or Fatuus, the pronouncer of fate whose name is etymologically linked to the likely origin of the word 'fairy'.

Spirits intent on seducing both men and women were identified as a problem in England as early as the eighth century, since Bede mentions incubi (which he identifies with *dusii* – according to Augustine, the Gaulish equivalent of fauns) seducing both sexes in Anglo-Saxon Northumbria.[49] Elves were often used to explain 'socially unsanctioned pregnancy' in Anglo-Saxon England,[50] a tradition that survived the Norman Conquest. On the one hand, Thomas of Monmouth's use of the word *faunus* to describe the spirit seducing the young woman of Dunwich linked a prevalent contemporary folk belief with its closest Classical equivalent, the sexually rampant fauns; but it also echoed earlier Anglo-Saxon beliefs that may have been linked (as I argued in Chapter 4 above) with *wudewasan*.

The belief that intercourse with an incubus might result in serious illness or death seems to have persisted throughout the Middle Ages in England. According to the *Early South-English Legendary*, 'their members soon swell', usually resulting in death,[51] while Walter of Hemingburgh recorded the case of a woman named

---

[48] Thomas of Monmouth, *Life and Miracles of St William of Norwich*, pp. 79–85.
[49] Bede, *In Lucae evangelium expositio* (*PL* 92.438B).
[50] Hall, *Elves*, p. 117.
[51] Horstman (ed.), *Early South-English Legendary*, p. 306.

Johanna from Kingsley, Hampshire, who used to meet an incubus in Woolmer Forest. Three days after intercourse with the incubus in 1337, her body swelled up and her stomach and lips turned black before she died.[52] By far the most famous British tale of seduction by an incubus, however, was that told by Geoffrey of Monmouth to account for the parentage of Merlin (Plate 16). Geoffrey has Merlin's mother confess that

> when the chambers were closed and the gates bolted, someone used to stand before me in the form of a youth, beautiful of face and comely in all things; he used to give me repeated kisses and playfully to wrestle with me; his wrestling gave me pleasure. Beaten, but not unwilling, I submitted to and endured ravishment, but enjoyed what I suffered, which was not rape or violation. Then he retreated, melting into the thin breezes.

King Vortigern's magician, Maguncius, seeks to explain the nature of Merlin's father: 'The moon is below the sun, and they are separated by a space; this space is allotted to demons, who often assume the shape of men and so deceive and impregnate foolish girls. Perhaps an incubus of that sort was this boy's father'.[53] Merlin's conception by an incubus was extensively discussed in medieval literature,[54] but in Geoffrey's portrayal Merlin's father is a sublunar daemon – a category of being rooted in Platonic philosophy and developed by the philosopher Xenocrates, who succeeded Plato and Speusippus as head of the Academy of Athens. Xenocrates divided the cosmos into

---

[52] Walter of Hemingburgh, *Chronicon*, vol. 2, pp. 314–15; see also Thomas of Walsingham, *Historia Anglicana*, vol. 1, pp. 199–200.
[53] Geoffrey of Monmouth, *Historia Regum*, pp. 141–43.
[54] Green, *Elf Queens*, pp. 85–97.

the supercelestial realm of the gods, the celestial realm of the stars and planets and the sublunar realm inhabited by daemons and humans. Daemons were intermediate between gods and human beings, possessed of both divine power and human affections – and consequently daemons could be good or evil.[55] Xenocrates' views were influential on Plutarch, Proclus and the fifth-century Christian theologian Theodoret of Cyrrhus, among others.[56]

Although often marginalised, what might be termed 'philosophical daemons' continued to exist alongside the demons of theology, who were fallen angels under the dominion of Satan in hell. In the *Metrical Chronicle of Robert of Gloucester* (c. 1300), King Vortigern's clerks tell him about the incubus that fathered Merlin, explicitly eliding the daemons of the philosophers with the elves of popular belief:

> The clerks said that it is in philosophy found
> That there be in the air and high, far from the ground,
> As a manner ghosts, wights as it be,
> And we may them oft on earth in wild places see;
> And oft in man's form, women he cometh to;
> And oft in women's form he cometh to men also,
> That men calleth elven …[57]

Anne Lawrence-Mathers has observed that Geoffrey's creation of Merlin came at a time when Christian demonology was still in flux, and there was still the possibility

---

[55] Schibli, 'Xenocrates' Daemons', pp. 146–49.
[56] Schibli, 'Xenocrates' Daemons', p. 154; Luck (ed.), *Arcana Mundi*, pp. 207–20.
[57] Wright (ed.), *Metrical Chronicle*, vol. 1, p. 196 (spelling and language lightly modernised).

of distinguishing Platonic daemons from the unclean spirits of the New Testament. By the time theologians came to clarify such matters, the figure of Merlin was already well established.[58] Though the exact nature of Merlin's father was understood, Merlin's conception by an incubus put him in the curious category of a demi-godling; in his descent into madness after the Battle of Arthuret (when Merlin lived like a wild animal in the woods),[59] Merlin becomes a *homo silvestris*, like a woodwose or faun.[60]

Curiously, Geoffrey of Monmouth associated belief in fauns with the pagan Saxons. The Saxon Hengist tells King Vortigern that 'We worship the deities of heaven: Jupiter, Juno, Mars, Pallas, old Saturn, the Satyrs, the Fauns, the Lares, and others without number; above all of them we value Mercury, who guides us and our actions'.[61] Germanic Mercury is Woden, and in this respect Geoffrey was right in giving primacy to Mercury in his *interpretatio Romana* of Anglo-Saxon religion. However, the addition of beings like satyrs, fauns and lares was probably intended simply to emphasise that the pagan Anglo-Saxons observed an unrestricted form of idolatry that deified anything, including spirits of nature. The satyrs and fauns thus make an appearance as a satire on pagans for worshipping unworthy beings.

The woodwose, *homo silvestris* or wildman, as we have seen in Chapter 4 above, was at least in part a medieval re-imagining of satyrs, since some of the key texts on

[58] Lawrence-Mathers, *True History*, p. 142.
[59] Lawrence-Mathers, *True History*, p. 51.
[60] Thomas, 'The Celtic Wild Man Tradition', pp. 27–42.
[61] Geoffrey of Monmouth, *Historia Regum*, p. 129.

satyrs transmitted in the Middle Ages failed to mention the satyrs' horns and hooves. Some of the woodwoses in medieval art may portray humans in fancy dress, but at least one *homo silvestris* was encountered as real in the twelfth-century Suffolk coastal town of Orford, where fishermen came across such a being swimming in the sea. According to the chronicler Ralph of Coggeshall,

> he was completely naked, and appeared to be of the human species in all his members. He had hair, but on the surface it seemed to have fallen out or been torn off, but his beard was copious and pointed; he was excessively hairy and shaggy on his chest.[62]

The wildman was captured by the fishermen, held captive and tortured before his eventual escape back to the sea. Ralph was unsure whether the wildman was 'a mortal man, or some kind of fish shaped like a human being, or … some evil spirit lurking in the body of some drowned man, such as we read of in the life of the blessed Audoen'.[63] While Ralph's wildman is not a supernatural being, the striking feature of the story is the wildman's strong association with the sea when he is called a *homo silvestris*. On the one hand, Ralph's story came from the coast, and for people living on the coast the frightening wilderness embodied and represented by the figure of the wildman was the sea. On the other hand, as I explored in

---

[62] Ralph of Coggeshall, *Chronicon*, pp. 117–18: *Ex omni parte nudus erat, ac speciem humanam in omnibus membris praetendebat. Capillos autem habebat, sed in superficie quasi divulsi et demoliti videbantur, barba vero prolixa erat et pineata, circa pectus nimium pilosus et hispidus.*

[63] *Si autem hic mortalis homo exstiterit, sive aliquis piscis humanam praetendens speciem, sive aliquis malignus spiritus fuerit in aliquo corpore submersi hominis latitans, sicut de quodam legitur in vita beati Audoeni …*

Chapter 1 above, traditions of godlings associated with water seem to have been the longest lasting and the most persistent, and there was an old tradition of malevolent hairy spirits of waters in medieval East Anglia.[64] Whether England's freshwater mermaids – who are generally portrayed as malevolent beings – should be regarded as degraded nymphs can only be speculation.

Parcae, Fates and Nymphs

There is some evidence for the ongoing significance of the Parcae or their equivalents, the Matres, Norns or Wyrd Sisters in medieval Britain – 'the Werdys that we clepen Destiné', as Chaucer called them.[65] In twelfth-century Devon and Cornwall, Bartholomew Iscanus imposed penances on 'those who have prepared a table with three knives for persons in their household, so that arriving there, they would foretell good things',[66] which mirrored Burchard's prohibition on preparing a table for the Parcae.[67] The similarity of the phrasing and the mention of three knives leaves little doubt that *personarum* in Bartholomew's penitential was a euphemism for (or even a mistranscription of) *Parcarum*. Similarly, Bartholomew imposed penances on 'those who have made a vow to a tree or water',[68] and 'those who have believed that

---

[64] Young, *Suffolk Fairylore*, p. 47.
[65] Jones and Pennick, *History of Pagan Europe*, p. 150.
[66] Wright and Halliwell-Phillipps (eds.), *Reliquiae Antiquae*, vol. 1, p. 285: *Qui mensam praeparavit cum tribus cultellis in famulatum personarum, ut ibi nascentibus bona praedestinent.*
[67] Schmitz (ed.), *Bussbücher*, vol. 1, p. 460.
[68] Wright and Halliwell-Phillipps (eds.), *Reliquiae Antiquae*, vol. 1, p. 285: *Qui votum fecerit ad arborem vel aquam.*

men or women may be transformed into the image of a wolf or other animal'.[69] Here as elsewhere, however, it is difficult to judge the extent to which the material in Bartholomew's penitential reflected popular beliefs in his diocese; when Bartholomew followed Burchard by imposing penances on those who believed that they rode at night with Diana or Herodias, it is rather unlikely that people in England believed this, unless some people believed they could join the supernatural ride of the *hægtessan* described in one Old English charm against sudden stitch.[70]

To a large extent, it is likely that portrayals of the Parcae or Fates in Britain's medieval literature resulted not from the preservation of pre-Christian beliefs, but from self-conscious Classicism. After all, it makes little sense for the Parcae themselves to have survived alongside the fairies that personified the decrees of the Parcae and took their place. The Parcae make an appearance in the classicising satirical Latin poem *Speculum stultorum* ('The Mirror of Fools') by Nigel Wireker (fl. 1190), where they are portrayed as 'three sister-fates' in a section entitled *narratio de tribus sororibus fatalibus* ('account of the three sister-fates'). The three sisters are called goddesses but never actually named as the Parcae by Nigel, nor as nymphs, but they are clearly personifications of fate. As the fairies often do, Nigel's Parcae serve a narrative function of making sure people receive their just desserts, even if in a slightly perverse way.

---

[69] Wright and Halliwell-Phillipps (eds.), *Reliquiae Antiquae*, vol. 1, p. 286: *Qui masculam vel feminam in lupinam effigiem alicuius animalis transformari posse crediderit*.

[70] Niles, 'Pagan Survivals', p. 130.

Nigel's three sisters first encounter a wealthy and beautiful maiden weeping, and the first two goddesses propose helping her, but the third counsels against this, warning that some people do not make the best use of their good fortune. The second maiden encountered by the fates is also wealthy and beautiful, but disabled and unable to walk. Again, the first two goddesses propose restoring her mobility, but the third objects that the maiden already had more advantages than most other people. Close to the city gates, at a crossroads, the goddesses encounter a third poor maiden who defecates in public. The first two goddesses want to flee the unpleasant sight, but the third persuades them to reward the young woman with wealth and influence, since her condition can truly be improved. Nigel Wireker then reveals the meaning of the fable: many of the senior clergy are like the defecating young woman, frequently undeserving of the reward of high office, and yet fate seems to favour them.[71]

In the twelfth century the Parcae were also discussed by Alberic of London (perhaps to be identified with a Master Alberic who was a canon of St Paul's Cathedral in around 1160),[72] who wrote an influential treatise on mythography, the *Liber imaginum deorum* ('Book of the Images of the Gods'), which would one day inform the work of Bocaccio:[73]

For the Fates are three, whom we call Parcae by antiphrasis, because they spare (*parcere*) none. Of these, according to Servius, one speaks; another writes; and a third draws out a

---

[71] de Longchamps, *Speculum stultorum*, pp. 104–7 (lines 3281–3457).
[72] Pepin (ed.), *Vatican Mythographers*, p. 9.
[73] Lummus, 'Boccaccio's Poetic Anthropology', p. 724.

thread. According to Homer one bears the thread, another pulls it, the third severs it. These, who may be considered the recorders and librarians of Jupiter, bring the supreme dispositions of the gods into effect. However, we give them to Pluto on account of these tasks, since their doings are greatly seen upon the earth. But Clotho is to be interpreted as 'bringing forth', Lachesis as 'lot', and Atropos as 'without order'; by which names the whole of human life is indicated in its disposition. For at first men are brought forth from non-being into being, or from their mother's womb into the light. Then comes lot, as to how each one must live; and at last death brings an end to life – which is therefore said to be 'without order', since it observes no dignity, sparing no age, and draws all to it indifferently.[74]

Alberic's account references Isidore of Seville in his interpretation of the etymology of the name *Parcae*, and displays the extent of his knowledge of ancient literature on the fates. By placing his discussion of the Parcae under the heading of the realm of Pluto, Alberic reinforced their association with the underworld, which may have been one factor that fed into their transformation into fairies. Alberic also offered an account of the nymphs, enumerating the different categories of nymph, and described

---

[74] Bode (ed.), *Scriptores rerum mythicarum*, vol. 1, pp. 187–88: *Tria enim Fata, quae per antiphrasis, quod nulli parcant, Parcas appellamus ... Harum, secundum Servium, una loquitur, altera scribit, tertia fila deducit. Secundum Homerum una colem hajulat, trahit altera, tertia rumpit. Has, licet exceptrices et librariae Jovis sint, quod summi scilicet dei dispositiones ad effectum ducunt, Plutoni tamen ob hoc ministras damus, quia earum in terris maxime officia videntur. Interpretatur autem Clotho evocatio, Lachesis sors, Atropos sine ordine; per quae nomina tota humanae vitae innuitur disposition. Evocantur enim primo homines ex non esse in esse, sive de matris utero in lucem; deinde sors, qualiter cuique vivendum sit, succedit; postremo mors vitae finem importat; quae ideo sine ordine dicitur, quod nullam observans dignitatem, nulli parcens aetati, indifferenter omnia ad se trahit.*

the cult of genii in some detail, but here as elsewhere he portrayed the gods as a superstition of a former world,[75] without direct relevance to his own time. This is not altogether surprising; the genre of mythography within which Alberic wrote was focussed on the beliefs of the ancients as testified in their writings, and it is unlikely that it would have occurred to a twelfth-century mythographer to consider the degraded traces of mythology in contemporary folk belief – that was a matter for the preachers and the writers of penitentials.

Nevertheless, medieval Latin writers used the word *nymphae* to refer to fairies, in spite of the Latin word's exclusively feminine connotations. Thus we encounter *candela nympharum* for 'fairy lights' in a twelfth-century life of Hereward the Wake.[76] While we cannot be certain what vernacular term was glossed by *candela nympharum*, in one case we know that *nympha* glossed 'elf'. A mid-twelfth-century compilation of the miracles of St Withburga, the *Miracula Sancte Wihtburge*, alludes to a cleric 'from the countryside belonging to the blessed king and martyr Edmund [that is, the territories of the abbey of Bury St Edmunds] which may be interpreted in the English tongue as "valley of the nymphs"',[77] meaning the Suffolk village of Elveden (*ælfdenu*). Since Anglo-Saxon elves had been both male and female (at least in the late pre-Conquest period), the use of an exclusively feminine Latin term for elves is noteworthy. The

---

[75] Bode (ed.), *Scriptores rerum mythicarum*, vol. 1, pp. 172, 184–85.
[76] Hardy and Martin (eds.), *Gesta Herwardi*, vol. 1, p. 396.
[77] Quoted in Hall, *Elves*, pp. 64–65: *ex rure ... quodam beatis regis et martyris EDMUNDI quod lingua uallem nunpharum interpretatur anglica*.

thirteenth-century *Early South-English Legendary* perhaps gives us a glimpse of this kind of elf belief, which emphasised elves as supernatural women:

> And oft in form of woman, in many a hidden way
> Great company men see of them, both happy and playing,
> That are called elves; and often they come to town,
> And by day much in woods they be, and by night upon high downs.[78]

However, the *Legendary* also affirmed that elves could choose to appear as either men or women in order to seduce members of either sex,[79] and it is possible that it was this belief in the ambiguous gender of fairies, rather than a belief that they were always female, that emboldened Latin authors to adopt a feminine term. Their readers might be expected to understand that *nymphae* were simply elves in the form of women, and not that all elves were women.

Fairy Kings and Fairy Otherworlds

It was a persistent feature of medieval popular religion that the doctrine of a hell where Satan ruled and sinners were eternally punished by fire never quite displaced – and therefore existed alongside – ideas of a paradise-like underworld realm presided over by the fairies.[80] It is unclear, however, whether we should see the chthonic fairyland as a survival of pre-Christian belief or as part

---

[78] Horstman (ed.), *Early South-English Legendary*, p. 307.
[79] Horstman (ed.), *Early South-English Legendary*, p. 306.
[80] Green, *Elf Queens*, pp. 147–93.

of a process of 'undemonisation', as people began to entertain the possibility of a less threatening underworld than that described by preachers. Looked at in one way, a fairy underworld was a natural development from the widespread belief that fairies lived inside hills, although Patrick Sims-Williams has noted that such a development did not take place in Ireland, where the hills and burial mounds inhabited by the *aos sí* remained distinct territories rather than points of access to a single fairy realm.[81] This suggests that there was a degree of British cultural specificity to belief in an underground otherworld fairy realm. Hutton's suggestion that the idea of a fairy kingdom ruled by a fairy monarch derived from romance literature at the end of the thirteenth century is most unlikely,[82] given that otherworld monarchs are already present in the stories of King Herla and Eliodorus recounted, respectively, by Walter Map and Gerald of Wales.

The *Buchedd Collin*, a Welsh life of St Collen dating from 1536, shows the extent to which Annwn was synonymous with fairyland and Gwyn ap Nudd with the king of the fairies in late medieval Wales. Although this particular story was recorded on the eve of the Reformation, it may well draw on earlier tales:

As [St Collen] was in his cell one day, he heard two men talking about Gwyn ap Nudd, and saying that he was the King of Annwn (the Under-World) and the Fairies. Collen put his head out, and told them to hold their peace, and those were only demons. They told him to hold his peace, and, besides, he

---

[81] Sims-Williams, *Irish Influence*, p. 59.
[82] Hutton, *Queens of the Wild*, p. 79.

would have to meet Gwyn face to face. By-and-by Collen heard a knocking at his door, and in answer got the reply, 'It is I, the messenger of Gwyn ap Nudd, King of Annwn, bidding you to come to speak with him on the top of the hill by mid-day'. The saint persistently refused to go day after day, until at last he was threatened with the words, 'If you don't come, Collen, it will be the worse for you'. This disconcerted him, and, taking some holy water with him, he went. On reaching the place, Collen beheld there the most beautiful castle that he had ever seen, with the best-appointed troops; a great number of musicians with all manner of instruments; horses with young men riding them; handsome, sprightly maidens, and everything that became the court of a sumptuous king. When Collen entered, he found the king sitting in a chair of gold. Collen was welcomed by him, and asked to seat himself at the table to eat, adding that beside what he saw thereon, he should have the rarest of all dainties, and plenty of every kind of drink. Collen said, 'I will not eat the tree-leaves'. 'Hast thou ever'. asked the king, 'seen men better dressed than these in red and blue?' Collen said, 'Their dress is good enough, for such kind as it is'. 'What kind is that?' asked the king. Collen said that the red on the one side meant burning, and the other, cold. Then he sprinkled holy water over them, and they all vanished, leaving behind them nothing but green tumps.[83]

Although Collen is confident that Gwyn ap Nudd is nothing more than a demon, and that the fairies are suffering torment in hell, the idea that the Fairy King is able to conceal the truth by fairy glamour is itself a deviation of popular religion from the standard Christian portrayal of hell. One of the earliest appearances of the Fairy King in English literature is in the Middle English

---

[83] Baring-Gould (ed.), *The Lives of the Saints*, vol. 16, p. 224.

poem *Sir Orfeo*, whose earliest surviving manuscript can be dated to around 1330.[84] *Sir Orfeo* is, first and foremost, a reimagining of the tale of Orpheus and Eurydice (here called Heurodis) as medieval romance, where Orfeo is the king of Winchester and the Fairy King takes on a role similar to that of Pluto or Hades in the ancient myth of Persephone. While Angana Moitra has argued that the Fairy King is partly an evolution of Pluto/Hades and partly a 'creole' entity (following Jane Webster's approach to Romano-British religion),[85] there are a number of different possible reasons for the substitution of fairies for gods in medieval romance. In the first place, fairies were more readily comprehensible within a medieval Christian culture than was the alien concept of pagan gods. Secondly, fairies were less likely to attract religious controversy than the representation of deities. And thirdly, the gods belonged to a different register of literature – Latin poetry imitative of classical authors, like Nigel Wireker's *Speculum* – while fairies belonged to the register of vernacular literature.

Moitra has argued that the figure of the Fairy King underwent a process of 'cultural translation' between the Classical and medieval worlds,[86] and this might be true. However, it is important to be careful about assuming the survival of identities over time on the basis of similar functions served by characters in different stories. The Fairy King is perhaps better interpreted as a narrative substitute for Pluto than as a development of the same

[84] Bliss (ed.), *Sir Orfeo*, p. x.
[85] Moitra, 'From Pagan God to Magical Being', pp. 27–30.
[86] Moitra, 'From Graeco-Roman Underworld to the Celtic Otherworld', p. 86.

character; if so, the question we should be asking is why such a substitution might have been made. *Sir Orfeo* is a literary work, and in the same way that the characters of Orpheus and Eurydice were adapted for the genre of romance, so the Fairy King may have been a character more suitable for a romance set in England than a Classical god of the underworld. In the same way, in the eighteenth century Alexander Pope chose to introduce sylphs, gnomes and elves to his satirical poem *The Rape of the Lock* (instead of the gods of the Classical world, or John Milton's angels) for reasons of genre; satire was unworthy of higher beings, so Pope largely confected a cosmology of his own, suitable for his purpose.[87]

Where Moitra is undoubtedly correct, however, is in identifying the Fairy King as a 'Celtic' figure. Presumably a Fairy King figure featured in the lost Breton *lai* of Orpheus, cognate with the Welsh figure of Gwyn ap Nudd whom we encountered in the story from the life of St Collen. Rather than being a purely literary process, however, the borrowing of a Fairy King figure may have been underway in English culture by the twelfth century, in response to the integration of British myths into the new Anglo-Norman culture. Moitra has suggested that the Pan-like pygmy king of the story of King Herla recorded by Walter Map (whom we encountered in Chapter 4 above) was an earlier incarnation of the Fairy King of *Sir Orfeo*,[88] whose more animalistic and zoomorphic characteristics come to be downplayed in subsequent portrayals (much as satyrs and fauns in Roman sculpture

---

[87] Young, *English Catholics*, pp. 64–67.
[88] Moitra, 'From Pagan God to Magical Being', pp. 32–36.

were sometimes portrayed as fully human, with only a suggestion of the animal in their facial expression or the inclusion of pointed ears).

Medieval Folklore

The category of 'folklore' is a modern one, with the term 'folk-lore' coined in 1846 to replace the older term 'popular antiquities', and thus the idea of 'medieval folklore' is something of a conscious anachronism. However, there is a long tradition of attempting to extract information about popular belief from medieval texts. The particular difficulties associated with extracting such information from works of literature will be examined separately later in this chapter, while the perils of taking beliefs cited in medieval penitentials at face value has already been mentioned; however, the search for popular belief in chronicles and courtly collections of anecdotes like Gervase of Tilbury's *Otia imperialia* (composed c. 1210–1214) and Walter Map's *De nugis curialium* (composed c. 1191) is equally fraught with difficulty. Setting aside questions of truthfulness and exaggeration in writers' representation of popular belief (which, at this distance in time, are very difficult to deal with), it is important to bear in mind that medieval writers did not report beliefs as fact with anything resembling the same intent as Victorian folklorists. Gervase and Walter wrote for entertainment, while chroniclers like Ralph of Coggeshall were engaged in the reporting of prodigies of nature that they considered in some way morally instructive or worthy of wonder.

Furthermore, while these writers were of English or Welsh birth, the 'folklore' they reported was not always native to Britain. Gervase and Walter spent long periods abroad, and while they sometimes specified that the beliefs they reported were British, the extent to which they were really in touch with English and Welsh popular belief is open to question. On the other hand, both men surely filtered their perceptions of folklore, wherever they encountered it, through their upbringings and particular cultural preconceptions. Among the supernatural beings identified as specifically English by Gervase of Tilbury are the Portunes, whose name evokes the Roman deity Portunus, the god of harbours. However, the Portunes' behaviour combines features of later domestic and night-riding fairies:

> Just as nature produces certain marvels among men, thus spirits in aerial bodies (which they assume by divine permission) play tricks upon them. For there are in England certain demons – I do not know if I should say they are demons, or that they are ghosts of secret and unknown origin – whom the Gauls call Neptunes and the English Portunes. It is their nature to embrace the simple life of fortunate farmers; and when, on account of their domestic work, they are awake at night, the doors are suddenly closed and they warm themselves at the fire, and eat little frogs from their laps, having roasted them on the coals. They are old in appearance, with a wrinkled face, small in stature, not having half a thumb's length. They wear little patched coats, and if anything was to be done in the house, or burdensome work to be undertaken, they bind themselves to doing it, completing it more easily than any human. It is their nature that they are able to obey, and are not able to harm. They have, however, one little way of annoying. For when in the uncertain shadows of night the English are riding somewhere alone, a Portune (not seen at all) joins himself, unwanted, to the horseman. And when he has accompanied him for a long time, at last he takes the reins

and leads the horse into a marsh at hand; and when he is stuck in it, wallowing, the departing Portune laughs, and by this trick makes fun of human simplicity.[89]

Portunus was originally the Roman god of doors and keys, as well as being associated with farming, barns and harvest.[90] However, there is no evidence of a cult of Portunus in Roman Britain, and the idea that this obscure god's association with agriculture survived into the thirteenth century is implausible. One interpretation of the name of the Portunes is that it was only indirectly linked to the god, deriving instead from the adjective *opportunus* (with the original sense of 'one who pushes at the door' or 'one who arrives at the right time').[91] The Portunes could thus be understood as 'the opportune ones' who arrive to help on the farm when the farmer needs assistance, rendering 'Portune' similar to

---

[89] Gervase of Tilbury, *Otia Imperialia* 3.61: *Sicut inter homines mirabilia quaedam natura producit, ita spiritus in corporibus aereis quae assumunt ex divina permissione ludibria sui faciunt. Ecce enim in Anglia daemones quosdam habet, daemones inquam, nescio dixerim an secretas et ignotae generationis effigies, quos Galli Neptunos Angli Portunos nominant. Istis insitum est, quod simplicitatem fortunatorum colonorum amplectuntur, et nocturnas propter domesticas operas agunt vigilias, subito clausis januis ad ignem calefiunt, et ranunculas ex sinu projectas prunis impositas comedunt, senili vultu, facie corrugata, statura pusilli, dimidium pollicis non habentes. Panniculis consertis induuntur, et si quid gestandum in domo fuerit aut onerosi operis agendum, ad operandum se jungunt, citius humana facilitate expediunt. Id illis insitum est, ut obsequi possint, et obesse non possint. Verum unicum quasi modulum nocendi habent. Cum enim inter ambiguas noctis tenebras Angli solitarii quandoque equitant, Portunus nonnunquam invisus equitanti se copulat, et cum diutius comitatur euntem, tandem loris arreptis equum in lutum ad manum ducit, in quo dum infixus volutatur, Portunus exiens cachinnum facit, et hujuscemodi ludibrio humanam simplicitatem deridet.*
[90] Scullard, *Festivals and Ceremonies*, p. 176.
[91] Chabot, 'Portunus', p. 4.

the familiar euphemisms of later ages for folkloric beings like 'the good folk' and 'the good neighbours'.

On the other hand, Gervase's pairing of the *Portuni* of the English with the *Neptuni* of the Gauls does suggest a link with the respective aquatic deities Portunus and Neptune. Gervase's *Neptuni* are clearly the ancestors of the *lutins* of French folklore, whose name derives from Old French *netun*, meaning a marine monster (presumably from demonisation of the god of Neptune in the era of conversion).[92] The aquatic origins of medieval folkloric beings is a recurring feature across different cultures. As we saw in Chapter 1 above, St Samson encountered a trident-wielding supernatural woman in an eighth-century Breton hagiography, suggesting a land-based monstrous nereid much like those encountered in modern Greek folklore. Similarly, the Irish *lúchorpáin* (leprechauns) are water spirits in the earliest sources, and the word *abac* (cognate with Welsh *afanc*, 'aquatic monster') is used interchangeably with *luchorpán* for these beings.[93] The modern leprechaun is, however, a being that has migrated entirely to the land, and has no strong connection with water in Irish folklore.

It is important to remember that Gervase does not here give the actual names of the *Neptuni* and *Portuni* but uses Latin terms to stand for English (or, more likely, Norman French names) that he does not record. If *Neptuni* stood for *netuns* or *lutins*, it is just possible that *Portuni* stood for an otherwise unattested Norman French word that was something like *portuns*, and which was an alternative

[92] Chabot, 'Portunus', p. 5.
[93] Bisagni, '*Leprechaun*', pp. 63–64.

name for mischievous spirits derived, like *netun*, from demonisation of the aquatic deity Portunus. However, it is also possible that the absence of any other attestation of this term derives from the fact that Gervase simply made it up. Aware that mischievous spirits were called *netuns* in France (*Neptuni* in Latin), did Gervase simply pick the name of another Roman aquatic deity to refer to English supernatural beings, for the sake of literary symmetry?

Whatever the truth about their name, the frogs eaten by the Portunes seem to link them to their aquatic origins. The detail evokes the fourth-century Christian poet Prudentius' mockery of the nymphs 'located beneath a deep lake in the manner of frogs' (*sitas sub alto more ranarum lacu*).[94] However, the Portunes' behaviour as domestic helpers on the farm is reminiscent of the pucks and brownies of later English and Scottish tradition, even if they differ from these later figures by acting together and appearing as a group. However, groups of household spirits appear elsewhere in Europe, like the Lithuanian barstukai.[95] The Portunes' tricks on riders, meanwhile, evoke later traditions about 'hag-ridden' and 'fairy-ridden' horses, as well as fairy deceit leading astray riders and pedestrians. Again, the Portunes' penchant for leading riders into marshes could be a nod to their historic aquatic origins.

A character somewhat like Gervase's Portunes appears in Thomas of Walsingham's *Historia Anglicana* for the year 1343: a 'little red man' (*homunculum rubeum*) who

---

[94] Prudentius, *Peristephanon* 10.243–44 quoted in Cameron, *Last Pagans of Rome*, p. 283.
[95] Young (ed.), *Pagans in the Early Modern Baltic*, p. 123.

appeared in a wheat field somewhere in the north of England and led astray a son of Lord Greystoke. The young nobleman was riding in a field when he saw the wheat moving and the little man emerge; the man then grew in stature, seized the nobleman's reins and 'whether he wanted to or not', led him into the wheat 'to a place where, as it seemed to him, a most beautiful lady dwelt with many young women similar to her. The woman cut off the nobleman's head – or so it seemed to him – and caused him to go mad until his senses were eventually restored by St John of Beverley.[96] Here a gnome-like supernatural man, who seems intent on leading riders astray, becomes linked to a fairy otherworld accessed by a portal from our world (in this case, through a field of wheat) and inhabited by beautiful supernatural women. Thomas of Walsingham's account thus suggests that two very different kinds of fairy had been brought together by the fourteenth century – a diminutive, ugly, male spirit that operates in our world, and an otherworld inhabited by beautiful female elves.

Gervase's original Portunes are clearly not elves – at least as elves were understood in the late Anglo-Saxon period – since they are not beautiful, and they are diminutive in size. The Portunes are monstrous in combining the facial features of old men with their small size, and in this respect they resemble dwarfs. On the other hand, the Portunes are fairly unthreatening beings in comparison with dwarfs, who were usually linked with harm in Anglo-Saxon belief and considered undesirable beings. While the Portunes apparently have their own society, and their

---

[96] Thomas of Walsingham, *Historia Anglicana*, vol. 1, pp. 261–62.

own distinctive food source in the form of frogs, there is no hint in Gervase's account that the Portunes have their own kingdom or realm, or that it is located under the earth. However, they are certainly magical beings insofar as they can perform domestic tasks faster than any human being and can become invisible at will.

Another kind of English supernatural being mentioned by Gervase is the 'gyant', which sounds a great deal like many of the equiform bogies of later English folklore:

There is in England a certain kind of demon, which they call in their speech 'Gyant', like a one-year-old foal, standing on its hindlegs, with sparkling eyes. This kind of demon very often appears on streets, in the very heat of the day or around sunset. And any time it appears, when there will be danger in that town that day or night, having run about the streets it provokes the dogs to bark; and while it simulates flight, it draws the dogs after it in the vain hope of following it. This illusion constitutes a warning of fire to the inhabitants, and thus this dutiful kind of demon, while it terrifies those who catch sight of it, puts the ignorant on their guard by its arrival.[97]

The English (or Norman French) name 'gyant' that Gervase gives for this being is rather surprising, since there is no indication in Anglo-Saxon lore that giants ever took an equine form, nor in the medieval giant lore

[97] Gervase of Tilbury, *Otia Imperialia* 3.62: *Est in Anglia quoddam daemonum genus, quod suo idiomate Gyant nominant, adinstar pulli equini anniculi, tibiis erectum, oculis scintillantibus. Istud daemonum genus saepissime comparet in plateis, in ipsius diei fervore aut circa solis occiduum. Et quoties apparet, futurum in urbe illa die vel nocte instat periculum, in plateis discursu facto canes provocat ad latrandum, et dum fugam simulat, sequentes canes ad insequendum spe vana consequendi invitat. Huiusmodi illusio convicaneis de ignis custodia cautelam facit, et sic officiosum daemonum genus, dum conspicientes terret, suo adventu munire ignorantes solet.*

discussed in Chapter 4 above. Yet while the idea that bogies served a useful function of warning people against fire seems to have disappeared in subsequent folklore, the idea that bogies encountered by travellers on lonely roads resembled horses is a widespread one throughout Britain and Ireland, with the being in question variously identified as the pooka, kelpie, or 'shagfoal'. The example of Gervase's 'gyant' serves as a salutary reminder not to invest too much in the names given to supernatural beings, since from an etymological point of view the word 'giant' or *gigas* reveals almost nothing about the true nature of this being or its relationship to subsequent folklore.

Gervase's account of follets evokes later accounts of 'poltergeists' (which were usually seen as fairies in medieval and early modern literature[98]), since the follets are never seen and only heard, throw things in people's houses, and are impervious to attempts to exorcise them:

And there are other [spirits], which the common people call follets, who inhabit the homes of simple rustics and are repelled neither by water nor exorcisms; and since they are not seen, they afflict those going in with stones, wood and domestic utensils; their words are heard in the same way as human words, even though their forms do not appear.[99]

The term 'follet' is prefigured by the *folez* of Benoît de Saint-Maure, whom Green interprets as 'wild men' – that

---

[98] Cameron, *Enchanted Europe*, p. 46.
[99] Gervase, *Otia imperialia* 1.18: *Sunt et alii, quos Folletos vulgus nominat, qui domos simplicium rusticorum inhabitant et nec aqua nec exorcismis arcentur, et quia non videntur, ingredientes lapidibus, lignis et domestica suppellectile affligunt, quorum verba utique humano more audiuntur, etsi effigies non comparent.*

is, the mad men of the woods.[100] While Gervase's follets properly belong to the folklore of northern France, one of the best-known 'fairy poltergeists' of the Middle Ages is from England: the tale of the 'fantastic spirit' Malekin, recounted by Ralph of Coggeshall in around 1218 but situated in the reign of Richard I (1189–1199). At Dagworth in Suffolk, the children of Sir Osberne de Bradwell found themselves joined at play by the voice of a little girl who called herself Malekin and was able to move objects, but only revealed her physical form once when Sir Osberne's daughter begged her to do so. Malekin reported that she had been born a human child, but was taken by 'others' when her mother left her sleeping in the fields near Lavenham. She now lived in a parallel society with these 'others', with whom she had to remain for seven years. Although invisible, Malekin was a physical being; she ate and drank and was in possession of a magical hat that made her invisible when she wore it. Malekin also had supernatural knowledge beyond her years, and was able to converse with the family's chaplain in Latin about the Scriptures.[101]

The story of Malekin seems to be an early attestation of the theme of the fairy changeling, although Malekin herself is not the changeling but the stolen child; we never learn whether the 'others' replaced Malekin with a fairy replica whom her mother found again in the fields. Rose Sawyer has argued that it was not until the fifteenth century that elves were first explicitly identified as beings

---

[100] Green, *Elf Queens*, p. 79.
[101] Ralph of Coggeshall, *Chronicon*, pp. 120–21; Young, *Suffolk Fairylore*, pp. 48–51.

who stole children in mystery plays – even though the idea that there were child-stealing demons and fauns was much older.[102] Once again, the labelling of child-stealing spirits as 'elves' may represent the elision of a more complex ecosystem of supernatural beings into a single category. However, the late medieval emergence of child-stealing fairies was but one example of the way in which medieval fairies were in some respects dependent (or parasitic) on human beings and human society. Fairies seduced and sometimes even married humans, stole their children and sometimes kidnapped human midwives. In this respect the medieval fairy did not resemble the godlings of the ancient world who were characterised by their distance from human society rather than their interaction with it. Whether this shift can be put down in some way to Christian efforts at demonisation or a late medieval cultural emphasis on materiality can only be speculation.

Fairies and Romance

The fairies of medieval romance have been the focus of much speculation about the nature and origins of medieval fairy belief since the publication of Lucy Allen Paton's *Studies in the Mythology of Arthurian Romance* (1903), which was followed by numerous studies seeking to trace fairy characters in romance back to supposed 'Celtic' or 'Teutonic' origins. C. S. Lewis rejected this approach, arguing that intermediate beings like fairies were integrated within medieval cosmologies in their own right, and therefore appeals to the 'original cultures' within

---

[102] Sawyer, 'Child Substitution', pp. 156–57.

which fairies originated were not necessary.[103] However, both approaches proceeded on the assumption that it was possible to excavate folklore from the romances, and that their writers used fairies in ways determined by prevailing cultural assumptions about these beings. To assume this, however, is to ignore that medieval romances were works of uninhibited creative fiction, whose writers were just as capable of freely drawing on and adapting cultural themes as any contemporary author of fantasy.

Euan Cameron has argued that just as no-one should infer widespread belief in magic in twenty-first-century Britain and America from the popularity of the *Harry Potter* books, so we ought not to take medieval literary themes as indicative of the nature of popular belief.[104] In James Wade's view, medieval romance was shaped by the creativity and world-building of its authors rather than fixed and determined by historical or political conditions. Medieval authors fashioned and used fairies as and when they needed them, and while it is possible to study the 'internal folklore' of romances, there is little to be gained from trying to extract folklore from them that corresponds to beliefs attested beyond the text itself.[105] Richard Firth Green has been critical of this 'functionalist' trend of insisting that magic and fairies were primarily deployed in romance as literary devices.[106] As a result, scholarship on fairies in medieval romance does little to advance our knowledge of fairy belief; if the prevailing assumption is that fairies and their magic were merely

---

[103] Lewis, *Discarded Image*, p. 126.
[104] Cameron, *Enchanted Europe*, p. 74.
[105] Wade, *Fairies in Medieval Romance*, pp. 5–6.
[106] Green, *Elf Queens*, p. 12.

used as a *deus ex machina* to resolve otherwise awkward plots, then there is little reason to pursue in detail what medieval people actually believed about fairies, and why.

The cultural relationship between literature and popular belief in the post-Enlightenment, post-Romantic, postmodern twenty-first century is clearly not the same as the relationship between literature and belief in the Middle Ages, when clear lines between documentary narrative and imaginative fiction were more rarely (or at least less self-consciously) drawn. In the debate over literary influence on fairies, literary scholars tend to be more likely to advance a case for strong literary influence, while intellectual historians and historians of belief may be more cautious in conceding much influence to literature. However, the fault line between the literary scholars and the historians is not an exact one, with at least one prominent historian (Ronald Hutton) making the case – albeit with important qualifications – for literary influence on fairy belief.[107] The case for literature influencing fairy belief is easier to make, in fact, than the case for real-world fairy belief determining the portrayal of literary fairies. While Green laments the functionalism of much criticism of medieval fairy literature, it is hard to escape the versatility of fairies as a literary *deus ex machina* with the capacity to supply fantastical narrative elements that could not easily be obtained elsewhere. Furthermore, the romances present no coherent picture of who or what the fairies are, or even whether they are human or non-human beings.[108]

---

[107] Hutton, 'Making of the Early Modern British Fairy Tradition', pp. 1140–41.
[108] Hutton, 'Making of the Early Modern British Fairy Tradition', p. 1140.

However, while tracing the precise inspirations for literary fairies may be impossible, the female godlings who became the fairies were entwined with the idea of narrative long before they became a *deus ex machina* to provoke or resolve the narratives of the authors of medieval romance. From the beginning, the Parcae were goddesses of the narrative of human life, determining the circumstances of a person's birth, fortune and death through their weaving of the thread of destiny. In this sense the Parcae and their re-personified successors the *fata* – ironically, while lacking a narrative myth of their own – are deities of narrative and resolvers of story, a role they take on in folktales as well as literary romance. In the same way that 'fairy tales' are about choice, destiny and enchantment rather than about fairies, so romances are fairy narratives because they are set in an imaginative world determined by the forces of fate, destiny and fortune that are the province of the fairies and bear little relation to the cosmos of Christian theologians. The prominence of actual fairy characters in romances or folktales is, arguably, an incidental matter in comparison with the prominence of *fatalitas* (as destiny and enchantment) within the narrative.

Katharine Briggs believed that the fairies of romance had begun life as humans possessed of magical powers, and observed that 'It is rather paradoxical that the word "fairy" now generally used to describe non-human and non-angelic creatures should have been first used about the illusions conjured up by these human enchantresses'.[109] Briggs was right that, until the fifteenth century, the

---

[109] Briggs, *Fairies in Tradition and Literature*, p. 10.

word *fée/fay* was more often used as a participle (meaning 'enchanted') than as a noun, and its use is thus not reliably diagnostic of whether beings so described were human or nonhuman entities.[110] Fairies were simply 'enchanting/ enchanted ones'. However, it is also possible that non-human fairies became euhemerised as humans with magical powers, if human enchanters were more acceptable to a particular audience than supernatural beings with no clear place in the Christian cosmos. The question of whether the fairies of romance began life as human or supernatural is essentially an irresolvable 'chicken and egg' problem, but if Briggs was right that literary fairies began as human, then their relationship with the fairies of medieval folklore is tenuous indeed.

It was not only those characters explicitly identified as fairies in the medieval romances who belonged to the fairy realm. On one interpretation, the entire chivalric fantasy is a kind of fairyland, since its human heroes – even if they had once lived on earth – were now believed to inhabit the fairy realm. A fourteenth-century Dominican preacher denounced 'superstitious wretches' who believed the heroes Onewyn, Wade and (according to a later manuscript) 'King Arthur and his retainers' lived in 'elvenland',[111] and Chaucer's Wife of Bath famously declared that 'In olde days of the king Arthour,/ Of which that Britons speake great honour,/All was this

---

[110] Hutton, 'Making of the Early Modern British Fairy Tradition', pp. 1140–41.

[111] Green, 'Refighting Carlo Ginzburg's Night Battles', p. 394. The idea that Arthur was taken to fairyland can be found in Stephen of Rouen's *Draco Normannicus* (c. 1167–1169); see Tatlock, 'Geoffrey and King Arthur', pp. 113–25.

land full fill'd of faerie'.[112] The distinction between an imagined past inhabited by characters with magical powers and fairies, and a fairyland inhabited by both human and non-human heroes, may not have been as clear cut to late medieval writers and preachers as it is to us, with our clearly defined literary distinction between low and high fantasy.

By the fourteenth century romance was a clearly defined genre with its own conventions, yet it also formed part of a wider elite culture in which the surviving literature of Greece and Rome was most valued and prestigious. Since the gods of Classical literature were unequivocally identified with demons by most medieval theologians, there was little scope for medieval authors to elaborate new stories about the deities of Olympus; but the morally ambiguous fairies may have provided an outlet for the classicising impulse under a different and genre-appropriate guise. Thus Sir Orfeo of Winchester takes the place of Orpheus, and the Fairy King stands in for Pluto/Hades in *Sir Orfeo*. It is clear that some of the fairies of romance are little more than thinly veiled Classical gods, such as Chaucer's fairy king and queen in *The Merchant's Tale*, named Pluto and Proserpina, while Morgan le Fay bears many characteristics of Circe and Medea.[113] It is possible, therefore, that one of the many versatile literary purposes of fairies in medieval romance was to introduce figures with the capacity to act like Classical deities while keeping them at arm's length from the contested realm of theology.

---

[112] Quoted in Kassell, 'All Was This Land Full Fill'd of Faerie', pp. 118–19.
[113] Hutton, *Queens of the Wild*, pp. 83, 86–87.

Fairies in Ritual Magic

The conjuration of fairies in ritual magic (as opposed to the conjuration of demons common in medieval clerical magic) was largely a phenomenon of the late sixteenth century (and thus beyond the scope of this book),[114] but it was rooted in much older medieval fantasies of a fairy magic practiced in literature by women (even if real-world learned magic was practised almost entirely by men).[115] In the sixteenth century, for whatever reason, fantasy crossed over into reality (or at least an attempted realisation of an imagined reality), as male magicians tried to conjure the beautiful fairy women of romance in the hope of gaining sexual control over them.[116] If fairy-conjuring was a new phenomenon, however, the involvement of fairies in magic was not. As we have seen, the very word 'faierie' in Middle English had the double meaning of the fairy realm and the state of enchantment, and Owen Davies has argued that the fairies provided a way for unlearned magical practitioners to account for their powers,[117] such as the Clerk family whom we met at the beginning of this chapter.

Magic in medieval Europe was often both highly transgressive and deeply conservative: transgressive in its willingness to invoke beings whose veneration was forbidden, such as pagan deities and apocryphal or invented angels; and conservative in its preservation of earlier religious practices as magical rites. Whether or not we view magic

---

[114] Harms, 'Hell and Fairy', pp. 55–77.
[115] Green, *Elf Queens*, p. 107.
[116] Klaassen and Bens, 'Achieving Invisibility', p. 4.
[117] Davies, *Popular Magic*, pp. 183–84.

as a degraded or degenerate form of religion – which is a controversial thesis – it is clear that a belief or practice that may have originated in religion may be preserved in magical tradition, shorn of its religious meaning.[118] Yet the existence of magical traditions, in and of itself, need not be of any religious significance; the appearance of garbled Arabic prayers in medieval British grimoires, for instance, does not mean British magicians were Muslims.[119] This kind of religion-to-magic transformation is one available model for explaining medieval fairy belief; the 'faerie' (the enchanted and enchanting ones) were embodiments of the idea of magic itself, and they perpetuated pagan gods and godlings in a vestigial form, but as magical rather than as cultic figures. Fairies are thus better understood as artefacts of medieval magic rather than artefacts of deviant religiosity, even if they were assembled from elements drawn from pre-Christian religion.

As early as the fifteenth century, a verse tract on alchemy portrayed the Fairy Queen, named as Elchyyell, as a revealer and teacher of alchemical secrets.[120] However, claiming to have received magical assistance from the fairies or conceiving of the fairies as the embodiment of magic was rather different from claiming to be able to conjure fairies at will. While the Reformation had a limited impact on ritual magic and discouraged some ritual magicians from invoking the Virgin Mary and the saints (for example), there is no good reason to believe that fairy-conjuring was a product of the Reformation, since

---

[118] Hutton, *Pagan Religions*, p. 295; Hutton, *Queens of the Wild*, pp. 31–32.
[119] Young, *Magic in Merlin's Realm*, p. 46.
[120] Hutton, *Queens of the Wild*, p. 102.

there are plenty of pre-Reformation examples of fairies evoked in ritual magical practice from the eve of England's religious upheavals in the 1520s and 1530s. When the monk William Stapleton conjured spirits in Norfolk in the 1520s one of them was called Oberion, echoing the name of Shakespeare's fairy king in *A Midsummer Night's Dream*; (c. 1595/1596);[121] the same spirit was also conjured by a group of Yorkshire treasure-hunters in 1510.[122] In 1532 Edward Legh reported to Thomas Cromwell a conversation with William Neville about the magician William Wade, who 'had his knowledge of the fairies' and offered sacrifices to them.[123]

Legh's mention of sacrifices to the fairies is interesting in the context of rites of conjuration that seem to imitate, albeit in a more elaborate form, much older ritual behaviours mentioned by Burchard of Worms and Bartholomew Iscanus: the laying of a table with three knives for the Parcae. While such a practice is better understood as folk religion than ritual magic, the summoning of three fairy women by laying a table for them either survived or was revived as a magical practice in the sixteenth century.[124] However, fairies were also conjured singly as well as in groups of three. One of the first fairies to be conjured in English magic may have been Sibylla or Sibyllia; a form of conjuration of Sybilla appears in Cambridge University Library MS Add. 3544, a working

---

[121] Young, *Magic in Merlin's Realm*, pp. 145–46. Hutton, 'Making of the Early Modern British Fairy Tradition', p. 1147, traces the name to the dwarf ruler Auberon in the romance *Huon of Bordeaux*.
[122] Klaassen and Wright, *Magic of Rogues*, pp. 120–21.
[123] Klaassen and Wright, *Magic of Rogues*, p. 33.
[124] Klaassen and Bens, 'Achieving Invisibility', p. 6.

magician's grimoire dating probably to the 1530s, where she is identified as a 'prophetess' but not named as a fairy.[125] In the 1580s Reginald Scot explained that Sibylia was 'a sister of the fairies',[126] but the use of the name for fairy characters goes back at least to the fifteenth century, when the French writer Antoine de la Sale wrote about a visit to a cave that, he was told, would give him access to 'the paradise of Queen Sibyl' (who is clearly the fairy queen).[127] In medieval England, 'Sibyl' was a generic term for a female seer, and in the romances it was frequently applied to fairies.[128]

Lauren Kassell has suggested that the appearance of fairies in magical practice coincided with the decline of fairy belief in society at large (or, at least, a great deal of talk of its decline).[129] As Jan Veenstra and Karin Olsen have observed, fairies 'could thrive in the world of magic and the world of art where the boundaries between fiction and reality were seriously blurred' even when their existence was questioned elsewhere in an increasingly sceptical culture.[130] Magic thrives on transgression, and it is possible that the growth of fairy conjuring among ritual magicians was encouraged in part by Reformation attempts to suppress fairy belief. It is equally possible that some magicians chose to conjure fairies because, in the heated religious atmosphere of the Reformation, they were less controversial than demons and angels. But the

[125] Foreman, *Cambridge Book of Magic*, pp. 54–55.
[126] Scot, *Discoverie of Witchcraft*, pp. 246–48.
[127] Green, *Elf Queens*, p. 40.
[128] Green, *Elf Queens*, pp. 142–43.
[129] Kassell, 'All Was This Land Full Fill'd of Faerie', pp. 107–22.
[130] Veenstra and Olsen, 'Introduction', p. viii.

appearance of fairy conjuring before the watershed of the Reformation suggests that, at root, it may be an epiphenomenon of the arrival of fairy belief in its modern form in the early sixteenth century: a complex composite of earlier beliefs about distinct groups of supernatural beings that had finally taken on a life of its own and penetrated the lives of those for whom fairies were real.

William Stapleton's attempted conjurations of the spirit Incubus in Norfolk, a few miles away from where, eleven centuries earlier, devotees of the god Faunus-Incubo had performed esoteric rites in his honour provides an apt illustration of the limitations and opportunities of history in the *longue durée*. On the one hand, explaining the causal relationship between these two ritual acts is a difficult and complex task, perhaps yielding no definitive answer; but on the other, and setting aside questions of causal relationship, a comparison of these two moments separated by many ages shows that they share much in common – even down to a preoccupation with magical rings and the offering of sacrifice. This does not mean that the paganism of fourth-century Norfolk 'survived' into the sixteenth century, of course, but it does point to the existence of deep and persistent cultural currents drawing religious believers to transgressive ritual practices invoking and placating beings connected with buried treasure, prophecy and good fortune.

Conclusion

Those beings that came to be known as 'elves' and later 'fairies' in medieval Britain were a composite cultural creation whose origins are probably to be found in a synthesis of British (that is, Breton, Welsh and Cornish) and English popular culture that occurred in the aftermath of the Norman Conquest. It is not so much that the fairies were a novel creation at this time, but that the word 'elf' proved resilient (for whatever reason) at a time when the range of supernatural beings people believed in seemed to be contracting. In default of other terms, a miscellaneous range of beings came to be named as 'elves', and the fairies of medieval Britain are best viewed not as a singular class of beings, but as a ragtag alliance of supernatural beings from various sources – not unlike the chaotic jumble of grotesque forms in the fairy illustrations of Arthur Rackham or Brian Froud. Over time, the characteristics of elves/fairies stabilised and new characteristics emerged, such as the idea that fairies might be in some way dependent on human beings for certain needs and, at the very end of the Middle Ages, the notion that fairies could be conjured by magicians.

Older characteristics acquired by elves/fairies in the Middle Ages included their penchant for stealing children (borrowed from the lamiae of the ancient world); their helpfulness in the home (acquired, perhaps, from the Lares and Penates) – including, sometimes, less welcome poltergeist-like activity; their desire to have intercourse with men and women, especially in wild places (borrowed from the fauns, dusii, incubi and succubi) and, of course, their association with fate and destiny – extending into the realm of magic and enchantment – derived ultimately from the Parcae. Furthermore, the Middle Ages crystallised the idea that the fairies lived in an otherworld kingdom (usually underground), an idea that seems to have originated in Welsh folklore and British belief.

Occasionally, the fairies were portrayed as diminutive in stature, and the idea that they were dangerous persisted from the threatening Anglo-Saxon elves. Over time, the concept of *fatalitas/faerie* that gave the fairies their name developed into complex ideas about magic and enchantment; however, while the fairies of romance were clearly inspired in some way by folklore, there is no reliable way to trace the ultimate origins of literary fairies or establish their relationship with widespread popular belief. However, by 1500 the British fairy had taken the form in which it would meet the Reformation, and ultimately the Enlightenment.

Epilogue

The Fairy Legacy

~

It has been the argument of this book that a plausible history of Britain's godlings – albeit with a number of problematic lacunae – can be told in the *longue durée* from the Iron Age to the late Middle Ages. The 'small gods' of Britain are supernatural beings with a history, once we are prepared to accept that they are culturally constructed beings with a place both in folklore and learned culture, and influenced by the interaction and interplay of both. The introduction of the concept of the *longue durée* makes it possible to set aside some of the stronger claims that have been made in favour of the survival of pagan gods as demoted nature spirits. Godlings are ancient, and a feature of popular religion in both the pre-Christian and the Christian period, but this does not make them an ark preserving earlier strata of belief. As noted in Chapter 1 above, Britain's lesser supernatural beings are rather a ship of Theseus where every part has undergone restoration, reinvention and replacement. Nevertheless, just as a survey of the new parts of Theseus' ship gives some sense of the character of that ship in earlier phases of its existence, so Britain's godlings are not without some continuity.

There is a case for long-term survival from the distant past to be made for spirits associated with water sources such as wells and streams, but the keynote of Britain's godlings is reinvention and innovation for particular historical circumstances. While the survival of some elements of Romano-British belief is not impossible, this book has argued that the godlings we know as the fairies and their immediate antecedents are creations of the Christian era – even if it would be misleading to describe them as Christian beings. The writings of Church Fathers such as Isidore of Seville, Jerome and Augustine on fauns, nymphs, the Parcae, pygmies and heroes were crucial in forming learned discourses that fed eventually into popular culture. Britain's godlings were thus transmitted indirectly from the Classical world through patristic writings, which fed in turn into pastoral literature such as penitentials and sermons. The godlings were also subjected to complex processes of demonisation, undemonisation and – in some cases – 're-personification' that often transformed them entirely.

The reinvention of gods as ciphers, symbols and embodiments of abstract qualities began at the very moment the veneration of the gods as objects of genuine worship ceased. The evidence from Roman Britain suggests that while in some places Christians may have been perpetrating iconoclasm against images of the gods, in other places Christians were creating new portrayals of Classical mythology in which gods and heroes became abstracted representations of Christian virtue. Clearly, while some perceived the legacy of pagan religion as a threat, to others it was nothing more than a spent force; and it was into the space created by this difference of Christian opinion that deities crept back. It is a short step from portraying abstract concepts via images of the gods to personifying those concepts as gods; and thus godlings seem to have been rescued from the brink of destruction at the hands of Christians by the processes of re-invention and re-personification. Having been disassembled and demonised, godlings re-assembled themselves; the Parcae were dead, but the speech of the Parcae, the *fata* ('things uttered'), became personified and took on a life of their own as the children (or grandchildren) of the Parcae: the fairies.

Throughout this book, I have been careful about using the term 'survival' for Britain's godlings. While the term is not always inappropriate, it risks implying that 'small gods' belong by rights to the past, and obscures the fact that such beings are always evolving and adapting in the collective cultural imagination. There is nothing archaic about belief in such beings, and nothing especially surprising about their 'survival'; even under Christianity, organised hostility to belief in small gods has been rare. Rather, the idea that belief in godlings has survived against the odds – rather than being a near-universal feature of human religious experience – represents a projection of the distinctive cultural norms of contemporary Western society onto the past. In other words, there is general acceptance that belief in fairies is particularly ridiculous, even set beside other supernatural beliefs, so explaining why people in the past took them seriously requires special explanations to be invoked. Yet the fact that fairies are risible in modern British culture says more about the peculiar features of modern British religious culture than about the cultures of the past. Furthermore, the idea that fairies are in some way archaic, and barely survive into the present, is itself part of the fairy tradition. As Carole Silver observed, 'The fairies have been leaving England since the fourteenth century ... but despite their perpetual farewells they had not completely vanished from Great Britain by the 1920s'.[1] Yet the idea that the godlings were gone is even older; as we have seen, Gildas was already convinced in the sixth century that veneration paid to the spirits of mountains, valleys and rivers was a thing long gone from Britain.

The belief that godlings are always on the way out may be down to the low or unclear status they enjoy within religious cosmologies; even in Ovid's *Fasti*, the numen Faunus is unsure whether he will have any power to influence Jupiter. The chthonic *di nemorum*, the gods of the groves, always occupy a position subordinate to the celestial Olympians, and then subordinate to the Olympians' transcendent Christian successor as supreme deity. The theory advocated by Emma Wilby and Michael Ostling that godlings represent and embody a more basic substratum of animistic belief beneath later polytheisms is not without merit, although it is largely unproveable. In the specific case of Roman religion, godlings of nature do indeed seem to be older than the Greek-influenced official pantheon, but projecting this Roman situation onto Britain is perilous. Fairies may or may not be survivals of pre-Christian animism in some attenuated form, but they certainly embody the survival of a pre-Christian mode of thought in which fate, rather than divine providence, determines human destiny. *Fatalitas*, whether understood as the enactment of destiny or as enchantment, and characterised by brutal fairy justice, stands as a counterpoint to the merciful *providentia* of Christ's economy of

---

[1] Silver, *Strange and Secret Peoples*, p. 185.

salvation. In this sense, the answer to the question 'Are fairies pagan?' must be yes – they are beings who belong in the pre-Christian world, even if the nature of their historical origination in that world can be contested.

Britain's folkloric beings have been through many adaptations, re-fashionings and re-inventions – and at this distance in time it is often difficult to distinguish which of these has occurred. The spirits of Iron Age Britain, whoever and whatever they truly were, were made to conform to the patterns of Roman religion; then the gods of Roman Britain, demonised by Christianity, were re-fashioned by folklore into the little-understood godlings of post-Roman Britain and Anglo-Saxon England, before the Norman Conquest occasioned yet another re-invention based on an imagined or constructed 'British' past. By the fourteenth century, the elves of medieval England included traces of other forgotten beings, and a fairly coherent idea of a fairy otherworld was beginning to form. The elves or fairies were embodied, morally ambivalent beings, living in a realm beneath the earth and possessing powers of magic; exempt, at least in part, from the passage of time, they were nevertheless occasionally in need of human beings. Fairies seduced human men and women, and they stole children and caused illness in people and animals. Sometimes ethereally beautiful and sometimes ugly and diminutive, the fairies were associated with rocks, hills and springs but might also take up residence in domestic dwellings.

Although it lies beyond the scope of this book, the Reformation in the sixteenth century occasioned another refashioning of folkloric beings, who were relentlessly demonised until they became witches' imps and familiars, mere terrestrial devils distinguishable only from the demons of hell by their gross materiality – at least, for those who did not deny the existence of the fairies altogether as a delusion of the age of popery. While traces of fairy belief survived this onslaught to be recorded by nineteenth-century folklorists, ridicule and the Victorian tendency to associate fairies with children meant that active belief in fairies as folkloric beings was largely extinct by around 1900. Yet even then another reinvention awaited, as fairies were picked up by Theosophists and Spiritualists and then by global mass popular culture and fantasy fiction, creating varieties of 'international fairy' that are rarely objects of heartfelt belief, but continue to serve as a canvas for the projection of human dreams about the almost-human.[2]

The Classicising Legacy

One of the most prominent re-constructed buildings at Vindolanda Roman fort on Hadrian's Wall is a nymphaeum in the form of a small temple placed in a picturesque landscape next to a small stream (Plate 17). A decorative feature and an evocation of Roman religion rather than a re-construction of any specific building, the nymphaeum echoes the many ornamental 'temples', often dedicated to the nymphs, that are scattered throughout Britain's eighteenth-century landscape gardens. While such structures were no doubt little more than aesthetic affectations for many landowners, not every lover of

---

[2] On contemporary fairy belief see Magliocco, "'Reconnecting to Everything'", pp. 325–48.

the Classical world was disconnected from its spiritual dimension. When he visited the Roman fort at Papcastle, the eighteenth-century antiquary William Stukeley went so far as to make an offering to the nymphs, pouring a libation of wine into a spring,[3] and the sight of modern offerings of coins inside the patera (the dish-shaped depression) of a Roman altar is a common sight at Roman sites throughout Britain. The interpretation of such apparent ritual activities at ancient sacred sites is a subject of academic debate, but just as Stukeley felt compelled in some way to honour the spirits of place, so many modern visitors find themselves offering some token recognition of the sacredness of a location in the landscape. Yet it is noteworthy that, for Stukeley at Papcastle in the eighteenth century and for the Vindolanda Trust in the twentieth, the cult of the nymphs as spirits of place became the focus of re-constructions of Roman religion rather than, say, the burnt offerings of cattle to Jupiter. When the notorious libertine Sir Francis Dashwood dedicated a portico on his West Wycombe estate to Bacchus, the festivities featured a re-creation of the Bacchic *thiasos* of 'Bacchanals, Priests, Priestess[es], Pan, Fawns, Satyrs, Silenus, &c. all adorned in proper habits, and skins wreathed with vine leaves, ivy, oak, &c.' and culminated in an ode dedicated 'to the Deity of the place' rather than any form of sacrifice.[4]

While Roman state religion has little meaning to modern Britons, and the gods of Olympus are little

---

[3] Henig, *Religion in Roman Britain*, p. 115.
[4] 'A Description of the Grand Jubilee at Lord Le Despencer's, at West-Wycombe', p. 409.

more than characters in children's stories, the appeal of godlings like the nymphs seems to remain – in part, perhaps, because it is rooted in the landscape itself rather than culturally specific religious abstractions. When, in the late eighteenth century, the Romantic movement re-ignited a sense of the numinous value of landscapes and the natural world, a revival of a more or less ironic 'cult' of ancient rustic godlings was not far behind. Yet, in all likelihood, some of the tenants of Georgian estates who laboured to build temples to the nymphs for the aesthetic pleasure of landowners were themselves believers in those godlings of nature and the land who had never departed. At the start of this book we saw how John Aubrey identified fairy belief as a remnant of Roman religion, and many early modern authors did not hesitate to treat ancient godlings and the fairies of their own world in the same breath. In John Milton's poem 'On the Morning of Christ's Nativity', densely packed with Classical allusions, the godlings of the ancient world are sent packing by the infant Christ: 'The parting Genius is with sighing sent', 'The Nymphs in twilight shade of tangled thickets mourn', 'The Lars and Lemures moan with midnight plaint'. But Milton does not restrict himself to Classical beings; Christ evicts the fairies too: 'And the yellow-skirted fays/Fly after the night-steeds, leaving their moon-lov'd maze'.[5]

In a similar way, in Robert Burton's *Anatomy of Melancholy*, the Classical nymphs and satyrs appear alongside the fairies of contemporary popular belief in an

---

[5] Milton, *Poems*, pp. 10–12.

anachronistic flattening of history,[6] while fauns made it into the title of the Scottish minister Robert Kirk's celebrated book about fairies, *The Secret Commonwealth of Elves, Fauns and Fairies* (1691), even if he never discussed fauns in the text. One possible reason for these odd juxtapositions of Classical learning and folklore was that the Classical godlings were more acceptable subjects of learned discussion than the fairies, and therefore a discussion of both sets of beings was potentially more accessible, and more palatable, to a learned early modern audience. Jan Veenstra and Karin Olsen have noted, 'The spirits of woods, fields, mountains, rivers and lakes, the little folk from fairy stories, the familiar spirits of witchcraft lore and the ghostly inhabitants of the four elements' did not become objects of serious intellectual enquiry and learned speculation until the Renaissance.[7]

It was the supposed Classical antecedents of the fairies that may have saved them from total demonisation at the time of the Reformation, which saw a redoubling of those efforts already made by medieval theologians and preachers to classify the supernatural world into good angels and evil demons. Protestant theologians persistently associated fairy belief with the era of 'popery', to the point where the fairies became an emblem of the follies of the vanished Catholic world.[8] Furthermore, Emma Wilby has traced much of the imagery of early modern witchcraft confessions to fairy lore, arguing that people

---

[6] Burton, *Anatomie of Melancholy*, pp. 46–47, 245, 560.
[7] Veenstra and Olsen, 'Introduction', p. vii.
[8] On fairies in the Reformation era see Buccola, *Fairies, Fractious Women and the Old Faith*; Oldridge, 'Fairies and the Devil', pp. 1–15.

were compelled to use language acceptable to the judicial authorities and re-frame fairy beliefs in demonological and infernal terms.[9] The possibility that fairy belief would be crushed entirely under the weight of Protestant demonological opprobrium was averted, however, by a simultaneous revival of self-conscious Classicism in early modern England, which made it acceptable not only to talk about gods and godlings, but also to elide other supernatural beings with them. A striking example of such elision was Charles Hoole's English-Latin dictionary of 1649, where Hoole translated 'Angel-guardian' as *Genius*,[10] while proposing *lamiae* for fairies and *Lamia* for the Fairy Queen. Elves were *larvae*, while *Fauni* were 'Fairies of the wood', *Dryades* 'Fairies of the Okes', *Nymphae* 'Fairies of the Springs', *Naiades* 'Fairies of the Streams' (mermaids?) and *Oreades* 'Fairies of the Hills'. 'Fairies of the house' (presumably pucks and brownies) were *Lares*, while 'Spirits in the Air', in a probable mistranscription of *dusii*, were *Clusii*.[11]

Hoole was not alone in thinking it acceptable to identify the guardian angel of Christian belief with the genius,[12] and there are indications that this kind of language went beyond cosmetic aesthetic Classicism. Some people seem to have entertained the idea that the godlings of the ancient world still lurked in the English countryside. As part of a discussion of Robin Goodfellow, whom John Aubrey had already identified with the god Faunus,

---

[9] Wilby, *Cunning-Folk*, pp. 50–57; see also Young, *Suffolk Fairylore*, pp. 67–75.
[10] Hoole, *Easie Entrance*, p. 145.
[11] Hoole, *Easie Entrance*, p. 146.
[12] See, for example, 'Pen', *A Pleasant Treatise of Witches*, pp. 120–26.

the Wiltshire antiquary noted that Virgil had spoken in the *Georgics* 'of Voyces heard louder than a Man's',[13] and reported that his friend Lancelot Morehouse 'did averre to me *super verbum sacerdotis* [on his word as a priest], that he did once heare such a loud Laugh on the other side of a hedge; and was sure that no Human voice could afford such Laugh'.[14] Aubrey's implication was that if Robin Goodfellow really existed, he could be expected to act like the Roman fauns, producing strange noises in wild nature. When an image of Robin Goodfellow appeared on the frontispiece of the 1639 chapbook *Robin Goodfellow, His Merry Prankes and Mad Jests* he was portrayed as a priapic, moustachioed Pan, faun or satyr dancing in a ring of diminutive fairies, and holding a candle and broom – emblems, presumably, of his status as a domestic fairy who helped with housework (Plate 18).[15] The bizarre image combines Classical speculations like Aubrey's with the most prosaic ideas about Robin Goodfellow as a domestic sprite.

The juxtaposition of Classical divinities with folkloric beings was a cultural artefact of the Renaissance, and in the aftermath of the Romantic rediscovery of 'Celtic' fairy belief it was forgotten by many – yet not all. In the late nineteenth century, the distinctive portrayal of the supernatural by the Welsh writer Arthur Machen (1863–1947) was inspired not only by Arthurian legend but also by the Roman remains in the midst of which he grew up in

---

[13] Perhaps a reference to Virgil, *Georgics* 3.45, *et vox adsensu nemorum ingeminata remugit* ('and a vast voice was heard widely through the silent groves').
[14] Aubrey, *Remaines*, p. 81.
[15] Robichaud, *Pan*, pp. 61–63.

Caerleon. The source of the uncanny in Machen's supernatural tales is often unease about relics of ancient rites left behind from Roman Britain. Machen took an active interest in Roman archaeology; in his story 'The Great God Pan' (1894), for example, Machen drew on W. M. Hiley Bathurst's commentary on archaeological discoveries at Lydney when he identified the god Nodens (whom Machen seems to have viewed as a British analogue of Pan) as 'the god of the Great Deep or Abyss'.[16] In the story 'The White People' (1904), in a typical elision of the folkloric and the Classical, a girl learns to speak 'the fairy language', yet the beings she encounters are identified as nymphs.[17] Similarly, in John Buchan's novel *Witch Wood* (1927), in which a seventeenth-century Scottish Presbyterian minister exposes secret pagan worship in his local community, the focus of the abominable cult of a zoomorphic god named Abiron turns out to be a Roman altar inscribed with the letters 'I. O. M.' (*Iovi optimo maximo*, 'to Jupiter best and greatest') – evidence that 'the mysteries of the heathen had been here'.[18]

While the idea that the roots of British folklore and popular religion could be traced back to Roman Britain still held appeal for authors such as Machen and Buchan, and indeed for C. S. Lewis, for many others the scramble to discern the origins of the fairies as decayed Celtic gods or a peculiarity of Celtic belief had the effect of squeezing out any sense of Britain's folkloric beings as

---

[16] Machen, *The Great God Pan*, p. 53; Hiley Bathurst, *Roman Antiquities*, p. 39.
[17] Machen, *The White People*, pp. 111–47.
[18] Buchan, *Witch Wood*, p. 86.

members of a broad, international, cross-cultural category of 'small gods'. Yet while early modern commentators like Aubrey were wrong about the exact nature of the relationship between Faunus and Robin Goodfellow and between the nymphs of Arcadia and the dancing fairies of rural England, it is the contention of this book that they were right in perceiving fauns, nymphs and fairies as the same sort of beings (Plate 19). Now that the phantasm of a universal 'Celtic' culture has been banished from scholarship, it is possible to explore once again the possibility that Britain's godlings can ultimately be traced to Greece and Rome – at least as their inspiration.

Almost Human, Not Quite Divine

Many years ago, a friend who works as a conservationist in Vietnam told me about an unexpected encounter he once had with an orangutan in the rainforest of Borneo, while he was climbing a tree in order to observe birds. As the conservationist approached the level of the canopy he heard the orangutan's approach and then saw her at close quarters, fixing him with an intent and human-like stare of curiosity. The human observer of nature was conscious of an abrupt reversal, as he became the one observed – and observed on equal terms by a being of near-human intelligence, a dweller in the world of the forest canopy into which he had intruded. When Europeans first encountered great apes in the sixteenth and seventeenth centuries they sometimes approached them via a conceptual framework grounded in the medieval tradition of *naturalia*, in which strange human-like creatures like satyrs and pygmies were supposed to dwell in remote lands. As we have seen in Chapter 4 above, in the medieval tradition the satyr was primarily a *pilosus*, with the bestiaries omitting mention of its horns and hooves, and therefore it is not altogether surprising that great apes such as gorillas and orangutans came to be named by some early commentators as the 'Indian satyr' (*satyrus Indicus*).[19] At the same time, the Malay name of the orangutan was rendered literally into Latin as *homo silvestris*, 'man of the woods', evoking folkloric beings, while others described apes as 'pygmies', recalling a long tradition of commentary on diminutive human or semi-human races reaching back to Herodotus.[20]

The seventeenth-century clergyman and physician John Webster did not hesitate to identify the satyrs, fauns and pans of the ancients with misinterpreted or exaggerated apes, and even suggested that belief in fairies arose from misidentified pygmies.[21] A surviving late seventeenth- or early eighteenth-century handbill advertised 'A most Astonishing Creature, called the Ethiopian SATYR, or Real wild-Man of the Woods' at Holborn Hill, in language apparently calculated to appeal to an audience interested in folkloric beings (Plate 20).[22] Francis Moran has noted early modern commentators' intense desire to see the humanity (or semi-humanity) of gorillas, chimpanzees and orangutans,[23] which might

---

[19] See, for example, Tulp, *Observationum medicarum libri*, pp. 274–75; Dapper, *Description de l'Afrique*, p. 257
[20] Moran, 'Between Primates and Primitives', pp. 39–42.
[21] Webster, *Displaying of Supposed Witchcraft*, pp. 280–84.
[22] Wellcome Collection, wellcomecollection.org/works/z4x3bu35, accessed 27 April 2022.
[23] Moran, 'Between Primates and Primitives', pp. 39–42.

seem at first surprising in light of Christian beliefs about the uniqueness of human beings as the only creatures made in God's image. However, medieval works of *naturalia* were suffused with ambiguity about the line between the human and the non-human and, for that matter, the non-human and the supernatural. In a world where sincere belief in human-like fairies was still possible, the idea that humans and apes might share a single or a similar nature was scarcely a strange one.

The observation that aliens, alien abduction narratives and UFO encounters are the modern equivalents of encounters with fairies has been made so often that it is almost a cliché of writing about fairy belief.[24] Yet aliens are really more like angels or demons than fairies. They are inhabitants of a completely different realm, characterised by their difference rather than by their similarity to human beings. It is the longings of cryptozoology, and in particular the desire to believe in human-like cryptids, that more nearly match the fairy lore of the past; like fairies, cryptids are imagined to co-exist on earth with human beings, even if they are hidden from us, and they represent the almost-human rather than the radically different. Furthermore, like fairies, cryptids seem to embody much the same anxieties about humans' relationship with nature and with the animal world that may have given rise to belief in the *di nemorum*, those godlings who were always entwined with nature like the nymphs and fauns. The first Europeans to meet our closest evolutionary relatives processed those anxieties, at least in part, by falling back on language drawn from a medieval tradition

---

[24] Green, *Elf Queens*, p. 41.

of *naturalia* where the natural, the marvellous and the supernatural overlapped, as they frequently do in modern cryptozoology.[25]

Yet the cryptozoologists' longing to believe that we share our world with mysterious, almost-human beings is also a kind of denial. Rather than grappling with the difficult question of how we relate to real-world sentient animals of near-human intelligence, human beings take refuge in cultural constructions of imagined, hidden beings who always lie beyond the fringe of scientific knowledge, or beyond our ability to detect them, like the monsters who people the edges of old maps. Our reluctance to rethink our relationship to the animal world seems, in turn, to be just one expression of a broader dysfunctionality in humans' interaction with our natural environment. As Chris Gosden has argued, whether we choose to acknowledge it or not, we dwell within 'sensate ecologies' that include other non-human sentient beings, and 'it is often difficult to say where the body stops and its surroundings start'.[26] It is increasingly clear that the unease many people feel at the exploitation of sentient animals, the felling of ancient trees or the poisoning and destruction of habitats is moral and spiritual as well as emerging from a sense of global civic responsibility or a self-interested, pragmatic fear for the survival of the human species as we lay waste to non-renewable resources.

In ages past, the collective human cultural imagination constructed intermediate beings who bridged the gap between the human and the non-human, and between the

[25] Turner 'The Place of Cryptids in Taxonomic Debates', pp. 12–31.
[26] Gosden, *History of Magic*, p. 416.

human and the divine: morally ambivalent, often frightening beings who became the focus for anxieties about the threats posed by nature – and by untamed human nature – but who also held out the possibility that humans could gain access to a knowledge and wisdom that lay beyond the human realm. Just as human encounters with the 'almost human' great apes expose the nature as well as the shortcomings of human beings, so past encounters with the culturally constructed 'almost human' are revealing of human nature. It may be that cultures that have largely abandoned or hopelessly caricatured the stories we tell about these almost human beings, consigning them to the nursery or to literary and cinematic fantasy, have lost an important means of negotiating humanity's relationship with the environment and with ourselves. But whatever tides of belief may have receded in the society of contemporary Britain, there are still brief moments of stillness when, somehow, the natural environment inexplicably seems to be gazing back. It is at those times that the words of Ovid may still be apt: *numen inest*, 'a spirit is in it'.

BIBLIOGRAPHY

Manuscript Sources

Aberdeen, UK, Aberdeen University Library MS 24
Aberystwyth, UK, National Library of Wales MS Cardiff 2.629
London, UK, British Library, MS Cotton Nero E 1
London, UK, British Library, MS Harley 3244
London, UK, British Library, MS Royal 12 C XIX
New York, USA, Morgan Library MS M.81

Primary Printed Sources

Ap Gwilym, Dafydd (ed. H. Idris Bell and David Bell), *Fifty Poems* (London: Honourable Society of Cymmrodorion, 1942)
Aubrey, John (ed. James Britten), *Remaines of Gentilisme and Judaisme* (London: Satchell, Peyton, and Co., 1881)
Baring-Gould, Sabine (ed.), *The Lives of the Saints* (London: John Hodges, 1872–77), 16 vols
Bieler, Ludwig (ed.), *Libri epistolarum Sancti Patricii episcopi: Introduction, Text and Commentary*, 2nd edn (Dublin: Royal Irish Academy, 1993)
Blake, E. O. (ed.), *Liber Eliensis*, Camden Third Series 92 (London: Royal Historical Society, 1962)
Bliss, A. J. (ed.), *Sir Orfeo*, 2nd edn (Oxford: Clarendon Press, 1966)
Bode, Georg Heinrich (ed.), *Scriptores rerum mythicarum latini tres Romae nuper reperti* (Celle: E. H. C. Schulze, 1834), 2 vols
Bradley, Sidney A. J. (ed.), *Anglo-Saxon Poetry* (London: J. M. Dent, 1982)

Bromwich, Rachel (ed.), *Trioedd Ynys Prydain: The Triads of the Island of Britain*, 4th edn (Cardiff: University of Wales Press, 2014)

Burton, Robert, *The Anatomie of Melancholy*, 6th edn (Oxford: Henry Cripps, 1651)

Calder, George (ed.), *Imtheachta Æniasa: The Irish Aeneid* (London: Irish Texts Society, 1907)

Camden, William (trans. Edmund Gibson), *Camden's Britannia Newly Translated into English* (London: F. Collins, 1695)

Cicero (trans. H. Rackham), *On the Nature of the Gods (De Natura Deorum) Academica*, Loeb Classical Library 268 (Cambridge, MA: Harvard University Press, 1933)

D'Achery, Luc and Mabillon, Jean (eds.), *Acta Sanctorum Ordinis S. Benedicti ... Pars Prima* (Venice: Sebastian Colet, 1734)

Dapper, Olfert, *Description de l'Afrique* (Amsterdam: W. Waesberge, 1686)

Darlington, Reginald B. (ed.), *The Vita Wulfstani of William of Malmesbury* (London: Offices of the Society, 1928)

'Description of the Grand Jubilee at Lord Le Despencer's, at West-Wycombe', *The Gentleman's Magazine* 41 (1771): 409

Foreman, Paul (ed. Francis Young), *The Cambridge Book of Magic: A Tudor Necromancer's Manual* (Cambridge: Texts in Early Modern Magic, 2015)

Forshall, Josiah and Madden, Frederic (eds.), *The Holy Bible, Containing the Old and New Testaments, with the Apocryphal Books, in the Earliest English Versions Made from the Latin Vulgate by John Wycliffe and His Followers* (Oxford: Oxford University Press, 1850), 4 vols

Fowler, Roger (ed.), *Wulfstan's Canons of Edgar* (London: Early English Text Society, 1972)

Gellius, Aulus (ed. John C. Rolfe), *Attic Nights, Volume I: Books 1–5*, Loeb Classical Library 195 (Cambridge, MA: Harvard University Press, 1927)

Geoffrey of Monmouth (trans. Neil Wright), *The Historia Regum Britanniae of Geoffrey of Monmouth* (Cambridge: D. S. Brewer, 1991)

Gerald of Wales (ed. James F. Dimock), *Giraldi Cambrensis opera* (London: Longmans, Green and Co., 1861–77), 8 vols

Gerald of Wales (trans. L. Thorpe), *The Journey through Wales and the Description of Wales* (Harmondsworth: Penguin, 1978)

Gervase of Tilbury (ed. Felix Liebrecht), *Des Gervasius von Tilbury Otia imperialia* (Hanover: Carl Rümpler, 1856)

Gunton, Symon (ed. Simon Patrick), *The History of the Church of Peterburgh* (London: Richard Chiswell, 1686)

Gwynn, John (ed.), *The Book of Armagh* (Dublin: Royal Irish Academy, 1913)

Hardy, Thomas D. and Martin, C. T. (eds.), *Gesta Herwardi incliti exulis et militis in Geoffroy Gaimar, Lestorie des Engles* (London: Her Majesty's Stationery Office, 1888), 2 vols

Harper-Bill, Christopher (ed.), *The Register of John Morton, Archbishop of Canterbury 1486–1500. Volume 3: Norwich sede vacante, 1499* (Woodbridge: Canterbury and York Society, 2000)

Herrick, Robert, *Hesperides* (London: John Williams, 1648)

Hoole, Charles, *An Easie Entrance to the Latine Tongue* (London: William Dugard, 1649)

Horstman, Carl (ed.), *The Early South-English Legendary* (London: Early English Text Society, 1887)

Isidore (ed. Stephen A. Barney, W. J. Lewis, J. A. Beach and Oliver Berghof), *The Etymologies of Isidore of Seville* (Cambridge: Cambridge University Press, 2006)

Jordanes (ed. Alfred Holder), *De origine et actibus Getarum* (Leipzig: Mohr, 1895)

Kirk, Robert, *The Secret Commonwealth of Elves, Fauns and Fairies* (London: David Nutt, 1893)

Lambarde, William, *A Perambulation of Kent* (London: Edmund Bollifant, 1596)

Lapidge, Michael (ed.), *The Roman Martyrs: Introduction, Translations, and Commentary* (Oxford: Oxford University Press, 2018)

Lapidge, Michael and Rosier, James L. (eds.), *Aldhelm: The Poetic Works* (Cambridge: D. S. Brewer, 1985)

Bibliography

Latham, Ronald E. (ed.), *Revised Medieval Latin Word List from British and Irish Sources* (Oxford: Oxford University Press, 1965)

Luck, George (ed.), *Arcana Mundi: Magic and the Occult in the Greek and Roman Worlds*, 2nd edn (Baltimore, MD: Johns Hopkins University Press, 2006)

Map, Walter (ed. M. R. James, C. N. L. Brooke and R. A. B. Mynors), *Walter Map: De Nugis Curialium: Courtiers' Trifles* (Oxford: Oxford University Press, 1983)

McNeill, John T. and Gamer, Helena A. (eds.), *Medieval Handbooks of Penance: A Translation of the Principal* libri poenitentiales *and Selections from Related Documents*, 2nd edn (New York: Columbia University Press, 1990)

Migne, Jacques-Paul. (ed.), *Patrologia Latina* (Paris: Jacques-Paul Migne, 1844–64), 221 vols

Milton, John, *Poems, &c. on Several Occasions* (London: Thomas Dring, 1673)

Morris-Jones, John and Rhys, John (eds.), *The Elucidarium and Other Tracts in Welsh from Llyvyr Agkyr Llandewivrevi, A. D. 1346* (Oxford: Clarendon Press, 1894)

Napier, Arthur S. (ed.), *Old English Glosses* (Oxford: Clarendon Press, 1900)

Nigel de Longchamps (ed. John H. Mozley and Robert R. Raymo), *Speculum stultorum* (Berkeley, CA: University of California Press, 1960)

Ovid (trans. J. G. Frazer), *Fasti*, Loeb Classical Library 253 (Cambridge, MA: Harvard University Press, 1931)

'Pen, A', *A Pleasant Treatise of Witches* (London, 1673)

Penry, John, *A Treatise Containing the Aequity of an Humble Supplication Which Is to Be Exhibited unto Hir Gracious Maiesty and This High Court of Parliament in the Behalfe of the Countrey of Wales* (Oxford: J. Barnes, 1587)

Pepin, Ronald E. (ed.), *The Vatican Mythographers* (New York: Fordham University Press, 2008)

Ralph of Coggeshall (ed. J. Stevenson), *Radulphi de Coggeshall Chronicon Anglicanum* (London: Her Majesty's Stationery Office, 1875)

Sabatier, Pierre (ed.), *Bibliorum Sacrorum versiones antiquae* (Rheims: Reginald Florentain, 1743), 3 vols

Salesbury, William, *A Dictionary in Englyshe and Welshe* (London: John Waley, 1547)

Schmitz, Hermann Joseph (ed.), *Die Bussbücher und die Bussdisciplin der Kirche* (Mainz: Verlag von Franz Kirchheim, 1883), 2 vols

Scot, Reginald, *The Discoverie of Witchcraft* (London: A Clark, 1665)

Scott, Walter, *Letters on Demonology and Witchcraft* (London: John Murray, 1830)

Scott, Walter, *Minstrelsy of the Scottish Border* (Kelso: James Ballantyne, 1802), 2 vols

Statius (ed. D. R. Shackleton Bailey), *Thebaid: Books 1–7*, Loeb Classical Library 207 (Cambridge, MA: Harvard University Press, 2004)

Steiner, Johann Wilhelm (ed.), *Codex inscriptionum Romanarum Danubii et Rheni* (Seligenstadt: Verfassers, 1854), 2 vols

Surius, Laurentius, *De probatis sanctorum historiis* (Cologne: Gervinus Calenius, 1570–75), 5 vols

Thomas of Monmouth (ed. A. Jessopp and M. R. James), *The Life and Miracles of St William of Norwich* (Cambridge: Cambridge University Press, 1896)

Thomas of Walsingham (ed. Henry Thomas Riley), *Thomae Walsingham, quondam monachi S. Albani, Historia Anglicana* (London: Longman, Green, Longman, Roberts and Green, 1863), 2 vols

Tulp, Nicolaes, *Observationum medicarum libri tres* (Amsterdam: Louis Elzevir, 1641)

Van Hoof, Lieve and Van Nuffelen, Peter (eds.), *Fragmentary Latin Histories (AD 300–620): Edition, Translation and Commentary* (Cambridge: Cambridge University Press, 2020)

Varro (ed. Roland G. Kent), *On the Latin Language* (Cambridge, MA: Harvard University Press, 1938), 2 vols

Virgil (ed. H. R. Fairclough), *Eclogues, Georgics, Aeneid 1–6*, Loeb Classical Library 63 (Cambridge, MA: Harvard University Press, 1989)

Walter of Hemingburgh (ed. H. C. Hamilton), *Chronicon domini Walteri de Hemingburgh* (London: Sumptibus Societatis, 1849), 2 vols

Webster, John, *The Displaying of Supposed Witchcraft* (London: J. M., 1677)

Wenzel, Siegfried (ed.), *Fasciculus Morum: A Fourteenth-Century Preacher's Handbook* (University Park, PA: Pennsylvania State University Press, 1989)

Williams, Hugh (ed.), *Gildae De Excidio Britanniae* (London: Honourable Society of Cymmrodorion, 1899)

Worcestre, William (ed. Frances Neale), *The Topography of Medieval Bristol* (Bristol: Bristol Records Society, 2000)

Wright, William A. (ed.), *The Metrical Chronicle of Robert of Gloucester* (London: Her Majesty's Stationery Office, 1887), 2 vols

Wright, Thomas and Halliwell-Phillipps, James Orchard (eds.), *Reliquiae Antiquae: Scraps from Ancient Manuscripts, Illustrating Chiefly Early English Literature and the English Language* (London: John Russell Smith, 1845), 2 vols

Young, Francis (ed.), *Pagans in the Early Modern Baltic: Sixteenth-Century Ethnographic Accounts of Baltic Paganism* (Leeds: Arc Humanities Press, 2022)

Secondary Printed Sources

[Aldhouse-]Green, Miranda J., *Exploring the World of the Druids* (London: Thames and Hudson, 2005)

Aldhouse-Green, Miranda J., *Sacred Britannia: The Gods and Rituals of Roman Britain* (London: Thames and Hudson, 2018)

Ambrose, Kirk, *The Marvellous and the Monstrous in the Sculpture of Twelfth-Century Europe* (Woodbridge: Boydell, 2013)

Anderson, Duncan, *History of the Abbey and Palace of Holyrood* (Edinburgh: Duncan Anderson, 1849)

Anderson, Earl R., *Folk Taxonomies in Early English* (London: Associated University Presses, 2003)

Ando, Clifford, 'Interpretatio Romana' in Lukas de Blois, Peter Funke, and Johannes Hahn (eds.), *The Impact of Imperial Rome on Religions, Ritual and Religious Life in the Roman Empire* (Leiden: Brill, 2006), pp. 51–65

Antonov, Dmitriy, 'Between Fallen Angels and Nature Spirits: Russian Demonology of the Early Modern Period' in Michael Ostling (ed.), *Fairies, Demons, and Nature Spirits: 'Small Gods' at the Margins of Christendom* (Basingstoke: Palgrave MacMillan, 2018), pp. 123–44

Aramburu, Francisca, Despres, Catherine, Aguiriano, Begoña and Benito, Javier, 'Deux faces de la femme merveilleuse au Moyen Age: la magicienne et la fée' in Francisca Aramburu, Catherine Despres, Begoña Aguiriano and Javier Benito (eds.), *Bien dire et bien aprandre: fées, dieux et déesses au Moyen Age* (Lille: Centre d'Études Médiévales et Dialectales de Lille III, 1994), pp. 7–22

Arthur, Ciaran, *'Charms', Liturgies and Secret Rites in Early Medieval England* (Woodbridge: Boydell, 2018)

Avarvarei, Simona C., 'Shakespeare's Weird Sisters: In Between Outlandish Womanhood and Prophesying *Moirae*', *Linguaculture* 8:2 (2017): 108–11

Bargan, Andrea, 'The Probable Old Germanic Origin of Romanian *iele* "(Evil) Fairies"', *Messages, Sages, and Ages* 2:2 (2015): 13–18

Baronas, Darius, 'Christians in Late Pagan, and Pagans in Early Christian Lithuania: The Fourteenth and Fifteenth Centuries', *Lithuanian Historical Studies* 19 (2014): 51–81

Barrett, Anthony A., 'Saint Germanus and the British Missions', *Britannia* 40 (2009): 197–217

Bassett, Steven, 'How the West Was Won: The Anglo-Saxon Takeover of the West Midlands', *Anglo-Saxon Studies in Archaeology and History* 11 (2000): 107–18

Batten, Caroline R., 'Dark Riders: Disease, Sexual Violence, and Gender Performance in the Old English *Mære* and Old Norse *Mara*', *Journal of English and Germanic Philology* 120:3 (2021): 352–80

Beard, Mary, North, J. and Price, S., *Religions of Rome* (Cambridge: Cambridge University Press, 1998), 2 vols

Ben-Amos, Dan, *Folklore Concepts: Histories and Critiques* (Bloomington, IN: Indiana University Press, 2020)

Bernstein, Alan E., *The Formation of Hell: Death and Retribution in the Ancient and Early Christian Worlds* (Ithaca, NY: Cornell University Press, 1993)

Bisagni, Jacopo, '*Leprechaun*: A New Etymology', *Cambrian Medieval Celtic Studies* 64 (2012): 47–84

Bitel, Lisa L., 'Secrets of the *Síd*: The Supernatural in Medieval Irish Texts' in Michael Ostling (ed.), *Fairies, Demons, and Nature Spirits: 'Small Gods' at the Margins of Christendom* (Basingstoke: Palgrave MacMillan, 2018), pp. 79–101

Bonner, Campbell, 'Some Phases of Religious Feeling in Later Paganism', *Harvard Theological Review* 30:3 (1937): 119–40

Breeze, David J., *Maryport: A Roman Fort and Its Community* (Oxford: Archaeopress, 2018)

Brett, Caroline, Edmonds, Fiona and Russell, Paul, *Brittany and the Atlantic Archipelago, 450–1200: Contact, Myth and History* (Cambridge: Cambridge University Press, 2022)

Briggs, Katharine M., 'The English Fairies', *Folklore* 68:1 (1957): 270–87

Briggs, Katharine M., *The Vanishing People: A Study of Traditional Fairy Beliefs* (London: Batsford, 1978)

Briggs, Katharine M., *The Fairies in Tradition and Literature*, 2nd edn (London: Routledge, 2002)

Brown, Jim, 'A Middle Iron Age Enclosure and a Romano-British Shrine Complex near Egleton, Rutland', *Transactions of the Leicestershire Archaeological and Historical Society* 90 (2016): 67–101

Buccola, Regina, *Fairies, Fractious Women and the Old Faith: Fairy Lore in Early Modern British Drama and Culture* (Selinsgrove, PA: Susquehanna University Press, 2006)

Buchan, John, *Witch Wood* (Edinburgh: Birlinn, 2020)

Cambry, Jacques, *Monumens Celtques, ou Recherches sur le Culte des Pierres* (Paris: Johanneau, 1805)

Cameron, Alan, *The Last Pagans of Rome* (Oxford: Oxford University Press, 2010)
Cameron, Averil, *The Mediterranean World in Late Antiquity, AD 395–700*, 2nd edn (London: Routledge, 2012)
Cameron, Euan, *Enchanted Europe: Superstition, Reason, and Religion, 1250–1750* (Oxford: Oxford University Press, 2010)
Chaney, William A., *The Cult of Kingship in Anglo-Saxon England* (Berkeley, CA: University of California Press, 1970)
Charles-Edwards, Thomas M., *Wales and the Britons, 350–1064* (Oxford: Oxford University Press, 2012)
Charnell-White, Cathy A., *Bardic Circles: National, Regional and Personal Identity in the Bardic Vision of Iolo Morganwg* (Cardiff: University of Wales Press, 2007)
Christol, Michel and Janon, Michel, 'Révision d'inscriptions de Nîmes, I *CIL*, XII, 5890', *Revue archéologique de Narbonnaise* 19 (1986): 259–67
Clark, Stuart, *Thinking with Demons: The Idea of Witchcraft in Early Modern Europe* (Oxford: Oxford University Press, 1997)
Coates, Richard, 'The Name of the Hwicce: A Discussion', *Anglo-Saxon England* 42 (2013): 51–61
Constantine, Mary-Ann, 'Welsh Literary History and the Making of the Myvyrian Archaiology of Wales' in Dirk van Hulle and Joep Leerssen (eds.), *Editing the Nation's Memory: Textual Scholarship and Nation-Building in Nineteenth-Century Europe* (Leiden: Brill, 2008), pp. 109–28
Coombe, Penny, Hayward, Kevin and Henig, Martin, 'A Relief Depicting Two Dancing Deities and Other Roman Stonework from Peterborough Cathedral' in Ron Baxter, Jackie Hall and Claudia Marx (eds.), *Peterborough and the Soke: Art, Architecture and Archaeology* (London: Routledge, 2019), pp. 26–42
Cottam, Elizabeth, De Jersey, Philip, Rudd, Chris and Sills, John, *Ancient British Coins* (Aylsham: Chris Rudd, 2010)
Cousins, Eleri H., *The Sanctuary at Bath in the Roman Empire* (Cambridge: Cambridge University Press, 2020)
Creighton, John, *Coins and Power in Late Iron Age Britain* (Cambridge: Cambridge University Press, 2000)

Cunliffe, Barry, *Iron Age Britain* (London: Batsford, 1995)
Curry, Jo Norton, 'A Commentary on the *Orphic Argonautica*' in Malcolm Heath, Christopher T. Green and Fabio Serranito (eds.), *Religion and Belief: A Moral Landscape* (Newcastle-upon-Tyne: Cambridge Scholars Publishing, 2014), pp. 76–93
Dark, Ken R., *Britain and the End of the Roman Empire* (Stroud: Tempus, 2000)
Davenport, Peter, *Medieval Bath Uncovered* (Stroud: Tempus, 2002)
Davidson, Hilda, *Katharine Briggs: Story-Teller* (Cambridge: Lutterworth Press, 1986)
Davies, Owen, *Popular Magic: Cunning-Folk in English History*, 2nd edn (London: Continuum, 2007)
Davies, Owen, *A Supernatural War: Magic, Divination, and Faith during the First World War* (Oxford: Oxford University Press, 2019)
Davies, Surekha, *Renaissance Ethnography and the Invention of the Human: New Worlds, Maps and Monsters* (Cambridge: Cambridge University Press, 2016)
De la Bédoyère, Guy, *Gods with Thunderbolts: Religion in Roman Britain* (Stroud: Tempus, 2002)
De la Bédoyère, Guy, *The Real Lives of Roman Britain* (New Haven, CT: Yale University Press, 2015)
Delamarre, Xavier, *Dictionnaire de la langue gauloise* (Paris: Éditions Errance, 2003)
Demacopoulos, George, 'Gregory the Great and the Pagan Shrines of Kent', *Journal of Late Antiquity* 1:2 (2008): 353–69
Dempsey, Charles, *Inventing the Renaissance Putto* (Chapel Hill, NC: University of North Carolina Press, 2001)
Ditchfield, Simon, 'Thinking with Saints: Sanctity and Society in the Early Modern World' in F. Meltzer and J. Elsner (eds.), *Saints: Faith without Borders* (Chicago, IL: University of Chicago Press, 2011), pp. 157–89
Dorcey, Peter F., *The Cult of Silvanus: A Study in Roman Folk Religion* (Leiden: Brill, 1992)

Dowden, Ken, *European Paganism: The Realities of Cult from Antiquity to the Middle Ages* (London: Routledge, 2000)

Edmonds, Radcliffe G., *Redefining Ancient Orphism: A Study in Greek Religion* (Cambridge: Cambridge University Press, 2013)

Egeler, Matthias, 'A Note on the Dedication *lamiis tribus* (RIB 1331) as Represented on the Seal of the Society', *Archaeologia Aeliana*, 5th Series 39 (2010): 15–23

Ellis, H. D., 'The Wodewose in East Anglian Church Decoration', *Proceedings of the Suffolk Institute of Archaeology* 14:3 (1912): 287–93

Faulkner, *The Decline and Fall of Roman Britain* (Stroud: History Press, 2001)

Filotas, Bernadette, *Pagans Survivals, Superstitions and Popular Cultures* (Toronto: Pontifical Institute of Medieval Studies, 2005)

Flight, Tim, *Basilisks and Beowulf: Monsters in the Anglo-Saxon World* (London: Reaktion, 2021)

Flood, Victoria, 'Political Prodigies: Incubi and Succubi in Walter Map's *De nugis curialium* and Gerald of Wales's *Itinerarium Cambriae*', *Nottingham Medieval Studies* 57 (2013): 21–46

Flower, Harriet I., *The Dancing Lares and the Serpent in the Garden: Religion at the Roman Street Corner* (Princeton, NJ: Princeton University Press, 2017)

Fontes, Manuel da Costa, *Folklore and Literature: Studies in the Portuguese, Brazilian, Sephardic, and Hispanic Oral Traditions* (Albany, NY: State University of New York Press, 2000)

Foster, Jennifer, *The Lexden Tumulus: A Re-appraisal of an Iron Age Burial from Colchester, Essex* (London: BAR Publishing, 1986)

Foster, Michael Dylan and Tolbert, Jeffrey A. (eds.), *The Folkloresque: Reframing Folklore in a Popular Culture World* (Boulder, CO: Utah State University Press, 2016)

Frankfurter, David, 'Where the Spirits Dwell: Possession, Christianization, and Saints' Shrines in Late Antiquity', *Harvard Theological Review* 103:1 (2010): 27–46

Frend, William H. C., 'Pagans, Christians, and "the Barbarian Conspiracy" of A.D. 367 in Roman Britain', *Britannia* 23 (1992): 121–31

Bibliography

Frick, David A., *Polish Sacred Philology in the Reformation and the Counter-Reformation: Chapters in the History of Controversies* (Berkeley, CA: University of California Press, 1989)

Friedman, John Block, 'Eurydice, Heurodis, and the Noon-Day Demon', *Speculum* 41:1 (1966): 22–29

Fulton, Helen (ed.), *A Companion to Arthurian Literature* (Oxford: Blackwell, 2012)

Gallais, Pierre, *La fée à la fontaine et à l'arbre: un archetype du conte merveilleux et du récit courtois* (Amsterdam: Rodopi, 1992)

Garstad, Joseph, 'Joseph as a Model for Faunus-Hermes: Myth, History and Fiction in the Fourth Century', *Vigiliae Christianae* 63:5 (2009): 493–521

Gay, David E., 'Anglo-Saxon Metrical Charm 3 against a Dwarf: A Charm against Witch-Riding?', *Folklore* 99:2 (1988): 174–77

Gerrard, James, 'Wells and Belief Systems at the End of Roman Britain: A Case Study from Roman London', *Late Antique Archaeology* 7 (2009): 551–72

Gerrard, James, *The Ruin of Roman Britain: An Archaeological Perspective* (Cambridge: Cambridge University Press, 2013)

Glickman, Gabriel, *The English Catholic Community 1688–1745* (Woodbridge: Boydell and Brewer, 2009)

Goodchild, Richard G., 'The Farley Heath Sceptre', *The Antiquaries Journal* 27:1–2 (1947): 83–85

Gorgievski, Sandra, *Face to Face with Angels: Images in Medieval Art and in Film* (Jefferson, NC: McFarland and Co., 2010)

Gorla, Silvia, 'Some Remarks about the Latin *Physiologus* Extracts Transmitted in the *Liber Glossarum*', *Mnemosyne* 71:1 (2018): 145–67

Gosden, Chris, *The History of Magic: From Alchemy to Witchcraft, from the Ice Age to the Present* (London: Viking, 2020)

Gray, Douglas, *Simple Forms: Essays on Medieval English Popular Literature* (Oxford: Oxford University Press, 2015)

Green, Richard Firth, *Elf Queens and Holy Friars: Fairy Beliefs and the Medieval Church* (Philadelphia, PA: University of Pennsylvania Press, 2016)

Green, Richard Firth, 'Refighting Carlo Ginzburg's *Night Battles*' in Craig M. Nakashian and D. P. Franke (eds.), *Prowess, Piety, and Public Order in Medieval Society: Essays in Honor of Richard W. Kaeuper* (Leiden: Brill, 2017), pp. 381–402

Greimas, Algirdas J. (trans. Milda Newman), *Of Gods and Men: Studies in Lithuanian Mythology* (Bloomington, IN: Indiana University Press, 1992)

Grinsell, Leslie V., *Folklore of Prehistoric Sites in Britain* (London: David and Charles, 1976)

Guy, Ben, 'Constantine, Helena, Maximus: On the Appropriation of Roman History in Medieval Wales, c.800–1250', *Journal of Medieval History* 44:4 (2018): 381–405

Hall, Alaric, *Elves in Anglo-Saxon England: Matters of Belief, Health, Gender and Identity* (Woodbridge: Boydell, 2007)

Hall, Alaric, 'The Evidence for *Maran*, the Anglo-Saxon "Nightmares"', *Neophilologus* 91:2 (2007): 299–317

Harding, Phil A. and Lewis, C., 'Archaeological Investigations at Tockenham, 1994', *Wiltshire Archaeology and History Magazine* 90 (1997): 26–41

Harf-Lancner, Laurence, *Les fées au moyen âge: Morgane et Mélusine, la naissance des fées* (Paris: Librairie Honoré Champion, 1984)

Harms, Daniel, 'Hell and Fairy: The Differentiation of Fairies and Demons within British Ritual Magic of the Early Modern Period' in Michelle D. Brock, Richard Raiswell and David R. Winter (eds.), *Knowing Demons, Knowing Spirits in the Early Modern Period* (Basingstoke: Palgrave MacMillan, 2018), pp. 55–77

Harte, Jeremy, 'Fairy Barrows and Cunning Folk' in Simon Young and Ceri Houlbrook (eds.), *Magical Folk: British and Irish Fairies 500 AD to the Present* (London: Gibson Square, 2018), pp. 65–78

Harvey, Antony, 'Cambro-Romance? Celtic Britain's Counterpart to Hiberno Latin' in Pádraic Moran and Immo Warntjes (eds.), *Early Medieval Ireland and Europe: Chronology, Contacts, Scholarship*, Studia Traditionis Theologiae 14 (Turnhout: Brepols, 2015), pp. 179–202

Hassall, Mark W. C. and Tomlin, R. S. O., 'Roman Britain in 1980: II. Inscriptions', *Britannia* 12 (1981): 369–96

Häussler, Ralph, 'La religion en Bretagne' in Frédéric Hurlet (ed.), *Rome et l'Occident: Gouverner l'Empire (IIe siècle av. J.-C.–IIe siècle ap. J.-C.)* (Rennes: Presses Universitaires de Rennes, 2009), pp. 491–523

Hawkes, Jane, 'Anglo-Saxon Romanitas: The Transmission and Use of Early Christian Art in Anglo-Saxon England' in Peregrin Horden (ed.), *Freedom of Movement in the Middle Ages* (Donnington: Paul Watkins Publishing, 2007), pp. 19–36

Henig, Martin, 'The Maiden Castle "Diana": A Case of Mistaken Identity? = Bacchus?', *Proceedings of the Dorset Natural History and Archaeology Society* 105 (1983): 160–62

Henig, Martin, *Religion in Roman Britain* (London: Routledge, 1984)

Henig, Martin, '*Ita intellexit numine inductus tuo*: Some Personal Interpretations of Deity in Roman Religion' in Martin Henig and Anthony King (eds.), *Pagan Gods and Shrines of the Roman Empire* (Oxford: Oxford University Committee for Archaeology, 1986), pp. 159–69

Henig, Martin, '*Murum civitatis, et fontem in ea a Romanis olim constructum*: The Arts of Rome in Carlisle and the *civitates* of the Carvetii and their Significance' in Mike R. McCarthey and D. Weston (eds.), *Carlisle and Cumbria: Roman and Medieval Architecture, Art, and Archaeology* (London: British Archaeological Association, 2004), pp. 11–28

Herren, Michael W., 'The Transmission and Reception of Graeco-Roman Mythology in Anglo-Saxon England, 670–800', *Anglo-Saxon England* 27 (1998): 87–103

Higgins, Charlotte, *Under Another Sky: Journeys in Roman Britain* (London: Jonathan Cape, 2013)

Higham, Nicholas, *Rome, Britain and the Anglo-Saxons* (London: Seaby, 1992)

Hiley Bathurst, William M., *Roman Antiquities at Lydney Park, Gloucestershire* (London: Longmans, Green and Co., 1879)

Hilts, Carly, 'A Landscape Revealed: Exploring 6,000 Years of Cambridgeshire's Past along the A14', *Current Archaeology* 339 (June 2018): 18–25

Hines, John, 'Practical Runic Literacy in the Late Anglo-Saxon Period: Inscriptions on Lead Sheet' in Ursula Lenker and Lucia Kornexl (eds.), *Anglo-Saxon Micro-Texts* (Berlin: De Gruyter, 2019), pp. 29–60

Hitch, Sarah, Naiden, Fred and Rutherford, Ian, 'Introduction' in Sarah Hitch and Ian Rutherford (eds.), *Animal Sacrifice in the Ancient Greek World* (Cambridge: Cambridge University Press, 2017), pp. 1–12

Hoggett, Richard, *The Archaeology of the East Anglian Conversion* (Woodbridge: Boydell and Brewer, 2010)

Hooke, Della, *Trees in Anglo-Saxon England: Literature, Lore and Landscape* (Woodbridge: Boydell, 2011)

Hraste, Daniel Nečas and Vuković, Krešimir, 'Rudra-Shiva and Silvanus-Faunus: Savage and Propitious', *Journal of Indo-European Studies* 39:1/2 (2011): 100–15

Hubbard, Edward, *The Buildings of Wales: Clwyd (Denbighshire and Flintshire)*, 2nd edn (London: Penguin, 1994)

Hunt, Ailsa, 'Pagan Animism: A Modern Myth for a Green Age' in Ailsa Hunt and Hilary Marlow (eds.), *Ecology and Theology in the Ancient World: Cross-disciplinary Perspectives* (London: Bloomsbury, 2019), pp. 137–52

Hutton, Ronald, *Pagan Religions of the Ancient British Isles: Their Nature and Legacy* (Oxford: Blackwell, 1991)

Hutton, Ronald, *Shamans: Siberian Spirituality and the Western Imagination* (London: Hambledon Continuum, 2007)

Hutton, Ronald, 'How Pagan Were Medieval English Peasants?' *Folklore* 122:3 (2011): 235–49

Hutton, Ronald, *Pagan Britain* (New Haven, CT: Yale University Press, 2013)

Hutton, Ronald, 'The Making of the Early Modern British Fairy Tradition', *The Historical Journal* 57:4 (2014): 1135–56

Hutton, Ronald, 'The Wild Hunt and the Witches' Sabbath', *Folklore* 125:4 (2014): 161–78

Hutton, Ronald, *The Witch: A History of Fear, from Ancient Times to the Present* (New Haven, CT: Yale University Press, 2017)

Hutton, Ronald, 'Afterword' in Michael Ostling (ed.), *Fairies, Demons, and Nature Spirits: 'Small Gods' at the Margins of Christendom* (Basingstoke: Palgrave MacMillan, 2018), pp. 349–56

Hutton, Ronald, *Queens of the Wild: Pagan Goddesses in Christian Europe: An Investigation* (New Haven, CT: Yale University Press, 2022)

Huws, John Owen, *Y Tylwyth Teg* (Dyffryn Conwy: Gwasg Carreg Gwalch, 1987)

Insoll, Timothy, 'Introduction' in Timothy Insoll (ed.), *Archaeology and World Religion* (London: Routledge, 2001), pp. 1–32

Jahner, Jennifer, Steiner, Emily and Tyler, Elizabeth M. (eds.), *Medieval Historical Writing: Britain and Ireland, 500–1500* (Cambridge: Cambridge University Press, 2019)

Johns, Catherine, 'Faunus at Thetford' in Martin Henig and Anthony King (eds.), *Pagan Gods and Shrines of the Roman Empire* (Oxford: Oxford University Committee for Archaeology, 1986), pp. 93–104

Johns, Catherine and Potter, Timothy W., *The Thetford Treasure: Roman Jewellery and Silver* (London: British Museum, 1983)

Jones, Barri and Mattingly, David, *An Atlas of Roman Britain* (Oxford: Blackwell, 1990)

Jones, Michael E., *The End of Roman Britain* (Ithaca, NY: Cornell University Press, 1998)

Jones, Pollyanna, 'Pucks and Lights: Worcestershire' in Simon Young and Ceri Houlbrook (eds.), *Magical Folk: British and Irish Fairies 500 AD to the Present* (London: Gibson Square, 2018), pp. 31–41

Jones, Prudence and Pennick, Nigel, *A History of Pagan Europe* (London: Routledge, 1995)

Josephson, Joseph Ananda, *The Invention of Religion in Japan* (Chicago, IL: University of Chicago Press, 2012)

Kassell, Lauren, '"All Was This Land Full Fill'd of Faerie", or Magic and the Past in Early Modern England', *Journal of the History of Ideas* 67:1 (2006): 107–22

Keightley, Thomas, *The Fairy Mythology, Illustrative of the Romance and Superstition of Various Countries* (London: Bohn, 1850)

Klaassen, Frank and Bens, Katrina, 'Achieving Invisibility and Having Sex with Spirits: Six Operations from an English Magic Collection ca. 1600', *Opuscula* 3:1 (2013): 1–14

Klaassen, Frank and Wright, Sharon Hubbs, *The Magic of Rogues: Necromancers in Early Tudor England* (University Park, PA: Pennsylvania State University Press, 2021)

Kling, David W., *A History of Christian Conversion* (Oxford: Oxford University Press, 2020)

Knutsen, Roald, *Tengu: The Shamanic and Esoteric Origins of the Japanese Martial Arts* (Leiden: Brill, 2011)

Laing, Gordon J., *Survivals of Roman Religion* (London: Longmans, Green and Co., 1931)

Lambert, Pierre-Yves, *La langue gauloise* (Paris: Errance, 2002)

Lapidge, Michael, 'Latin Learning in Dark Ages Wales: Some Prolegomena' in D. Ellis Evans, John G. Griffith, and Edward Martin Jope (eds.), *Proceedings of the Seventh International Congress of Celtic Studies* (Oxford: International Congress of Celtic Studies, 1985), pp. 91–107

Lapidge, Michael, *The Cult of St Swithun* (Oxford: Clarendon Press, 2003)

Larson, Jennifer, *Greek Nymphs: Myth, Cult, Lore* (Oxford: Oxford University Press, 2001)

Lawrence-Mathers, Anne, *The True History of Merlin the Magician* (New Haven, CT: Yale University Press, 2012)

Laycock, Stuart, *Britannia the Failed State: Tribal Conflict and the End of Roman Britain* (Stroud: History Press, 2008)

Lecouteux, Claude, *Fées, sorcières et loups-garous au moyen âge* (Paris: Imago, 1992)

Lewis, C. S., *The Discarded Image: An Introduction to Medieval and Renaissance Literature* (Cambridge: Cambridge University Press, 1964)

Lewis-Williams, J. David, *A Cosmos in Stone: Interpreting Religion and Society through Rock Art* (Oxford: AltaMira Press, 2002)

Lindow, John, *Norse Mythology: A Guide to Gods, Heroes, Rituals, and Beliefs* (Oxford: Oxford University Press, 2002)

Liversedge, Joan, Smith, David J. and Stead, Ian M., 'Brantingham Roman Villa: Discoveries in 1962', *Britannia* 4 (1973): 84–106

Lummus, David, 'Boccaccio's Poetic Anthropology: Allegories of History in the *Genealogie deorum gentilium libri*', *Speculum* 87:3 (2012): 724–65

Machen, Arthur (ed. S. T. Joshi), *The White People and Other Weird Stories* (London: Penguin, 2012)

Machen, Arthur (ed. Aaron Worth), *The Great God Pan and Other Horror Stories* (Oxford: Oxford University Press, 2018)

MacKillop, James, *A Dictionary of Celtic Mythology* (Oxford: Oxford University Press, 2000)

Magliocco, Sabina, '"Reconnecting to Everything": Fairies in Contemporary Paganism' in Michael Ostling (ed.), *Fairies, Demons, and Nature Spirits: 'Small Gods' at the Margins of Christendom* (Basingstoke: Palgrave MacMillan, 2018), pp. 325–48

Manjarrés, Julio Mangas, 'El ara de las *Parcae* de *Termes* (Tiermes, Soria): nuevo documento y análisis sobre un probable sincretismo', *Gérion* 31 (2013): 331–61

Mann, Richard, 'Silchester, the Roman Calleva', *Quarterly Journal of the Berks Archaeological and Architectural* 2 (1891): 45–46

Maraschi, Andrea, 'The Tree of the Bourlémonts: Gendered beliefs in fairies and their transmission from old to young women in Joan of Arc's Domrémy' in Marina Montesano (ed.), *Folklore, Magic, and Witchcraft: Cultural Exchanges from the Twelfth to Eighteenth Century* (London: Routledge, 2022), pp. 21–32

Marzella, Francesco, '*Hirsuta et cornuta cum lancea trisulcata*: Three Stories of Witchcraft and Magic in Twelfth-Century Britain' in Fabrizio Conti (ed.), *Civilizations of the Supernatural: Witchcraft, Ritual, and Religious Experience in*

Late Antique, Medieval, and Renaissance Traditions (Budapest: Trivent, 2020), pp. 221–46

Mattingly, David, *An Imperial Possession: Britain in the Roman Empire, 54 BC–AD 409*, 2nd edn (London: Penguin, 2007)

Meaney, Audrey L., 'Bede and Anglo-Saxon Paganism', *Parergon* 3 (1985): 1–29

Meens, Rob, 'A Background to Augustine's Mission to Anglo-Saxon England', *Anglo-Saxon England* 23 (1994): 5–17

Merritt, Herbert D., 'Conceivable Clues to Twelve Old English Words', *Anglo-Saxon England* 1 (1972): 193–205

Meserve, Margaret, *Empires of Islam in Renaissance Historical Thought* (Cambridge, MA: Harvard University Press, 2008)

Mills, A. David (ed.), *A Dictionary of English Place-Names* (Oxford: Oxford University Press, 1993)

Moitra, Angana, 'From Pagan God to Magical Being: The Changing Face of the Faerie King and Its Cultural Implications' in Désirée Cappa, James E. Christie, Lorenza Gay, Hanna Gentili and Finn Schulze-Feldmann (eds.), *Cultural Encounters: Cross-Disciplinary Studies from the Late Middle Ages to the Enlightenment* (Wilmington, DE: Vernon Press, 2018), pp. 23–40

Moitra, Angana, 'From Graeco-Roman Underworld to the Celtic Otherworld: The Cultural Translation of a Pagan Deity', *Oxford Research in English* 11 (Autumn 2020): 85–106

Moran III, Francis, 'Between Primates and Primitives: Natural Man as the Missing Link in Rousseau's *Second Discourse*', *Journal of the History of Ideas* 54:1 (1993): 37–58

Mylonopoulos, Joannis, 'Odysseus with a Trident? The Use of Attributes in Ancient Greek Imagery' in Joannis Mylonopoulos (ed.), *Divine Images and Human Imaginations in Ancient Greece and Rome* (Leiden: Brill, 2010), pp. 171–204

Newman, Barbara, *God and the Goddesses: Vision, Poetry and Belief in the Middle Ages* (Philadelphia, PA: University of Pennsylvania Press, 2016)

Newman, Coree, 'The Good, the Bad and the Unholy: Ambivalent Angels in the Middle Ages' in Michael Ostling (ed.), *Fairies, Demons, and Nature Spirits: 'Small Gods' at the Margins of Christendom* (Basingstoke: Palgrave MacMillan, 2018), pp. 103–22

Niles, John D., 'Pagan Survivals and Popular Belief' in M. Godden and M. Lapidge (eds.), *The Cambridge Companion to Old English Literature*, 2nd edn (Cambridge: Cambridge University Press, 2013), pp. 120–36

Ogden, Daniel, *The Dragon in the West* (Oxford: Oxford University Press, 2021)

Oldridge, Darren, *The Devil in Tudor and Stuart England* (Stroud: History Press, 2011)

Oldridge, Darren, 'Fairies and the Devil in Early Modern England', *The Seventeenth Century* 31:1 (2016): 1–15

Oosthuizen, Susan, *The Emergence of the English* (Leeds: Arc Humanities Press, 2019)

Ostling, Michael (ed.), *Fairies, Demons, and Nature Spirits: 'Small Gods' at the Margins of Christendom* (Basingstoke: Palgrave MacMillan, 2018)

Ostling, Michael, 'Introduction: Where've All the Good People Gone?' in Michael Ostling (ed.), *Fairies, Demons, and Nature Spirits: 'Small Gods' at the Margins of Christendom* (Basingstoke: Palgrave MacMillan, 2018), pp. 1–53

Padel, O. J., 'Geoffrey of Monmouth and Cornwall', *Cambridge Medieval Celtic Studies* 8 (1984): 1–28

Parish, Helen, 'Magic and Priestcraft: Reformers and Reformation' in David J. Collins (ed.), *The Cambridge History of Magic and Witchcraft in the West from Antiquity to the Present* (Cambridge: Cambridge University Press, 2015), pp. 393–425

Parish, Helen, *Superstition and Magic in Early Modern Europe: A Reader* (London: Bloomsbury, 2015)

Parker, Eleanor, *Winters in the World: A Journey through the Anglo-Saxon Year* (London: Reaktion, 2022)

Paxson, James J., *The Poetics of Personification* (Cambridge: Cambridge University Press, 1994)

Perring, Dominic, *The Roman House in Britain* (London: Routledge, 2002)

Perring, Dominic, '"Gnosticism" in Fourth-Century Britain: The Frampton Mosaics Reconsidered', *Britannia* 34 (2003): 97–127

Petts, David, *Pagan and Christian: Religious Change in Early Medieval Europe* (London: Bristol Classical Press, 2011)

Pollard, Richard M., '"Lucan" and "Aethicus Ister"', *Notes and Queries* 53:1 (2006): 7–10

Powicke, Frederick M., 'The Christian Life' in Charles G. Crump and E. F. Jacob (eds.), *The Legacy of the Middle Ages* (Oxford: Clarendon Press, 1926), pp. 23–57

Purkiss, Diane, *Troublesome Things: A History of Fairies and Fairy Stories* (London: Allen Lane, 2000)

Rahtz, Philip and Harris, Leslie, 'The Temple Well and Other Buildings at Pagans Hill, Chew Stoke, North Somerset', *Proceedings of the Somerset Archaeological and Natural History Society* 101/102 (1967): 15–51

Rahtz, Philip and Watts, Lorna, 'Pagans Hill Revisited', *The Archaeological Journal* 146 (1989): 330–71

Raiswell, Peter and Dendle, Richard, 'Demon Possession in Anglo-Saxon and Early Modern England: Continuity and Evolution in Social Context', *Journal of British Studies* 47:4 (2008): 738–67

Rattue, James, *The Living Stream: Wells in Historical Context* (Woodbridge: Boydell, 2001)

Raymond, Joad, 'Introduction' in Joad Raymond (ed.), *Conversations with Angels: Essays Towards a History of Spiritual Communication, 1100–1700* (Basingstoke: Palgrave MacMillan, 2011), pp. 1–21

Rippon, Stephen, *Territoriality and the Early Medieval Landscape: The Countryside of the East Saxon Kingdom* (Woodbridge: Boydell Press, 2022)

Rippon, Stephen, Smart, Chris, and Pears, Ben, *The Fields of Britannia: Continuity and Change in the Late Roman and Early Medieval Landscape* (Oxford: Oxford University Press, 2015)

Robbins, 'Crypto-Religion and the Study of Cultural Mixtures: Anthropology, Value, and the Nature of Syncretism', *Journal of the American Academy of Religion* 79:2 (2011): 408–24

Robichaud, Paul, *Pan: The Great God's Modern Return* (London: Reaktion, 2021)

Rose, Herbert J., 'Faunus' in Nicholas G. L. Hammond and Howard H. Scullard (eds.), *The Oxford Classical Dictionary*, 2nd edn (Oxford: Clarendon Press, 1970), p. 432

Ross, Leslie, *Medieval Art: A Topical Dictionary* (Westport, CN: Greenwood Press, 1996)

Russell, Jeffrey Burton, *Lucifer: The Devil in the Middle Ages* (Ithaca, NY: Cornell University Press, 1986)

Russell, Paul, '"Go and Look in the Latin Books": Latin and the Vernacular in Medieval Wales' in Richard Ashdowne and Carolinne White (eds.), *Latin in Medieval Britain* (Oxford: Oxford University Press, 2017), pp. 213–46

Russell, Miles and Laycock, Stuart, *UnRoman Britain: Exposing the Great Myth of Britannia* (Stroud: History Press, 2010)

Ryan, Martin J., 'Isidore Amongst the Islands: The Reception and Use of Isidore of Seville in Britain and Ireland in the Early Middle Ages' in Andrew Fear and Jamie Wood (eds.), *A Companion to Isidore of Seville* (Leiden: Brill, 2020), pp. 424–56

Salisbury, Joyce E., *Iberian Popular Religion 600 B.C. to 700 A.D.: Celts, Romans and Visigoths* (New York: Edwin Mellen Press, 1985)

Salisbury, Joyce E., 'Before the Standing Stones: From Land Forms to Religious Attitudes and Monumentality' in Marta Díaz-Guardamino, Leonardo García Sanjuán and David Wheatley (eds.), *The Lives of Prehistoric Monuments in Iron Age, Roman, and Medieval Europe* (Oxford: Oxford University Press, 2015), pp. 19–30

Sauer, Eberhard, 'Sacred Springs and a Pervasive Roman Ritual', *ARA: The Bulletin for the Association for Roman Archaeology* 21 (2012): 51–55

Sayers, William, 'Middle English *wodewose* "Wilderness Being": A Hybrid Etymology?', *American Notes and Queries* 17:3 (2004): 12–19

Sayers, William, 'Puck and the Bogymen as Reflexes of Indo-European Conceptions of Fear and Flight', *Tradition Today* 8 (June 2019): 52–56

Schibli, Hermann S., 'Xenocrates' Daemons and the Irrational Soul', *The Classical Quarterly* 43:1 (1993): 143–67

Scull, Christina and Hammond, Wayne G. (eds.), *The J. R. R. Tolkien Companion and Guide: Volume 1* (Boston, MA: Houghton Miffin, 2006)

Scullard, Howard Hayes, *Festivals and Ceremonies of the Roman Republic* (London: Thames and Hudson, 1981)

Sébillot, Paul, *Traditions et Superstitions de la Haute-Bretagne* (Paris: Maisonneuve and Co., 1882), 2 vols

Semple, Sarah, *Perceptions of the Prehistoric in Anglo-Saxon England: Religion, Ritual, and Rulership in the Landscape* (Cambridge: Cambridge University Press, 2013)

Shamas, Laura A., *'We Three': The Mythology of Shakespeare's Weird Sisters* (New York: Peter Lang, 2007)

Shorrock, Robert, *The Myth of Paganism: Nonnus, Dionysus and the World of Late Antiquity* (London: Bloomsbury, 2011)

Silver, Carole G., 'On the Origin of Fairies: Victorians, Romantics and Folk Belief', *Browning Institute Studies* 14 (1986): 141–56

Silver, Carole G., *Strange and Secret Peoples: Fairies and Victorian Consciousness* (Oxford: Oxford University Press, 1999)

Simpson, Jacqueline, 'On the Ambiguity of Elves [1]', *Folklore* 122:1 (2011): 76–83

Sims-Williams, Patrick, 'The Visionary Celt: The Construction of an "Ethnic Preconception"', *Cambridge Medieval Celtic Studies* 11 (1986): 71–96

Sims-Williams, Patrick, *Irish Influence on Medieval Welsh Literature* (Oxford: Oxford University Press, 2010)

Snyder, Christopher A., *An Age of Tyrants: Britain and the Britons, A.D. 400–600* (University Park, PA: Pennsylvania State University Press, 1998)

Spence, Lewis, *British Fairy Origins* (London: Watts and Co., 1946)

Sugg, Richard, *Fairies: A Dangerous History* (London: Reaktion, 2018)

Suggett, Richard, 'The Fair Folk and Enchanters: Wales' in Simon Young and Ceri Houlbrook (eds.), *Magical Folk:*

British and Irish Fairies, 500 AD to the Present (London: Gibson Square, 2018), pp. 137–50

Tatlock, John S. P., 'Geoffrey and King Arthur in *Normannicus Draco* [Concluded]', *Modern Philology* 31:2 (1933): 113–25

'The Third Country Meeting of the Society', *Proceedings of the Society of Antiquaries of Newcastle-upon-Tyne* 3:30 (1888): 311–22

Thomas, Charles, *Christianity in Roman Britain to AD 500* (Berkeley, CA: University of California Press, 1981)

Thomas, Charles, *Celtic Britain* (London: Thames and Hudson, 1986)

Thomas, Keith, *Religion and the Decline of Magic*, 4th edn (London: Penguin, 1991)

Thomas, Neil, 'The Celtic Wild Man Tradition and Geoffrey of Monmouth's *Vita Merlini*: Madness or *Contemptus Mundi*?', *Arthuriana* 10:1 (2000): 27–42

Turner, Stephanie S., 'The Place of Cryptids in Taxonomic Debates' in Samantha Hurd (ed.), *Anthropology and Crytozoology: Exploring Encounters with Mysterious Creatures* (London: Routledge, 2017), pp. 12–31

Van der Horst, Pieter C., 'Fatum, Tria Fata; Parca, Tres Parcae', *Mnemosyne* 11 (1943): 217–27

Veenstra, Jan R. and Olsen, Karin, 'Introduction' in Jan R. Veenstra and Karin Olsen (eds.), *Airy Nothings: Imagining the Otherworld of Faerie from the Middle Ages to the Age of Reason, Essays in Honour of Alasdair A. MacDonald* (Leiden: Brill, 2014), pp. vii–xvi

Vėlius, Norbertas, *Chtoniškasis lietuvių mitologijos pasaulis* (Vilnius: Vaga, 1987)

Wade, James, *Fairies in Medieval Romance* (Basingstoke: Palgrave MacMillan, 2011)

Warner, Marina, *Joan of Arc: The Image of Female Heroism*, 2nd edn (Oxford: Oxford University Press, 2013)

Watts, Dorothy J., 'The Thetford Treasure: A Reappraisal', *The Antiquaries Journal* 68:1 (1988): 55–68

Watts, Dorothy J., *Christians and Pagans in Roman Britain* (London: Routledge, 1991)

Webb, Simon, *On the Origins of Wizards, Witches and Fairies* (Barnsley: Pen and Sword, 2022)

Webster, Jane, 'A Dirty Window on the Iron Age? Recent Developments in the Archaeology of pre-Roman Celtic Religion' in Katja Ritari and Alexandra Bergholm (eds.), *Understanding Celtic Religion: Revisiting the Pagan Past* (Cardiff: University of Wales Press, 2015), pp. 121–54

Wedlake, William J., *Exacavations at Camerton, Somerset: A Record of Thirty Years' Excavation, Covering the Period from Neolithic to Saxon Times, 1925–56* (Camerton: Camerton Excavation Club, 1958)

Wedlake, William J., *The Excavation of the Shrine of Apollo at Nettleton, Wiltshire, 1956–1971* (London: Thames and Hudson, 1982)

Wheeler, Mortimer, *Maiden Castle, Dorset* (Oxford: The Society of Antiquaries, 1943)

Wilby, Emma, *Cunning-Folk and Familiar Spirits: Shamanistic Visionary Traditions in Early Modern British Witchcraft and Magic* (Eastbourne: Sussex Academic Press, 2005)

Wilby, Emma, 'Burchard's *strigae*, the Witches' Sabbath, and Shamanistic Cannibalism in Early Modern Europe', *Magic, Ritual and Witchcraft* 8:1 (2013): 18–49

Williams, Kelsey J., *The Antiquary: John Aubrey's Historical Scholarship* (Oxford: Oxford University Press, 2016)

Williams, Noel, 'The Semantics of the Word "Fairy": Making Meaning Out of Thin Air' in Peter Narváez (ed.), *The Good People: New Fairylore Essays* (New York: Garland, 1991), pp. 457–78

Wiseman, Timothy P., 'The God of the Lupercal', *The Journal of Roman Studies* 85 (1995): 1–22

Wiseman, T. P., *Unwritten Rome* (Liverpool: Liverpool University Press, 2008)

Wright, Thomas, *A Volume of Vocabularies* (London: Privately Printed, 1857)

Yeates, Stephen J., *The Tribe of Witches: The Religion of the Dobunni and Hwicce* (Oxford: Oxbow, 2008)

Young, Francis, *English Catholics and the Supernatural, 1553–1829* (Farnham: Ashgate, 2013)
Young, Francis, *A History of Exorcism in Catholic Christianity* (Basingstoke: Palgrave MacMillan, 2016)
Young, Francis, *Magic as a Political Crime in Medieval and Early Modern England: A History of Sorcery and Treason* (London: I. B. Tauris, 2017)
Young, Francis, *Peterborough Folklore* (Norwich: Lasse Press, 2017)
Young, Francis, *Suffolk Fairylore* (Norwich: Lasse Press, 2018)
Young, Francis, *Athassel Priory and the Cult of St Edmund in Medieval Ireland* (Dublin: Four Courts Press, 2020)
Young, Francis, *Witchcraft and the Modern Roman Catholic Church* (Cambridge: Cambridge University Press, 2022)
Young, Francis, *Magic in Merlin's Realm: A History of Occult Politics in Britain* (Cambridge: Cambridge University Press, 2022)
Young, Simon, 'In Search of England's Fairy Trees: The Fair Oak of Bowland', *Northern Earth* 147 (2016): 16–21
Young, Simon, 'Fairy Holes and Fairy Butter: Cumbria' in Simon Young and Ceri Houlbrook (eds.), *Magical Folk: British and Irish Fairies 500 AD to the Present* (London: Gibson Square, 2018), pp. 79–94
Young, Simon, *The Boggart: Folklore, History, Place-Names and Dialect* (Exeter: University of Exeter Press, 2022)
Zochios, Stamatios, 'Lamia: A Sorceress, A Fairy or a Revenant?', *Caietele Echinox* 21 (2011): 20–31

Unpublished Theses

Chabot, Jean-R., 'Portunus', unpublished MA thesis (Ottawa: University of Ottawa, 1984)
Fergus, Emily, 'Goblinlike, Fantastic: Little People and Deep Time at the Fin de Siècle', unpublished MPhil thesis (London: Birkbeck University of London, 2019)
Sawyer, Rose A., 'Child Substitution: A New Approach to the Changeling Motif in Medieval European Culture', unpublished PhD thesis (Leeds: University of Leeds, 2018)

Smith, Alexander, 'The Differentiated Use of Constructed Sacred Space in Southern Britain, from the Late Iron Age to the 4th Century AD', unpublished PhD thesis (Newport: University of Wales College, 2000), 2 vols

Web Sources

Bosworth Toller's Anglo-Saxon Dictionary Online, bosworthtoller.com

'Calne Fates Sculpture', Wiltshire Museum, wiltshiremuseum.org.uk/?artwork=calne-fates-sculpture

Debusmann, Bernd, 'How "Saint Javelin" raised over $1 million for Ukraine', *BBC News*, 10 March 2022: bbc.co.uk/news/world-us-canada-60700906

Geiriadur Prifysgol Cymru, geiriadur.ac.uk/gpc/gpc.html

Kingsbury, Kate and Chesnut, Andrew R., 'Syncretic Santa Muerte: Holy Death and Religious Bricolage', *Religions* 12:3 (2021), doi.org/10.3390/rel12030220

The Oxford Dictionary of National Biography (online edition), oxforddnb.com

Oxford English Dictionary, oed.com

Portable Antiquities Scheme, finds.org.uk

Roman Inscriptions of Britain, romaninscriptionsofbritain.org

'Wooden Roman Figure Found at Twyford during HS2 dig', *BBC News*, 13 January 2022, bbc.co.uk/news/uk-england-beds-bucks-herts-59972275

INDEX

Abandinus (deity), 96
abduction, child, 129, 149, 150,
    265, 292, 303, 309
Abraham, 123
Abundantia (deity), 108, 211
Adam of Bremen, 157
Ælfric of Eynsham, 219, 265
ælfscyne (elf-like beauty), 222,
    233
ælfsiden (elf magic), 222
Æsir, 46
aetiologies, 7
Alberic of London, 153,
    275–77
alchemy, 299
Aldhelm, 83, 216, 217, 221,
    226
Alexander the Great, 123
álfar. See elves
aliens, 319
allegory, 18
altars, 72, 79, 82, 89, 97, 100,
    102, 105–7, 109, 111, 130,
    188, 210, 226, 311, 316
Ambia, 198
America, United States of, 66
amphitheatres, 107
Ancaster, Lincolnshire, 96
ancestors, cults of, 16, 18, 91,
    111, 145, 146, 153, 156
angels, 4, 41, 58, 60, 76, 86, 152,
    234, 236, 253, 282, 298,
    301, 313, 319
    fall of, 184, 198, 267, 270
    guardian, 314

anglicisation, 194
Anglo-Saxons, 16, 180, 187,
    195, 196, 198, 223, 227,
    245, 257
    conversion of, 139
    religion of, 29, 30, 89, 140,
    178–79, 187–92, 208, 231,
    271
Anicilla, 168
animism, 21, 23, 24, 34, 38, 44,
    45, 54, 60–61, 65, 67, 70,
    88, 98, 127–28, 138, 162,
    164, 308
Anne, St, 86
Annwn, 81–82, 152, 204,
    208–10, 279–80
Antenociticus (deity), 96
Anthony, St, 213, 215, 218
anthropology, 25, 28, 44, 47, 51,
    62, 63, 139, 145, 164
anthropomorphism, 61, 63, 66,
    67, 70
Antinous, 124
antiquarians, 7, 13, 79, 311, 315
antlers, 63
Antoine de la Sale, 301
Ap Gwilym, Dafydd, 204
apes, 12, 317–19, 321
Apollo (deity), 95
Apollo Cunomaglus (deity), 92,
    96, 127, 175
Apollonius of Tyana, 123
Apuleius, 40
Aquinas, Thomas, 267
Arawn, 209, 210

349

Index

archaeology, xv, 24, 26, 28–30, 34, 50, 62, 68, 78–82, 89, 91–92, 102, 112, 121, 132, 142, 143, 167, 168, 171, 172, 177, 178, 190–93, 202, 239, 240, 316
archangels, 183, 250, 256
Arden, Forest of, 235
Ardennes, France, 235
Arduinna (deity), 235
Arianism, 169
Arles, France, 149
Arnemetia (deity), 86
Arthur, king, 9, 263, 296
Arthuret, battle of, 271
Arubianus (deity), 209
Ashton, Rutland, 175
Athens, Academy of, 269
Atropos. See *under* Parcae
Aubrey, John, 7–10, 86, 312, 314–15, 317
Auchendavy, East Dunbartonshire, 106, 130
Audoen, St, 272
augenblickgötter, 43
augurs, 68
Augustine, St, 43, 117, 129, 184, 213–14, 218, 221, 268, 306
Augustus, emperor, 68
Aulus Gellius, 108
Aurelius Ursicinus, 170
Avalon, 263
Avon, river, 80, 100

Bacchus (deity), 74, 94, 116, 135, 153, 174, 311
Badb, 110
Baltic languages, 186, 207
Baltic region, 7
Baltic religion, 98, 148, 162
baptism, 157, 161, 162
baptisteries, 159, 175
bardic tradition, 201

Barkway, Hertfordshire, 92
barrows, 16, 63, 82, 83, 189, 245
barstukai, 266, 287
Bath, Somerset, 71, 73, 79, 80, 92, 123, 169, 176, 243–45
baths, Roman, 170, 176, 188
Becnait, 198
Bellerophon, 168
Bellona (deity), 114
Benoît de Saint-Maure, 290
Benwell, Tyne and Wear, 97, 109–10, 119
Bertram, St, 165
bestiaries, 221, 318
Bethesda, Pool of, 86
Binchester, Co. Durham, 71
birth, 22, 105, 295
Bladud, king, 243
boggarts, 25, 207
bogies, 56, 149, 289, 290
Bona Dea. *See* Fauna
Bonus Eventus (deity), 106
Borneo, 317
Boudiccan Revolt, 121
Brading, Isle of Wight, 63
Brampton, Cumbria, 97
Brandon, Suffolk, 84–85
Brantingham, Yorkshire, 101
Braudel, Ferdinand, 27, 47
Brazil, 145
bread ovens, 267
brenin, 97–98
Breton language, 13, 77, 185, 200
Bretons, 13, 36, 75, 257–59
Brigantes, 106
Brigantia (deity), 97–98, 101, 106
Briggs, Katharine, xv, 15–17, 21, 58, 70, 295–96
Britannia (personification), 97, 106
British Museum, 112

350

Index

Brittany, 19, 22, 81, 129, 173, 194, 206, 286, 303
Brittonic languages, 22, 96, 116, 118, 194, 195, 200–11, 242, 257
Bromham, Bedfordshire, 79
Bromswold, forest of, 237
Bromyard, John, 256
Bronze Age, 49, 63
Brooks, Arthur, 112
brownies, 70, 287, 314
Bruttius, 125
Bryennios, Joseph, 150
Buchan, John, 12, 316
Burchard of Worms, 263, 266, 273, 274, 300
burgrunan, 77, 187, 192, 227, 229, 230, 235, 262
burials, 63, 68, 160, 170, 177, 189, 190, 192, 279
  deviant, 105
Burton, Robert, 312
Bury St Edmunds, Suffolk, 277
Buxton, Derbyshire, 86
Byrhtferth of Ramsey, 231–37

Cadbury Congresbury, Somerset, 176
Caelestis (deity), 101
Caelius Aurelianus, 45
Caerleon, Gwent, 107, 316
Caerwent, Monmouthshire, 170
Cain, 197–98, 224
Caldey Island, 75
Calne, Wiltshire, 108
Cambry, Jacques, 13–14
Camden, William, 7, 246, 247
Camerton, Somerset, 174
Camulus. *See* Mars Camulus
cannibalism, 109
Canterbury
  St Pancras' church, 191
Canterbury, Kent, 140

capricorns, 69
Cardea (deity), 43
Carrawburgh, Northumberland, 72, 79, 100–2
Castellio, Sebastian, 45
Castleford, Yorkshire, 100
Catholicism, 60, 145, 146, 164, 171, 313
Cathubodua (deity), 110
Celtiberians, 53, 104
Celtic languages, 186, 207
Celticism, 9–10, 21, 23–24, 28–30, 57, 104, 110, 133, 200, 282, 292, 315–17
cemeteries, 16, 170, 175, 189
centaurs, 69, 135
Ceres (deity), 95, 106, 153
changelings, 291
charms, 221, 242, 243, 274
charters, 83
Chaucer, Geoffrey, 10, 273, 296, 297
Chedworth, Gloucestershire, 159
Chepstow, Monmouthshire, 100
Cherwell, river, 80
Chester, Cheshire, 100, 107, 137
Cheyne, Thomas, 73
Chi Rho monogram, 122, 159, 167, 168
chimpanzees, 318
Christianisation, 30, 33, 35, 54, 74, 76, 82–83, 129, 134, 138–45, 155, 158–63, 167, 172, 173, 185, 186, 193, 198–99, 211, 231, 234, 244, 249, 262
  of wells, 80–81, 86, 87
Christianity
  cosmology of, 20, 42, 145, 148, 251, 292, 308
  Gnostic. *See* Gnosticism
  popular, 125, 143–44, 198, 255

351

Index

chronicles, 31, 251, 252, 270, 272, 283
chthonic, godlings as, 58, 81, 82, 88, 152, 244, 245, 278, 308
church courts, 164, 250, 254–55
Church Fathers, 30, 35, 134, 249, 267, 306
Churn, River, 65
Cicero, 44, 114
Circe, 297
Cirencester, Gloucestershire, 65, 71, 73, 131
clairvoyance, 41
Clark, Stuart, 4
classicising, 263, 264, 274, 297, 310–17
Claudian invasion, 3, 68, 69, 90, 94, 96, 99
Clerk family, 250–51, 253, 255–56, 298
Cocceius Firmus, Marcus, 130
Cocceius Nigrinus, Marcus, 97
Cockersand Moss, Lancashire, 170
coins
   deposition of, 80, 169, 176, 311
   Iron Age, 62, 68–69
   Roman, 82, 239, 246
Colchester, Essex, 69, 117
colepixy, 55–56
Collen, St, 279–80, 282
colonialism, 11, 59, 145, 156
   Roman, 66
columns, sacred, 144
commentaries, 30, 31, 35, 70, 76, 196, 197, 213, 218, 220, 221, 238, 241, 242, 249, 264, 318
Conan Doyle, Arthur, 14
Constantine, emperor, 202, 246
constructions, cultural, 4, 26, 30, 50, 51, 153, 155, 252, 305, 320, 321

conversion, 137, 139, 156, 158, 171–72, 177, 191, 195, 286
   stages of, 160, 162–63
coraniaid, 238–40, 243
Corbridge, Northumberland, 127
Cornish language, 194, 200, 204, 242, 257, 266, 303
Cornwall, 36, 81, 257, 259, 266, 273
Cotswolds, 64, 103, 132
Cottingley Fairies, 14
Coventina (deity), 72, 79, 96, 100, 102, 176
creolisation, religious, 99, 281
Cromwell, Thomas, 300
crosses, standing, 144
crossroads, 101, 275
crowns, ritual, 63
crypto-religion, 144–45
cryptozoology, 319–20
Cuda (deity), 132
Cumbric language, 194
curse tablets, 123, 169
curses, 53, 85, 198, 218
Cybele (deity), 241
Cymbeline (Cunobelinus), king, 9, 68–69

daemons, Platonic, 5, 39–41, 43, 254, 269–71
Dagworth, Suffolk, 291
Danelaw, 177, 224, 251
Danu (deity), 132
Darent, river, 101
Dashwood, Francis, 311
David I, king of Scots, 236
dead, fairies as the, 16–17, 60, 184, 242, 266
Deae Matres (deities), 22, 71, 73, 77, 93, 96, 103–5, 202–3, 205, 206, 225, 226, 231, 235, 273

Deal, Kent, 63, 82
decapitation, 87, 170
de-Christianisation, 175, 178
demigods, 45, 46, 58
demonisation, 32, 35, 74, 83–84, 128–29, 142–55, 186, 193, 196, 198, 209, 214, 230, 231, 253, 262, 286, 287, 292, 306, 307, 309, 313
demonology, 40, 60, 148, 151, 187, 204, 214, 252, 267, 270, 314
demotion, divine, 9, 148–49, 238, 305
destiny, 22, 59, 88, 103, 110, 227, 263, 295, 303, 308
devil, the. *See* Satan
Devon, 257, 266, 273
Diana (deity), 174, 183, 235, 274
Dionysus (deity), 74, 119–20, 124
Dis Pater (deity), 127, 244
dissolution of the monasteries, 52
divination, 86, 146, 150
Dobunni, 127, 141, 234
Dominicans, 256, 296
Domrémy, France, 255
Donar, oak of, 165
doubles, psychic, 22
dragons, 25, 245
dreams, 22, 102, 114, 119, 237
druids, 38, 56–57, 62, 91, 207
dryads, 235, 314
dualism, cosmic, 42, 151, 152
Dunwich, Suffolk, 267, 268
Dusii (spirits), 117, 129, 183–86, 220–21, 268, 303, 314
dwarfs, 132, 238, 239, 242–43, 246, 288

earthworks, 17, 142, 178
Edgar, Canons of, 84

Edmund of Abingdon, St, archbishop of Canterbury, 86
Edmund, St, 237, 277
Edward III, king of England, 167
Edward the Confessor, king of England, 165, 167
Egeria (nymph), 86, 115
Egleton, Rutland, 190
Egwin, St, bishop of Worcester, 231–34, 236
Egyptians, 57, 72, 125
Eleusinian Mysteries, 119
elf-shot, 266, 267
Eliodorus, 241, 242, 279
elites, role of, 25–27, 30, 32, 137, 167, 168, 180, 188, 251, 256, 260, 297
Elsi, 165–66
Elveden, Suffolk, 277
elves, 20–21, 30, 35, 36, 46, 196, 197, 234, 242, 248, 249, 259, 266, 270, 282, 288, 291–92, 302–3, 314
 Anglo-Saxon, 222–24, 268, 304
 gender of, 73, 234–35, 277–78
 medieval, 249, 250–52, 260, 262–63, 309
Ely, Cambridgeshire, 84, 85
emperor-worship, 42, 59, 92, 133
enchantment, 81, 84, 154, 205, 260, 263, 295–96, 298, 299, 303, 304, 308
Enlightenment, 11, 156, 304
Eof, 231, 232, 234–37
Ephialtes, 213
epigraphy, 31, 34, 42, 66, 81, 82, 89, 91–92, 94, 97, 111, 126, 210, 244

epithets, divine, 96, 101, 116, 117
Epona (deity), 63, 96, 99
eroticism, 263
Erriapus (deity), 66
Estonia, 23
Ethiopia, 221, 318
Ethnography, 6–7
etymology, 5, 14, 55–56, 215, 226, 227, 230, 247, 261, 268, 276, 290
euhemerisation, 11, 12, 77, 113, 125, 152–53, 296
euphemism, 115, 147, 203–6, 213, 219, 226, 249, 253, 262, 273, 286
Eurydice, 18, 281, 282
Eusebius of Caesarea, 41
Evesham, Worcestershire, 231, 235, 236
execution, places of, 128
exorcism, 205, 224, 254, 290

fairies
  as animistic spirits, 21, 60, 308
  as bogies, 149
  as diminished gods, 8, 9, 17, 21, 51, 316
  domestic, 266, 284, 287, 289, 309, 314, 315
  etymology of, 13–14, 154–55, 260–62, 268
  euphemisms for. *See* euphemism
  gender of. *See* gender
  in magic. *See under* magic
  Latin terms for, 45
  as literary construct, 14, 32–33, 292–97
  lore of, 8, 10, 18, 23, 24, 31, 33, 36, 51, 77, 87, 226, 240, 252, 253, 313, 319
  as psychic doubles, 22
  'pygmy theory' of, 11–12
  relationship with witches, 75
  size of, 238–39
  as social beings, 70
  solitary, 15, 70
  Spiritualist beliefs about, 14
  as synthetic beings, 36, 249–304
fairy rings, 2, 315
fairy tales, 295
fairy trees, 165, 255
fairyland, 15, 19, 128, 208, 211, 246, 247, 254, 260, 278, 279, 296–98
Fakenham, Norfolk, 242
familiar spirits, 61, 309, 313
fantasy, 2, 22, 293, 296–98, 310, 321
Farley Heath, Surrey, 127
fate, 2, 36, 59, 83, 88, 103–7, 109, 114, 128, 155, 192, 225, 227, 229, 248, 251, 261, 268, 274, 275, 295, 303, 308
Fates. *See* Parcae
Fauna (deity), 13, 115
Faunalia, 115
fauns, 2, 35, 38, 47, 59, 71, 74, 114, 115, 117, 122, 129, 148, 159, 184, 212–22, 239–42, 248, 264–68, 271, 282, 292, 303, 306, 313–15, 317–19
  fauni ficarii, 212, 214, 219, 238, 265
Faunus (deity), 8, 10, 43–45, 71, 94, 205, 213, 215, 268, 302, 308, 314, 317
  cult of, 34, 112–29
Faustus of Riez, 199
Faversham, Kent, 191
feathers, votive, 92, 123, 167

Index

Felmingham, Norfolk, 111
Feltwell, Norfolk, 176
fens, 245
fertility, 18
festivals, 142–43, 164, 203, 213
Finnish language, 207
folklore, study of, 2–3, 6, 7, 13, 15, 25, 47, 283
folkloresque, 185–86
follets, 267, 290–91
Fomoir, 198
Forculus (deity), 43
Fortuna (deity), 106, 108, 154, 170
fountains, 85, 100, 102, 130
Frampton, Dorset, 122, 168
Frazer, James, 47
frogs, 284, 287, 289
Froud, Brian, 303
Fumsup, 154
functionalism, 13, 16, 293, 294
Furies, 192, 228–31, 233

Gabriel, archangel, 250
Gaelic language, 194, 195
Gage, Thomas, 171
Galicia, 54, 78, 82, 151
Gaul, 94, 104, 129, 140, 173, 182, 183, 186, 188, 194, 284, 286
    religion of, 22, 57, 95, 117, 127, 184–85, 202, 210, 264
Gaulish language, 81–82, 110, 186, 208
gender, 34, 59, 73, 88, 95, 113, 220, 234–35, 278
genealogy, 48, 202
genii, 38, 42, 52, 65, 94, 100, 111, 183, 234, 277, 312, 314
Genii Cucullati, 73, 131–32
genii loci, 34, 105, 106, 129–32
Geniscus, 183

Geoffrey of Monmouth, 9, 36, 201, 243–44, 257–58, 269–71
Gerald of Wales, 36, 146, 241, 258, 279
Germanic languages, 207, 222, 224
Germanic tribes, 47, 95, 142, 173, 180–81, 194, 196, 227
    religion of, 3, 72, 75, 93, 140, 174, 178–79, 182, 187, 193, 226, 231, 242, 271
Germanus of Auxerre, 181
Germany, 103, 131, 265, 266
    conversion of, 157
Gervase of Tilbury, 150, 261, 267, 283–91
ghosts, 18, 52–53, 60, 83, 205, 266, 270, 284, 313
Ghyst, 247–48
giants, 30, 35, 77, 197, 198, 207, 239, 243–48, 289, 290
Gildas, 136–37, 141, 181, 182, 193, 199, 308
Glastonbury, Somerset, 217
glosses, 20, 31, 37, 45, 55–56, 83, 93, 192, 219–20, 223, 224, 227, 229, 230, 238, 239, 249, 263, 265, 266, 277
Glywys, 131
Glywysyng, kingdom of, 131
gnomes, 2, 282, 288
Gnosticism, 168
Gobannos (deity), 202
goblins, 11, 132, 204, 259
Goddess, the (Wicca), 58
godling, definition of, 2, 38–40
Godmanchester, Cambridgeshire, 96
Gofannon, 202
gorillas, 318
Gothic language, 46
Graces, 52

355

granaries, 82, 100, 265, 267
Great Ashfield, Suffolk, 250
Great Witcombe,
    Gloucestershire, 101
Greece, 5, 9, 14, 22, 39–41, 45,
    61, 76, 99, 102, 129, 144,
    148, 150, 159, 160, 286,
    297, 308, 317
  folklore of, 149
Green Children of Woolpit, 87
Gregory I, pope, 190–91
Gresford, Clwyd, 107, 108
Greta Bridge, Co. Durham, 100
Greystoke, lord, 288
griffins, 69, 135
Grimm, Brothers, 13
grimoires, 299, 301
groves, sacred, 44, 61, 91, 115,
    120, 121, 127–29, 161,
    178–79, 215, 308
Gwynn ap Nudd, 210
gyant, 289–90

Hades (deity), 18, 244, 281, 297
Hadrian, emperor, 124
Hadrian's Wall, 72, 79, 92, 97,
    100, 102, 103, 127, 132, 310
hægtessan, 75, 77, 187, 227,
    229–30, 262, 274
hagiography, 235–36, 251, 286
hags, 34, 74–75, 77, 207, 230,
    262
Hancock, Alice, 255
Harlow, Essex, 68
Hastings, battle of, 257
Hayling Island, Hampshire, 68
head cults, 87, 170, 202
healing, 250, 251, 255
Hearne, Thomas, 246–47
Hecate (deity), 230
Helena, St, 202
hell, 152, 208–9, 244, 254, 270,
    278, 280, 310

Hellequin, 211
Hercules, 45, 69
heresy, 151, 172, 174, 252, 254
  belief in fairies as, 160
Hereward the Wake, 84–85, 237
Hergest, Red Book of, 9
Herla, king, 240, 242, 279, 282
hermits, 54
Herodias, 274
Herodotus, 6, 318
heroes, 18, 36, 41, 45, 58, 153,
    160, 210, 226, 246–48, 251,
    296–97, 306
Herrick, Robert, 14
Hiley Bathurst, William, 240,
    316
hillforts, 67, 142, 247
hills, 12, 17, 112, 128, 149, 189,
    191, 195, 209, 228–29, 239,
    240, 279, 280, 309, 314
Hinduism, 146
Hinton St Mary, Dorset, 168
historical-realist interpretations,
    11, 16
Holyrood Abbey, Midlothian,
    236
Honorius of Autun, 241
Hoole, Charles, 314
Horned God (Wicca), 58
horns, 63, 215, 216, 221, 272,
    318
horses, 63, 99, 280, 285
  'hag-ridden', 287
  spirits in the form of, 290
Houghton, Huntingdonshire,
    192
household, spirits of. *See under*
    fairies
Housesteads, Northumberland,
    127
Hoxne Treasure, 112, 124, 170
hunting, gods of, 126–28, 178,
    248

Index

Hwicce, 141, 234
hypocausts, 240

Iao (deity), 123
Iberia, 53, 54, 104, 151, 182, 183
Iceland, 157
Icklingham, Suffolk, 175
iconoclasm, 55, 159, 170–71, 306
idolatry, accusations of, 60, 125, 136–37, 147, 149, 153, 166–67, 182–83, 255, 271
Ilam, Staffordshire, 165
incubation, 119
incubi, 45, 184, 185, 205, 212–15, 219–21, 252, 258, 267–71, 302, 303
  female (incubae, succubi), 219–21
Incubo (deity), 45, 213, 302
inscribed stones, post-Roman, 188, 199, 214
insects, fairies as, 14
interpretatio Romana, 8, 65, 92–99, 117, 124, 264, 271
Inuus (deity), 213
Ireland, 19, 29, 37–38, 56, 109–10, 138, 140, 144, 148, 172–73, 194, 198, 200–1, 203, 211, 217, 219, 223, 238, 279, 290
Irish language, 29, 204
Iron Age, 5, 29, 34, 38, 50, 54, 57–58, 60–70, 78, 80, 89–91, 93, 95, 98, 121, 124, 133, 142, 170, 201, 305, 309
Iscanus, Bartholomew, bishop of Exeter, 265–67, 273–74, 300
Isidore of Seville, 35, 84, 153, 214–17, 219, 221, 225–27, 238, 247, 249, 267, 276, 306
Islam, 42, 299

Istanbul, Turkey, 6
Italy, 137, 182, 188
Itchen, river, 228, 229
Ixworth, Suffolk, 250

James, M. R., 268
Japan, 66
Javelin, Saint, 107
Jerome, St, 199, 212–15, 219, 221, 249, 306
Jews, 148, 247–48
jinn, 42
Joan of Arc, 255
John of Beverley, St, 288
Jordanes, 46
Joseph (patriarch), 125
Julian, emperor, 34, 119, 121, 133, 169, 172, 174, 175
Julius Caesar, 94, 264
Juno (deity), 271
Jupiter (deity), 44, 95, 111, 144, 183, 210, 225, 244, 271, 276, 308, 311, 316
Jupiter Ammon (deity), 69

Keightley, Thomas, 12–14
kelpies, 290
Kenchester, Herefordshire, 239
Kennet, river, 80
Kimmeridge, Dorset, 105
King, Fairy, 22, 210, 211, 278–83, 297, 300
Kingsley, Hampshire, 269
Kirk, Robert, 8, 313
Kouretes, 241

Lailoken, 215
lais, Breton, 259
lamiae, 109–10, 119, 149–50, 183, 220, 226, 263, 265, 303, 314
Lamyatt Beacon, Somerset, 189
Lantfred, 227, 229, 231, 233

Index

Lares, 71, 94, 110–12, 137, 271, 303, 314
　Compitales, 111
Larzac, France, 81
Łasicki, Jan, 98
Latin language, 30–32, 41, 45, 118, 137, 194–96, 199, 200, 205, 212, 241, 257, 261, 263–65, 277, 286, 291, 314
Latium, 113, 118
Laimės, 105
Lavatris, Co. Durham, 127
Lavenham, Suffolk, 291
Layamon, 262
Lea, river, 80
Lear, king, 9
lectio facilior, 56
Legh, Edward, 300
leprechauns, 55, 198, 218, 238, 286
Leshii, 169
Lewis, C. S., 39, 292, 316
Lexden, Essex, 68
lexicography, 30
Leyton Low, Essex, 81
libations, 108, 182, 311
Liberal Arts, Seven, 52
Limentinus (deity), 43
literacy, 50, 91, 95, 173, 199
Lithuania, 71, 98, 104, 120, 152, 266, 287
　conversion of, 160–62
Little Dean, Gloucestershire, 79
Litton Cheney, Dorset, 79
Livius Andronicus, 108
Llanllyr, Ceredigion, 214
Lleu Llaw Gyffes, 210, 211
Lludd and Llefelys (story), 238, 239
Lollardy, 254
London, 153
　Drapers' Gardens, 126

Holborn, 318
　St Paul's Cathedral, 275
longaevi, 39
Longney, Gloucestershire, 164–66
longue durée, concept of, 3, 5, 22, 24, 27–28, 33, 38, 40, 47–59, 81, 88, 302, 305
Lucan (poet), 216–17, 221
Lugus (deity), 210
Lullingstone, Kent, 100–1, 111, 169, 175
Lupercalia, 43, 213, 218
lutins, 76, 286
Lydney, Gloucestershire, 64, 102, 108, 210–11, 240, 316

Mabinogion, 9, 202
Mabon, 202
Macha, 110
Machen, Arthur, 12, 315–16
MacRitchie, David, 12
Macrobius, 113, 115
mære, 219–21
magic, 84, 85, 88, 119, 123, 125, 151, 160, 216, 222, 239, 243, 255, 262–63, 269, 289, 291, 293–97, 303–4, 309
　conjuration of fairies in, 298–303
　harmful, 105
Magnus Maximus, 202
Maguncius, 269
Maiden Castle, Dorset, 63, 174
Malekin, 267, 291
Man, Isle of, 194
manes (spirits), 16, 41, 110, 183, 205
Map, Walter, 36, 240–41, 258, 279, 282, 283
Maponos (deity), 202
Mars (deity), 69, 95, 120, 127, 271

Index

Mars Belatucadrus (deity), 96
Mars Camulus (deity), 92, 96
Mars Cocidius (deity), 127
Mars Rigonemetus (deity), 120
Martianus Capella, 52
Martin of Braga, 109, 149
Martin of Tours, St, 173
Mary, Virgin, 87, 233, 235, 236, 255, 299
Maryport, Cumbria, 105, 111–12
Matrona (deity), 202–3
Matronalia, 203
mausolea, 108, 170, 188
mavones, 183
Medea, 297
medicine, 45, 243
Medusa, 69
  jet pendants depicting, 192
Meilyr of Caerleon, 146
Meinulf, St, 236
Mellitus, bishop, 190
Mercury (deity), 170, 183, 191, 271
Mercury, Gaulish (deity), 95, 264
Merlin, 257, 269–71
  conception of, 258
mermaids, 273, 314
metalwork, deposition of, 67, 79–80
Michael, archangel, 183
Mictēcacihuātl (deity), 154
Midir, 218
Mildenhall Treasure, 74, 112, 115, 124, 168
Milton, John, 282, 312
Minerva (deity), 137, 183, 243
mining, 11, 108
missionaries, 37–38, 139–40, 147, 149–51, 156–57, 160–62, 172–73, 190, 193, 208

Mithraea, 176
Mithras (deity), 160, 171
Mocuxsoma, 72
Modraniht, 230
Modron, 202–3
Mogons (deity), 72
monasteries, 52, 80, 177, 199, 214, 257
Mongols, 7
monotheism, 41–42, 70
monsters, 77, 150, 195, 216, 223, 238, 239, 241, 245, 286, 288, 320
Moon, Sphere of the, 254, 269, 270
Morehouse, Lancelot, 315
Morgan le Fay, 297
Morganwg, Iolo, 10, 207
Mormo, 149
Morrigan, 110
mosaics, 63, 94, 101, 115–16, 122, 127, 168, 170
Mother Earth, 153
mother goddesses. *See* Deae Matres
mountains, 12, 44, 54, 78, 82, 136, 137, 150, 193, 308, 313
Muerte, Santa, 154
Murray, Margaret, 58
Muses, 52
Myrddin Wyllt. *See* Merlin
mystery cults, 119–20, 126
mystery plays, 292
mythography, 275, 277
mythology, comparative, 3, 7, 13, 23, 56

Nacton, Suffolk, 222
Narbonne, France, 102
narcotics, 114, 119
naturalia, literature on, 221, 238, 239, 241, 249, 317, 319, 320
Nebuchadnezzar, 217

necromancy, 84
Neighbridge, Gloucestershire, 240
Neine (nymph), 99
Nemesis, 107–8
Nemesis (deity), 106
Nene, river, 1, 80, 123
Nennius, 165
Neoplatonism, 148
Neptune (deity), 76, 114, 168, 183
Neptuni. See lutins
Neratius Proxsimus, Quintus, 120
nereids, 75–76, 149, 150
Nettleham, Lincolnshire, 120
Nettleton Shrub, Wiltshire, 171, 175
Nettleton, Gloucestershire, 175
Neville, William, 300
New World, 7
Newnham-on-Severn, Gloucestershire, 68
Nicomachus Flavianus, Virius, 114
nightmare, 114, 119, 128, 205, 219, 260, 262
Nodens (deity), 108, 210–11, 316
Norfolk, 112, 129, 192, 300, 302
Norman Conquest, 3, 36, 80, 187, 194, 203, 249, 251, 252, 256–60, 268, 303, 309
Norman French language, 261, 286, 289
Norns, 77, 227, 273
Norse religion, 46–47, 177
Northumbria, kingdom of, 268
Núadu (deity), 211
Nudd (Lludd) Llaw Ereint, 210, 211
Nuits-Saint-Georges, France, 104
Numa, king of Rome, 43–44, 86, 114–15
numen, 44–46, 61, 92

Nustles, Gloucestershire, 210
nymphaea, 100–1, 159, 169, 310
nympholepsy, 102
nymphs, 1, 2, 8, 32, 34, 38, 47, 59, 65, 71–74, 76, 77, 79, 84, 86–87, 94, 97, 99–102, 113–14, 122, 148–50, 159, 176, 207, 208, 224, 235, 237, 252, 264–65, 273, 274, 276–78, 287, 306, 310–14, 316, 317, 319

obelisks, 57
Oberion, 300
Old English language, 20, 31–32, 192, 194, 195, 219–20, 226, 227, 229, 230, 242, 244, 245, 249, 257
Ollototae, Matres, 103
oracles, 44, 114, 120, 128
orality, 24, 50, 57, 72, 159, 196, 201, 243
orangutans, 317–18
Orcus, 244
Orcus (deity), 183
Orderic Vitalis, 258
Orford, Suffolk, 272
Orford, wild man of, 219, 272–73
Orpheus, 18, 116, 123, 127, 135, 217, 259, 281, 282, 297
Orphic cults, 116, 120, 168
orthopraxy, 182
Osberne de Bradwell, 291
Ostrogoths, 188, 246
otherworlds, 65, 79, 138, 208, 252, 309
    underground, 36, 74, 81–82, 87, 208–9, 223, 248, 251, 279, 288, 303
Ottoman Turks, 6, 150
Ovid, 7, 31, 42–44, 67, 114, 119, 308, 321

Index

Pagans Hill, Somerset, 191
Pan (deity), 43, 44, 114, 115,
    119–20, 124, 213, 241, 282,
    311, 315, 316
panitae, 74, 184, 213, 215, 221,
    318
Papcastle, Cumbria, 311
Parcae, 52, 104, 120, 225, 275,
    306
    Morta (Atropos), 108, 234, 276
Parcae (deities), 22, 38, 59, 71,
    77, 103–5, 107–8, 114,
    154–55, 183, 187, 206,
    225–27, 229–31, 233–35,
    249, 261–63, 273–77, 295,
    300, 303, 307
Parentalia, 170
pastoral literature, 24, 306
Patrick, St, 37, 173, 179, 199
Pegasus, 69
Pelagius, 199
Penates, 71, 110, 111, 303
penitentials, 31, 181–87, 226,
    265–67, 273, 274, 277, 283,
    306
Penry, John, 205, 206
Persephone, 281
Persia, 13, 14, 158
personification, 19, 43, 52–53,
    59, 68, 97, 103, 104, 106–7,
    120, 204, 206, 227, 229,
    262, 274
    re-personification, 35, 51–52,
    153–55, 227, 262, 263, 295,
    306–7
Peter, St, 202, 237
Peterborough, Cambridgeshire,
    1, 2, 237
phytanthropy, 66
Pictish language, 195
Picts, 181
Picus (deity), 43, 113, 120–21,
    125

pilosi, 183, 212–13, 215, 219–21,
    265–66, 318
place-names, significance of, 31
plague, 105
Plato, 40, 269
Pliny the Elder, 8, 238
Plutarch, 40, 270
Pluto (deity), 218, 244, 276, 281,
    297
poltergeists, 290, 291, 303
polytheism, 61, 70, 124, 308
pooka, 290
Pope, Alexander, 282
Portunes, 267, 284–89
Portunus (deity), 284, 285
possession, spirit, 146
post-Roman era, 3, 28, 47, 61,
    64, 80, 98, 128, 129, 131,
    138–39, 140–42, 173, 174,
    176–81, 182–83, 188–89,
    191, 193, 196, 199, 214,
    217, 309
Poundbury, Dorset, 170
Pratchett, Terry, 2
prehistory, 16, 17, 28, 69–70, 88,
    134, 138, 140, 164, 211, 219
Prester John, 241
printing, 197
Priscillian, 151
Proclus, 270
prophecy, 36, 41, 146, 208, 215,
    248, 250, 251, 258, 301, 302
Protestantism, 205, 313–14
providence, 52, 308
Prudentius, 114, 287
puck, 71, 83, 186, 207, 260, 287,
    314
pygmies, 11–12, 35, 36, 238–43,
    282, 306, 317, 318

Quadriviae, 101
Queen, Fairy, 24, 73, 297, 299,
    301, 314

Rackham, Arthur, 303
Ralph of Coggeshall, 219, 267, 272, 283, 291
reductivism, xvi, 5, 58, 253
Reformation, 143, 164, 279, 299, 301–2, 304, 309, 313
religion, popular, 21, 31, 35, 47–48, 50, 53–54, 70, 88, 99, 137, 151, 278, 280, 305, 316
  Frankish, 226
  Roman, 67, 99, 133, 211
Renaissance, 115, 313, 315
Rhiannon, 202
Rhineland, 210
Rhydderch, White Book of, 9
Richard I, king of England, 291
Rigina (deity), 202
rings, 119, 121, 123, 126, 302
Risingham, Northumberland, 102, 248
rivers, 65, 78, 80, 136, 193, 308, 313
  deification of, 64, 137
Robin Goodfellow, 8, 10, 71, 314, 315, 317
Robin Hood, 248
Robin of Risingham, 248
Roma (deity), 106
Roman Britain, 3, 5, 8, 29, 69, 88, 141, 192, 193, 196, 200, 226, 243–48, 306, 316
  Christianity in, 29, 139, 167–81, 199
  religion in, 1, 2, 16, 27, 28, 30–31, 34–35, 61, 57, 58, 62–68, 71–74, 78–82, 89–135, 137, 145, 193, 202, 203, 210, 211, 225, 231, 234, 259, 285, 309, 316
Roman religion, 7, 8, 9, 33–34, 41–44, 59, 61, 77, 88, 210, 308–12

romance (literary genre), 15, 18, 22, 33, 36, 250, 258–59, 279–82, 292–98, 301, 304
Romanisation, 5, 49, 68–69, 91, 133
Romanitas, 69, 140, 141, 180
Romanticism, 10, 53, 312, 315
roundhouses, 91, 176
Ruin, The (poem), 245
Russia, 107, 169

Sabrina (deity), 64
sacrifices, 59, 62, 114, 115, 149, 157, 182, 300, 302, 311
  human, 66, 91
sacrilege, 52–53
Salesbury, William, 204, 205
Samnites, 120
Samogitians, 162
Samson of Dol, St, 75–77, 184, 216, 286
Satan, 60, 150–52, 211, 224, 254, 270, 278
satire, 271, 282
Saturn (deity), 115, 178, 271
Saturnalia, 115
satyrs, 2, 12, 74, 77, 115, 122, 183, 207, 212, 213, 215, 219–22, 239–43, 266, 271–72, 282, 311, 312, 315, 317–18
schrätlein, 266
Scot, Reginald, 151, 301
Scotland, 2, 19, 21, 75, 77, 215, 223, 227, 287
Scott, Walter, 10–11
scucca, 83
Severn Bore, 68
Severn, river, 64, 68
Severus Alexander, emperor, 123
sexuality, 36, 109, 114, 184, 214, 219–21, 263, 268, 278, 298
shagfoal, 290

Index

Shakespeare, William, 10, 15, 25, 71, 74, 300
shamanism, 21, 34, 38, 61–65, 69, 70, 88, 109, 217
shape-shifting, 62
shrines, 1, 64, 68, 72, 79, 89, 91, 100–2, 110, 123, 130, 137, 145, 146, 159, 169, 174–75, 179, 189–91, 240
Siberia, 61
Sibylla (spirit), 300–1
sídhe, 37–38, 209, 223, 238, 279
Silchester, Hampshire, 123, 245–47
sileni, 219, 221
Silenus (deity), 311
silvani, 71, 74, 101, 184, 214, 221
Silvanus (deity), 71, 126–27, 129
Sir Orfeo, 18, 259, 280–82, 297
sleep paralysis, 214
snakes, 111–12, 162, 192
soldiers, 72, 92, 96, 102, 103, 110, 130, 133
Spain, 102, 109
sphinxes, 69
Spiritualism, 14, 310
springs, 37, 78–81, 83–87, 92, 100, 114, 130, 149, 169, 176, 202, 243, 245, 252, 309, 311, 314
Sri Lanka, 146
St Albans, Hertfordshire, 101
St Paul-de-Varax, France, 218
Stamford, Lincolnshire, 237
Stapleton, William, 300, 302
stature, fairy, 11, 223, 238–39, 241, 251, 284, 304
Stephen, St, 250
stitch, sudden, 229, 230, 274
Strabo, 241
Stukeley, William, 311
succubae. *See under* incubi
Sucellus (deity), 127
Suleviae, 71, 73, 103
Sulis Minerva (deity), 71, 73, 92, 103, 123, 169, 245
superstition, idea of, 53, 54, 66, 153, 156, 255
survivalism, concept of, 40, 47, 49, 50, 155
Susanna, St, 45
Swithun, St, 227, 233
sylphs, 282
syncretism, 99, 104, 112, 122–24, 133, 145, 156, 162, 175, 177, 201

tanks, baptismal, 175
Taranis (deity), 127
Tatars, 7
temples, 44, 59, 69, 121, 123, 125, 137, 188
closure of, 119, 170, 171, 174
Iron Age, 68
ornamental, 310, 312
re-use of, 189–92
Romano-British, 63, 73, 89, 91, 108, 118, 127, 176, 189, 210, 240
Thames, river, 64, 80
Theocritus, 8
Theodoret of Cyrrhus, 270
Theodosius I, emperor, 119, 174
theomacha, 75–77, 184, 216
Theosophy, 310
therianthropy, 34, 58, 62, 64, 70, 216, 217, 221, 224, 264
Theseus, Ship of, 48, 305
Thetford Treasure, 34, 112–29, 134
Thetford, Norfolk, 112
thiasos, Bacchic, 74, 115–16, 122, 135, 311
Thistleton, Rutland, 72
Thomas of Monmouth, 268

Index

Thomas of Walsingham, 287, 288
Thor (deity), 46
three, number. *See* triads
Thurtaston, Cheshire, 189
Tincomarus, king, 68
Tiora, grove of, 120
Tíréchan, 37–38
Tockenham, Wiltshire, 130
Tolkien, J. R. R., 210, 245
Tramarinae, Matres, 103
trance-states, 62, 102
transgression, ritual, 119, 298, 301, 302
treasure, buried, 34, 74, 112, 114–16, 118, 119, 121, 124, 126, 128, 134, 167, 168, 170, 250, 251, 300, 302
trees, sacred, 61, 84, 98, 127, 161, 162, 164–66, 182, 255, 273
triads, 36, 71, 77, 104, 108, 110, 203, 237, 248, 251
Trioedd Ynys Prydein, 201
troglodytes, 12
Tuatha Dé Danaan, 238
Twyford, Buckinghamshire, 90
Tyche (deity), 101, 130–1
Tyne, river, 64

Ukraine, 107
Uley, Gloucestershire, 170, 171, 191, 240
undemonisation, 35, 83, 150, 193, 208, 209, 279, 306
underworld, 18, 71, 74, 81–82, 135, 152, 204, 208, 211, 218, 262, 276, 278–79, 282
Unwen (hero), 245–47, 296

Vanir, 46
Varro, 67, 113, 115, 215, 225, 244

Vedic tradition, 71
Velnias (deity), 71, 152
Venus (deity), 123
Verbeia (deity), 64
Verica, king, 68, 69
Veteres (deity), 72–73, 96
Vetus Latina (Bible translation), 212
Victories (deities), 68, 107
Victricius of Rouen, 173
Vietnam, 317
villas, Roman, 79, 101, 124–25, 169, 188
Vindolanda (Chesterholm), Northumberland, 203, 310, 311
Vinotonus (deity), 127
Viridius (deity), 96
Visigoths, 188, 265
Vodyanye, 169
Vortigern, king, 269, 270, 271
Vulcan (deity), 92, 114
Vulgate, 199, 205, 212, 213, 221, 244, 265
Vytautas, grand duke of Lithuania, 161

Wade (hero), 296
Wade, William, 300
Waden Hill, Wiltshire, 189
Waldringfield, Suffolk, 222
Wales, 2, 9–10, 19, 36, 75, 98, 131, 140, 172, 194, 199, 201–6, 257, 258, 279–80
Walter of Hemingburgh, 268
Walter, king of Aquitaine, 265
Wanborough, Surrey, 68
Water Newton, Cambridgeshire, 123, 167–68
water, deities of, 1, 19, 34, 38, 65, 78–88, 99–101, 169, 175, 195, 218, 249, 272–73, 286, 305

Index

Way, river, 80
Webster, John, 11–12, 318
weeks, days of the, 178
Weird (Wyrd) Sisters, 77, 227, 273
wells, 16, 78–81, 83, 101, 126, 165, 175, 176, 182, 192, 305
   worship of, 84, 86–87
Welsh language, 29, 131, 147, 194, 200, 204, 208, 239, 241–42, 249, 257, 303
Wendens Ambo, Essex, 126
werewolves, 274
Wessex, kingdom of, 216
West Wycombe, Buckinghamshire, 311
Westerwood, North Lanarkshire, 101
Wharfe, river, 64
Wheeler, Mortimer, 174
Wicca (religion), 58
Widsith (poem), 246
wild men. *See* woodwoses
William I, king of England, 84, 247, 257
William of Auvergne, 211
Wilmington, Long Man of, 245
Winchester, Hampshire, 227–28, 281, 297
Wireker, Nigel, 274–75, 281
witch trials, 21, 61
witchcraft, 76, 77, 84, 183, 230, 262, 313
witches, 34, 38, 60, 74–76, 84–85, 261, 309
witchfinders, 151
Witham, river, 80
Withburga, St, 277
Woden (deity), 178–79, 271
wolves, 237
Woodburn, Northumberland, 248
Woodeaton, Oxfordshire, 189, 240
woodpeckers, 120–21
woods, wild men of the. *See* woodwoses
woodwoses, 212, 219, 221–22, 248, 265, 271–72
Woolmer, forest of, 269
Woolpit, Suffolk, 87
Worcestre, William, 247–48
Wulfstan, bishop of Worcester, 165, 166
Wycliffe, John, 219, 265
Wye, river, 100
wyrd, 227

Xenocrates, 270

York, Yorkshire, 111, 130, 131
Yorkshire, 300

Zambia, 23
zoomorphism, 63, 99, 282, 316